BLACKBERRY PIE MURDER

Hannah didn't feel the rain that pelted down with the force of a spewing faucet. She didn't flinch as a second and then a third bolt of lightning arced down from where they were standing. She was concentrating solely on the motionless figure on the gravel.

"I can't quite tell what . . . oh, no!" Lisa was clearly badly shaken as she arrived at the front of the truck. "It's a man, Hannah. And I think he's . . . he's . . . dead!"

Hannah heard the panic in Lisa's voice, but she was too busy to deal with it now. She knelt down beside the man on the ground and with cold and wet fingers, she felt for a pulse. For one brief moment, she thought she felt a slight sign of life, but that hope quickly faded when she saw that the man's neck was bent at an impossible angle . . .

Books by Joanne Fluke

Hannah Swensen Mysteries

CHOCOLATE CHIP COOKIE MURDER
STRAWBERRY SHORTCAKE MURDER
BLUEBERRY MUFFIN MURDER
LEMON MERINGUE PIE MURDER
FUDGE CUPCAKE MURDER
SUGAR COOKIE MURDER
PEACH COBBLER MURDER
CHERRY CHEESECAKE MURDER
KEY LIME PIE MURDER
CANDY CANE MURDER
CARROT CAKE MURDER
CREAM PUFF MURDER
PLUM PUDDING MURDER
APPLE TURNOVER MURDER
DEVIL'S FOOD CAKE MURDER
GINGERBREAD COOKIE MURDER
CINNAMON ROLL MURDER
RED VELVET CUPCAKE MURDER
BLACKBERRY PIE MURDER
DOUBLE FUDGE BROWNIE MURDER
JOANNE FLUKE'S LAKE EDEN COOKBOOK

Suspense Novels

VIDEO KILL
WINTER CHILL
DEAD GIVEAWAY
THE OTHER CHILD
COLD JUDGMENT
FATAL IDENTITY

Published by Kensington Publishing Corporation

BLACKBERRY PIE MURDER

JOANNE FLUKE

KENSINGTON BOOKS
www.kensingtonbooks.com

KENSINGTON BOOKS are published by

Kensington Publishing Corp.
119 West 40th Street
New York, NY 10018

All Kensington titles, imprints and distributed lines are available at special quantity discounts for bulk purchases for sales promotion, premiums, fund-raising, educational or institutional use. Special book excerpts or customized printings can also be created to fit specific needs. For details, write or phone the office of the Kensington Special Sales Manager: Kensington Publishing Corp., 119 West 40th Street, New York, NY 10018. Attn. Special Sales Department. Phone: 1-800-221-2647.

Kensington and the K logo Reg. U.S. Pat. & TM Off.

ISBN-13: 978-0-7582-8038-1
ISBN-10: 0-7582-8038-6
First Kensington Hardcover/Trade Edition: March 2014
First Kensington Mass Market Edition: February 2015

eISBN-13: 978-1-61773-869-2
eISBN-10: 1-61773-869-7
Kensington Electronic Edition: February 2015

10 9 8 7 6 5 4 3 2 1

Printed in the United States of America

This book is for Ruel,
for my God-Daughter Amanda Joanne,
and for my friend Arlene Gorman.
I will never forget you.

Acknowledgments

Big hugs to the kids and the grandkids who know that the most important ingredient in home-baked cookies is love.

Thank you to my friends and neighbors: Mel & Kurt, Lyn & Bill, Lu, Gina, Adrienne, Jay, Bob, Laura Levine & Mark, Judy Q., Richard Jordan, Dr. Bob & Sue, Richard & Krista, Dan Grimm, Mark B., Angelique, Dan Arnold at Claim Jumper, Paige at Maggiano's, Mark & Mandy at Faux Library, Rosemary at the Elks Club, Gene at SDSA, Daryl and her staff at Groves Accountancy, and everyone at Boston Private Bank.

Thank you to my Minnesota friends: Lois & Neal, Bev & Jim, Lois & Jack, Val, Ruthann, Lowell, Dorothy & Sister Sue, Mary & Jim, and Tim Hedges.

Special thanks to my supremely talented and incredibly patient Editor-in-Chief and friend, John Scognamiglio.

Hugs all around to Steve, Laurie, Doug, Helen, Adam, Vida, Karen, Robin, Lesleigh, Alex, Darla, Peter, and all the other good folks at Kensington Publishing who keep Hannah sleuthing and baking up a storm.

Thanks to John at *Placed4Success.com* for Hannah's movie and TV spots, the recipe for the Blackberry Pie Martini, and for spearheading Hannah's social media.

Thanks to Meg Ruley at the Jane Rotrosen Agency for her constant support and her wise advice.

Thanks to Hiro Kimura, my superb cover artist. Every time I see that blackberry pie on the cover, I want to cut a big piece, top it with a scoop of vanilla ice cream, and ditch my diet for as long as it takes to gobble it up!

And thank you to Lou Malcangi at Kensington, for designing all of Hannah's delicious covers in hardcover and in paperback, and the remarkable covers for the Joanne Fluke Suspense Thrillers.

Thanks to Rudy at *Z'Kana Studios* in Richmond, Virginia for the amazing brag reel of my televised interviews and baking segments.

Thanks to Kathy Allen for the final testing of Hannah's recipes.
It's an incredible ego trip to have someone bake for me for a change!

Hugs to my friend Trudi Nash for going with me on book tours, taking great photos, and for convincing me that she loves doing it.

Thanks to Nancy and her fabulous cookie recipes.

Thank you to JoAnn Hecht for making Hannah's recipes look beautiful and taste great at launch parties.

Hugs to Fern and Leah for all their work on the *Joanne Fluke* Facebook page and the *I Love Joanne Fluke* Facebook page. And thank you to all of the Hannah Fanatics and fans of Team Swensen.

Thank you to Dr. Rahhal, Dr. and Cathy Line, Dr. Wallen, Dr. Niemeyer, and Rita & Dr. Lack for helping with my pesky book-related medical and dental questions.

Special thanks to Vida Engstrand at Kensington for planning and booking my appearances and media interviews for book tours and conventions.

Thanks to Tracy at *Suzi Davis Travel* for making great travel arrangements for Trudi, John, and me.

Last, but certainly not least, a big hug to all of the Hannah fans who send in their favorite family recipes for Hannah to try. I'm going to remind her to stock up on extra butter, sugar, and chocolate before the next blizzard hits Lake Eden, Minnesota!

 **Chapter One**

"**A**nd you actually *believed* Mother?!" Hannah Swensen stared at her sister in complete amazement.

"Well . . . yes." Andrea shifted slightly on her stool at the stainless steel work island in Hannah's industrial kitchen at The Cookie Jar.

"Let me get this straight." Hannah's youngest sister, Michelle, looked every bit as astounded as Hannah did. "You trusted Mother when she promised not to interfere with the plans we're making for her wedding?"

"Yes. I know it sounds stupid of me, but Mother said it in front of everyone at the table. And she seemed completely sincere."

"I'm sure she was sincere . . . at the time," Hannah agreed. "But sincerity isn't the issue here. Personality is. Mother's a buttinski. That's the way she is and she can't help it."

Michelle nodded. "All you have to do is look at her track record. Did you really believe she'd let us arrange everything and just show up for the ceremony?"

"Well . . . no. Not when you put it that way. But she said she wanted a fall wedding and I chose fall colors for the flowers. I had beautiful bronze asters and yellow and orange chrysanthemums. Mother loves chrysanthemums. She told me they were her favorite flower just last week!"

Hannah gave a little snort. "Maybe they were . . . *last*

week. But this is this week. Why don't you try her out on roses? They come in all sorts of designer colors."

"Do you think she'll go for it?" Andrea asked, but neither of her sisters replied. Instead, they simply stared at her in utter disbelief. Then, almost in tandem, they shook their heads. It took a moment, but Andrea started to laugh. "You're right. Mother won't approve of any flowers I choose, at least not today. I'll suggest the roses and let her reject them."

"Makes sense to me," Hannah said, exchanging smiles with Michelle. Hannah's youngest sister was on a summer break from college and she was in town for two weeks before she had to go back to start the fall semester. She'd spent the previous night with her friend, Carly Richardson, who was undergoing a big change in her family dynamics.

"I didn't get a chance to ask you when I came in," Andrea addressed Michelle. "How's Jennifer Richardson doing?"

"She's doing a lot better than I expected. She's fitting right in, almost as if she never left. And I could tell that Loretta's really happy she's home. Carly told me she really likes Jennifer, but I know it's a big adjustment for her. For most of her life, Carly was like an only child."

"How old was Carly when Jennifer ran away?"

"She was four. There's almost ten years between them, and Jennifer ran away right after her fourteenth birthday."

"Then Loretta is handling it all right?" Hannah asked.

"Oh, yes. Carly says it was a big shock when her mother got that call from Jennifer, but she always believed that Jennifer would come back home someday."

All three Swensen daughters were silent for a moment, thinking about the troubles that the Richardson family had endured. It had started when Jennifer had run away from home, and it had reached a crescendo of hurt when Loretta's husband and Carly's father, Wes Richardson, had fatally shot himself in the hayloft of the barn six months to the day after Jennifer had run away. Somehow, through it all, Loretta had carried on, raising Carly and supporting them both by using the life insurance money that Wes had left her to become a full partner at Trudi's Fabrics.

"Will you tell Carly to call me if there's anything I can do for them?" Andrea asked Michelle.

"Sure. I'll tell Carly."

"The same goes for me," Hannah said. Michelle, Carly and Tricia Barthel had been fast friends in school, and Hannah had always been fond of Carly. "Now let's get back to the wedding plans before Mother gets here," she said, bringing them back to the subject at hand. "How are you coming along with the bridesmaid dresses, Michelle?"

"I'm not. Mother says she wants our dresses to match the flowers so I have to wait until she makes up her mind about them. The only thing is, Claire says it'll be a special order if we want three dresses exactly the same, and special orders take at least three weeks."

"No flowers and no dresses." Andrea was clearly frustrated as she ticked them off on her fingers. "If Mother doesn't start cooperating with us, this wedding isn't going to happen."

"At least she finally approved the menu for the reception," Michelle said, obviously trying to look on the bright side. But then she noticed Hannah's exasperated expression. "The menu's *not* set?"

"Not anymore. Mother called me yesterday and said she didn't want the standing rib roast. So far, she's rejected beef, pork, lamb, and poultry including Doc's favorite, Rock Cornish Game Hens."

"Then the only thing left is fish," Andrea pointed out.

"I know. I'm going to try to talk her into poached salmon with champagne sauce. Sally says she can do that for a large crowd."

"I think Mother likes salmon," Michelle said, but she didn't look convinced. "Do you think she'll go for it?"

"We'll find out in a couple of min . . ." Hannah stopped in mid-sentence when there was a sharp knock at the back door. "That must be Mother now. Andrea? Will you please get the door? And if you'll pour her coffee, Michelle, I'll dish up some Chocolate-Covered Cherry Cookies. Maybe a couple of her favorite cookies will make her more cooperative."

Hannah had just finished plating the cookies when the kitchen door opened and she heard Andrea greet their mother.

"I've never been so embarrassed in my life!" Delores Swensen swept into the kitchen with the force of a hurricane. "This is absolutely ridiculous!"

"Sit down, Mother." Andrea gestured toward a stool at the work island.

"I poured your coffee, Mother," Michelle said, setting the mug in front of her mother.

"And I baked your favorite cookies," Hannah added, setting the plate directly in front of her mother.

"I'm far too upset to eat. Or sit. Or even drink coffee, for that matter."

All three sisters exchanged puzzled glances. Their mother was obviously agitated. Delores Swensen was always perfectly dressed and coiffed when she left her house, but this morning the scarf at her neck was crooked, her blouse wasn't tucked in all the way, and even more alarming, she wasn't wearing any makeup!

"You're not wearing makeup," Hannah said, commenting on her mother's less-than-perfect appearance.

"I didn't have time to put it on. I just rushed right over here to show you. Have you girls seen this *atrocity*?"

Hannah looked up at the paper Delores was waving over her head like a saber. "Is that the *Lake Eden Journal*?" she hazarded a guess.

"Yes! And I'm never going to speak to Rod Metcalf

again!" Delores named the editor and owner of the town newspaper. "He's nothing but a . . . a snake in the grass!"

Hannah didn't want to ask, but her younger sisters were silent and someone had to find out what was wrong. "I'm not sure what you're talking about, Mother. What did Rod do?"

"He wrote this!" Delores slammed the paper down on the stainless steel surface in front of Hannah. "Just read it and you'll see what I mean!"

Hannah glanced at the headline. "*Jordan High Gulls Win Three Games in a Row?*" she asked, reading it aloud.

"Not that one!"

"Loretta Richardson Never Lost Hope That Her Daughter Would Come Home?"

"Not that one, either! Read the article below it. I've never been so mortified in my entire life!"

"*When Is the Next One? No Body Nose!*" Hannah read the heading on the article halfway down the page.

"Yes! That awful man ridiculed us! I don't know what you girls are going to do about this, but I plan to pull the curtains closed and never leave my house again! I don't appreciate being the object of public mockery!"

Hannah's sisters were regarding her curiously and Hannah began reading the article aloud. "It's been over four months since a member of the Swensen family has sniffed out the body of a murder victim," she began, but Delores held up a hand to stop her.

"Reading it once was quite enough for me. I don't want to hear it again!"

"I understand," Hannah said, even though she was secretly amused at Rod's heading *No Body Nose* and his reference to sniffing out murder victims. Although it took a great deal of restraint on her part, she kept a solemn expression on her face as she pushed the cookie plate a bit closer to her mother. "I baked these just for you, Mother."

"All right, dear. I'll have one. I wouldn't want to hurt your feelings."

Hannah breathed a sigh of relief as her mother reached for a cookie. Perhaps the endorphins in the chocolate would have a calming effect. Then she spread out the newspaper in the center of the worktable and motioned for her sisters to crowd around her so that all three of them could read it silently.

The article continued in the same vein, pointing out that with the exception of Coach Watson, every other Lake Eden homicide victim had been discovered by someone in the Swensen family. There was even a tally sheet, arranged like a baseball box score, showing Hannah with the most "hits," followed by Delores and Andrea. Michelle was in last place with nothing but strikeouts. Under the score box was a quote from Andrea's husband, Bill Todd, the Winnetka County Sheriff, who said that the drop in the murder rate had made it possible for his deputies to take care of routine matters like serving warrants for smaller crimes and tracking down citizens who had failed to show up for jury duty. Then Rod quoted one of Hannah's boyfriends, Deputy Mike Kingston, who said his homicide detectives were almost caught up on paperwork. The article ended with another quote from Mike that had Hannah wincing slightly because he speculated that perhaps Hannah's uncanny ability to find murder victims, an attribute he called her "*slaydar,*" was on the blink.

There was an awkward moment of silence as they all finished reading and then Hannah spoke. "We really shouldn't be that upset over this," she said, attempting to put the best spin on what she'd just read. "Rod didn't have enough real news so he put this in as one of his little jokes."

"It's *not* funny!" Delores said, and her tone was icy. "It's cruel. And after Doc reads it, he'll be just as embarrassed as I am. I wouldn't blame him a bit if he called off the wedding!"

"Doc would never do that," Hannah told her. "He loves you. You know that. And Doc knows Rod well enough to realize that this is just another one of his spoofs. Nobody's going to take it seriously, Mother." Hannah turned to her sisters. "Right, girls?"

"Right!" Michelle agreed quickly.

"Everybody in Lake Eden knows that Rod has a strange sense of humor," Andrea said. "Remember when he ran that awful picture of Bill right after he was elected sheriff?"

"The one that said *Law Enforcement at Its Finest*?" Hannah asked, unable to keep the grin off her face as she remembered the photo of her brother-in-law dressed in the bank robber outfit he'd worn when he took Tracey and her friends out to Trick or Treat for Halloween.

"Yes. Bill knew it was a joke. He even thought it was funny. And so did everybody else at the sheriff's station."

"That's not the same thing!" Delores said, giving Andrea the look that all three girls had named *Mother's Death Ray*. "You girls may think this is funny, but I'll never be able to hold my head up in this town again!"

The sisters exchanged glances, but no one was about to argue the point. Despite the fact that she'd reached for another cookie, their mother was still in a terrible mood. The silence stretched on for several more seconds and finally Michelle spoke up.

"Where's Lisa?" Michelle asked in an obvious attempt to change the subject.

"At Cyril's garage," Hannah told her. "Her car was supposed to be ready by seven and Herb dropped her off there on his way to work."

Andrea glanced at the clock on the kitchen wall. "It's eight-thirty. I guess Cyril didn't have it ready on time."

"That's not surprising." Delores gave a little laugh. "The last time I took my car in for an oil change, it took two days. What's wrong with Lisa's car?"

Hannah's spirits lifted considerably as her mother helped herself to a third cookie. "Her fuel pump went out. She was going to call if Cyril couldn't have it ready to go by nine."

As if on cue, the phone rang and Michelle got up to answer it. Hannah listened to Michelle's end of the conversation for a beat and then she got up to retrieve her car keys.

"It's not ready?" Andrea asked, as Michelle hung up the phone.

"Not yet. I'll open the coffee shop if you want to drive out there, Hannah."

"And I'll help," Andrea added. "I'm good at pouring coffee and talking to people."

Delores nodded. "I'll help too, but I'm going to stay out here in the kitchen so I don't have to talk about Rod's horrid article. I'll fill the display jars and you girls can carry the cookies into the coffee shop."

"Thanks for helping," Hannah said sincerely. Her family had never failed to volunteer whenever she needed help. She glanced out the window and frowned slightly as she realized the sky was overcast. "I wonder if it's going to . . ." Hannah stopped speaking abruptly as they all heard a crashing boom outside. A few seconds later, a blinding flash lit up the darkening sky.

"You'd better take an umbrella, dear," Delores warned her. "I was listening to KCOW radio in the car on my way here and Rayne Phillips said that there was a sixty-percent chance of a summer storm this morning."

"He should have made that a hundred percent chance," Andrea commented as raindrops began to pelt against the windowpane.

Hannah grabbed an umbrella from the coatrack by the back door. "I'd better hurry. If Lisa calls, tell her I'm on the way and I've got an extra umbrella in the car for her."

"Just a minute," Delores said, stopping Hannah before she could leave.

"What is it?" Hannah asked, turning to face her mother.

"I want you to promise me you won't find any dead bodies on your way out to Cyril's garage."

There was a smile on her mother's face and Hannah was glad. The chocolate in the cookies must have helped. Delores was getting her sense of humor back.

"I promise," Hannah said.

"Or on your way back, either."

"Yes, Mother," Hannah promised, heading out the door and into the rain.

Chapter
Two

A rainy morning in August presented problems that appeared almost insurmountable just as soon as Hannah drove out of the parking lot in back of The Cookie Jar. It was so muggy that the windows in her Suburban were already starting to fog up. By the time she got to the end of the alley, she'd used her hand to wipe off a clear space to peer through, and she had to lower the driver's side window to keep it from fogging up again. This meant the rain came in, but she figured that a little rain was better than running into a building or another vehicle.

Naturally, the air conditioner wasn't working. It seemed the only time it worked was in the winter when she didn't need it. Ditto for the heater, which seemed to work best in the summer. In order to keep the windshield from fogging up so much that she couldn't see the pavement, she had to endure a wet left sleeve. "At least I don't wear glasses," Hannah muttered as she turned right on First Street and headed for the highway that would lead her to Murphy's Motors.

At highway speeds, the rain no longer came in the window and Hannah breathed a sigh of relief. She couldn't go as fast as she would have liked because it hadn't rained in over a week and the asphalt was slick with oil from the trucks that barreled down this route every day. Every time the lightning flashed, she could see an answering gleam in the surface of the wet roadway and the rumbling of thunder outside her open window made listening to the radio impossible.

The giants in the sky are bowling, Hannah thought, smiling as she remembered her father's reassuring words when the booming thunder had frightened her as a child. *But why is it flashing?* she'd asked him, pointing up at the lightning. *Because their bowling balls have flashing lights in them*, he'd answered. And from that moment on, Hannah had wished for a toy bowling ball with lights in it each and every Christmas until she was old enough to realize that it was all a figment of her father's imagination.

She was almost there. Hannah pulled off at the next exit and took the access road to the turnoff that led to Cyril's garage. It was two miles down a gravel road and even though it was bumpy, she was glad to be off the highway. She pulled in past the gas pumps, past the metal shed where the limousines were kept for Cyril's second business, Shamrock Limo, and pulled up close to the door that led to the customer waiting room.

Lisa must have been watching for her because she dashed out the door almost before Hannah's truck stopped, holding a newspaper over her head as an umbrella. "We're going to be late," she said, climbing into the passenger seat. "It's almost nine."

"No problem. Andrea and Michelle are opening for us and Mother offered to fill the cookie jars. Everything's under control."

"Oh, good!" Lisa buckled her seatbelt. "Cyril thought he'd be finished by now, but they sent the wrong fuel pump and he had to order a new one. He promised to have my car ready by five and I can pick it up when I get off work today."

"I'll give you a ride out here," Hannah offered, glancing down at the newspaper that Lisa had dropped to the floorboards. "Is that the *Lake Eden Journal*?"

"Yes. I think you should buy up all the copies so your mother doesn't see the article."

"Too late. Mother came in this morning waving the paper and spitting nails."

"I can understand that. But everybody knows that Rod tends to go too far when he tries to be funny. Did you manage to calm her down before you left?"

"I think so. She ate four Chocolate-Covered Cherry Cookies."

"And that did it?"

"It seemed to. Before I left The Cookie Jar, she actually smiled and made me promise not to find any more dead bodies."

"Okay then." Lisa frowned slightly. "I'm sorry I missed the wedding planning meeting, but maybe it's a good thing I did. I just don't have any more ideas for the wedding cake and the table decorations. It's hard to plan when she hasn't settled on the wedding colors yet."

"That's okay. We didn't have time for the meeting anyway." Hannah came to the entrance that led to the highway, but she bypassed it to continue down the gravel road.

"Aren't we taking the highway?"

"No. My windshield wipers need replacing and I was practically blinded every time someone passed me. I figured we're better off taking the back roads to town."

"Fine with me." Lisa rolled down her window and breathed in the cool air.

"You're going to get wet," Hannah warned her.

"I know, but I've got another blouse at the shop. And it's like a sauna in here. It's too bad you can't get your climate-control system fixed."

Hannah laughed. "What climate-control system? They didn't call it that when my cookie truck was built. And even if I had one, it probably wouldn't work. At least Mike had the heater fixed . . . sort of. And the air-conditioning has never worked right. Cyril says I need a whole new unit and it's just not worth sinking the money into something this old."

"Time for a new cookie truck?"

"Yes, but only when I can afford it. I don't want to take on any big car payments while I'm still paying off my condo."

"I can understand that. Herb and I were talking about getting something newer for me when the fuel pump went out, but we decided to nurse my car along for as long as we could."

"That's exactly the way I feel. I'm going to hang on to this truck . . ." Hannah paused for a moment as thunder rumbled loudly overhead. With the windows up, it had been quieter, but the advantages of cool air outweighed the ease of conversation. ". . . just as long as I can," she finished.

Lisa gave a little gasp as a blinding flash of lightning struck a tree in a nearby field. "It's really bad out there," she said, reaching up to cover her ears as the thunder boomed.

"That's another reason I decided to take the back way," Hannah told her once the volley of thunder had reached its crescendo and faded. "This road is lined with trees and lightning will hit them before it'll hit us."

"So all we have to worry about is a tree getting struck by lightning and toppling in front of us?"

"Right." Hannah listened to the rain drumming on the roof of her truck for a moment and then she gave a little laugh. "That and the road washing out."

"I don't think that'll happen. It's only been raining for . . ." Lisa paused as the thunder boomed again, and then she continued, ". . . less than half an hour."

Hannah picked up speed as they entered an open area and slowed down when the road was tree-lined again. "At least we're not the tallest thing on the road right now."

The two women rode in silence for a moment, safely en-

sconced in their metal cocoon and listening to the electrical
storm raging outside. Then Lisa spoke. "I wonder if we'll get
any customers at all today."

"My guess is not many."

"That's exactly what I think. Maybe we'll have time to sit
and have a cup of coffee, and talk about something *besides*
your mother's wedding."

"That would be a welcome change." Hannah gripped the
wheel tightly as they passed another open area. The blinding
lightning flashes and crashing thunder were unnerving. She
steered to avoid a puddle that was building up in a low spot
on the road and her truck fishtailed slightly. There was a
sharp bend ahead and she regained control barely in time to
make the turn.

"Watch out!" Lisa hollered as she saw a large branch that
had fallen in the center of the road.

"Hold on!" Hannah called out almost simultaneously as
she spotted the obstacle and hit the brakes as hard as she
could. The Suburban fishtailed again on the loose, wet gravel
as she swerved to avoid the branch and then there was a sick-
ening thump as Hannah's front bumper hit something on the
shoulder of the road.

Hannah uttered a phrase she never would have voiced if
her nieces had been within earshot. "Sorry, Lisa. Are you
okay?"

"I'm fine. You weren't going that fast. And don't worry
about what you said. It's exactly what I was thinking. Did
you hit that tree branch?"

"I don't think so. I'm almost sure I avoided it. It must
have been something else."

Hannah leaned forward to wipe fog from the inside of the
windshield and Lisa did the same. Then both of them peered
out into the driving rain. "Can you see anything?"

"Not much. There's something there and I think part of it
is light-colored, but . . ." Lisa stopped her description as

lightning flashed and then she gave a little cry. "Oh, Hannah! I think it's . . . it's a *person!*"

As if of one mind, both women opened their doors and jumped out into the elements. Hannah didn't feel the rain that pelted down with the force of a spewing faucet. She didn't flinch as a second and then a third bolt of lightning arced down only feet from where they were standing. She was concentrating solely on the motionless figure on the gravel.

"I can't quite tell what . . . Oh, no!" Lisa was clearly badly shaken as she arrived at the front of the truck. "It's a man, Hannah! And I think he's . . . he's . . . dead!"

Hannah heard the panic in her partner's voice, but she was too busy to deal with it now. She knelt down beside the man on the ground and with cold and wet fingers, she felt for a pulse. For one brief moment, she thought she felt a slight sign of life, but that hope quickly faded when she saw that the man's neck was bent at an impossible angle.

"Is he . . . ?" Lisa attempted to ask the question again.

"He's dead," Hannah answered.

Lisa swallowed hard, and then she asked another question. "Who is it?"

"I don't know. I've never seen him before."

"A stranger," Lisa said in a shaking voice.

"Come on, Lisa." Hannah motioned to her partner as she got up and walked back to the truck. "We need to call this in to the sheriff's station."

A few moments later, the call had been made and the two partners were silent, sitting in their respective seats, staring out at the rain splattering big, fat drops against the windshield. Tree branches were dipping low with the weight of the rain, thunder was rumbling like a prehistoric beast, and flashes of lightning caught the scene outside in freeze frame. It was a bad storm, a nasty storm. Inside the truck, they were lucky to be protected from the elements.

"Where are you going?" Lisa asked as Hannah grabbed

her umbrella from the back seat and opened the driver's door.

Hannah didn't answer. She couldn't find the words. Head bent, her eyes on the ground, she walked around to the front of her truck, opened the umbrella, and propped it up over the dead man's face. No one should have to be outside and unprotected in this storm. It just wasn't right.

Tears were running down Lisa's face as Hannah climbed back in the truck. She reached over to pat Hannah's hand and then she reached in her purse for a tissue. Hannah handed her the box that she always kept on the console.

"I'm glad you did that," Lisa said, wiping her eyes.

"I had to," Hannah replied, and then she began to shake almost uncontrollably. She knew it was a combination of the rain, the cold, and the wet clothing she was wearing. It was also the fact that despite her promise to her mother at The Cookie Jar, she'd found another dead body. And this time it was even worse because she'd killed him herself!

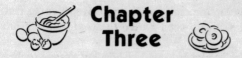

Chapter Three

It didn't take long for the ambulance to arrive since the hospital was only a few miles away. Hannah watched from the driver's seat as Doc Knight, clad in a yellow slicker and hat, checked for vital signs. It took him awhile, Doc was nothing if not thorough, but she knew there was no hope because of the grim expression on his face when he came around to her side of the car.

"He's dead?" she asked, fearing the worst.

"Yes."

But before Doc could do more than pat her on the shoulder, Mike Kingston and Lonnie Murphy pulled up. Even though Hannah dated Mike occasionally and usually felt a surge of excitement when she saw him, today it was different. She wasn't sure why, but perhaps it was because she felt heartsick and guilty about the accident and the fact that a man had died. Looking back, she didn't think she could have anticipated and avoided it, but she was utterly miserable all the same. Coupled with the fact that she was shivering almost uncontrollably from shock and thoroughly chilled from wearing wet clothing, there was no joy at seeing one of her boyfriends.

"Hannah," Mike said and there was a warmth in his voice that she would have gloried in under any other circumstances. "What happened, Hannah?"

"It was raining really hard, and I wasn't going fast, but my truck skidded when I tried to avoid that tree branch, and . . ."

"Hold it," Mike ordered, reaching out to squeeze her arm as he pulled out his notebook. "Start from the beginning and don't leave anything out. Lisa? Lonnie's going to take your statement in the squad car, so please go with him."

As Lisa opened the passenger door to get out of the truck, Hannah had the crazy urge to beg her not to leave. But before she could act on her impulse, Mike patted her shoulder.

"It's okay. You're going to be all right, Hannah. Just start from the beginning and tell me exactly what happened."

The next period of time seemed impossibly long as Hannah described the details of the accident and Mike proceeded to ask questions. The volleys of questions and answers seemed endless and Hannah wished she could just go back to her condo, climb into bed, and pull the covers over her head. This wasn't real. It couldn't be. When she got up this morning, the sky was clear and she'd looked forward to the day. Now, less than four hours later, she was guilty of causing a man's death!

"Okay, Mike. That's enough," Doc Knight called out, walking up to the open window of Hannah's truck. "I need to take Hannah and Lisa back to The Cookie Jar now."

"But I'm not finished taking . . ."

"Yes, you are." Doc glanced at Hannah. "Do you have dry clothes at work?"

Hannah nodded. Her teeth were chattering so hard it was difficult to speak.

"All right then. I left the heater on in my car and Lisa's already inside. Leave your keys for Mike, hop out, and go join her. I'll be there in just a second." He turned to Mike. "You'll make sure that Hannah gets her truck back when you're through with it?"

"Yes, but I really need to . . ." Mike started to object, but Doc shook his head.

"Whatever you need to do, you can do later at The Cookie Jar when they're dry and warm. You wouldn't want to be responsible for two cases of pneumonia compounded by severe shock, would you?"

"Of course not, but . . ."

"Good!" Doc opened Hannah's door and helped her out. "Come along, Hannah. You need to leave right now, doctor's orders."

"Oh, Hannah!" Delores gave a little cry of distress as Doc led Hannah and Lisa into the kitchen.

Here it comes, Hannah thought, taking a deep breath in preparation. Her mother was going to chew her out royally for not only finding another dead body, but actually causing his death. "I'm sorry, Mother," she said.

"Sorry for what?"

"I promised you I wouldn't find another dead body."

"Don't be silly, dear. I was talking about murder victims. I'm just so glad you're both all right!"

"So am I, but I feel terrible about hitting that man. I was trying to avoid a branch in the road and I didn't see him."

Delores rushed over to give Hannah a hug in spite of her daughter's drenched clothes and wet hair. "Just remember that it was an accident. You certainly didn't mean to hit that man. When Doc called me he said it was raining so hard and visibility was so bad, he almost hit *your* truck."

"I should have pulled over and stopped," Hannah said, stating the obvious.

"But you couldn't," Lisa reminded her. "You were trying to get around the bend and under the trees so that we wouldn't be struck by lightning."

"This is not the time to lay blame," Delores said, and Hannah recognized the no-nonsense, mother-knows-best tone of voice. "Hannah?" She pointed to the tiny bathroom off the kitchen. "You get straight into that shower and get warm. Then put on dry clothes and come out here."

"But Lisa should . . ."

"I turned on the oven for Lisa. You know how much heat that puts out. All she has to do is stand in front of it while you shower and dress and then she can do the same."

Doc walked over to give Delores a hug. "No wedding talk today, Lori. The girls are too upset."

"I know that. We won't even mention it."

"Good. I'll need you at the hospital later if you're free. A couple of board members are coming in from Minneapolis and I always behave better if you're there."

Hannah was on her way to the tiny bathroom off the kitchen, but she turned in time to see her mother smile. It was a beautiful smile, an appreciative smile that came from the heart. Just seeing the expression on her mother's face assured her that they'd have a loving marriage.

It didn't take long for Hannah to shower and dress. She turned the bathroom over to Lisa, who didn't take more than ten minutes, either, and then they sat down at the workstation with Delores to have a bracing cup of coffee.

"Michelle and I baked something for you while you were gone," Delores told them.

"*You* baked?" Hannah felt her eyebrows shoot up in surprise. Delores hadn't baked when they were growing up and, as far as she knew, her mother hadn't baked since.

"Well . . . I didn't actually do the baking, but I measured the ingredients."

"And I'll bet you did a wonderful job," Lisa said diplomatically.

"That's what Michelle said. Of course she had to explain that a stick and a half of butter equaled three-quarters of a cup, but there's no way I could have known that without softening it up and measuring it."

"Absolutely right," Hannah told her, feeling absurdly pleased that her mother had measured ingredients to help Michelle bake for them. "What did you bake?"

"Tio Tito's Sublime Lime Bars."

"Who's Tio Tito?" Lisa asked her.

"He's the man who makes the vodka that we put in the cookie bars. Tito is his nickname and *tio* means *uncle* in Spanish."

"How did you come up with the name?" Lisa asked her.

"Michelle named them. She took a summer school class in Spanish and she thought it sounded cute."

"We can't sell those to minors, Mother," Hannah reminded her, "not with alcohol in them."

"Oh, they're not for sale. They're for you and Lisa. When Doc called, he told me to run across to the Municipal Liquor Store and buy a bottle of brandy to put in your coffee. But Hank had so many different kinds of brandy, I couldn't decide. Then I noticed that one bottle had a copper top and it was different from all the rest so I bought that. I didn't realize that it was vodka and not brandy until I got back here."

"What made you decide to bake with it instead of pouring it in our coffee?" Lisa asked her.

"It was Michelle's idea. She remembered the Double Whammy Lemon Cake you made for my last party and she decided to try it in lime cookie bars."

Hannah smiled at her mother to show she was about to tease her. "They sound wonderful. Are we going to talk about them, or do we actually get to taste them?"

"You get to taste them." Delores laughed as she reached for the foil-covered plate at the end of the workstation. "Wait just a second. I'm going to get Michelle. She wanted to be here when you tasted them."

The moment the swinging restaurant-style door between

the kitchen and the coffee shop had shut, Hannah reached for the foil-covered plate and pulled off the foil. "They're pretty."

"You're not going to taste one until Michelle gets here, are you?" Lisa sounded worried.

"Nope. It was sweet of them to bake for us and I can wait if you can."

"I don't know if I can, or not. They smell really good."

"Yes, they do! Maybe we could just take a little bit off the bottom and . . . " Hannah halted in mid-reach as the door swung open and Michelle and Delores came in.

"You didn't taste them yet, did you?" Delores asked.

Hannah shook her head. "No, but it was close. It's a good thing you came in when you did."

A moment later, all four of them were munching on Michelle's creation. Hannah popped the rest of her bar cookie in her mouth and gave a happy sigh. "Incredibly delicious," she pronounced.

"Just wonderful!" Lisa added. "Do you think we could make them without the vodka so we could sell them in the coffee shop?"

Michelle looked thoughtful for a moment. "I don't see why not. There's one-third cup of vodka in the whole pan of bars. And we used one-third cup of lime juice. I don't see why you couldn't use one-third cup of whole milk for the vodka and leave the lime juice as it is."

"How about increasing the lime juice to two-thirds of a cup?" Delores asked her. "I really like lime."

"So do I, but that might make it too limey . . . if *limey* is a word, that is."

"It is," Hannah told her. "It's a term that was used for English sailors back in the early days. They were at sea for months, sometimes years, and they used to carry barrels of limes on a ship for sailors to eat to keep from getting scurvy.

I like limes as much as you do, Mother, but I agree with Michelle. It could be a little too limey."

"That's why I'm just the measurer and not the baker," Delores said. "These are just perfect, Michelle. It's really a delightful recipe and I know Doc would absolutely love to taste them."

Hannah caught her mother's not so subtle hint. "I get it, Mother. Let's all have one more and save a couple for Lisa to take home to Herb. And then, if you like, you can take the rest out to the hospital for Doc."

"Not just Doc," Delores explained. "I was thinking about that lunch with the board members. Doc needs their approval on a couple of things, and I don't think a little vodka ever hurts when you're dealing with board members."

TIO TITO'S SUBLIME LIME BAR COOKIES

Preheat oven to 350 degrees F., rack in the middle position.

- ½ cup finely-chopped coconut *(measure after chopping—pack it down when you measure it)*
- 1 cup cold salted butter *(2 sticks, 8 ounces, ½ pound)*
- ½ cup powdered *(confectioners)* sugar *(no need to sift unless it's got big lumps)*
- 2 cups all-purpose flour *(pack it down when you measure it)*

- 4 beaten eggs *(just whip them up with a fork)*
- 2 cups white *(granulated)* sugar
- ⅓ cup lime juice *(freshly squeezed is best)*
- ⅓ cup vodka *(I used Tito's Handmade Vodka)*
- ½ teaspoon salt
- 1 teaspoon baking powder
- ½ cup all-purpose flour *(pack it down when you measure it)*

Powdered *(confectioners)* sugar to sprinkle on top

Coconut Crust:

To get your half-cup of finely-chopped coconut, you will need to put approximately ¾ cup of shredded coconut in the bowl of a food processor. *(The coconut will pack down more when it's finely-chopped so you'll need more of the stuff out of the package to get the half-cup you need for this recipe.)* Chop the shredded coconut up finely with the steel blade. Pour it out into a bowl and measure out ½ cup, packing it down when you measure it. Return the half-cup of finely chopped coconut to the food processor. *(You can also do this by spreading out the shredded coconut on a cutting board and chopping it finely by hand.)*

Cut each stick of butter into eight pieces and arrange them in the bowl of the food processor on top of the chopped coconut. Sprinkle the powdered sugar and the flour on top of that. Zoop it all up with an on-and-off motion of the steel blade until it resembles coarse cornmeal.

Prepare a 9-inch by 13-inch rectangular cake pan by spraying it with Pam or another nonstick cooking spray. Alternatively, for even easier removal, line the cake pan with heavy-duty foil and spray that with Pam. *(Then all you have to do is lift the bar cookies out when they're cool, peel off the foil, and cut them up into pieces.)*

Sprinkle the crust mixture into the prepared cake pan and spread it out with your fingers. Pat it down with a large spatula or with the palms of your impeccably clean hands.

Hannah's 1ˢᵗ Note: If your butter is a bit too soft, you may end up with a mass that balls up and clings to the food processor bowl. That's okay. Just scoop it up and spread it out in the bottom of your prepared pan. (You can also do this in a bowl with a fork or a pie crust blender if you prefer.)

Hannah's 2ⁿᵈ Note: Don't wash your food processor quite yet. You'll need it to make the lime layer. (The same applies to your bowl and fork if you make the crust by hand.)

Bake your coconut crust at 350 degrees F. for 15 minutes. While your crust is baking, prepare the lime layer.

Lime Layer:

Combine the eggs with the white sugar. *(You can use your food processor and the steel blade to do this, or you can do it by hand in a bowl.)* Add the lime juice, vodka, salt, and baking powder. Mix thoroughly. Add the flour and mix until everything is incorpo-

rated. *(This mixture will be runny—it's supposed to be.)*

When your crust has baked for 15 minutes, remove the pan from the oven and set it on a cold stovetop burner or a wire rack. **Don't shut off the oven! Just leave it on at 350 degrees F.**

Pour the lime layer mixture on top of the crust you just baked. Use potholders to pick up the pan and return it to the oven. Bake your Sublime Lime Bar Cookies for an additional 30 minutes.

Remove the pan from the oven and cool your lime bars in the pan on a cold stovetop burner or a wire rack. When the pan has cooled to room temperature, cover it with foil and refrigerate it until you're ready to serve.

Cut the bars into brownie-sized pieces, place them on a pretty platter, and sprinkle them lightly with powdered sugar. Yum!

Hannah's 3rd Note: If you would prefer not to use alcohol in these bar cookies, simply substitute whole milk for the vodka. This recipe works both ways and I can honestly tell you that I've never met anyone who doesn't like my Sublime Lime Bar Cookies!

 # Chapter
Four

There was a knock at the back door, and Hannah glanced at the clock. It was eleven in the morning and her mother had left twenty minutes ago, Tio Tito's Sublime Lime Bar Cookies tucked under her arm for the board member luncheon. It would have taken her at least ten minutes to drive to the hospital, and if her mother's best friend, Carrie Rhodes, was working with the Rainbow Ladies at the hospital this morning, the news of her accident would be all over town.

"Bad news travels fast," Hannah repeated one of her great-grandmother's favorite homilies as she headed across the kitchen floor to open the door. "Might as well get it over with." She added the phrase she'd been repeating to herself ever since she'd realized that the stranger she'd struck was dead, and then she winced a bit at her grammar. It was probably Bertie Straub from the Cut n' Curl at the end of the block. Bertie was on the third tier of the Lake Eden Gossip Hotline, the phone tree Delores and Carrie had established to disseminate breaking news in Lake Eden, and Bertie would have heard about the accident by now. She was undoubtedly arriving to get the full details from Hannah so that she could repeat them to her morning clients.

"Hi, Ber . . . Norman!" Hannah changed names in mid-speech as she saw the other man she dated, Norman Rhodes, standing there. "Come in, Norman."

Norman closed his umbrella and stepped inside, placing it on the rug Hannah always kept by the back door when it was raining. "I wasn't sure you'd want to talk to anybody."

"You're not just anybody," Hannah told him, stepping into his arms for a most welcome hug. His arms tightened around her and she realized that this was the first time she'd felt completely safe and thoroughly comforted since Doc had confirmed that the man she'd struck on the road was dead. Norman was her haven, her safe harbor from the calamities of life. Was she a fool for not marrying him and staying secure with him for the rest of her life? Some said yes, and some said no, and Hannah knew that both sides were right. She was a fool. She had everything she needed right here in Norman's arms. And she wasn't a fool because no woman should marry when she still had strong feelings she couldn't ignore for a different man. She pulled away slightly as if in reaction to her last thought.

And as if Norman somehow sensed her mood, he released her so that she could step back.

"So tell me about it," Norman said, and then he paused for a moment. "But only if you want to, of course."

"I want to. Just let me get you a cup of coffee first." Hannah gestured toward the stainless steel workstation. "Have a seat. I'll get you a couple of cookies, too."

"Great! I didn't have time for breakfast. Cuddles learned how to chase a ball this morning and we played longer than we should have."

Hannah felt the corners of her mouth turn up in a smile on her way to the kitchen coffeepot. Norman was a great kitty-daddy. "I thought Cuddles knew how to chase a ball."

"Oh, she did. But she finally figured out that I'd throw it again if she brought it back and dropped it in front of me."

As she plucked a Chocolate Chip Crunch Cookie, a Lovely Lemon Bar Cookie, and a Molasses Crackle from the bakers rack, Hannah thought about how her cat, Moishe, brought his toy mouse back to her every time she threw it. "Do you think she learned it from Moishe?"

"She must have. I didn't try to teach her to do it. I'm almost sure she learned it last night when I brought her over to your place to play."

It had been a wonderful night and for a brief moment, Hannah wished she could go back in time to the exact instant that Norman had arrived at her condo, and live it all over again. Perhaps things would be different the second time around and Cyril would have Lisa's car ready. Of course, then Lisa might have hit the stranger on her way back to The Cookie Jar and she wouldn't wish the guilt of taking someone's life on anyone else, especially not her good friend and partner.

"What is it?" Norman asked her when she set their cups of coffee and the plate of cookies down. "You look very serious."

"It was nothing really. I was just thinking that you can't mess with fate."

"What were you doing? Wishing that you could go back in time so that you wouldn't have the accident?"

"Exactly. I keep wishing that things were different and wondering what would have happened if I'd left five minutes later, or if I'd decided to take the highway to town instead of going the back way. I wonder if anyone else does that."

"I do. I scraped my side mirror backing out of the garage right after I moved into our house, and I kept wishing I could go back a couple of seconds in time so that I'd back up straighter and I wouldn't scrape it."

"It's good to know I'm not alone," Hannah said, but her mind was fixed on two words that Norman had used. *Our house*. Norman had called it their house and that made her feel sad. In a way, it *was* their house. They'd designed it together for a contest in the Minneapolis paper and they'd won first prize. But she'd never, in her wildest imagination, dreamed that Norman would build it and ask her to marry him!

Norman reached out to cover her hand with his. "You're never alone when I'm around."

There was silence between them for a long moment, but it wasn't an uncomfortable silence. At last Hannah sat up a little straighter and sighed. "I killed him, you know," she said.

"It wasn't your fault. You couldn't have seen him in the pouring rain."

"Then I should have pulled over."

"Perhaps. Why didn't you?"

"I was trying to get under the trees so we'd have some shelter from the lightning."

"That makes sense to me."

"And then I came around the bend and there was a fallen tree branch in the middle of the road. I swerved to avoid it, but the truck skidded and headed for the side of the road and . . . and before I could straighten it out, I hit him."

"You didn't see him standing there?"

"No. It all happened so fast and all I could do was react when I saw the branch. I had no idea he was standing on the shoulder of the road."

Norman looked thoughtful. "I wonder why he was standing there. If he saw you coming, he should have jumped out of the way. Were you going fast?"

"No. I slowed way down because it was raining so hard that I couldn't see well."

"You did the right thing then."

Hannah thought about that for a moment. "Maybe. But if I did the right thing, why did I hit him?"

"Because you couldn't help it. It was an accident, Hannah. It's not like you set out to hit him on purpose."

"I know that, but I still feel awful. I wonder who he was."

"You didn't recognize him?"

"No. I wonder if Doc Knight knows."

Norman shrugged. "If he ever lived around here, Doc would know. He's lived here for years. And if Doc doesn't know, he was probably a stranger."

"I'd feel better if I knew who he was," Hannah said, and then she paused. "At least I *think* I'd feel better."

"Then call Doc and ask."

Hannah glanced up at the clock. Delores had said Doc's lunch was at one and it was only eleven-thirty. "Good idea," she said. "I think I will."

A moment later, Hannah was standing by the kitchen phone, talking to her mother in Doc Knight's office.

"Sorry, dear," Delores told her. "Doc's not here right now."

"That's okay. I just wanted to know if he knew the man I hit. I didn't recognize him."

"Neither did Doc. I asked him about that. I do know there wasn't any identification on him so he could have been a transient."

"You've been in Lake Eden longer than Doc. Did you recognize him?"

"I didn't see him, dear."

Of course her mother hadn't seen him! Hannah kicked herself mentally for asking the question in the first place. Delores wasn't the type to pull off a sheet in the morgue to view a dead body.

"I can look at the photos if you really want me to," Delores offered and Hannah knew she was making a huge concession for her daughter.

"No, that's okay. But would you ask Doc if anybody else

who saw him recognized him? And would you call me and let me know what he says?"

"I'll do that, dear. I'll call you right after the lunch with the board members is over." There was a long pause and then Delores sighed. "You're still at The Cookie Jar, aren't you?"

"Yes, Mother."

"And you're not alone?"

"No. Norman's with me right now and Andrea and Michelle are in the coffee shop. I gave Lisa the rest of the day off to be with Herb. She's pretty upset over this whole thing."

"Of course she is. You should probably take the afternoon off, too. Why don't you go home and take a little nap?"

Hannah shuddered slightly. She knew exactly what would happen if she went home and attempted to nap. She'd dream about the stranger she'd hit and it would be even more frightening than it had been when it actually happened.

"I think I'll stay here, Mother. I'm better off doing some work. Maybe I'll bake. That always calms me down."

"Good idea. Has Michelle told you about Winnie Henderson's party yet?"

"No, but I haven't really seen her. She's been really busy in the coffee shop."

"I'll tell you then. Winnie called while I was there and she ordered six dozen pirate cookies for her grandson's birthday party. She said they were having a pirate party and she was hoping you could make something that fit into that theme."

"Pirate cookies," Hannah repeated, frowning slightly. "I've never made a pirate cookie before."

"I didn't think you had and that's why I wanted to give you plenty of advance warning. What are you going to do? Put skulls and crossbones on them?"

"Winnie's grandson might like that, but I'm not sure Winnie would. Thanks for telling me about it, Mother. It'll give me something to think about here in the kitchen. And please don't forget to call after the lunch is over."

"I won't, dear. I doubt lunch will take that long. Doc ordered poached salmon from the hospital kitchen and you know how I feel about salmon. I'll probably just push it around my plate and eat two of the lime bars for dessert."

When they'd said their goodbyes and hung up, Hannah headed back to the workstation and Norman. "Mother said Doc doesn't know who the man was. She's going to ask Doc if anybody else recognized him when they brought him into the hospital. She'll call me when Doc gets back to the office after his meeting."

"What was that about pirates?" Norman asked and then he looked a little sheepish. "Sorry, but I couldn't help but hearing your end of the conversation."

"That's okay. Winnie Henderson is giving a pirate party for her grandson's birthday and she ordered some designer cookies."

"Cookies that look like pirates?"

Hannah shook her head. "That would be much too hard unless I had a pirate cookie cutter and Lisa frosted them. And I don't. I think all it has to do is remind him of pirates."

Norman drained his coffee cup and stood up. "Sorry, Hannah. I'm not going to be much help on this one. I can stay for another few minutes if you need me, but I have a noon appointment at the clinic. Rose McDermott's coming in for an impression. She has a couple of bridges that need to be replaced."

"Would you like to take a couple of cookies with you?" Hannah asked, noticing that he'd eaten everything she'd placed on the plate.

"No thanks. I don't want to spoil my dinner. And that reminds me . . . would you like to go out to the Lake Eden Inn for dinner tonight?"

Hannah's mouth watered even though she wasn't a bit hungry. It was an instinctive thing. Sally Laughlin, the chef at the restaurant in the Lake Eden Inn, was one of the best cooks she'd ever met.

"It might do you some good to get out," Norman said, noticing her hesitation. "How about if I bring Cuddles out to play with Moishe when I come to pick you up?"

"Great!" Hannah agreed and it wasn't just the thought of Sally's cuisine that prompted her decision. She had to tell Sally that Delores hated poached salmon and they'd better start thinking of other choices for the menu at the wedding reception.

"Six-thirty?" Norman asked.

"Perfect." Hannah crossed the kitchen floor to open the door for him. "I'll be ready and so will Moishe."

Norman stopped, turned in the doorway and pulled Hannah into his arms. "It wasn't your fault and no one will blame you. Remember that."

"I'll try," Hannah promised as he kissed her good-bye. She always felt safe and cherished in Norman's arms, and after he'd gone out the door, she closed it behind him and gave a contented sigh. She really ought to marry Norman. He made her feel wonderful and he was perfect for her.

Less than five minutes later, Hannah was talking to Winnie on the phone. After the initial pleasantries were exchanged, Hannah waited for Winnie to ask about the accident. Since there were no questions forthcoming, either, Winnie was exercising uncharacteristic restraint or she'd been busy on the farm and hadn't answered her call from the Lake Eden Gossip Hotline.

"Good to hear from you, Hannah, but why did you call?" Winnie asked in her forthright way.

"I wanted to find out more about the party you're giving for your grandson. Mother said it was this weekend?"

"That's right."

"And you want six dozen pirate cookies?"

"That's exactly what I want."

"Why pirate cookies?"

"Because Little Matt's favorite movie series is *Pirates of the Caribbean* and he says he wants to grow up to be Jack Sparrow. That's why we're having a pirate party. It's going to be a real big deal. Connor drew a treasure map and all the kids are dressing up like pirates. They're going to follow the clues and dig up the treasure we buried in the pasture."

"That sounds like fun."

"Oh, it will be. Connor makes a great pirate leader and all of my kids just love him."

Hannah heard the warmth in Winnie's voice and she smiled. After several bad marriages, perhaps Winnie's horse trainer was going to be the perfect man for her. "How old is Matt?" she asked, pen poised over the stenographer's book she kept by the kitchen phone.

"He'll be six this weekend, and he's a real pistol. That kid's got more energy than the new stallion that Connor's trying to break. He went to Janice Cox's preschool last year and she told me he was inquisitive and extremely verbal. I think he's going to grow up to be a lawyer."

"Do you know what else you're going to serve at the party?"

"I sure do. Little Matt told his mother and me exactly what he wanted. We're having pepperoni pizza from Bertanelli's, root beer, and potato chips. It's not exactly a healthy meal, but it *is* his birthday and we promised him he could choose."

Hannah jotted another note, *potato chips, pizza, and root beer*. "Are you having a cake?"

"We're having a cake *and* pie. Little Matt just loves my Blackberry Pie. He calls it Blackbeard Pie."

"That's funny. You'll have to give me the recipe sometime." Hannah stopped and realized that she was asking for a family recipe. "If you want to, that is," she added.

"It's no secret and it's real simple. I'll give you some blackberries, too. I'm the only one who grows them around here. I stake 'em so they're easy to pick and I've got a big patch on the edge of the north field. And that reminds me. When Connor comes in for lunch, I have to ask him to pick me some more. I baked the pies for Little Matt's birthday party real early this morning and would you believe? Somebody stole one right off my kitchen window ledge when they were cooling! I guess that'll teach me not to leave my kitchen window open."

Hannah smiled. The "thief" was probably one of the hired hands Winnie hired for the summer. "You said you're having a cake, too?"

"You betcha. Those six-year-olds can really eat."

"What kind of cake?"

"I don't know. I was thinking of ordering a cake from the place at the mall that puts pictures on top. I figured I'd take in a picture of Johnny Depp as Jack Sparrow so they could put it on the icing, but Connor was worried that Little Matt would be upset when we cut the cake."

"Upset?"

"Yes. He idolizes Jack Sparrow as being the best pirate ever. Connor didn't think he'd like it when he saw us cut Jack Sparrow into little pieces."

"Connor's probably right."

"I know he's right. I thought about it and decided not to buy that cake. But now I don't know what we're going to serve with the Blackbeard Pie and the clock is ticking as loud as that crocodile in *Peter Pan*."

"How about a Rummy Tum Tum Cake?" Hannah asked her. "Pirates drink rum, don't they?"

"They sure do. Do you make it?"

"No, but Sally does out at the Lake Eden Inn. She puts real rum in hers, but I bet she could make it with rum flavoring."

"That's a great idea, Hannah. I'll call her right after I get off the phone with you. Do you want to know what I got Little Matt for his birthday present?"

"Definitely. What did you get?"

"I found one of those standup cutouts of Johnny Depp as Jack Sparrow and I hired a photographer from Holdingford to take a picture of Little Matt standing right next to it. That photographer did a real good job. I'm going to give Little Matt the standup cutout and the photographer made a big print of that picture. I had it framed so that Little Matt can hang it in his bedroom."

"That's a wonderful present, Winnie."

"I thought so, too. And I checked with his mother since she'll probably be the one to hang the picture and she thought it was a real good present, too." Winnie was silent for a moment. "Do you think you can make a pirate cookie, Hannah?"

"Absolutely. You don't have to worry about that. Lisa and I will have them ready to go tomorrow in time for the party."

When she hung up the phone Hannah had another cup of coffee at the workstation and thought about what Winnie had said. "A pirate cookie," she said with a sigh, attempting to think of what type of cookies she could bake. Nothing came to mind so she thought about pirates and what they did. They made enemies walk the plank, some of them wore gold earrings and had parrots on their shoulders, and they said *Ho, ho, ho,* and *Arggggh.* None of those things brought any particular type of cookie to mind. What else did pirates do?

Hannah got up to get one of the Cocoa Snap Cookies she'd baked early this morning. Perhaps the chocolate would jump start her thought process. She took a bite of the cookie and imagined she was on a pirate ship, watching the crew.

What would they do next? They would board a merchant ship and steal bounty, or perhaps they would wait until the captain had turned over his payload and collected from the buyer. Then they would steal the gold pieces that had been given in payment. Gold pieces. Was there anything she could do in gold pieces? Hannah thought about it for a minute and drew a blank. Perhaps she should concentrate on the pirates themselves, rather than their lifestyle.

A mental image of a pirate, even though it was fueled by movies and Halloween costumes, was easily forthcoming. Pirates wore eye patches, and brandished black powder pistols. They had jeweled or hoop earrings, tight pants, and shirts unbuttoned practically to their waists. Sometimes they were missing a tooth or had a gold cap over one of their front teeth. If the pirate was Captain Hook, he had a hook for a hand.

"Nothing there," Hannah said aloud, shaking her head. "There aren't any romantic pirates except Jack Sparrow . . . and Jean Lafitte, the hero of New Orleans."

Perhaps the pantry would give her some ideas. Hannah got up and walked across the kitchen to the pantry. She was surveying the shelves with a frown on her face when she heard someone calling her name.

"Hannah?"

Hannah recognized the voice immediately. It was Lisa and she was in the kitchen. But what was Lisa doing here when she had the rest of the day off?

"In here," Hannah said, sticking her head out the pantry door. "What are you doing back here? I thought you were going home to relax this afternoon."

"I changed my plans. Herb's got a meeting with Mayor Bascomb at noon and he's not sure how long it'll last. He's taking Dillon with him, and Sammy's got a play date with Vespers at the parsonage. I dropped him off at Grandma Knudson's and I just couldn't face the idea of going home alone. So I came here." Lisa stopped speaking and gave a little sigh. "Besides, I keep thinking about that man and wishing I'd seen him there by the side of the road so I could have warned you."

"It was raining too hard to see much of anything, Lisa."

"I know that, but I keep wishing anyway. I knew I'd get depressed if I just stayed home and then I remembered how you bake whenever you're upset. I thought I might as well try that here."

"Makes sense to me. You can help me come up with a new cookie." Hannah stepped out of the pantry and reached behind her to turn off the light.

"What kind of a cookie?"

"A pirate cookie. Winnie Henderson is having a pirate birthday party for her grandson and we have to come up with a theme cookie."

Lisa poured herself a cup of coffee from the kitchen pot, sat down at the workstation, and waited for Hannah to join her. "Can you use your Berried Treasure Bar Cookies?" she asked.

"That won't work. Winnie wants a cookie, not a bar cookie."

Both women sat there thinking for several minutes and then Lisa began to smile.

"What did you just think of?" Hannah asked her.

"I thought of our Surprise Cookies. And then I thought of Little Snowballs. Why can't we combine the two into one new cookie no one's ever had before?"

"You mean . . . Little Snowballs made bigger with surprises inside of them?" Hannah asked her.

"Yes. We could put all sorts of things inside if they were a little bigger. How many do we need?"

"Six dozen."

"By when?"

"By Saturday morning."

"Plenty of time."

"But that's tomorrow!"

Lisa didn't look concerned. "Piece of cake . . ." she said. "Or maybe I should say piece of *cookie*."

"Very funny, Lisa."

As Hannah watched, Lisa's eyes began to sparkle. "It's going to work, Hannah. We can call them Treasure Chest Cookies and they'll be perfect for a pirate party. They all have different little gems of sweetness inside."

"That sounds perfect to me. I wonder if we can make some kind of treasure chest to hold them."

"Herb can," Lisa quickly volunteered her husband. "He's got the garage all outfitted for woodworking and he's very creative. I know he can make something that looks like a treasure chest."

"Aunt Hannah!" Tracey, Hannah's eldest niece, came running into the kitchen from the coffee shop. "Mom said you were okay, but I needed to see you to make sure."

"You don't need to worry," Hannah said, realizing that Andrea must have told Tracey about the accident. "I'm fine."

"But it must feel awful to kill somebody!"

"Your mother told you *that*?!"

"Oh, no. Mom wouldn't tell me anything like that. She thinks I'm too young to hear it. I found out at Vacation Bible School."

"Who told you?" Lisa asked, clearly intrigued by the dissemination of gossip at the Holy Redeemer Lutheran Church.

"Well, Mrs. Reverend Bob didn't tell me, if that's what you're thinking." Tracey shook her head so hard her shoulder-length blond hair swept her cheeks. "She's my teacher this year and she says we should never repeat anything that hurts anyone else. But this can't really hurt that man because he's already dead." She paused and turned to Hannah. "He is dead, isn't he?"

"That's what Doc Knight said," Hannah confirmed.

"How about you, Aunt Lisa?" Tracey asked, turning to her. "I should have asked you before. You were there with Aunt Hannah and I didn't even ask you how you were." She hurried over to Lisa and gave her a hug. "I'm so sorry I was . . . negligent. That's the right word, isn't it?"

"That's the right word, but you weren't negligent. You were just too worried about your Aunt Hannah to think about anyone else. But I still want to know who told you about the accident."

"It was Karen Dunwright. She's in my class. And she heard it from Calvin Janowski. We were out for recess this morning and Calvin's mother called him to tell him she might be late to pick him up because the road was still blocked off for the crime scene investigation. She even sent him a picture of all the police cars parked on the road."

"Cell phones strike again," Hannah said in a tone that she thought was under her breath, but Tracey turned to look at her.

"Most of the kids have them," she explained. "I have one too, but I can't use it except in emergencies." She stopped speaking and looked worried again. "You weren't talking on your cell phone when you had the accident, were you, Aunt Hannah?"

"No."

"And you weren't texting either?"

"No."

"Oh, good. Dad says at least half of the accidents around here are caused by people texting."

"You don't have to worry about me texting, Tracey. My cell phone is old and I don't think it has that capability."

"You have a phone that can't text?" Tracey asked, looking shocked.

"I think so. And even if it can, I don't know how to do it."

"I could teach you. I know how to text."

Now it was Hannah's turn to be shocked. "Your parents let you text?"

"No, but I know how. I watched some of the older kids and it's easy. You just have to know all the abbreviations like LOL and TC."

"I know LOL is laughing out loud," Lisa said. "What's TC?"

"Teacher coming. That's for if you're texting in class." Tracey stopped and looked a bit apprehensive. "You won't tell Mom I know how to text, will you, Aunt Hannah?"

"Not as long as you don't do it when you're not supposed to."

"Oh, good. I dodged a bullet *that* time, huh?"

Hannah glanced at Lisa who was biting her lip to keep from laughing. "I guess you did."

"Anyway, can I help you and Aunt Lisa bake? Bethie's down for a nap and Grandma McCann can't come to pick me up for at least a half hour."

"Of course you can help. You can be our official stirrer. Lisa and I are going to test a recipe for Treasure Chest Cookies."

"Oh boy!" Tracey said, clearly delighted as she ran to get the extra apron that Hannah kept in a drawer for her. "I think today is my lucky day because I've never even heard of a Treasure Chest Cookie before!"

TREASURE CHEST COOKIES
(Lisa's Aunt Nancy's Babysitter's Cookies)

Preheat oven to 350 degrees F., rack in the middle position.

The Cookie Dough:

> ½ cup *(1 stick, 4 ounces, ¼ pound)* salted butter, room temperature
>
> ¾ cup powdered sugar *(plus 1 and ½ cups more for rolling the cookies in and making the glaze)*
>
> ¼ teaspoon salt
>
> 2 tablespoons milk *(that's ⅛ cup)*
>
> 1 teaspoon vanilla extract
>
> 1 and ½ cups all-purpose flour *(pack it down when you measure it)*

The "Treasure":

Well-drained Maraschino cherries, chunks of well-drained canned pineapple, small pieces of chocolate, a walnut or pecan half, ¼ teaspoon of any fruit jam, or any small soft candy or treat that will fit inside your cookie dough balls.

The Topping:

1 cup powdered *(confectioners)* sugar

To make the cookie dough: Mix the softened butter and ¾ cup powdered sugar together in a medium-sized mixing bowl. Beat them until the mixture is light and fluffy.

Add the salt and mix it in.

Add the milk and the vanilla extract. Beat until they're thoroughly blended.

Add the flour in half-cup increments, mixing well after each addition.

Divide the dough into 4 equal quarters. *(You don't have to weigh it or measure it, or anything like that. It's not that critical.)*

Roll each quarter into a log shape and then cut each log into 6 even pieces. *(The easy way to do this is to cut it in half first and then cut each half into thirds.)*

Roll the pieces into balls about the size of a walnut with its shell on, or a little larger.

Flatten each ball with your impeccably clean hands.

Wrap the dough around a "treasure" of your choice. If you use jam, don't use over a quarter-teaspoon as it

will leak out if there's too much jam inside the dough ball.

Pat the resulting "package" into a ball shape and place it on an <u>ungreased</u> cookie sheet, 12 balls to a standard-size sheet. Push the dough balls down just slightly so they don't roll off on their way to your oven.

Hannah's 1ˢᵗ Note: I use baking sheets with sides and line them with parchment paper when I bake these with jam. If part of the jam leaks out, the parchment paper contains it and I don't have sticky jam on my baking sheets or in the bottom of my oven.

Bake the Treasure Chest Cookies at 350° F. for approximately 18 minutes, or until the bottom edge is just beginning to brown when you raise it with a spatula.

Remove the cookies from the oven and allow them to cool on the sheets for about 5 minutes.

Place ½ cup of powdered sugar in a small bowl.

Place wax paper or parchment paper under the wire racks.

Roll the still-warm cookies in the powdered sugar. The sugar will stick to the warm cookies. Coat them evenly and then return them to the wire racks to cool completely. *(You'll notice that the powdered sugar*

will "soak" into the warm cookie balls. That's okay. You're going to roll them in powdered sugar again for a final coat when they're cool.)

When the cookies are completely cool, place another $\frac{1}{2}$ cup powdered sugar in your bowl. Roll the cooled cookies in the powdered sugar again. Then transfer them to a cookie jar or another container and store them in a cool, dry place.

Hannah's 2nd Note: I tried putting a couple of miniature marshmallows or half of a regular-size marshmallow in the center of my cookies for the "treasure". It didn't work. The marshmallows in the center completely melted away.

Lisa's Note: I'm going to try my Treasure Chest Cookies with a roll of Rollo's next time I make them. Herb just adores those chocolate covered soft caramels. He wants me to try the miniature Reese's Pieces, too.

Yield: 2 dozen delicious cookies that both kids and adults will love to eat.

Chapter
Five

It seemed like forever, but at last Hannah's day was almost over. As Delores had promised, she had called after the board member luncheon to say that none of Doc Knight's paramedics or hospital staff had recognized the man that Hannah had hit. She'd also said that, just as Hannah had suspected, the man's neck had been broken. Doc was planning to perform an autopsy later in the afternoon to ascertain the exact cause of death.

Everyone else was gone and the shop was closed. Andrea had left when they locked the front door and Herb had come to get Lisa. Lisa's car was ready. Herb had checked, and they were picking it up at Murphy's Motors before they went home. Hannah and Michelle had done the prep work for the morning and, except for the two of them, The Cookie Jar was deserted.

"Are you almost ready to go, Hannah?" Michelle came out of the walk-in cooler after stashing the final batch of cookie dough for the morning's baking.

"I'm ready, but my truck's not here yet."

"I know. Lonnie just called me on my cell and said that they need to keep it overnight."

"Oh, great!" Hannah said sarcastically. "What are we going to do for transportation?"

"Lonnie took care of that. He checked with his dad and a

couple of Cyril's mechanics are dropping off a loaner for you from the shop. You can keep it until you get your truck back."

"That's nice of Cyril, but I wonder why they need to keep my truck so long."

"Lonnie said something about waiting for the autopsy report so they could make sure the man's injuries were consistent with the damage to your truck."

Hannah thought about that for a moment. "Okay. I guess that makes sense."

Both sisters sat down at the workstation and propped their feet up on neighboring stools. They munched on a couple of Treasure Chest Cookies, which both of them agreed were perfect for Little Matt's party, until there was a knock on the back door and the mechanics with the loaner arrived. Less than twenty-five minutes after that, the two sisters were pulling into Hannah's condo complex. Michelle was driving. Hannah had explained that she didn't want to drive any motor vehicle quite yet, and Michelle had volunteered.

"Home never looked so good!" Hannah said as her sister drove down the ramp of her underground garage and pulled into her parking spot.

"Home's a good place to be after a rough day." There was empathy in Michelle's voice. "And you had a very rough day."

"Not as rough as the man I hit." Hannah got out of Cyril's loaner, which was a newer model Buick with air-conditioning that actually worked, and started up the stairs. For the first time she wished her garage didn't have stairs to the street level and her condo wasn't on the second floor. She felt like a zombie and she simply had to get back some energy before Norman arrived to take her out to dinner.

"Your turn, or mine?" Michelle asked when they arrived at Hannah's door.

"Yours. I'll unlock and open. You brace yourself."

"Ready."

Hannah opened the door and quickly stepped to the side. Michelle jumped into position in front of the doorway and braced herself for what was about to happen. Both of them heard the thump as Moishe jumped off the back of the living room couch and streaked toward the door. A second later, he was airborne until he landed in Michelle's outstretched arms.

"That was a good one, Moishe," Michelle said, giving him a scratch under the chin as she carried him inside and placed him in his favorite position on the back of the couch. Then she turned to Hannah. "Is he getting heavier?"

"I don't know. He could be. He's been really hungry lately. Maybe I'd better put him on a diet."

As if in response to Hannah's comment, Moishe let out a yowl. Then he turned to give Hannah a baleful look.

"I think he knows that word," Michelle said.

"I think you're right. He just gave me the same death ray glance Mother used to give us when we did something really bad. I should have said that I might have to change his eating habits."

Both sisters turned to look at Moishe, but his expression was perfectly neutral and he made no sound. "That works," Michelle said.

"It works for now, but he'll figure it out. Moishe's a really smart cat. I'll call Dr. Bob and see if I can get an appointment for tomorrow. They can check him out and put him on the scale."

Moishe gave another yowl and the fur on his back began to bristle.

"He doesn't like Dr. Bob anymore?" Michelle asked, staring at the cat who had narrowed his eyes and laid back his ears.

"He adores Dr. Bob. And Sue, too. That's not it. He just heard me say the word . . ." Hannah stopped until she thought of another word . . . "weighing device. I think he caught that particular phobia from me. I don't like to step on the weighing device either." Hannah gave Moishe a little pat and headed for the kitchen. "Since I'm going out with Norman, you're going to need something for dinner. I'll see what's in the refrigerator."

"Don't worry about me. I'm sure there's something. And if there's not, I can always call out for a pizza. Lonnie said Bertanelli's delivers in the summer."

"That's true. They hire high school kids with their own cars and pay them mileage. It's good for the kids and Bert told me that it's great for their business."

Hannah had just stepped into the kitchen when the phone rang. "I'll get it," she called out to Michelle, and picked up the wall phone by the kitchen table. "The Cookie Jar. This is Hannah speak . . . oops!"

There was laughter on the other end of the line. "Did you forget you'd left work?" her caller asked.

"I did. Hi Ken." Hannah recognized Kenneth Purvis, the Jordan High principal's voice. "What's up at the school?"

"The combined sports teams just held the drawing for their annual raffle."

"That's nice," Hannah said, wondering why Ken was calling to tell her about it.

"I'm calling to tell you that you won the grand prize, Hannah!" Ken answered her unspoken question.

"I did?" Hannah was completely astounded. She vaguely remembered buying raffle tickets from several members of the Gulls football team when they came into The Cookie Jar. The Jordan High combined sports teams held a big raffle every year to raise money for athletic uniforms and sports supplies, but she didn't remember anything about the prizes for this year. "That's just fantastic, Ken! What did I win?"

"You don't remember what the grand prize was?"

"Actually . . . no. I didn't think I'd win and I really didn't pay any attention to the flyer. I just bought the tickets the way I do every year to help out the school."

"Well, you're in for a big surprise then. The grand prize is magnificent and it's worth over a thousand dollars!"

"Wow!" Hannah could feel her excitement grow. "Tell me, Ken. What is it?"

There was silence for a moment and then Ken chuckled. "I'm not going to tell you. I'm just going to let them deliver it on Monday and surprise you. Can you be home between one and two?"

"No, but can't you deliver it to me at The Cookie Jar?"

"It's too bulky for that, and too heavy, too. You'd never get it home on your own. Besides, the boys have to assemble it, set it up, and plug it in. Do you have anyone that can let us in? A friend? A neighbor who lives in the complex?"

Hannah thought fast. "My downstairs neighbor could do it, but she works afternoons for Janice Cox at Kiddie Korner. Her husband's home, but he works the night shift at DelRay Manufacturing and he'll be sleeping. Maybe Norman could come out to let them in, but I really hate to ask him. Doc Bennett's on vacation and Norman's been really busy at the dental clinic."

"Not a problem. How about if we stop by your shop and pick up a key? The four boys delivering it are trustworthy and I'll ride along in the truck to supervise."

"That'll work. Just be careful of Moishe. I don't want him to get out."

"That won't be a problem. I'll recruit Kathy. She loves cats and she'll ride along to take care of Moishe."

"Perfect," Hannah declared, remembering how enamored Ken's wife had been with Moishe when he'd spent his days at The Cookie Jar during the production of the independent feature that Ross Barton had filmed in Lake Eden.

"One other question," Ken said. "Where do you want us to put it?"

Several of the words Ken had used to describe her prize flashed through Hannah's mind. *Assemble. Set up. Plug in.* Her thousand dollar prize could be anything from a new big screen television to a refrigerator with a water and ice dispenser in the door. "I have to know what it is before I can tell you where to put it."

"And I'm not going to tell you and spoil the surprise. Do you trust us to decide? I'll consult with Kathy to get the woman's viewpoint. And if you don't like the place we choose, all you have to do is call us and we'll move it to wherever you'd rather have it."

"That works for me. Thanks, Ken. This is exciting. I'll expect you at The Cookie Jar on Monday. And when I get home from work, I can ooh and ahh over my wonderful grand prize."

When Hannah had replaced the receiver in the cradle, she turned to see Michelle standing behind her.

"I heard," Michelle said. "You'd better buy a lottery ticket tonight. The jackpot is way up there and your luck's changing for the better."

"Thank goodness for that! It certainly didn't start out being very lucky."

"I know, but it's a lot better now. You won a raffle and you're going to have dinner at the best restaurant in the Lake Eden area with a man you love. What could be better than that?"

Nothing unless I can go back to this morning and avoid killing that man, Hannah thought, but she didn't say it. That thought was depressing and she didn't want to voice it. "Let's put your theory to the test. I'll open the refrigerator door and see if I can find something perfect for you to eat," she said, crossing to the refrigerator, opening the door, and perusing the contents of the shelves inside.

"Do you have any bread?" Michelle asked, peering around her.

"Yes."

"How about butter?"

"I always have butter."

"Then I've got the perfect dinner if that box behind the sour cream is what I think it is."

"This one?" Hannah moved a box of Velveeta cheese to the front of the shelf.

"Yes. I'll have a grilled cheese with some sliced tomatoes on the side. It's one of my favorite meals. And I saw the ketchup so I'm all set. I just love grilled cheese cut in quarters and dipped in ketchup."

"Okay. There's half a bag of potato chips in the cupboard so you can have some of those, too. I made Chip Chip Hooray Cookies a couple of nights ago and they were left over. If you want some cookies for dessert, they're in the cookie jar."

"I love those cookies. That's perfect, Hannah. I'm going to be having a gourmet meal." Michelle glanced up at the clock and frowned. "I'll feed Moishe. You don't have time. If Norman's picking you up at six-thirty and you want to shower and change, you'd better get cracking. It's already ten after six. And don't forget to buy that lottery ticket before you come back."

CHIP CHIP HOORAY COOKIES

Preheat oven to 350 degrees F., rack in the middle position.

1 and ½ cups softened butter *(3 sticks,
    ¾ pound, 12 ounces)*
1 and ¼ cups white *(granulated)* sugar
2 large egg yolks *(Save the whites in a small,
    covered plastic container to make Angel
    Kiss Cookies or Angel Pillow Cookies)*
½ teaspoon salt
2 teaspoons vanilla extract
2 and ½ cups all-purpose flour *(pack it down in
    the cup when you measure it)*
1 and ½ cups finely crushed plain regular
    potato chips *(measure AFTER crushing—I
    used Lay's, put them in a plastic zip-lock
    bag and crushed them with my hands)*
¾ cup white chocolate chips *(I used Nestle Pre-
    mium White)*
¾ cup semi-sweet chocolate chips *(I used Nes-
    tle)*

—————————

⅓ cup white *(granulated)* sugar for dipping

Hannah's 1ˢᵗ Note: Use regular potato chips, the thin salty ones. Don't use baked chips, or rippled chips, or chips with the peels on, or kettle fried, or flavored, or anything that's supposed to be better for you than those wonderfully greasy, salty old-fashioned crunchy potato chips.

Lisa's Note: I made these for the 4th of July picnic at Eden Lake and rolled them in a combination of white, red, and blue sugar.

In a large mixing bowl, beat the butter, sugar, egg yolks, salt, and vanilla extract until the mixture is light and fluffy. *(You can do this by hand, but it's a lot easier with an electric mixer.)*

Add the flour in one-half cup increments, mixing well after each addition.

Add the crushed potato chips and mix well.

Take the bowl out of the mixer and add the white and semi-sweet chips by hand. Stir them in so that they are evenly distributed.

Form one-inch dough balls with your hands and place them on an UNGREASED cookie sheet, 12 to a standard-sized sheet. *(As an alternative, you can line your cookie sheets with parchment paper.)*

Place the sugar in a small bowl. Spray the flat bottom of a drinking glass with Pam or another nonstick cooking spray, dip it in the sugar, and use it to flatten each dough ball. *(Dip the glass in the sugar for each cookie ball.)*

Bake your cookies at 350 degrees F., for 10 to 12 minutes, or until the cookies are starting to turn golden at the edges. *(Mine took the full 12 minutes.)*

Let the Chip Chip Hooray Cookies cool on the cookie sheet for 2 minutes and then remove them to a wire rack to cool completely. *(If you used parchment paper, all you have to do is pull it over to the wire rack and let the cookies cool right on the paper.)*

Yield: Approximately 6 to 7 dozen crunchy, shortbread-like cookies, depending on cookie size.

Chapter Six

"**D**id I tell you how good you look tonight, Hannah?" Norman asked as he reached for the decanter of chilled water on their table and poured glasses for both of them.

"Yes, you did. And I thanked you. That's what Mother always says a woman should do when a man compliments her appearance. She's supposed to say that and nothing more. But then I spoiled your compliment by saying that of course you thought I looked good because you gave me this outfit for my birthday."

Norman laughed. "I know I did. Claire picked it out for me. But that's not all I was talking about. You're also happier than you were this morning and when you're happy, you're beautiful."

Several responses flew through Hannah's mind, the first of which was *Have you had your eyes checked lately? You obviously need glasses*. The second response was *Don't be silly. I know I'm not beautiful*, and the third was *Are you trying to butter me up for some reason?* But Hannah decided to follow her mother's instructions and she didn't say any of those. "Thank you, Norman," she said. And then she reached out to cover his hand with hers.

Sally Laughlin approached their table and Hannah pulled

her hand back. She was a bit uncomfortable with public displays of affection. "Hi, Sally," she said.

"Hello, Hannah. Good to see you, Norman." Sally was dressed in one of her signature chef's jackets that were trimmed in the same colorful pattern as the aprons the kitchen staff wore. Hannah knew that because the kitchen was visible through a large plate glass window so that diners could watch their food being prepared. "I heard about your accident," Sally told her. "Are you all right?"

"I'm okay," Hannah said and she left it at that. She really didn't want to discuss the accident. She just wanted to forget what had happened in the rain this morning, or at least put it out of her mind for the present. There was no point in discussing it again and again, and talking about it might depress her and spoil her nice evening with Norman.

"Your mother and Doc are on their way here," Sally said, changing the subject when Hannah didn't elaborate. "She just called me to make sure you were here."

"Mother and Doc are joining us for dinner?" Hannah turned to Norman.

"I'm not sure. They're certainly welcome to join us, but this is the first I've heard about it."

Hannah turned back to Sally. "Did Mother say anything else?"

"Just that they had something important to tell you and it couldn't wait."

Hannah and Norman exchanged glances. The phrase *something important* to Delores could be used to describe almost anything that affected her from the new acquisition at her antique store to the announcement that she'd actually agreed to something they'd suggested for her wedding.

"Thanks for the early warning," Hannah told her. "We'll expect them in twenty minutes or so."

Norman gave Hannah a questioning look and she responded with a little nod. She knew exactly what his silent query meant.

"Please invite them to join us for dinner," Norman said, correctly interpreting Hannah's nod.

"I'll do that." Sally turned back to Hannah. "There's a new dessert tonight. It's Buttermilk Pie."

"I've never heard of Buttermilk Pie," Norman told her. "I'm going to order it."

"Isn't that a Southern dessert?" Hannah asked.

"Yes. My assistant chef has relatives in the South and this is his grandmother's recipe."

"Please save a piece for me, too," Hannah added her request to Norman's. "I've never tasted Buttermilk Pie, either."

Sally leaned a little closer so that she couldn't be overheard. "Did your mother like my entrée suggestion for her wedding reception?"

"I've got bad news on that score," Hannah said, giving a little sigh. "I haven't mentioned it to her yet. This morning she told me that she wasn't that fond of salmon. It's a great idea, Sally, but she'll never go for it."

"What did you suggest?" Norman asked Sally, and Hannah knew he was feeling a little out of the loop when it came to the wedding plans.

"Filet of salmon with champagne sauce," Sally told him. "I've been suggesting everything I can think of that I can manage with such a large crowd, but Delores has rejected everything."

"But why?" Norman asked, turning to Hannah. "Everything Sally makes is delicious."

"You know that, and I know that. Mother knows it too, but absolutely nothing we suggest pleases her lately."

"Maybe it does please her, but the problem is that she doesn't want to relinquish the reins," Norman guessed.

"That's exactly right. She doesn't want to plan the wedding, but she still wants to run the show."

"It sounds like you've got a real problem," Sally offered her opinion. "I just wish I had that salmon dish on the menu tonight. Then Delores could have tasted it *before* you suggested it."

"Do you think it would have worked?" Norman asked.

"Maybe, especially if I sprinkled a little of her favorite caviar on top of the champagne sauce. That might have been enough to make her suggest it to you instead of the other way around."

"That might have worked," Hannah said, but she wasn't convinced. "What's the special tonight, Sally?"

"Coq au vin. And I also have a petite filet with wild mushroom sauce."

"I'll have the coq au vin," Norman told her. "It's one of my favorites."

"Mine, too," Hannah said. She debated between the filet and the chicken for a second or two, and then she decided on the chicken. "Make that two, Sally," she said.

When Sally left to go back to the kitchen, Dot Larson, Sally's head waitress, appeared at tableside almost miraculously. It was one of Dot's talents. She hovered unobtrusively and there were times when she seemed to materialize out of thin air. Hannah gave a fleeting thought to how privy she must be to private conversations and how much value that could be in a murder investigation. Both Hannah and Lisa used that trick at The Cookie Jar, but it could be valuable here as well. Perhaps they should try to co-opt Dot in the next murder investigation.

"Hi, Dot," Hannah greeted her warmly.

Dot smiled at both of them. "Hello, Hannah. Hi, Norman. Good to see you here tonight."

"How's the baby, Dot?" Norman asked her.

"Growing like a weed. My mother has her hands full on the nights I work, I can tell you that!"

"But she doesn't mind . . . right?" Hannah asked her.

"That's right. Mom rocks him to sleep every night and Jimmy says she sings silly little songs to him about what a fine big boy he is."

Hannah hid a guilty grin. On several occasions she'd sung silly little songs to Moishe and told him what a fine big boy *he* was!

"Would you care for wine tonight?" Dot turned to Norman.

"Hannah?" Norman referred the answer to her.

"Not tonight," Hannah answered, and then she qualified it. "At least not for me. But Mother and Doc might want wine when they get here."

"I'll check back then. A mixed drink from the bar? Or water?"

"I'd like iced tea, please. And could I have a wedge of lemon with it?"

"Of course." Dot turned to Norman. "How about you?"

"I'll have the same."

"Shall I bring the bread basket now? Or wait until they get here?"

"Now." Hannah made a quick decision. She was really hungry, probably because she had been too upset to eat anything except the lime bar cookies Michelle and her mother had made this morning and one Cocoa Snap Cookie this afternoon.

"Give us a minute before you bring the bread," Sally said, arriving at their table as Dot was about to leave. "I want them to taste this first."

Hannah looked down at the plate Sally placed between

them. On it were two very thin slices of pie. "Is this your Buttermilk Pie?" she asked.

"Yes. It's just a sample to see if you like it."

Norman laughed. "I've never had dessert as an appetizer before."

"I don't think I have, either," Hannah said.

"Sure you have. Haven't you ever had cookies for breakfast?"

"I did this morning," Norman admitted. "I didn't have time for breakfast, and Hannah gave me cookies when I came to see her at work."

"No wonder we're so hungry!" Hannah admitted. "I did exactly the same thing."

The pie was calling out to her and Hannah took a bite. "Smooth, simple, and sweet with a little tang. It's absolutely delicious, Sally."

"The nutmeg is the perfect spice," Norman declared, cutting off another bite. "It's just wonderful, Sally."

"Thank you." Sally waited until the samples she'd brought were gone and then she handed the plate to Dot. "You can bring the bread basket now," she said. "If all they've had all day is dessert, they'll need something a bit more filling."

When the bread basket came a minute or two later, Hannah and Norman attacked it like starving wolves. The little taste of pie had definitely sparked their appetites. They split a muffin, devoured two slices of Sally's peach bread, and ate two mini scones apiece.

"It's empty," Hannah said, staring down at the red and white checked napkin that lined the bread basket. "I guess we'd better ask Dot to bring us another basket of bread before Mother and . . ."

"It's here," Dot interrupted her, setting a full basket on the table and whisking away the empty basket to hand to her busboy. "And so are your mother and Doc Knight. Sally's bringing them over right now. And here's the wine. Your mother called ahead to order it. She said something about the fact that they'd need it."

Hannah glanced at Norman, who looked every bit as clueless as she was. "I wonder what *that* means," she said.

"I don't know, but I think we're about to find out. Here they come and they don't look happy."

GRANDMA'S BUTTERMILK PIE

Preheat oven to 350 degrees F., rack in the center position.

Before you start, prepare <u>one</u> of the following:

Graham cracker crust *(either make your own, or buy one at the store)*
Shortbread cookie crust *(either make your own, or buy one at the store)*
9-inch deep-dish pie shell baked according to package directions

Hannah's 1st Note: Sally said her chef's grand-mother preferred this pie in a graham cracker crust. Personally, I like it in any of the above crusts.

6 Tablespoons *(¾ stick, 3 ounces)* salted butter, room temperature
1 cup brown sugar *(pack it down in the cup when you measure it)*
2 large eggs, separated *(the yolks in one bowl and the whites in another)*
¼ cup all-purpose flour *(pack it down when you measure it)*
1 Tablespoon fresh lemon or lime juice *(Sally says her chef's grandmother used lemon*

juice in the winter and lime juice in the
summer—she doesn't know why)

¼ teaspoon nutmeg *(freshly grated is so much
better!)*

¼ teaspoon cardamom *(if you don't have it, use
more nutmeg instead)*

¼ teaspoon salt

1 teaspoon vanilla extract

1 cup buttermilk, room temperature *(if you
don't want to wait for your buttermilk to
warm up to room temperature, pour it into
a microwave-safe measuring cup and heat
it for 20 seconds on HIGH in the
microwave.)*

Use a medium-size mixing bowl to combine the
butter and the sugar. Beat them until the sugar is completely incorporated and the mixture is light and
fluffy.

**Hannah's 2ⁿᵈ Note: Sally uses an electric mixer
when she does this. You can also do it by hand, but
it takes a bit of muscle.**

If you haven't done so already, separate the whites
of the eggs from the yolks. Add <u>only</u> the egg yolks to
the mixture and beat well.

Add the flour, lemon or lime juice, nutmeg, cardamom, salt, and vanilla extract. Mix them in thoroughly. The resulting mixture should be smooth with no lumps.

With the mixer running, add the buttermilk a bit at a time, pouring slowly and mixing it in until it is incorporated.

Use another bowl to whip the egg whites until they form soft peaks. *(Soft peaks droop at the tips when you stop mixing and raise the whisk or beaters.)*

When the egg whites have formed soft peaks, it's time to "temper" them with the heavier mixture. You do this by pouring a small amount of buttermilk pie batter into the bowl of whipped egg whites and folding it in gently, just until it's incorporated.

Hannah's 3rd Note: I use a rubber spatula to do this. The object is to incorporate the buttermilk batter, but to leave as much air as possible in the whipped egg whites.

Now it's time to reverse directions. Pick up the bowl with the tempered egg whites and fold them gently into the buttermilk mixture. Fold only until the egg whites have been incorporated. Again, your goal is to preserve as much air as possible in the mixture.

Pour the final mixture into the baked pie shell, smoothing the top if needed.

Bake the Buttermilk Pie at 350 degrees F. for 45 to 50 minutes, or until the filling is lightly browned and barely moves when the pie is jiggled *(with potholders, of course).*

Cool your pie on a cold stovetop burner or a wire rack until it reaches room temperature.

This pie can be served warm, or at room temperature.

Refrigerate any leftovers.

Hannah's 4th Note: When Sally serves this pie at the Lake Eden Inn, she centers the wedges on pie plates and decorates the rim of the pie plate with raspberry sauce and lemon or lime sauce. She also brings a bowl with sweetened, whipped cream to the table. When I serve it at home, I don't get that fancy. I simply place a mint leaf on top of each slice, and I double the recipe when I serve it to Mother. Even though it's not chocolate, she's crazy about it! Perhaps it's because she's always wanted to be a Southern Belle. And PLEASE don't tell her I said that!

Chapter Seven

When Doc filled a wineglass with her favorite white wine and handed it to Hannah before he served anyone else, Hannah knew that whatever they had to tell her wasn't good. She waited until everyone else had been served and then she spoke. "Something's wrong. What is it?"

Delores looked at Doc and Doc looked at Delores. For a moment, neither of them spoke. Then Delores gave a slight nod and Doc cleared his throat. "This isn't really appropriate conversation for dinner," he said. "We should wait until after we've eaten."

"No," Hannah said. "Whatever it is, I want to know now."

"It's that man you hit with your truck this morning," Delores said, and Hannah noticed that her mother wasn't quite able to meet her eyes. "Doc just finished the autopsy and . . . and . . ."

Delores stopped speaking, clearly unable to go on, and Hannah knew that whatever it was, it was deadly serious. "What?" she asked, turning to Doc.

"With the exception of a cracked cheekbone, the rest of his injuries were consistent with the damage to the front of your truck," Doc said.

"Did the cracked cheekbone cause his death?" Norman asked the question that Hannah was afraid to ask.

"No. He died almost instantly from massive trauma and an obstructed airway."

"So when I hit him, I broke his neck," Hannah said.

"Yes. I'm sorry, Hannah. I was hoping that there was some other explanation, but there isn't. When you hit him with your truck, you broke his neck and killed him."

Hannah swallowed hard and put down her wineglass without taking a sip. Even though she'd known that it was a long shot, she'd been hoping that Doc's autopsy would reveal that the man had died of something else. Of course it hadn't. She had killed him and now that Doc had performed the autopsy, it was official.

"It was an accident, dear." Delores reached across the table to pat Hannah's hand. "Nobody blames you."

"That's right," Norman said, reaching out to cover her other hand with his. "It was a terrible storm. You couldn't see him. And then there was the tree branch in the road when you came around the bend. You certainly didn't *mean* to hit him. Everyone knows that."

"There's more, Hannah," Doc said looking sad. "There are times when I hate some aspects of my job and this is one of them. I have a responsibility as the Winnetka County Coroner. I'm sorry, but I had to report it to the authorities."

"To the authorities," Hannah repeated, still not understanding exactly what Doc was trying to tell her. "Which authorities?"

"I had to file a report with the Winnetka County Sheriff's Department."

"But . . . why, Doc? It was an accident!"

"No one doubts that, Hannah. We know that you didn't intend to hit him, but you *did* hit him and he died as a result. Unfortunately in this case, whenever that happens there are consequences."

"Wha . . . what do you mean?" Hannah forced out the words.

"Excuse my language, but I'm very much afraid all hell is going to break loose."

Hannah reached for her water glass, but her hands began to shake. She was afraid she'd spill it if she picked it up so she didn't even try. Her mouth felt as if it were filled with sawdust and her throat was parched when she attempted to swallow. She needed to explain, to tell Doc that her truck had skidded on the wet gravel when she'd swerved to avoid the tree branch, that the pounding rain had reduced her visibility to almost zero, and the blinding flashes of lightning had made it impossible for her to see him standing there at the side of the road. She opened her mouth to tell him all that, but before she could even try to utter a word, she saw Mike rushing toward her across the dining room floor.

"I got here as soon as I could," he said, pulling Hannah to her feet and hugging her. "I'm so sorry, Hannah!"

He was holding her so tightly, she could barely move, but she managed to gasp out a question. "Sorry?"

"I'll try to delay them. Just go out through the kitchen and we'll figure out what to do later. Go now, Hannah! I called Michelle. She's coming to get you!"

"But, why should I . . ." Hannah started to ask, but then she spotted Andrea running through the dining room, dodging waitresses and busboys as if the meanest bull in Winnetka County were after her.

"Hannah!" Andrea gasped, jerking Hannah away from Mike and turning on him with fire in her eyes. "Get your hands off my sister! I'll never let you take her!"

Mike stared at her in surprise. "But I wasn't going to!"

Andrea made a sound that sounded a bit like a growl to Hannah's ears. "Oh, yes you were! Don't lie to me, you . . . you cop!"

Hannah stepped back, staring at one and then the other as they hurled accusations at each other. What in the world was going on?! And that was when Michelle came racing up to grab Hannah's hand.

"Quick! Come with me! Lonnie's in back and he's got the car running!"

"But . . . what in the world is . . . ?"

"No time!" Michelle interrupted her. "I'll explain later. He'll be here any minute and then . . . oh no! It's too late!"

Hannah glanced over Michelle's shoulder to see Bill striding toward their table looking grim.

"Go!" Andrea ordered Hannah and then she rushed to intercept her husband, grabbing his arm and attempting to slow his progress.

"Get away!" Hannah heard him say in a tone she'd never heard him use before. It was an officious tone, a commanding tone, a tone that brooked no nonsense.

"Don't you dare!" Andrea clung to his arm.

"I have to. It's my job. Get away or you'll go, too!"

Andrea just hung on harder. "I'm warning you, Bill. If you do this . . . if you even *try* to do this, I'll never speak to you again!"

"I have to do it. It's my job," Bill repeated, finally managing to shake her off. He made a beeline for the table and stopped in front of Hannah. "Hannah Louise Swensen," he continued in that same no-nonsense tone as he thrust an official-looking paper into Hannah's hand. "You have been served with a warrant for your arrest."

There was total silence for moment. Everyone at their table and the surrounding tables was completely quiet and motionless. It reminded Hannah of the game of statues they'd played in grade school on rainy days when they couldn't go out to the playground. They'd walked around the room until the teacher blew a whistle. That was the signal for everyone to freeze in place as if time had stopped. The best "statue" was awarded the whistle for the next round and the game resumed until recess was over.

"Mike!" Bill's voice broke what had, for a brief moment, seemed like a wicked witch's spell to Hannah. "Arrest her!"

Mike looked at Hannah and then he turned to face Bill squarely. "No," he said.

That threw Bill for a loop. He simply stared at Mike as if he couldn't believe his ears and then he repeated his order. "I said arrest her!"

"No."

Bill drew a deep breath and let it out again. "Michael Kingston, are you refusing my direct order?"

"Yes. I refuse to arrest her."

Hannah stared at Mike in shock. He was a by-the-book cop. Everyone in town knew that. Mike understood his duty and he did it regardless of his personal feelings. If his superior told him to jump, Mike asked *How high?* Hannah was almost positive that Mike had never refused a direct order in his whole career in law enforcement. Up to this point she'd been convinced that if there was a warrant for Mike's mother's arrest, he'd drive to the Kingston family home and fulfill his duty. And yet here Mike was, refusing to arrest her!

"If you refuse my direct order again, I am going to suspend you without pay. Do you understand?"

Mike nodded. "I understand."

"I'm ordering you to arrest Hannah Louise Swensen."

Mike looked Bill straight in the eye and shook his head. "No. I refuse to arrest her."

Bill uttered an oath under his breath that Hannah had never heard before. "Then I'll do it," Bill said, turning toward Hannah.

"Arrest me, Mike," Hannah said before Bill could utter the words. "Go ahead. The end result is going to be the same. There's no sense in losing your job when Bill's going to arrest me anyway."

"No. I won't be a part of it, Hannah. It's just not right. There are some things I'll do and some things I won't. And this is something I won't. There's no way I'm going to be the one to arrest you on this trumped up charge."

"Trumped up charge?" Hannah asked, even though Bill was right behind her.

"It's all politics, Hannah. These ridiculous charges won't stick. Ask Howie when he comes in to see you tonight. I called him and he knows all about it."

"You called Howie?" Hannah was doubly amazed. What happened to the one phone call people who were arrested were allowed to make? Cops weren't supposed to jump the gun and do it for them.

At that exact moment, Hannah realized that it was deathly quiet in the dining room of the Lake Eden Inn. There was no murmuring from the surrounding tables, no clink of silverware as diners enjoyed their food, not even a whisper or a rustle of clothing as people shifted in their chairs. Everyone around them was silent and still, staring in shock at the spectacle that was taking place right before their very eyes.

Oh boy! Hannah thought. *If Mother thinks today's article was mortifying, just wait until she sees tomorrow's* Lake Eden Journal. *Rod's going to have a heyday with this one!*

"Hannah Louise Swensen," Bill said, his voice loud in the silent dining room. "I have a warrant for your arrest on the charge of vehicular homicide. Come with me quietly, please."

Hannah glanced at the others at the table. Delores looked every bit as shocked as the other diners and Doc resembled a fish out of water with gaping mouth and a face drained of color. Michelle was staring at her with tears running down her cheeks, and Norman looked sick at heart and highly frustrated that he could do nothing to help her. Even Sally, who had come over to their table, looked as if she wished she were anywhere else but there. The only person who didn't look shocked, or sad, or completely helpless was Andrea. Andrea was staring at Bill with blazing eyes and a venomous look.

Better hide your service handgun tonight, Hannah thought as Bill marched her through the quiet dining room, across the lobby, and out the front door. *If Andrea finds it, I might not be the only Swensen sister charged with a homicide.*

Chapter Eight

Less than thirty minutes later, Hannah was being pro-
cessed at the Winnetka County Sheriff's Station. Bill
had taken her in, and ordered Lonnie's brother, Rick Murphy, to book her and lock her up in a cell. After informing
Rick that he would be personally responsible for the prisoner
for the night, Bill had turned his back on Hannah and gone
out the door. Hannah suspected that Bill would be heading
straight home to attempt to appease his angry wife. Of course,
there would be nothing Bill could say or do that would work,
at least not tonight. Hannah had grown up with Andrea and
she had never seen her sister this angry before. There was no
way Andrea would forgive Bill right away.

"I'm so sorry, Hannah," Rick said as he finished the
paperwork and took her to the holding cell. "I really don't
want to do this, you know."

"I know you don't. It's okay, Rick. You have to do your
duty."

"But that doesn't mean I have to like it." Rick walked her
past the small cells they kept for prisoners who were serving
short sentences or waiting for the next morning's arraignment in court. "At least the holding cell is empty tonight. It's
a whole lot bigger than these cells and you'll have room to
walk around. Not only that, you can see the desk from there

and that's where I'll be. You can just call out to me if you need anything."

A few minutes later, Hannah was incarcerated in the holding cell. Rick had apologized again for having to lock Hannah up, and Hannah knew he felt awful about it. He said he wished he could leave the cell door open, but he didn't dare do that because Bill might come back to check on him. Rick had clanged the cell door shut behind her, told her that he was going to make some phone calls to see if he could learn more about her situation, and left her alone in the holding cell with nothing but bars and concrete walls to look at.

The only thing she could do was pace across the floor, and that's what Hannah did until Rick came back ten minutes later. He was carrying a chair and he placed it right outside the cell door. "I've got some news," he said, sitting down to keep her company. And that was when Hannah learned that there was good news and there was bad news.

One piece of good news was that Howie Levine was on his way. Hannah's lawyer had been at the Guthrie in Minneapolis attending a play with his wife when he'd gotten Mike's phone call. Howie and Kitty had left the theater immediately and they were on their way back to Lake Eden. Howie told Rick that the traffic was horrible, but they should be back in town in less than an hour. Right after he dropped Kitty at home, Howie would come straight to the sheriff's station.

The other good news was that Delores was going to bring her dinner from the Lake Eden Inn. Hannah wouldn't go hungry tonight.

There was only one piece of bad news, but it was very bad. Since it was Friday night, Hannah would have to stay in the holding cell until she was arraigned on Monday morning. That meant she would spend three nights in jail. And even though the holding cell was large and there was room to move around, just knowing that she was locked in and couldn't get out left her feeling claustrophobic.

Hannah glanced at the clock on the wall outside her cell and sighed deeply. She'd only been in jail for fifteen minutes and time was passing much too slowly to suit her. She wished she were home on her couch in the living room, watching a vintage movie on television, munching buttered popcorn with Moishe purring beside her. She wished she were in her condo kitchen with Michelle, baking treats and laughing. She wished she were back at the Lake Eden Inn, enjoying her coq au vin with Norman, Doc, and her mother. She wished she were anywhere but here in this cell with steel bars between her and freedom.

"If wishes were horses, beggars could ride," she said aloud, repeating one of her Great-Grandmother Elsa's favorite sayings. She was in a cell at the Winnetka County Sheriff's Station and she had to try to make the best of it. Perhaps the time would pass more quickly if she had something to read, something to take her mind off this horrible situation.

"Rick?" she called out. "Is there anything around here to read?"

"I'll go see. Sometimes the secretaries leave magazines in the break room."

Hannah watched as he got up from behind the desk and left. She heard the sound of his footsteps echoing down the corridor and then stopping. She imagined him opening the door of the break room, switching on the lights, and checking to see if there were any magazines on the long wooden table in the center of the room. All too soon, she heard the door close and the sound of his footsteps increasing in volume as he walked back.

"Sorry, Hannah." Rick came up to her cell. "No one left any magazines. I'll check in Barbara's office. Maybe there's something to read in there."

Again Hannah waited, hoping that there was something, anything to get her mind off the events of this horrible day. It didn't really matter what it was. She'd settle for a book on police procedures, or a drivers manual, or a copy of the county statutes. Even a phone book would do although there weren't that many pages in the Lake Eden phone book.

Rick was coming back. Hannah listened eagerly as his footfalls approached. He simply *had* to have found something!

"Not much to choose from here," Rick said, arriving with several choices in his hand.

"That's okay. I'll take anything."

Rick laughed. "That's good." He reached through the bars to hand her part of a calendar with daily tear-off pages. "It's last year's, but it's got a knock-knock joke at the top of every page. Since it starts in November, it must have belonged to that temporary secretary we hired last year when Sandy was on maternity leave."

"Thanks, Rick," Hannah said, even though she wasn't very fond of knock-knock jokes. "What else have you got?"

"A booklet on . . . never mind. I shouldn't have brought that."

"What is it?"

"Something you probably don't want to read."

Now Hannah's curiosity was aroused. "Come on, Rick. Hand it over. I'll decide if I want to read it, or not."

"Okay, but don't say I didn't warn you."

Rick passed a slim booklet through the bars and Hannah read the title aloud. "*Symptoms and Treatment of Venereal Disease*?"

Rick's face colored slightly. "I don't know who brought that in. Actually, I don't think I *want* to know who brought that in."

"Me, either," Hannah said, handing it back to him. "Better put it back where it was."

"Good idea. Here's the other thing I found, Hannah. It looks pretty dull."

Hannah took the thick volume and began to smile. "*A Chronology of Minnesota Weather*," she read the title aloud. "This is absolutely perfect, Rick!"

"Really?" Rick sounded shocked. "Then you want to keep it?"

"You bet I do! That cot on the wall doesn't look very comfortable and I was afraid I'd be up all night. A couple pages of this and I'll be so bored, I'll go right to sleep."

Hannah was on her fourth week of bad knock-knock jokes when she heard her mother's voice. She looked up to see Delores and Andrea standing at the front desk. Andrea was carrying two large bags of food, and Delores was equally burdened.

"This one's for you, Rick," Delores said, handing him one of her bags. "Sally said you liked her prime rib dinner so she sent it for you."

"Thanks!"

Hannah couldn't see Rick's face but she knew he was wearing a big grin.

"It's okay if we take Hannah's dinner back to her, isn't it?" Andrea asked him.

"Sure. I'll let you in and you can talk to her while she eats. Follow me and I'll show you where she is."

Rick led the little procession and Hannah watched her mother and sister follow him down the hallway. When they arrived at the holding cell, Rick unlocked the door.

"There you go," he said. "I'll lock you in and then I'm going to get a cup of coffee and dig into my dinner before it gets cold."

"You're going to lock us in?!" Andrea turned to glare at him.

"Well . . . yeah, Mrs. Todd. I have to. Hannah's a prisoner and I can't leave the cell door open."

"But I'm the wife of your boss! Bill's not going to be happy with you if you lock my mother and me in a cell with my sister!"

Hannah watched as a myriad of expressions crossed Rick's face. First he looked as if he were about to object, and then he looked as if he'd thought better of it. He vacillated between the two extremes and Hannah knew exactly what was running through his mind. *It's true. She's Bill's wife and I don't want to make her mad. But that doesn't mean she can waltz in here and tell me what to do. My boss is the only one who can tell me what to do. But will he be mad at me if I don't follow procedure? Should I play it by the rules and tell her that I can't do that? She's got me between a rock and a hard place and I don't know what I should do. Bill suspended Mike without pay for not doing his duty, and I sure don't want to end up like that! Jessica will kill me if I come home suspended without pay!*

"I've got an idea," Hannah said, feeling sorry for Rick and his obvious dilemma. "Why don't you bring me the food, lock me up again, and get a couple of chairs so Mother and Andrea can sit right outside in the hall and visit with me while I eat."

"Yeah, that'll work!" Rick looked very relieved as he took the food from Delores and Andrea and carried it inside the cell. "Hold on, ladies. I'll get chairs for you."

Rick got the chairs in short order and rushed off to enjoy his dinner. Andrea didn't look happy at this turn of events, but she sat down right outside the holding cell with Delores.

"Oh, Hannah!" Delores sighed deeply. "I just knew something bad would happen today. And it did. I still can't believe that a daughter of mine is in jail!"

"And *my* husband locked you up!"

One look at Andrea's face and Hannah knew her brother-in-law wouldn't be forgiven soon.

"I am not going to read the paper tomorrow," Delores declared. "That snake in the grass was there and he heard the whole thing!"

"Rod Metcalf?" Hannah asked, unable to think of anyone else her mother might call a snake in the grass.

"That's right. And I think he took a picture of you with his cell phone as Bill led you out of the dining room."

"It'll probably be on the front page," Andrea said, frowning deeply. "I wish there was something we could do to kill that story, but I don't think asking Rod to do it will work."

There was a moment of silence and Hannah knew her mother and Andrea were thinking thoughts of public scandal and how they could possibly avert it. It was time to change the subject before all three of them got depressed. "So what did Sally send for my dinner?" Hannah asked.

"There's a new appetizer she made for you," Andrea replied quickly and Hannah knew she also wanted to change the subject. After all, her husband would be in the infamous article, too. "Open the bags and take a look."

Hannah opened the two bags of food and looked around for something to use as a table. There was nothing even remotely resembling a table in the cell. She finally settled for the cot nearest the door and then she began to explore the takeout boxes that Sally had sent.

"These are darling," she said, opening a box with four mini open-faced sandwiches spread with cream cheese that were topped with a small piece of smoked salmon.

"Aren't they though!" Delores looked pleased that Hannah liked them. "Do you think they'd work as an appetizer for the wedding reception?"

Hannah stared at her mother in shock. They'd been suggesting appetizers for weeks now and Delores had rejected every one of their suggestions. "I think these would be just perfect," she said, hoping that agreeing with her mother wouldn't mean that Delores would disagree.

"That's set then." Delores gave a quick nod. "I thought of it the moment I saw them. They're festive, and fancy, and not messy at all. I think that's important when the guests are wearing their best clothing and don't want to spill."

"That's very smart, Mother," Andrea complimented her.

"Yes, it is," Hannah agreed. "We'll have to keep that in mind when we figure out the rest of the menu."

"Thank you, dears." Delores looked pleased. "And by the way, I've also decided on the entrée."

"Really?" Hannah was amazed. If she'd only known that her mother would make decisions about the wedding the minute her eldest daughter was behind bars, she would have figured out a way to get locked up much earlier and saved them all the aggravation. "What did you decide on for an entrée, Mother?"

"Individual Beef Wellington. Sally told me she could make it for a crowd using small filets wrapped in puff pastry."

"What a good idea!"

"That's what Mother ordered tonight and she said it was just delicious," Andrea explained.

"Did she send one for me?" Hannah asked, hoping that Sally had given her a sample.

"No, dear. Sally said it wouldn't travel well. You have Fettuccini Porcini. It's a pasta dish Sally's cousin had when she was in Australia."

"It's really good. That's what I had tonight after you left," Andrea said. "I told Sally that there was a microwave in the break room here at the station and she told me that we could warm it up if it got too cold."

"It feels hot enough to me," Hannah said, pulling the pasta dish out of the hotbox and feeling the bottom. "How about dessert?"

"You have two desserts," Delores said. "Sally sent a slice of that Buttermilk Pie you tasted, and there's a slice of Rummy Tum Tum Cake."

The dessert box had a see-through plastic lid and Hannah's stomach growled as she gazed at the pie and the cake. "They both look absolutely wonderful."

"I had the cake for dessert," Andrea told her. "I was really upset and Mother thought I needed chocolate. It's delicious, but the slice you have is special."

Hannah picked up the fork that Sally had sent and pried the lid from the box. "I'll have a bite of the cake first."

"Careful!" Andrea warned her, getting up to move right up against the bars. "I said yours was special, Hannah. Don't eat it yet!"

"Why not? There's nothing wrong with having a bite of dessert before I start my entrée."

"Stop!" Delores hissed out the word, jumping up to join Andrea at the cell bars. "We said it was *special.*"

"That's why I wanted to taste it."

"Not special *that* way," Andrea tried to explain. "Special because . . ." she lowered her voice to a whisper. "It's special because it's got something in it."

"Of course it has something in it. All cakes have ingredients in them. Why are you whispering, Andrea?"

Andrea pressed right up against the bars. "This cake is special because we put a file in it," she whispered.

Hannah stared at her sister in amazement. "You're trying to help me break out of jail?"

"Yes!" Delores whispered. "It was my idea. I asked Sally if she had a file and she didn't, but Andrea had one in her purse."

"Andrea had a *file* in her purse?"

"Shhh!" Delores hissed. "It's right near the bottom and it's wrapped in foil. All you have to do is pull it out."

"The cake's still good. You can eat it," Andrea explained. "That's why we wrapped the file in foil."

Hannah stared down at the piece of cake. It was a big piece, but it wasn't big enough to contain a file. She felt around with the fork and found a hard object at the bottom, just as her mother had said. She pulled it out, unwrapped it, and began to laugh. "A *nail* file?"

Andrea looked highly embarrassed. "It was the only thing we could find."

Hannah was still laughing, but she managed to gasp out her questions. "What did you expect me to do? Pick the lock on the cell door?"

Delores shrugged. "No, but we wanted to bring *something*. And your nails are looking a bit ragged, dear."

"Then thank you. If Rick doesn't confiscate it, I'll file them. It's not like I don't have the time. I'll be in here for two more days before I'm arraigned."

"Oh, no!" Delores looked very concerned. "Will you be all right, dear? It's rather dreary in that cell."

"We should have stopped at my house and brought a nice bedspread," Andrea said. "And a few throw pillows to dress up the place."

"What a good idea! I'll do it tomorrow." Delores looked pleased that she had something she could do.

"They'll grant you bail, won't they?" Andrea asked Hannah. "I mean, you have strong ties to the community, you own a business and a condo here, and you're not a flight risk . . . are you?"

"Not really. For one thing, I wouldn't know where to go. And for another thing, I don't have the money to fly to a foreign country where they can't extradite me."

"Don't worry, dear," Delores told her, but Hannah saw the worried look in her mother's eyes. "They're bound to give you bail."

"That's another problem," Hannah told her. "I don't have the money to make bail."

"But I do. I'll be there at the arraignment, dear. And I'll bail you out."

"That's nice of you, Mother."

Delores shrugged again. "What else is a mother to do when her daughter's in jail? I'm certainly not going to leave you here! Now eat your dinner, my dear. You must keep up your strength."

Right, Mother, Hannah thought. *I won't be able to use my super powers and bend these steel bars if I'm as weak as a kitten.* But she smiled at her mother, anyway. Delores meant well. And then she dug into Sally's excellent dinner like there was no tomorrow.

CREAM CHEESE AND HERB SCONES

Preheat oven to 425 degrees F., rack in the middle position.

3 cups all-purpose flour *(pack it down in the cup when you measure it)*
2 teaspoons cream of tartar *(this is important)*
1 teaspoon baking powder
1 teaspoon baking soda
1 teaspoon salt
½ cup salted butter, softened to room temperature
(1 stick, 4 ounces, ¼ pound)

---

8 ounces *(by weight, not volume)* whipped cream cheese at room temperature *(I used Philadelphia brand, which is also 8 ounces by volume)*
6.5-ounce *(by weight)* package Boursin Cheese with Herbs at room temperature *(one package)*
2 large eggs, beaten *(just whip them up in a glass with a fork)*
1 cup sour cream

In a mixing bowl, combine the flour, cream of tartar, baking powder, baking soda, and salt. Mix thoroughly.

Mix in bits of salted butter with two forks or a piecrust blender, just as you would for piecrust dough.

Hannah's 1ˢᵗ Note: If you have a food processor, you can use it to do this. Cut ½ cup COLD salted butter into 8 chunks. Layer the chunks of butter with the dry ingredients in the bowl of the food processor. Process with the steel blade in an on-and-off motion until the mixture is the texture of cornmeal. Transfer the mixture to a mixing bowl and proceed to the next step.

Check your cheeses. If they haven't come up to room temperature, take them out of the packages, put them in a microwave-safe bowl, and soften them on HIGH for 20 seconds or so. Then take them out and add the beaten eggs and sour cream. Mix everything together thoroughly.

Add the cheese, egg, and sour cream mixture to the dry ingredients. Stir the dough with a fork until everything is thoroughly combined. The resulting mixture should be roughly the consistency of cottage cheese.

Use a large spoon to drop the biscuits onto an ungreased baking sheet. You can make 12 very large scones, 24 medium sized scones, or 4 to 5 dozen mini

scones. *(You can bake one sheet at a time with this dough—it'll be fine in the bowl for a half-hour or so while you wait for the first batch to bake.)*

Hannah's 2nd Note: I line my baking sheets with parchment paper for easy removal.

If your scones look a little ragged around the edges, wet your fingers and shape them into rounds.

Bake the scones at 425 degrees F. for 14 to 16 minutes for very large scones, 12 to14 minutes for medium-sized scones, or 8 to 10 minutes for mini scones baked in miniature cupcake tins sprayed with Pam or another nonstick cooking spray. To test for doneness, touch them with the back of a spoon to see if they're "set" on top.

Hannah's 3rd Note: DON'T OVERBAKE these scones. That will make them dry. My very large scones took a total of 15 minutes, the medium-sized scones took 14 minutes, and the mini scones in the miniature cupcake tins took 9 minutes. The rule of thumb here is that if they look done, they are done.

Cool the scones for at least 5 minutes on the cookie sheets, and then remove them with a spatula. *(If you used parchment paper, all you have to do is pull the paper off the baking sheet and peel off the scones.)*

The mini scones in the miniature cupcake tins should cool for at least 8 minutes before you remove them.

Serve the scones in a towel-lined basket so that they stay warm.

Yield: Makes 12 very large scones, 24 medium-sized scones, or 4 to 5 dozen mini scones. These scones are simply delicious served with extra cream cheese, capers, and smoked salmon.

Hannah's 4th Note: To serve mini scones as appetizers, simply cool them and cut them in half horizontally. Top them with more cream cheese, press on a few capers, and place a small slice of smoked salmon on top. You can either serve them that way, or spread a little more cream cheese on the top half and use it to make a mini sandwich the way Sally does.

FETTUCCINI "PORCINI"
(Australian Fettuccini)

Trudi's 1st Note: We just returned from a trip to Australia. This is my version of a recipe we experienced in Sydney. It's easy to make and a wonderful flavor.

For the Pasta:

Prepare a package of your favorite brand fettuccini pasta as instructed on the package. Use the size that serves 4. When the pasta is cooked, drain it, give it a stir to keep it from sticking together, cover it loosely with foil and set it aside on a cold burner to wait for its yummy sauce.

For the Sauce:

> ¼ pound bacon *(regular sliced, not thick)*
> ½ pound *(8 ounces)* fresh mushrooms sliced, or chopped
> ½ cup chopped onions *(regular yellow onions or green onions—if you use green onions, you can use up to 2 inches of the stem)*
> 4-inch square of fresh salmon filet

15-ounce *(approximate—if it's a bit more, that's okay)* jar of prepared Alfredo sauce

Pan fry the bacon until it's crispy and lift it out of the fat with a slotted spoon to drain it on paper towels.

Use the remaining bacon fat in the pan to fry the mushrooms until they are very well done.

Add the onions to the pan and continue to fry until the onions are translucent and fully cooked.

Cut the raw salmon into cubes and add it to the pan. Fry it until the salmon is fully cooked.

Add the drained bacon pieces to the pan and add the Alfredo sauce. Stir everything together until it's well-combined and heated through.

Arrange the pasta you've cooked on 4 plates. Ladle the delicious mixture in the frying pan over the pasta and serve to rave reviews!

Trudi's 2nd Note: The porcini is in quotes because I'm sure the restaurant used them, but regular mushrooms work just as well and are easier on the budget.

Fresh salmon works great but since it sort of falls apart in the cooking anyway, you probably could use

canned or packaged salmon and get the same results.

If you prefer, you could also use packaged Alfredo sauce mix and prepare it yourself.

RUMMY TUM TUM CAKE

Preheat oven to 350 degrees F., rack in the middle position.

- 1 box chocolate cake mix *(the size that makes a 9-inch by 13-inch cake) (DO NOT use cake mix with pudding in it because your cake will stick to the pan. I used Devil's Food Cake Mix when I tested this.)*
- 1 box chocolate instant pudding mix *(NOT sugar-free—the size that makes 4 half-cup servings)*
- ½ cup vegetable oil
- 1 cup sour cream
- ⅓ cup rum *(I used Appleton's Rum)*
- 2 teaspoons rum extract *(If your store doesn't have this, you can use vanilla extract instead)*
- 4 large eggs

6-ounce package semi-sweet chocolate chips
(approximately 1 cup)

Spray a Bundt pan with Pam or another nonstick cooking spray. Make sure to spray the little tube in the middle so the cake won't stick to that.

Place the dry chocolate cake mix and the dry chocolate pudding mix in the bowl of an electric mixer. Beat them together on low speed until they're combined.

Add the vegetable oil, sour cream, rum, and rum extract. Beat on LOW speed until thoroughly mixed.

Mix in the eggs, one at a time on MEDIUM speed, beating after each addition. When you're through, this batter should be nice and fluffy. If it's not, turn the mixer up to HIGH and beat for 2 additional minutes.

Take the bowl out of the mixer and add the chocolate chips by hand. Don't over-stir. You want to keep as much air as possible in the batter.

Spoon the batter into the prepared Bundt pan. Smooth the top with a rubber spatula.

Bake the cake at 350 degrees F. for 50 minutes or until a cake tester or a thin wooden skewer inserted in the center of the ring comes out clean. *(Mine took 53 minutes.)*

Cool the Rummy Tum Tum Cake for 20 minutes on a cold stovetop burner or a wire rack.

After 20 minutes, loosen the edges of the cake with a knife. Don't forget to run the knife around the tube in the center of the Bundt pan to loosen that, as well.

Invert a cake plate on top of the Bundt pan, flip the Bundt pan and the cake plate over, and unmold the cake. Let it cool completely on the plate before frosting it with Rummy Tum Tum Chocolate Frosting.

Hannah's Note: If you would prefer not to use alcohol in this cake, simply substitute ⅓ cup light cream for the rum. It's yummy that way, too.

RUMMY TUM TUM CHOCOLATE FROSTING

½ cup *(1 stick, ¼ pound, 4 ounces)* salted butter

1 cup white *(granulated)* sugar

⅓ cup rum *(I used Appleton's Rum)*

½ cup chocolate chips

1 teaspoon rum extract *(or vanilla extract if you can't find rum extract)*

½ to 1 cup powdered *(confectioner's)* sugar *(I
used a total of ¾ cup)*

Place the butter, sugar, and rum into a medium-size
saucepan. Bring the mixture to a boil, stirring constantly. Turn down the heat to medium and cook for
two minutes.

Add the half-cup chocolate chips, stir them in, and
remove the saucepan from the heat.

Stir in the rum extract.

Let the frosting cool to room temperature. If it hasn't
thickened enough, add enough powdered sugar to bring
it to spreading consistency. *(I started with ½ cup powdered sugar, but had to add another ¼ cup to make
my frosting the right consistency.)*

Frost the cake and don't forget the inside of the little crater in the middle. That's an added bonus for
frosting lovers.

Put the whole cake into the refrigerator so that the
frosting hardens completely. Cover it loosely with foil
if you intend to refrigerate it for more than 2 hours.

**Hannah's Note: If you would prefer not to use
alcohol in this frosting, simply substitute ⅓ cup
light cream for the rum.**

Chapter Nine

Howie was as good as his promise. He was at the sheriff's station within the hour. Delores and Andrea said their goodbyes so that Hannah could have privacy with her lawyer, but not before they'd promised to come back the next day. Rick let Howie inside the cell. Howie didn't seem to mind when Rick explained that he'd have to lock him inside the holding cell with Hannah, and Hannah surmised that this sort of thing had happened to Howie before.

"This is ridiculous, Hannah," Howie said, sitting down on the cot beside her.

"Then why did Judge Fleming issue a warrant for my arrest?"

"Judge Fleming didn't issue a warrant for your arrest. He's on vacation and Judge Colfax from Stearns County is filling in for him. He's the one who issued the warrant."

Hannah began to frown. "I don't know Judge Colfax."

"Believe me, you don't *want* to know him. Cross your fingers that this is the one and only time you ever have to appear before him."

"What's wrong with Judge Colfax?"

Howie gave a little laugh. "Let me see. Where do I start? Number one, he's hard of hearing and he won't wear his hearing aids. Number two, he's old. And just between you and me, he wasn't that good when he was younger. Number three, rumor has it that he pulled some strings and got drug charges against a state senator dismissed, and that's why he got his judgeship in the first place."

"He sounds awful!"

"That's putting it mildly, but for some strange reason, he likes me. And that worked to our advantage. I called him right before I came over here and I managed to convince him to arraign you early on Monday morning. That should be really good for us."

"Early is fine with me. The sooner I can get out of this cell, the better it'll be for me. But why would a later arraignment be bad?"

"Because Judge Colfax sleeps through most of the cases he hears in the afternoon and he gets testy when the bailiff wakes him. He's better in the mornings, especially if I make sure he's got a big cup of mocha java in his chambers."

"He'll give me bail, won't he?" Hannah voiced her biggest fear.

"I'm almost sure he will. The only reason he signed the warrant for your arrest in the first place is that Chad Norton is his nephew."

"And Chad Norton is the assistant district attorney?"

"That's right. You ran into a string of bad luck, Hannah. This never would have happened with Judge Fleming on the bench, but he's gone. And if Chad Norton's boss wasn't in Atlanta for his daughter's wedding, it wouldn't have happened either. The only reason it did is because Chad Norton needs the publicity prosecuting you will bring him."

"So I was railroaded?"

"You could say that. At least Judge Colfax will be long gone when your case comes to trial. *If* it comes to trial."

"You said *if* my case comes to trial?" Hannah felt her spirits rise. "Is there a chance it won't?"

"There's a very good chance it won't. A lot can happen in

the time between filing the charges and scheduling the trial. Judge Fleming could come back from vacation and decide to dismiss the case against you. Chad Norton's boss could get back from his daughter's wedding, take one look at the case, and tell Chad to drop it. Then there's Chad's plans to consider. He could get so much negative publicity for prosecuting you, he could decide the time wasn't right to run for his boss's job and drop your case like the hot potato it is."

Everything Howie had said made Hannah feel much better, but there was still one important question to ask. "If they don't drop the case and it does go to trial, do you think you can get me off?"

"Nothing's a sure thing when it comes to a jury trial, but I'm fairly certain I can. In the meantime, I want to schedule a meeting with you tomorrow so that you can tell me everything that happened. I need to have every detail that you can remember. "

"Okay," Hannah said, standing up when Howie did and wishing that he'd stay so that she wouldn't be left alone with her thoughts.

"I almost forgot," Howie said, handing her the bag he'd carried into the cell. "Kitty sent these for you. Rick already inspected everything and said you could have it. The only thing he wouldn't let you have was the handgun."

"What?!"

"Just kidding."

Hannah laughed. "You really had me going there for a second. Please thank Kitty for me. It's very sweet of her."

"She said to tell you that it's a care package. You should find some things in there to make you more comfortable while you're here. She'll drop by tomorrow afternoon to see you, and if there's anything else you need or want, just tell me when I see you in the morning and she'll bring it when she comes."

"Thanks, Howie."

Hannah felt a bit like crying as Rick came to let Howie out and they walked down the hallway together. It was strange how a little thing like walking down a hallway could mean so much when you were denied the opportunity to do it.

At least she had something to divert her. Hannah sat back down on the cot again and picked up the bag that Kitty had sent. She felt a surge of excitement that was surprisingly like opening presents as a child on Christmas morning.

"Wonderful!" Hannah breathed as she pulled out five paperback novels. There were two mysteries, a film star biography, a civil war history, and what looked like a very steamy romance. She flipped a few pages of the romance and then put it at the bottom of the stack she set by the head of the cot. It was true that she wanted some diversion but perhaps not quite that much.

The next item she pulled out of the bag was a bar of strawberry scented soap. She sniffed it and smiled, wondering if she'd be allowed to take a shower tomorrow. How did they do that anyway? Did a female deputy have to go in the shower room with her? Or would someone wait outside and let her shower in privacy?

There was no sense worrying about that problem now, and Hannah reached in the bag again. She found a brush and a comb, a toothbrush and toothpaste, and a small stick of deodorant. There were also several candy bars, a small package of potato chips, and a bottle of water. Kitty had thought of almost everything.

There was one item left in the bottom of the bag and Hannah reached inside again. This time she drew out a notebook with a pen stuck inside the spiral binding. How perfect! Now she could write down everything that had happened this morning and give it to Howie when he came for their meeting.

"Was it only this morning?" she questioned herself aloud. It seemed like ages ago. So much had happened, most of it bad, in one short day. And that one day wasn't even over yet!

Hannah had just finished writing down everything she remembered about the accident when she heard voices at the duty desk. Lonnie and Michelle were here.

"More visitors," Rick announced, leading them to the holding cell. "I guess I don't have to lock you inside this time since my brother's a deputy, too."

"Sorry it took us so long," Michelle said the moment she stepped inside the cell. "I brought you a couple of changes of clothes, another pair of shoes, and your slippers."

"Thanks," Hannah said, and then she turned to Lonnie. "I hope you didn't get in any trouble for what you tried to do for me."

"I didn't. Michelle sent me a text and said to take the car to the parking lot and wait for her there. And when I drove out, I saw Bill's cruiser and I figured out what had happened. I can't believe he actually arrested you."

"Well, he did. And here I am."

"Maybe I can get Rick to let you into the break room. We could all have coffee and talk."

Hannah considered it for a moment. It would be a real treat to walk down the hall to the break room. She was about to say yes when she considered the possible ramifications.

"I'd better stay here," she said.

"But don't you want to get out of here?" Michelle asked her.

"Of course I do! But I don't want to get Rick or Lonnie in any trouble. Mike's already suspended, and Andrea and Bill aren't speaking to each other. How am I going to get any inside police information if Rick and Lonnie are gone?"

Michelle gave her a questioning look. "What inside police information do you need?"

"I need to know who that man was and what he was doing here in Lake Eden. Doc Knight didn't know him and he's lived here for years. And neither did anybody who saw him when they brought him into the hospital."

"It's strange that Doc didn't know him, but maybe he was just passing through."

"Maybe. I just need to know more about him."

"So you want to investigate him?" Lonnie asked.

"No, not really. But I do want to know more. Maybe he has relatives somewhere we ought to notify."

"I understand," Michelle said. "You need to know for your own peace of mind."

"Yes, that's part of it. I also need to know because he's a mystery. I didn't know him, Lisa didn't know him, Doc didn't know him, and nobody at the hospital knew him."

"How about Mother?"

"I didn't ask her to look. You know how squeamish she is. There's no way I'd ask her to go down to the morgue and look at him."

"You're right," Michelle said. "She'd do it for you, but you'd hear about the huge favor she did for you for the rest of your life."

"Maybe the guy was a transient," Lonnie suggested. "He could have been some street person who hitchhiked here."

"I don't think so. He was dressed too well to be homeless."

"He was?" Michelle sounded surprised. "You didn't mention that before."

"That's because I didn't think of it before. I just wrote it all down for Howie. He told me he wanted every detail I could remember and I described what the man was wearing."

"What was he wearing?" Lonnie asked.

"Jeans and a white shirt. The jeans were expensive. I'm pretty sure I recognized the logo on the pocket."

"Do you think he could have gotten them from some charity that gives clothes to the needy?"

Hannah shook her head. "I don't think so. They fit too well for that. The shirt looked expensive, too. The only thing wrong with it were the stains on the front."

Michelle shivered. "Bloodstains?"

"No. The stains were reddish-purple, but I'm almost certain they weren't from blood. It was . . . thinner, a little like juice. And his shoes were expensive. I know that because I've seen them advertised and they're almost two hundred dollars a pair. I don't remember the brand, but I do remember the price."

"Anything else?" Lonnie asked, and Hannah could tell he was going into detective mode.

"He had a ring. I didn't get close enough to really see it, but it looked like a high school ring with a school seal on the front. Doc Knight probably still has it with his personal effects at the hospital. Either that, or Bill sent someone from the department to collect it."

Michelle and Lonnie exchanged glances. Then he turned to Hannah. "I'll check with Rick. If they're here in the evidence room, he'll know. And if they aren't, we'll run out to the hospital to look at them before we go back to your condo."

"There's one other thing. He had a diamond."

"In the high school ring?" Michelle asked.

"No, in his left front tooth. It was one of those embedded jewels like the fake ones Norman made for you."

"We should check with Norman to see which dentists do work like that," Michelle said. "And I'll call Doc and ask him if the hospital lab can figure out what that stain on his shirt is." She turned to Lonnie again. "Do you think the department is going to investigate?"

Lonnie shook his head. "Why should they? They know how he died. As far as the department is concerned, there's nothing to investigate."

"Then we'll investigate by ourselves," Michelle said, looking determined. "We'll find out who he was." She turned to Hannah. "You noticed a lot about him, Hannah."

"Not enough to figure out who he was," Hannah said, feeling very tired. It had been a long day.

"Maybe not, but you gave us plenty to go on," Lonnie pointed out. "I think Doc will let us take the guy's things. We can always return them if the guy's relatives show up. At least we can give it a try."

"But what if Doc can't release them to us?" Michelle asked.

"Then I'll take pictures of them with my cell phone. But I think he'll let me have them. It's not like they're evidence in a murder."

There was silence for a long moment while all three of them thought about that. It was true that the man's death wasn't a traditional murder, but Hannah *was* charged with vehicular homicide.

Hannah attempted to put all thoughts of homicides and trials out of her mind as she turned to Michelle. "If you can't get his actual belongings, please write down the brands on those clothes. I could be wrong about them being expensive."

"Okay. I can ask Andrea about the brands. She knows all the designers and she's going to stop by the condo when we get back there tonight."

Hannah put two and two together. "Andrea doesn't want to go home while Bill's still awake?"

"She didn't say anything like that, but that's the impression I got. I know she was with Mother and Doc at the hospital. She called me from there to see where I was. I'm supposed to call her on her cell phone when we're on our way back to your place."

"Thanks," Hannah said. "You two are a big help. You're making me feel much better."

Surprisingly, it was true. Even though she was still locked in a cell and facing criminal charges, Hannah *was* feeling much better. By attempting to learn the man's identity, she was taking an active part in something that was taking place outside of her jail cell. Learning the man's identity wouldn't bring him back or change the fact she'd killed him, but Hannah didn't like unanswered questions and there were several surrounding the man she'd killed. Who was he? Why had he come to Lake Eden in the first place? And why had he been standing at the side of the road nowhere near a farmhouse in the pouring rain?

"We'll find out who he was," Michelle addressed Hannah's unspoken questions. "And when you get out on bail, you can help us do it. Actually, you're helping us now. I wouldn't have known where to start. I just know if all three of us work together, we can do it."

"That's right," Lonnie said, and then he turned to Michelle, who was wearing shorts, with a grin. "You've got the legs, I've got the badge, and Hannah's got the brains. With the three of us working together, we're bound to figure everything out."

Hannah was halfway through the first chapter of a mystery that Kitty had sent her when Rick came down the hall again. "You've got another visitor, Hannah. It's Norman. Should I tell him you want to see him?"

"Oh, yes!" Hannah said, and then she hoped she hadn't sounded too eager. Rick and Lonnie's mother, Bridget Murphy, was a member of the Lake Eden Gossip Hotline. "I'd like to see him, Rick. Thank you very much."

Hannah just had time to run the hairbrush Kitty had sent through her hair and put a smile on her face before Rick arrived with Norman. "Here he is," Rick said, and then he turned back to Norman. "Sorry Norman, but I'll have to lock you in with Hannah."

"That's okay. I don't mind being locked in with Hannah. Anyone else, maybe. But with Hannah, it's just fine."

Oh, boy! Hannah thought. *This'll get on the gossip hotline in no time flat.* But did she really care if it did? Norman had paid her a compliment and she should accept it as such.

"How are you doing, Hannah?" Norman asked, sitting down on the cot next to her, slipping his arm around her to pull her close, and not even glancing at Rick as he locked the door and left.

"I'm all right." Hannah heard the slight tremor in her voice and hoped she wouldn't break into tears. Norman's arm felt so good around her.

"Don't lie to me, Hannah. I've been in jail and I know. It's no fun being locked up in a cell and not being able to get out."

"This cell is better than the others," Hannah said, trying to shed a good light on it.

"Maybe, but you're still locked in. Take a deep breath and try to remember that it's only for three days."

"I know. And now it's not even three days anymore. It's only two days and three nights."

"And when you wake up, it'll be only two days and two nights. Then you'll be out and back where you belong. Do you want to come and stay with me when you get out on bail? I've got the cats at our house and it would be a transition."

Our house. Norman was still calling it *our house.* He still wanted her even though she was now, technically, a jailbird. Idly, she wondered if there was anything that would make

Norman *not* want her. And she decided that there probably wasn't.

"Hannah?"

Norman was waiting for an answer and Hannah turned to smile at him. "Maybe," she said, leaving her options open. "You took Moishe to your place?"

"Yes. Moishe was a little anxious when you didn't come back to the condo with me, and he yowled when I tried to put Cuddles in her carrier. That's when I decided to take him home with me and I put them both in his carrier. By the way, it's big enough for both of them. And don't worry. I called Michelle on her cell phone and told her what I was doing."

"Thanks, Norman. I know Michelle would have taken good care of him, but he'll probably be happier with Cuddles."

"Both cats are happier. When I left, they were chasing up and down the staircase in the den and I left the animal channel on for them."

"Thanks, Norman. You don't know how much I . . ." Hannah stopped and blinked back the moisture that formed in her eyes. "You don't know how much I appreciate you."

Norman gave her another little hug and then he stood up to get the bag he'd brought with him. "Here, Hannah. I picked up something at the mall for you. I don't know if you need it, or not, but I thought you'd like to have it while you were here."

Hannah glanced at the package inside the bag. It was gift-wrapped and she couldn't see what was inside. "What is it?" she asked.

"You can open it when I leave. Right now I want to ask you a couple of questions."

"What questions?"

"Has Howie been here yet?"

"Yes. I have a meeting with him tomorrow morning and

Kitty sent me some things, too. He asked me to tell him everything I remembered about this morning and I wrote it all down for him."

"Good. When is the arraignment?"

"Monday morning. Howie managed to arrange an early arraignment because Judge Colfax is more alert then."

"You didn't get Judge Fleming?"

Hannah shook her head. "He's on vacation and Judge Colfax is filling in for him."

"Bad luck," Norman said, and then he must have seen the look on Hannah's face because he reached out to hug her again. "It'll be okay, Hannah. Howie's a good lawyer and there's no reason on earth that you won't get bail."

"I hope you're right."

"I am. Don't worry about that now. Is there anything you'd like me to do for you while you're in here?"

"Actually . . . yes! There *is* one thing. The man I killed had a diamond embedded in his front left tooth. Do you know any Minnesota dentists who do work like that?"

"No, but I can find out. All it'll take are a few phone calls. Was it a real diamond, or a fake diamond?"

Hannah shrugged. "I don't know. I only caught a glimpse of it and I might not know the difference anyway."

"Fair enough. I'm not sure I'd know the difference either. Why do you want to know which dentist did it?"

"Because I need to find out who the man was and the dentist might have his name. I really need to know, Norman."

"Of course you do. Does Doc still have him at the morgue?"

"I think so. I don't know where else he'd be. I could have asked Mother when she was here, but I didn't think of it then."

"I'll give Doc a ring and if he says it's okay, I'll run out there and take a look. I know quite a few dentists in Minnesota and I might recognize the work."

"Thanks, Norman. I hope this isn't a wild goose chase. I don't even know if the man was from Minnesota. He could have been from anywhere."

"That's true, but maybe I can narrow it down for you. I've been to quite a few dental conventions and dentists come from all over to attend those. As a matter of fact, there was a seminar about tooth jewelry and the techniques used to embed it at last year's dental convention. I didn't go to that particular seminar, but I'll check the program and see who taught it. And I'll call to see if I can get a list of which dentists attended." Norman gave her another hug and then he stood up. "I'd better go if I want to catch Doc while he's still awake. I'll see you tomorrow, Hannah."

Hannah walked him to the door, a far different procedure than she had performed at her condo countless times in the past. This time she couldn't open the door. Rick had locked it from the outside.

Norman gave her a final hug that felt so good, tears came to her eyes, and then Rick was there to let him out. Hannah walked back to her cot and sat down again, but, surprisingly, she didn't feel terribly bereft. She was alone, she was locked in, but all of her friends and relatives were helping her get the information she needed.

The bag Norman had brought was still sitting beside her on the cot. Hannah reached inside and pulled out the package. She tore off the gift wrap, felt slightly guilty for not saving the paper and the ribbon, and uncovered the prettiest, fluffiest blanket that she'd ever seen. It was patterned with cats, darling little cats, so many different breeds of cats that she couldn't name them all. They were romping and playing all over the surface of the blanket, and every single cat was as cute as it could be. They were all in different poses, chasing butterflies, and balls, and each other, and just looking at them made Hannah smile in delight.

She spent almost an hour looking at each cat, trying to decide which one was the cutest, and then she stretched out on the cot and picked up her book. Soon she was engrossed in the mystery again, and before the hands on the clock on the wall outside the holding cell had reached the hands-up position, she was fast sleep under the cat blanket that Norman had brought just for her.

Chapter Ten

It was wonderful being out of the cell! One of the female deputies had led her to the shower that the female prisoners used and waited for her just outside the door. Hannah hadn't even minded that there was an observation window as she unwrapped the strawberry-scented soap and used it to take her shower. Then she'd rinsed off, dried off on the not-so-soft towels the deputy had given her, and dressed in clean clothing.

Now she was sitting across from Howie Levine in the small room reserved for lawyers and their incarcerated clients.

"I've got to tell you, Hannah," Howie said. "I did some research last night and it doesn't look good."

Howie was frowning deeply and Hannah's heartbeat accelerated rapidly. "What do you mean?" she asked.

"I mean that you are clearly at fault."

Hannah couldn't help it. Her mouth dropped open in surprise. "But it was an accident! I couldn't help hitting that man. I wrote it all out for you to explain it."

"And I read it. I understand exactly what happened, Hannah. But I'm still telling you that you were clearly at fault when you killed that man."

"How can that *be*? I couldn't avoid him. There was no way! Are you saying that I should have run into that branch in the road?"

"No. I'm not telling you that at all."

"Then how can it be my fault that I hit that man and he's dead?"

Howie snapped open his briefcase and brought out a pamphlet. He flipped through the pages, stopped at one, and said, "This is the *Minnesota Drivers' Manual*. I'm going to read the pertinent section."

He cleared his throat and began to read aloud. " '*Your headlights, by law, must be used at times when you cannot see more than five-hundred feet ahead, and when it is raining, snowing, sleeting, or hailing.*' Did you turn on your headlights, Hannah?"

"No, but it was morning."

"Could you see at least five hundred feet ahead?"

"Well, no. But . . ."

"Was it raining, snowing, sleeting, or hailing?"

"Yes. I told you it was raining."

"Let me reiterate. It was raining and you could not see five hundred feet ahead. Is that correct?"

Hannah didn't want to answer, but Howie was her lawyer and she had to be truthful. "Yes."

"And yet you neglected to turn on your headlights?"

Hannah took a deep breath and nodded. "It wouldn't have helped if I'd turned them on, but . . . yes, I neglected to turn on my headlights."

"Thank you. Now on to the second part of the paragraph. The *Minnesota Drivers' Manual* reads '*If you cannot see a safe distance ahead, pull off the road and stop until visibility improves.*' Did you do that, Hannah?"

"You know I didn't."

"All right then. Do you see why Chad Norton had reason to file charges against you?"

"I admit he had a right to file charges, but give me a break, Howie! There were extenuating circumstances."

"What were those extenuating circumstances?"

"Lightning was striking all around us when we were driving past Winnie Henderson's pasture. The truck was the tallest object around and I wanted to go around the bend and pull over under the trees. I figured that if lightning continued to strike around us, one of the trees would be hit and not us. I was in reasonable fear for my life, Howie. And it wasn't just my life. Lisa was with me in the truck, and I was in reasonable fear for her life, also."

"That makes perfect sense to me," Howie said, giving her a quick smile.

"It does?" Hannah was surprised at the change that had come over Howie. Just seconds ago, he had sounded as if he were acting as the prosecuting attorney and not the counsel for her defense.

"Of course it makes sense. You were defending your life and the life of your passenger, Lisa Beeseman. If you'd pulled over right away, you would have put both of you in jeopardy from the lightning strikes."

"That's right!" Hannah was glad that Howie understood at last.

"And that's our case. You'll make a great witness, Hannah. And I didn't even have to prepare you."

"You mean the case is actually going forward? They're going to try me for vehicular homicide?"

Howie reached out to pat her hand. "Don't borrow trouble, Hannah. It might not happen. But if it does, I really don't think that twelve reasonable jurors will convict you."

"And you'll make certain that the jurors are reasonable?"

"As much as I can. I only have a limited number of preempts."

"That means peremptory challenges, doesn't it?"

"That's right. Each side has a fixed number of those and it means that they can dismiss a potential juror without stating a reason. The remainder of the dismissals have to be for cause."

"What would constitute cause?"

"There has to be a specific and forceful reason to believe that the potential juror cannot be fair, unbiased, or capable of serving as a juror."

"Okay, but what would those causes be?"

Howie gave a little shrug. "That's a bit complicated. The acceptable causes include an acquaintanceship with either of the parties, one of the attorneys, or a witness. Another is a potential juror's inability to be unbiased due to prior experience in a similar case. But all this isn't up to me, Hannah. The judge determines if the potential juror will be dismissed. Would you like me to put it all in a nutshell for you?"

Hannah's head was spinning. "Yes, please."

"It's a crap shoot, Hannah. I can control some things with my peremptory challenges, but once they run out, it's up to the judge. And that means the jury that'll be seated at your trial depends in large part on the judge you're lucky or unlucky enough to draw."

When Hannah got back to the holding cell after her meeting with Howie, she sat down on the edge of the cot with a sigh. It was a bit unsettling to realize that, at least as far as the driving statutes were concerned, she was guilty. Of course, there were extenuating circumstances. Howie had agreed with that. But would Judge Colfax give her bail, or would he order her to stay in county lockup until her case came to trial?

Hannah felt as if she were on a roller coaster, experiencing an upswing in her mood when Howie said she'd make a good witness, and a downswing when he told her that her case might go to trial and her acquittal wasn't a sure thing.

"Hannah?" One of the deputies she'd met, but didn't know well, arrived at the cell door. "You've got visitors. Shall I bring them down here to you?"

"Yes, please," Hannah said politely and the deputy went off to get her visitors.

A minute or two later, Delores and Doc arrived at her cell, along with the deputy who was carrying two chairs. "Hello, dear," Delores greeted her. "How was your meeting with Howie?"

"Fine," Hannah said, not wanting to worry her mother by confiding that the outcome of her case was uncertain.

"Sheriff said I can put these inside," the deputy informed them, unlocking the door and carrying the chairs inside. "I'm still going to have to lock you in, but since you're the only prisoner, you can keep the chairs here when your visitors leave."

"Thank you," Hannah smiled at him. Her mood was swinging up again and it felt great. With chairs in her cell, she wouldn't have to sit on the edge of the uncomfortable cot.

Once the deputy had left and Doc and Delores were seated, Doc set the large briefcase he'd been carrying on the cot and Delores put the large bag she'd brought on the floor. "Lonnie and Michelle examined the man's belongings and took some pictures," Doc told Hannah. "I released them to Lonnie since he was going to attempt to find the man's relatives."

"Great!" Hannah said, feeling her mood elevate even more. Her emotional roller coaster car was climbing even higher and it felt good.

"I looked at them, too," Delores said. "You were right, dear. They're definitely expensive. Andrea was there and she saw them, too. And she totally agreed with me. That man either stole them or spent some big money on his clothing and shoes."

Hannah was almost afraid to ask, but she needed to know the answer to another question. She just hoped it wouldn't send her mood on a downswing. "How about the stains on his shirt?"

"We're working on that," Doc said. "Some spots washed away in the rain, but that umbrella you put over the man's face preserved a portion of them. Marlene's examining them in the lab right now and she told me she thinks there's enough left to identify."

Hannah smiled, her good mood elevating again. Normally, she didn't like roller coasters, but the one she was imagining in her mind was a good one. Doc's intern, Marlene Aldrich, was a highly skilled lab technician. If anyone could identify that stain on the man's shirt, it was Marlene. "How about the tooth with the diamond? Did Norman get to see it?"

Doc nodded. "Yes, he did. He took quite a few photographs with that fancy equipment of his."

"Oh, good!" Hannah's smile grew even bigger. "Too bad we can't take that diamond to a jeweler to see if it's real."

"Oh, but we can," Delores said. "Doc called Bill this morning and asked if he had any objections if Norman extracted the tooth."

"And Bill said that they had crime scene photos, so it was perfectly okay with him," Doc finished the sentence for her.

The roller coaster car moved upward, but not as far as Hannah would have liked. It was stalled between up and down, hanging there like her vacillating mood. The phrase "crime scene photos" had stopped the car in its tracks. She'd never expected to be personally involved in anything that required crime scene photos! But the news that Bill had given Norman permission to extract the tooth was very good indeed.

You have to take the bad with the good, another of her great-grandmother's sayings ran through Hannah's mind. And for the first time she could recall, she envied those people with boring, predictable, and uneventful lives.

"They did find the man's car," Delores said, sending the roller coaster car upward again. "Unfortunately, something called the VIN was filed off so they don't have any way to track the owner. It's probably stolen, though. Judging by what I heard, it was a model, make, and color that's very popular with car thieves. Thousands of similar cars are stolen every year. I wonder what VIN stands for."

"Vehicle identification number," Hannah told her mother, trying not to react as the roller coaster car continued downward. Stolen car. No vehicle identification number. Even if they got lucky on their search through hundreds of stolen car reports, the man who had driven the car to Lake Eden wasn't the owner of record.

"I asked Bill about the man's body," Doc said. "The sheriff's department doesn't need it for any further testing, so we'll keep it in the hospital morgue for the present."

That meant they could take more photos if they needed them, or check if they thought of something else. Hannah's emotional roller coaster car stopped its descent and started up the slope again.

"Of course that will change if some relative comes forward to claim him," Doc added.

That wouldn't be a terrible thing, Hannah thought as the car climbed higher. *Then at least we'd know who he was.*

"But I don't think anyone in Lake Eden will," Delores continued, sending the roller coaster car downward again. "I activated the Lake Eden Gossip Hotline the moment that you were arrested. We asked everyone in town if they'd anticipated a visitor yesterday, a visitor who hadn't arrived, but we didn't get a single positive result."

The car on the tracks was descending lower and lower and Hannah gave a deep sigh. No one in Lake Eden knew who the man was.

"But don't lose hope, dear," Delores told her. "We widened the telephone tree to include three neighboring towns."

That was good! The car on the roller coaster slowed near the bottom, and started up a steep slope again. Things were looking up.

"I rode in with Doc," Delores continued, "and he has to get back to the hospital. We'll have to leave soon, but I brought you two throw pillows and a flowered bedspread. It's so dreary in here. And Doc carried in something else I thought you could use to distract you from your surroundings."

Distraction was good. Hannah's emotional roller coaster car climbed toward the top of the slope rapidly as she decided she would be grateful for whatever her mother had brought her. She knew that the pillows and bedspread must be in the bag at her mother's feet, but the briefcase that Doc had set on the cot was still a mystery. It was large enough to contain a portable DVD player with a half-dozen movies. Or perhaps it was music, a CD player with enough music to see her through two more nights. "Thank you, Mother. What else did you bring?"

"I brought you this," Delores said, snapping the briefcase open and lifting the lid. "I have two red pens and some of those marvelous sticky flags to mark the pages."

Hannah watched with interest as her mother drew out a thick sheaf of papers, bound together with several rubber bands, and placed them on Hannah's cot. Her roller coaster car was at the top of the slope now and it was all due to the surprise her mother had brought her.

"Here it is, dear!" Delores said, beaming at her.

"Here *what* is?"

"It's the manuscript for my newest Regency romance, *A Husband For Holly*. Since you're here for another two days, I knew you needed something to occupy your time and make you feel as if you were accomplishing something useful. Just read it, mark any corrections you have in red, and flag the pages. I wanted to help you, so I worked all night to finish it."

Hannah pictured the roller coaster car as it teetered on the very apex of the downslope. There was a moment when time stood still, at least in her mind, and then the car roared downward with full force, lurching, swaying, and descending so rapidly that Hannah felt her stomach drop down to her toes. This was a downswing, a real disaster. She'd been looking forward to reading the mystery she'd started the previous night, but now she had to proof her mother's manuscript.

"Aren't you glad I thought of it, dear? It's exactly what you needed."

Hannah stared at her mother. Delores looked so pleased with herself that she didn't have the heart to disappoint her.

"It's exactly what I needed," Hannah repeated, hoping she sounded sincere.

Midway through the third chapter, Hannah's roller coaster car was on its way up the track again. Her mother's newest romance was good, very good, and it was definitely well-written. Despite her earlier fit of pique . . . Hannah stopped in mid-thought and laughed out loud. *Fit of pique?* She was obviously enjoying her mother's book if she was spouting Regency phrases.

A few pages later, Hannah was actually disappointed at the interruption when the deputy came to tell her she had another visitor. She marked her place with a sticky red flag, and gazed down the hallway to see who would appear.

"Hi, Hannah," Lisa called out, hurrying toward the cell.

"Hello, Lisa." Hannah waited until the deputy had opened the cell, Lisa had entered, and they were both locked in. "Have a chair."

"Thanks. I've been on my feet all morning. Marge and Dad are helping Michelle in the coffee shop, so I decided to take my lunch now."

"You came *here* for lunch?"

"Yes, and I brought some for you, too. I stopped at Hal and Rose's Café right after I delivered the cookies to Winnie. You ought to see her dining room, Hannah. She's got those chocolates that look like gold coins scattered all over the tablecloth and placemats that look like pirate flags. And I saw the life-size standing cutout of Jack Sparrow. It looks just fantastic!"

"I'll bet it does!" Hannah eyed the bag that Lisa was carrying. "What did you bring for lunch?"

"Egg salad sandwiches and a big bag of Rose's French fries. She sent along mustard for me and a container of blue cheese dressing for you."

"Perfect," Hannah declared. She was hungry even though she'd eaten breakfast less than four hours ago.

"I almost forgot." Lisa stopped in the act of laying out their lunch on the seat of the empty chair she'd pulled up to the side of the cot, and reached into the bag again. "Winnie sent two copies of her Fresh Blackberry Pie recipe. Here's yours. It's really simple, Hannah. She gave me some black-berries, too. I'm going to go home tonight and make a pie so I can bring you a piece tomorrow."

"That would be nice," Hannah said, reading through the recipe quickly. "You're right, Lisa. It's a simple recipe, but I'll bet it's good."

"I *know* it's good. She let me taste a piece in the kitchen."

Lisa sat down and took a bite of her sandwich. Hannah did the same and they chewed in silence for several moments.

"Oops!" Lisa exclaimed, reaching in the bag again. "I almost forgot our milkshakes. They're chocolate. I figured you could use some chocolate about now."

"You figured right." Hannah picked up her straw, poked it through the slit on the lid, and took a big swallow. "I didn't realize how much I missed chocolate until right now."

The two partners ate for several minutes without speaking and then Lisa said, "I've got an idea about that man we hit."

Hannah heard the plural Lisa had used and shook her head. Lisa was sharing the blame and that wasn't fair. "I hit the man, not you. I was the one behind the wheel."

"Yes, but I was riding shotgun. I should have seen him and warned you."

"Impossible. You couldn't see any more than I could. It was raining too hard."

"Okay, but I still wish I'd seen him."

"So do I," Hannah said, "but we didn't. There's no sense in wishing if there's nothing you can do about it."

"I guess." Lisa took a swallow of her milkshake and sighed. "I want to help you find out who he was, Hannah. It's the least I can do."

"Okay," Hannah said, agreeing quickly with Lisa's offer since it might make her partner feel better.

"Good. What can I do?"

Hannah thought fast. What could Lisa do? And that was when a radical idea occurred to Hannah. "Tell the story of how I hit him."

"What?!"

"Tell it. The more people who hear it, the more buzz there'll be about it. You saw the man. Describe him. Describe his clothing and once you see the photo Norman took of the ring and the diamond in his tooth, describe those, too. Make it exciting and scary, and we're bound to get a crowd. If it's really exciting, everyone will repeat it."

"But are you sure you want me to talk about . . . *killing* him?"

"Yes. I'm already in trouble and we might as well take advantage of it. People will talk. They always do. And there's bound to be someone who knows who he is. We just don't know who that someone is yet. If the word gets around, whoever it is may come forward."

"Okay . . . if you're sure."

"I'm sure."

"All right then. I'd better get back and start baking cookies. I'll rehearse tonight and begin telling the story tomorrow."

"Tomorrow's Sunday, Lisa."

"I know, but we can still open the shop. I'll ask your mother to activate the gossip hotline and we'll do a special cookie sale, maybe a two-fer on Fresh Blackberry Cookies. That'll draw customers in."

"Fresh Blackberry Cookies? We don't make those, do we?"

"We do now. Winnie gave me the recipe. That's how she uses up the extra blackberries she doesn't bake in her pies. She told me they freeze really well and everybody loves them. If they're as good as she says they are, they're going to go like hotcakes. By the time you get out of here on Monday morning, almost everybody in town will know what happened. Maybe we'll even know who the man was by then."

"I hope so," Hannah said, but the car on her emotional roller coaster was starting down the slope again. What if no one knew? Would they ever know what her victim had been doing by the side of the road and why he'd come to Lake Eden?

WINNIE'S FRESH BLACKBERRY PIE
("Blackbeard Pie")

Preheat oven to 350 degrees F., rack in the middle position.

Hannah's 1st Note: Winnie told me to decide which top I wanted to have on my Fresh Blackberry Pie before I started. There are THREE ways to top your pie.

The Latticework Crust on top (like the one pictured on the cover) takes the most time and is the most difficult to do. Written instructions are confusing. There is a lattice cutter that you can order from cooking catalogues. That looks nice, but it's not woven. You can also use my friend Trudi's shortcut. She cuts little leaves out of piecrust and arranges them in lines that crisscross on top of her pies. If you choose to do a lattice top, you will need two rounds of piecrust to make this pie.

The French Crumble is easy and you need ONLY ONE round of piecrust if you decide to use it.

The Crust with the Slits cut in it is the easiest and fastest as long as you buy ready-made frozen pie crusts. You will need two rounds of piecrust for this top.

a package of 2 frozen 8-inch deep dish piecrusts *(or make your own from your favorite recipe)*

3 heaping cups whole blackberries *(approximately 3 grocery square berry boxes)*

¾ cup white *(granulated)* sugar

¼ cup all-purpose flour *(pack it down in the cup when you measure it)*

¼ teaspoon ground nutmeg *(freshly ground is best, of course)*

½ teaspoon ground cinnamon *(if it's been sitting in your cupboard for years, buy fresh!—cinnamon loses its flavor when it's old)*

¼ teaspoon salt

½ stick cold salted butter *(¼ cup, 2 ounces, ⅛ pound)*

Prepare your crust(s) according to the following instructions:

If you decided to use homemade piecrust, roll out one round and use it to line an 8-inch deep-dish pie pan *(or a 9-inch regular pie pan)*.

If you bought frozen piecrusts, leave one right in its pan and let it thaw on the counter. You'll use that for the bottom crust. If you decided to make the top Crust with Slits, loosen the second crust a bit in its pan, but leave it in the pan on the counter to thaw. If you decided to use the French Crumble top, return that second frozen piecrust to your freezer for the next time you bake a pie.

Rinse the blackberries, pat them dry with a paper towel, and put them in a large bowl.

Mix the sugar, flour, nutmeg, cinnamon, and salt together in a small bowl.

Dump the small bowl with the dry ingredients on top of the blackberries and toss them to coat the berries. *(Again, use your fingers and be as gentle as you can. You don't want the berries to break open so the juice runs out. There will be enough juice given off when your pie bakes.)*

Place a layer of coated blackberries in the bottom of the pan lined with piecrust. Arrange them with your fingers if there are any noticeable gaps. *(You want a nice foundation for the rest of the berries.)*

Place the rest of the coated berries in the pie pan. There should be enough to mound the top slightly. *(These berries will fill in and settle during baking.)*

There will probably be some leftover dry ingredients at the bottom of the bowl you used to mix the berries. Just sprinkle the remainder of the dry ingredients on top of the blackberries in the pie pan.

Cut the cold butter into 4 pieces and then cut those pieces in half. Place the pieces on top of the blackberries just as if you were dotting the blackberries with butter.

Top your pie with your choice of the Latticework Crust, the Crust with the Slits, or the French Crumble.

The Latticework Crust:

You're on your own with this one!

The Crust with Slits:

If you used a frozen piecrust, simply tip the pan it came in upside down over the berries in the bottom crust. Smooth it out with your impeccably clean fingers.

Squeeze the edges from the top crust and the edges from the bottom crust together. *(Use a little water for "glue" if the crust just won't cooperate.)*

With a sharp knife, cut 4 slits in the top crust about 3 inches long, starting near the middle of the pie and extending down toward the sides of the pie. *(This is a very important step. Not only does it let out the steam when the pie bakes, releasing a delicious aroma that'll have the neighbors knocking at your door, it also provides a way to sneak in those pieces of butter you forgot to put on the blackberries before you covered your pie with the top crust. Don't laugh. I've done it.)*

The French Crumble:

> 1 cup all-purpose flour
> ½ cup cold butter *(1 stick, 4 ounces, ¼ pound)*
> ½ cup brown sugar *(pack it down when you measure it)*

Put the flour into the bowl of a food processor with the steel blade attached. Cut the stick of butter into 8 pieces and add them to the bowl. Cover with the ½ cup of firmly-packed brown sugar.

Process with the steel blade in an on and off motion until the resulting mixture is in uniform small pieces.

Remove the mixture from the food processor and place it in a bowl.

Pat handfuls of the French Crumble in a mound over your pie. With a sharp knife, poke several slits near the top to let out the steam.

Winnie's 1st Note: If you used the Latticework Crust or the Crust with the Slits, you can make your pie look prettier by brushing a little water, milk, or cream on top of the crust and then sprinkling it with a little bit of white sugar. This will give it a sugary crunch with every bite.

Bake your Fresh Blackberry Pie at 350 degrees F. for 50 to 60 minutes *(mine took 55 minutes)*, or until the top crust or the French Crumble is a nice golden brown and the blackberries are tender when you pierce one with the tip of a sharp knife.

Cool your pie on a cold stove burner or a wire rack. This pie can be served warm with ice cream or sweetened whipped cream, or cold right out of the refrigerator.

Be sure to refrigerate any leftover pie. *(I've made this pie countless times and there have NEVER been any leftovers!)*

Winnie's 2nd Note: My grandson calls this "Bluebeard Pie" because he's crazy about pirates.

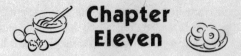

Chapter
Eleven

"All rise!" the bailiff called out in a loud voice, startling Hannah out of her worried thoughts.

Everyone in attendance in the small courtroom, not that many at eight o'clock on a Monday morning, rose as Judge Colfax walked in and took his place at the bench.

Hannah and Howie listened to the bailiff tell them that court was now in session, the honorable Judge Colfax presiding, and then they sat down again. Hannah felt the butterflies flutter wildly and churn into a miniature tornado in her stomach. What if Judge Colfax refused to give her bail? She'd be stuck in a cell until it was time for her trial. And Howie had told her that her trial could be delayed as long as six months, depending on the status of the court calendar. She could spend six months in jail. Or even worse, she could be found guilty of vehicular homicide and she didn't want to know how long a sentence that charge might have!

Could she survive six months in jail? Or could she endure even more time if she were convicted of the charges against her? After two grueling days in the holding cell at the sheriff's station, Hannah wasn't at all certain she'd make it. It had been bad enough in the larger holding cell, just knowing that she wasn't free to walk down the street, get into her truck, and drive anywhere she wanted to go. County lockup would be much worse. She'd heard horror stories about peo-

ple going stir-crazy in the county jail and trying to put themselves out of their misery by repeatedly banging their heads
against the concrete walls, hoping that they'd injure themselves so badly that they'd be taken to the hospital and would
at least have a window in the room.

There was a rustle in the back of the courtroom and Hannah craned her neck to see her mother and Andrea enter
through the double doors and take seats in the rear. They
looked very solemn and Hannah felt a lump grow in her
throat. Were they also worried that Judge Colfax wouldn't
grant her bail?

Norman was already in the courtroom. He had been seated
near the front when Howie had led Hannah in. Norman had
smiled at her and given her the high sign, and Hannah had
done her best to smile back.

The rustling of papers was loud in the silent courtroom as
Judge Colfax read through the agenda. It was as if everyone
was holding his or her breath, waiting for something to happen. A moment later, there was murmuring from the few
spectators who were there and Hannah turned to see Mike
enter the courtroom. A couple of the spectators glared at
him, and Hannah suspected that Mike had been one of the
officers who'd arrested their family member or loved one.

Hannah turned toward the front again. She'd looked at
Mike, but he hadn't met her eyes. Why was that? Did he
know something that she didn't know? Or was she simply
being paranoid? She sent up a silent plea that the reason was
her own paranoia.

Everyone who had told her they were coming was here.
She'd known that Doc Knight wouldn't be here. He had
surgery scheduled for seven this morning and it wouldn't be
over yet. Michelle and Lisa had come to see her yesterday
and explained that they would be at The Cookie Jar, handling the morning customers, but that Delores would call
them the moment the arraignment was over.

Howie motioned to her and Hannah leaned closer so that he could whisper in her ear. "Relax," he said. "You look like a deer caught in the headlights."

"That's because I *am* a deer caught in the headlights," Hannah whispered back.

"Not for long. It'll be over soon, Hannah. Just remember that when the judge asks you how you plead, you say, *Not guilty, Your Honor.* Don't say any more, and don't say any less. Just say, *Not guilty, Your Honor.* Are we clear on that?"

"Yes," Hannah said, and then she added, "Did you bring Judge Colfax his coffee this morning?"

"I did, and it was an extra-large mocha, exactly what he likes. Stop worrying, Hannah. We should be just fine."

Hannah thought about saying, *That's easy for you to say.* Even if things weren't fine, Howie wouldn't be the one who was locked up in jail. That would be her, and she had a perfect right to be worried. And then the bailiff was calling her name and Howie was motioning for her to stand up and face Judge Colfax on legs that were suddenly trembling like leaves in a windstorm.

The bailiff read the charges and Hannah did her best not to listen. There were more than she'd thought there would be, ranging from misdemeanors to a final charge of vehicular homicide. And then Howie was prodding her. The judge must have asked her how she pled. And Hannah said, "Not guilty, Your Honor," and clamped her lips shut.

Her words hung in the silent air and the room began to revolve slowly around her. Hannah knew she was close to fainting as Howie asked for bail. There was a buzzing in her ears that made listening impossible and she gripped the edge of the defense table tightly to keep from falling back into her chair. The judge wouldn't like that. She had to show the proper respect and keep standing and facing him with a polite and servile expression, even though she was weak-kneed and dizzy, and she'd never been so scared in her life.

The moment seemed to go on forever, as if the clock on the wall had stopped and everyone was frozen in place. And through the buzzing in her ears and the gulps of air she was taking so that she wouldn't do anything foolish like faint dead away, she heard the judge say, "Bail in the amount of fifty thousand dollars is granted. See the clerk."

His gavel banged loudly against the wooden surface, and then Howie turned to take her arm. "It's over, Hannah. I told you it would be all right. An officer of the court will escort you to the clerk's office and stay with you there while your mother makes bail. I'm sorry, but you'll have to be hand-cuffed until your bail is paid. It's not a secure area."

"That's okay," Hannah said, feeling a huge wave of relief wash over her, now that this part of her ordeal was over. "And once Mother pays my bail, they'll take off the hand-cuffs and I'll be free to go?"

"That's right. You'll be free to go."

Hannah turned so that the officer of the court could put on the handcuffs and guide her through a side door. She was afraid to say a word for fear it would be something that might hurt her later.

She stumbled once, walking down the hall, and the offi-cer gripped her arm. "Hey! Are you okay?"

"I . . . I think so."

"You should be. You're almost out of here. Your family went to the clerk's office to pay your bail and that's where we're going. I'll take these cuffs off the minute the paper-work's done."

Hannah swallowed hard. "Thanks. I was really scared. I've never been in court before."

The officer gave a little laugh. "I figured that. I saw your legs shaking when you stood up, and I was all ready to catch you if you passed out."

Hannah turned to look at the female officer, who couldn't

have weighed over a hundred pounds. "Thanks, but I probably would have taken you down with me."

"Not me," the officer said. "I've caught bigger ones than you and eased them down to the floor so they didn't hurt themselves."

They walked down the hallway in tandem for a few steps and then the officer spoke again. "You lucked out, that's for sure. I've never seen Judge Colfax give bail that light before."

"Really?" Hannah turned to her in shock. "I thought fifty thousand was a lot."

"Oh, no. Don't forget you only have to put up ten percent and sign a note for the rest. That's only five thousand. All the other homicide cases I've heard have been over a hundred thousand and more."

Hannah knew enough not to comment. To her, five thousand dollars seemed like a huge amount.

"Here we are," the officer said, opening the door and ushering Hannah in. "We stay in here, but the door is open to the clerk's office and you can hear what's going on. Sorry, but I have to stay with you."

"That's okay," Hannah said quickly. "I'm glad you're here. I've been all alone in a cell and I appreciate the company."

The officer turned to look at her in shock. "Nobody's ever told me *that* before! I can't do anything for you, you know. If your family doesn't make bail, I can't intercede."

"Oh, no. I wasn't thinking that at all. I'm just glad I have somebody to talk to." Hannah watched as a smile played over the officer's lips. And then she asked a question. "You don't have to answer this if you don't want to, but do you like your job? I'm just curious, that's all."

"I like it. It pays well and I'm a county employee. I get good bennies. That means a lot because my husband is out of work now."

"Oh, I'm sorry," Hannah said, feeling immediately sympathetic. "What kind of work does he do?"

"He's an auto mechanic."

Hannah thought fast. Lisa had mentioned that one of Cyril's mechanics had quit and he was looking for a replacement. "I don't know where you live, but is Lake Eden too far for him to drive?"

"No." The officer gave a little laugh. "We live out in the country and Lake Eden's only about ten miles. My husband's been applying for jobs all over the state. He even put out feelers in the Cities. He's got a sister down there and he figured he could stay with her during the week and come back home on weekends."

"Do you have a pen?" Hannah asked. "I think I have a lead for your husband."

The officer drew a pen from the pocket of her uniform, and reached into her other pocket for a small notebook. "That would be great. What is it?"

"Murphy's Motors in Lake Eden. They just lost one of their mechanics, and my partner said they were looking for someone to replace him. If your husband calls Cyril Murphy, tell him to say that Hannah Swensen recommended him for the job."

"I'll tell him to do that." The officer looked excited at the prospect of work for her husband so close to their home. "Thanks a lot, Miss Swensen. I appreciate it."

Hannah sat down in the chair the officer indicated and turned toward the open door to the clerk's office. Her mother was standing at the counter with her checkbook in her hand.

"What do you mean, you won't take a check?" Delores said, sounding irate. "I have ten times that in my account. Just call the bank and see."

"I'm sorry, ma'am, but we can't take checks. We're not

allowed. It's cash, money order, or cashier's check only." The clerk pointed to a sign on the desk that listed the approved ways to pay bail.

Hannah could read the sign from her chair in the waiting room. NO PERSONAL CHECKS. CASH, CASHIERS' CHECKS, OR MONEY ORDERS ONLY. NO EXCEPTIONS.

"That's ridiculous. I'm the mother-in-law of the Winnetka County Sheriff. Do you really think I'd give you a bad check?"

"I'm sorry, ma'am," the clerk stood firm. "We're not allowed to take personal checks."

Andrea stepped up to the counter. "My mother's upset," she said. "Surely you can understand that. This is the first time anyone in our family has ever been in court, and we didn't know about the rules for paying my sister's bail."

"I understand," the clerk said, "and I wish I could help you, but I can't take a personal check. It's not allowed."

"But I'm Andrea Todd, and I'm the wife of the Winnetka County Sheriff, Bill Todd. I'll personally guarantee that my mother's check is good."

The clerk looked as if she wished she were anywhere but standing behind the counter, but she shook her head. "I'm sure it's good, but I'm not allowed to accept it. Your sister will have to stay here in jail until you can produce cash, a money order, or a cashier's check for the entire amount. It's the rule and I'm not allowed to make any exceptions."

Delores pursed her lips and Hannah knew her mother's expression well. She was about to give the clerk a piece of her mind. Andrea stood by, seemingly a helpless witness to what was about to happen, and Hannah sent up a silent prayer that her mother would calm down. If Delores insulted the clerk or caused a scene, *she* might be the next person who had to go in front of Judge Colfax!

And that was when the white knight arrived, striding into

the clerk's office. "Let me," Norman said, silencing Delores with a glance and taking her arm. "I've got this handled."

Hannah watched in amazement as he turned to the clerk and gave her a smile. "Sorry for the trouble. They didn't realize how the system works, but I'm here to make Miss Swensen's bail."

"Thank you, sir," the clerk sounded very relieved. "Ten percent of the bail for Miss Swensen is five thousand dollars. You'll have to put up collateral for the rest."

"I'm prepared to do that," Norman said. Then he opened his wallet and drew out several cashier's checks. "I have one for five thousand dollars right here," he told the clerk, handing it over. "And if you give me the papers, I'll sign over my house for collateral."

The clerk examined the check and quickly wrote out a receipt. Then she handed Norman some papers, which he signed. "You're all set, sir. Miss Swensen may leave the courthouse."

My hero! Hannah thought, remembering the caption from a silent movie they'd seen only a few nights ago. The handsome hero had rescued the beautiful young woman that the villain had tied to the railroad tracks. She'd called him her hero as he'd untied her and lifted her into his arms. While it was true that she wasn't a beautiful young woman and Norman wasn't a handsome young man, he was still her hero.

The clerk stamped the papers and then she nodded at the officer in the other room. "Miss Swensen's bail has been met. Once you read her the restrictions and she collects her personal items, she is free to go."

"I'll meet you out front," Norman said, coming up to pat her shoulder. "Do you need help with your things?"

I can manage. Just keep the motor running for a quick getaway before the judge changes his mind, Hannah thought, but she didn't say it. Instead she said only, "I can manage. Thank you, Norman."

"You've got a nice boyfriend," the officer said as she helped Hannah collect her things. There wasn't much. The only things she'd brought with her were her purse and the blanket that Norman had given her. Everything else was still at the sheriff's station, and Lonnie had promised to take it to Michelle and Lisa at The Cookie Jar.

It took only a minute or two to hear the restrictions of her bail. And then she was walking out the front door of the courthouse, free at last, and Howie was there to meet her.

"Lisa sent these for you," he said, handing her one of the distinctive bags they used for takeout cookies at the shop. "She told me to tell you they were Fresh Blackberry Cookies."

"Thanks," Hannah said.

"Did you turn over your passport?" Howie asked.

"I don't have a passport. Should I have a passport?"

"Not now. You couldn't get one now. But don't worry about it. You weren't going anywhere anyway, were you?"

"No."

"Then it doesn't affect you one way or the other. They'll notify me when they set a court date, but it won't be for a while. You're free, Hannah."

"Free," Hannah repeated, smiling widely. Freedom was something you really didn't think about unless you lost it. And then it was the only thing that mattered. She caught sight of Norman's car and came close to running down the courthouse steps so that she could climb in beside him, but she wasn't entirely sure that her legs would hold her. Instead, she walked quickly down the steps and made her way to the curb. Her heart was still racing with the remnants of fear and she didn't completely relax until she was seated next to Norman in the passenger seat.

"Oh, Norman!" Hannah exclaimed, throwing her arms

around him and giving him a big kiss. "You really *are* my hero! Let's go to your house."

Norman pulled her closer and kissed her soundly. And then he chuckled.

"Why are you laughing?" Hannah asked him.

"If I'd only realized that all it took was five thousand dollars and a couple of signatures on some papers, I would have done this a long time ago!"

FRESH BLACKBERRY COOKIES

Preheat oven to 375 degrees F., rack in the middle position.

Hannah's Note: Winnie told Lisa that this recipe came from her daughter, Gina, who lives in Seattle. Gina developed this recipe while she was still at home on the ranch.

1 cup fresh blackberries *(you can also use frozen)*
1 cup white *(granulated)* sugar
½ cup salted butter, softened *(1 stick, 4 ounces, ¼ pound)*
1 teaspoon baking power
½ teaspoon salt
1 and ½ teaspoons grated lemon zest *(zest is the yellow part of the peel)*
1 large egg
2 cups all-purpose flour *(pack it down in the cup when you measure it)*
¼ cup milk

Rinse and thoroughly dry the blackberries. You can do this in a strainer and let them dry while you mix up the cookie dough. *(If you're using frozen blackberries, you don't have to rinse them—just put them in a strainer and let them thaw.)*

Prepare your baking sheets by lining them with parchment paper and then spraying the paper with Pam or another nonstick cooking spray.

Place the white sugar and the softened salted butter in the bowl of an electric mixer. Beat them together until they are light and fluffy.

Add the baking powder, salt, and grated lemon zest. Mix them in thoroughly.

Add the egg and mix until it is completely incorporated.

Add one cup of flour to your bowl. Mix it in.

Add the milk to your bowl. Mix that in.

Add the rest of the flour and mix until all the ingredients except the blackberries are combined.

Turn off the mixer, take out the bowl, and set it on the counter.

Pat the strained blackberries with a paper towel until they are thoroughly dry.

Add them to the dough in the bowl and gently fold them in with a rubber spatula. *The goal here is to keep as many whole, uncrushed berries as possible. Some will crush and juice. It's inevitable. Don't despair be-*

cause that is what will give your cookies streaks of lovely purple color.

Drop the cookies by teaspoonful onto the parchment covered cookie sheet, 12 cookies to a standard-size sheet. (Lisa and I use a 2-teaspoon cookie scoop to make these down at The Cookie Jar.)

Bake the Fresh Blackberry Cookies at 375 degrees F., for 12 to 15 minutes or until they are a light, golden brown color.

Yield: 4 to 5 dozen, depending on cookie size.

Chapter Twelve

It was one o'clock in the afternoon and Hannah was back at The Cookie Jar, mixing up cookie dough in the kitchen, and trying not to listen as Lisa told the story of how Hannah'd hit the stranger who'd been standing at the side of the road and killed him.

"He had on an expensive white shirt, designer jeans, and running shoes that sell for almost two hundred dollars a pair," Hannah heard Lisa say as she added ground oatmeal to her bowl and mixed it in.

"He must have had money, that's for sure!" It was Bertie Straub's voice and Hannah smiled. Bertie had probably left her clients under the dryers and dashed down the street to listen to Lisa's story so that she could go back and repeat it to them when she combed them out.

"Dark brown hair, hazel eyes, and not an ounce of fat on him. I saw him and he looked like he worked out almost every day," Lisa continued her description.

"How about jewelry?" It was Jon Walker from Lake Eden Neighborhood Pharmacy, just down the street. Jon must have walked up on his lunch break to hear Lisa's story.

"The man had a high school ring and we're working on identifying the school it came from," Lisa told them. "I have a photo right here if you want to see it. Why don't you pass it around? Maybe someone here will recognize the seal."

"Smart thinking," Hannah said under her breath. Lake Eden had quite a few residents who'd come from other towns and cities and perhaps one of them would recognize the seal on the ring.

As she zested an orange and added the zest to her bowl, Hannah listened for any response from Lisa's audience. All was silent for a minute or two and then Lisa went on with her story. "He had a diamond embedded in his left front tooth."

"Eeeuww!" Hannah heard a woman say, but she didn't recognize the voice from such a short exclamation.

"Do you think he was a gang member?" This time Hannah *did* recognize the speaker. It was her business neighbor, owner of Beau Monde Fashions next door, Claire Rodgers Knudson.

"Sounds more like a pimp to me, especially if it's a real diamond! Gang members don't usually have that kind of cash unless they deal drugs."

Hannah recognized the voice and she started to laugh. She couldn't help it. She laughed so hard, she had to clamp her hand over her mouth so that she wouldn't be heard by the customers in the coffee shop. The speaker had been Grandma Knudson, grandmother of Claire's husband, Reverend Bob Knudson, pastor of the Lake Eden Holy Redeemer Lutheran Church. Hannah had no idea how the matriarch of the church knew about pimps, gang members, and tooth jewelry, but she obviously did. There were times when Grandma Knudson surprised them all.

"Can someone get the diamond out to find out if it's real?" It was Bertie Straub's voice again.

"Norman Rhodes removed it on Saturday. And he's taking it out to the jewelry stores at the mall to have it appraised."

"Do you think it's real?" It was Grandma Knudson's voice again.

"Andrea does. Norman showed it to her."

"It's real then," Bertie Straub said. "Andrea knows her jewelry. Was it big?"

"Andrea said it was at least a carat, maybe more."

There was a whistle from someone that Hannah couldn't identify. She didn't think anyone could identify a whistler.

And then Grandma Knudson spoke up again. "Pimp," she said. "I knew it. He probably had one of his pieces steal it and he took it for himself."

Hannah cracked up again. Where in the world did Grandma Knudson get her information? It was a very good thing that Reverend Bob wasn't here to hear her. But Reverend Bob was a regular guy with a good sense of humor. If he were here, he'd probably laugh and that would only encourage his grandmother to be even more outspoken.

"Hush, Priscilla! You don't want to let this get back to Bobby. He'd be terribly embarrassed."

Hannah clamped her hand over her mouth again as she recognized the voice of the one person who could get away with chastising Grandma Knudson. It was Nola Koenig, who was visiting from Long Prairie, and the two women had been friends for more years than Hannah had been alive.

"You're right, Nola," Grandma Knudson said. "Sometimes my mouth has a will of its own. You folks won't tell Bob on me, will you?"

There was a chorus of no's from the crowd, and Hannah chuckled again. No one would tell on Grandma Knudson. Everyone loved her, and they all enjoyed her outrageous comments.

"Young lady? Do you have a picture of the man?" Nola asked Lisa.

"Yes, ma'am. I do," Lisa answered.

"I need some copies. Bobby's driving me back to Long Prairie tomorrow and I'll have my grandsons put them up all over town. You should do the same thing in the other towns around here, maybe even offer a contest with a prize for the first person who can identify him. Everyone loves contests with prizes."

There was murmuring from the crowd again and Hannah heard several people speak up to agree with Nola. Hannah thought it was a very good idea. People did seem to enjoy contests with prizes.

"We can do that." Lisa sounded excited at the prospect. "How about free coffee and cookies for a year to the first person who can identify him?"

"We've got a high-speed copier at the school." Hannah recognized Charlotte Roscoe's voice. Charlotte was the secretary at Jordan High. "I know Ken will let me use it if it's for a good cause. I can run copies of the photo."

"Is it gruesome?" Grandma Knudson asked Lisa. "We shouldn't put it up if it's too gruesome. Somebody's bound to complain and then we'll just have to take it down."

"It's not gruesome at all. It just looks like he's sleeping or something. Norman was careful about the angle and I think he photo-shopped out anything that looked bad. I'm not quite sure how he did it, but the man looks a lot better than he did when Hannah and I got out of the truck to see what she hit."

Hannah shivered slightly. She wished Lisa hadn't put it quite that way. She could still see the blood and the bruises in her mind.

"I've got an idea," Charlotte said. "Do you have any pictures of the ring or the tooth with the diamond?"

"I've got both of them," Lisa said. "Norman took a really good picture of the tooth, and Lonnie took a really good one of the ring."

"That's perfect," Charlotte told her. "We can put the photo of the man's face on the top half and the photo of the ring and the tooth side-by-side on the bottom half. Somebody's bound to recognize one of them."

There was a knock on the back kitchen door and Hannah hurried to answer it. She opened the door to see her mother standing there.

"Shhh! Lisa's telling her story in the coffee shop."

"Okay," Delores said, reaching out to hug her daughter. "I'm so sorry about that confusion with the check, dear. I had no idea they wouldn't accept my check. It was a good thing Norman was there."

"Yes, it was."

"Where did you go when you left the courthouse? I looked all over for you."

"I went to Norman's house."

"Of course you did. I forgot that Moishe was there and it never occurred to me that you'd gone out there with Norman to pick him up. Did you take him home?"

"No, he was having too much fun playing with Cuddles," Hannah said, and then she didn't say another word. She just motioned to a stool at the work island and went to the kitchen coffeepot to fill mugs for both of them.

"I'm just glad that's over!" Delores said, plucking a cookie from the plate of Orange Crisps that Hannah had carried to the table. Then she noticed the mixing bowl. "What are you making now, dear?"

"Chocolate Orange Crisps. It's the same recipe, but I decided to put miniature chocolate chips in them this time."

"These are good, but I think I'd like those even better," Delores said, finishing one cookie and taking another. "You could put miniature white chocolate chips in them and make another version."

"That's true. The only problem is that Florence doesn't carry miniature white chocolate chips at the Red Owl. She says they don't make them."

"That's what she always says when she doesn't carry something, dear. Everybody knows that. Why don't you just dump a package of regular white chocolate chips in the food processor and make smaller pieces?"

"Good idea. I'll do that with the next batch. Which one do you think you'd like best?"

"The ones with the miniature regular chocolate chips, dear."

"Of course you would," Hannah said, smiling at her mother. Although it had been a futile attempt, Delores had intended to bail her out and Hannah was sure that her mother would have been perfectly willing to put her house up for collateral. "You're a confirmed chocoholic, Mother," she said with a smile.

"There are worse holics to be," Delores said.

"That's not a word, Mother."

"Well, it should be! Everything's a *holic* nowadays. Besides alcoholics, there are workaholics, and sexaholics, and foodaholics, and shopaholics. I saw a commercial the other day that said if you honk the horn in your car too much, you're a honkaholic. What's next?"

"Textaholics, phoneaholics, and cyberholics, I guess. I'm not going to start worrying about it until they begin talking about cookieholics."

"They'll never do that in Lake Eden, dear. Your cookies are too good." Delores glanced over at the bowl again. "Haven't you stirred that cookie dough enough to make a test batch? If you do it now, I could critique them for you."

Hannah laughed. "Okay. Just let me scoop out enough for a pan and I'll stick them in the oven."

"How long do they have to bake?"

"Ten to twelve minutes. And they have to cool for five or you'll burn your tongue."

"Not five. Two and a half, dear. When they come out of

the oven, just stick them in the walk-in cooler and they'll take only half as long to cool down enough to eat."

Hannah laughed. "It would hurt the texture of some cookies, but not these. Good idea, Mother. I didn't even think of that."

"It's because I'm hungry. I came straight here on my lunch hour and I didn't stop to eat."

"*Necessity is the mother of invention*," Hannah said, quoting her great-grandmother Elsa.

"And invention is the mother of . . ." Delores stopped speaking and began to blush slightly. "I can't finish that one. I always cringed when your great-grandpa Swensen said it."

Hannah was puzzled. She couldn't recall her great-grandfather saying anything about invention. "I don't remember that one."

"Of course you don't. I asked great-grandpa Swensen to stop saying it when you were old enough to understand the words. And he did. He was a good man, Hannah." Her mother stopped speaking and looked pensive. "I wonder what he'd think if he knew his grandson was dead and he learned that I was getting married again."

Uh-oh! Guilt rears its ugly head, Hannah thought. *Mother's feeling guilty about marrying again.* And then she said the first thing that came into her head. "Great-grandpa Swensen used to have a saying for that, too. I remember him saying it when Shep died."

"Shep was the German shepherd they had for years and years. I remember when he died, but I don't remember what Great-grandpa said. What was it, dear?"

"'Life is for the living. Let's go out and rescue another dog.'"

"That's . . ." Delores stopped and swallowed hard. "That's a very good sentiment to remember, dear. I'm very glad you did."

"Me, too." Hannah scooped up the last cookie and put it on the cookie sheet. "Okay, Mother. Gird your loins. You're about to perform another taste test for me."

Delores gave a little laugh. "It's a grueling job, but someone has to do it. Hurry up and bake them, dear. I don't want to get fired as your taste-tester for not performing my duties."

ORANGE CRISPS

Preheat oven to 375 degrees F., rack in the middle position.

1 cup melted butter *(2 sticks, 8 ounces, ½ pound)*

2 cups white *(granulated)* sugar

2 teaspoons vanilla extract

½ teaspoon salt

2 teaspoons baking soda

2 large eggs, beaten *(just whip them up in a glass with a fork)*

2 and ½ cups all-purpose flour *(pack it down in the cup when you measure it)*

1 cup chopped nuts *(measure AFTER chopping—any nut you like will do—I used walnuts)*

Zest from one orange *(zest is the finely grated orange part of the peel)*

2 cups **GROUND** dry oatmeal *(measure BEFORE grinding—I used Quaker's Quick 1-Minute and zooped it up in my food processor with the steel blade)*

Melt the butter in a large microwave-safe bowl on HIGH for one minute. Let it sit for a few seconds and then stir it to see if it's melted. If the butter has not

melted, heat it again in increments of 20 seconds until it's melted.

Let the butter cool to room temperature.

Add the white sugar to the butter and beat until the mixture is thoroughly incorporated.

Mix in the vanilla extract, salt, and baking soda. Mix well.

Stir in the beaten eggs.

Add the flour in half-cup increments, mixing after each addition.

Mix in the chopped nuts. Try to distribute them evenly. You want some in each cookie.

Add the zest from one orange and mix it in thoroughly.

If you haven't already done so, measure your oatmeal and grind it with a food grinder, or in a food processor with the steel blade until it's the consistency of coarse sand.

Add the ground oatmeal to your bowl and mix it in. *(If you're not using an electric mixer, this will take a little muscle since the resulting dough will be fairly stiff.)*

Roll walnut-sized dough balls with your hands and place them on a cookie sheet sprayed with Pam or another nonstick cooking spray, 12 cookie balls to a standard sheet. You can also line your cookie sheets with parchment paper and spray that if you'd prefer.

If your dough is too sticky to roll, place the bowl in the refrigerator for thirty minutes and then try again.

Once the dough balls are on the cookie sheet, press them down with the tines of a fork in a crisscross pattern *(the way you'd do with peanut butter cookies.)*

Bake at 375 degrees F. for 10 minutes. Cool the cookies on the cookie sheet for 2 minutes and then remove them to a wire rack to cool completely.

Yield: 6 to 7 dozen delicious cookies, depending on cookie size.

CHOCOLATE ORANGE CRISPS

Preheat oven to 375 degrees F., rack in the middle position.

Follow the instructions for Orange Crisps **EXCEPT**:

Reduce the cup of chopped nuts to one-half cup of chopped nuts.

Add one cup of miniature semi-sweet chocolate chips *(a 6-ounce bag)* right after you mix in the chopped nuts. Then proceed as directed.

Yield: 7 to 8 dozen delicious cookies that Delores adores.

Chapter Thirteen

"I bet you're glad to get home," Michelle said as she drove down the ramp to the underground garage and parked in Hannah's space.

"I'm more than glad. I'm relieved, too. It's been a long day."

Hannah gave a little sigh as she got out of the car. They still had the loaner car that Lonnie had gotten for her from his father's garage. They would be driving it for a while. The authorities had released Hannah's cookie truck, but it had some front end damage. Mike had surprised her by picking it up on Saturday afternoon and taking it in to Murphy's Motors to be repaired.

Michelle led the way up the outside staircase with Hannah following behind her. When they reached the landing, she stopped and turned to face Hannah. "You're excited, aren't you?"

"About coming home, you mean?"

"No, about the grand prize. Mr. and Mrs. Purvis and the boys delivered it this afternoon. I handed them my key and Mrs. Purvis came into the coffee shop to bring it back. I gave her some cookies as a thank you. I hope that's all right."

"It's fine." Hannah smiled slightly. "The grand prize," she repeated, her smile growing a bit wider. "So much has happened in the past three days, I forgot all about it. I wonder what it is."

"You'll find out in a minute. Do you want to catch, or shall I?"

"There's nothing to catch. Norman's bringing Moishe back around seven tonight. I told him I'd fix him dinner."

"I'll help," Michelle said, unlocking the door and stepping inside. "Come on, Hannah. Let's go see your prize."

The first place Hannah went was the kitchen. Nothing new there. Her old refrigerator was still in place, and so was the stove and the dishwasher. The grand prize wasn't a fancy new kitchen appliance.

"I don't see anything in here," Michelle said, gazing around the living room.

"You're right," Hannah said, realizing that her old television set and stereo were still in place.

"Maybe we're just not seeing it," Michelle suggested. "It could be something small."

Hannah shook her head. "It's not small. They told me it would take at least three Jordan High football players to carry it in and set it up. And he said it had to be plugged in."

"Well . . . where is it?"

"Let's check the guest room. Maybe it's a new bedroom suite with a night-light built into the headboard or something like that."

Hannah opened the door to the room Michelle used when she visited. "It's not that," she said, stepping into the room and gesturing toward the bed and dresser.

"You're right. Same old, same old," Michelle said, and then, when she realized what she'd said, she added, "Not that I don't like the furniture in here. The mirror's nice and big and the bed is very comfortable."

Hannah chuckled slightly. Her baby sister was nothing if

not considerate. "It's Mother's old bedroom set and you know it."

"I know, but what I said is true. The bed *is* comfortable and the mirror's big. Do you think they could have put whatever it is it in the guest bathroom?"

"It's a tiny bathroom. It wouldn't take three football players to carry in anything that could have fit in there. They couldn't even get in there, at least not all three at once."

"A new toilet?" Michelle suggested. "They're really heavy. And a new toilet has to be set up and hooked to the plumbing. Maybe that's what Ken meant when he said it had to be plugged in."

Hannah shook her head. "No way. They couldn't put in a new toilet without getting permission from the homeowner's committee. I'm on the homeowner's committee and no one has asked permission for at least two months."

"You need permission just to put in a new toilet?"

"Yes, for a brand new one. You don't need permission if you're just doing repairs on the old one. Our handyman does that free of charge to the homeowner. The problem is that the condo association is responsible for the plumbing and the electrical in all of the condos. If something goes wrong, our handyman fixes it. If the job is too big for him, we pay a plumber or an electrician to come in."

"That's nice, but I still don't understand why you need permission to put in a new toilet."

"It's simple. People buy all sorts of fancy things with hookups in different spots like a bidet or whatever. The plumbing might need to be changed for those, and we want to check it out first to make sure that our handyman can do it. Changes to the plumbing are our responsibility and we don't want to pay for re-plumbing a whole bathroom to accommodate a fancy toilet."

"But what if you *want* a fancy toilet?"

"Then you have to pay for the plumbing and we have to authorize the permanent changes and inspect it when it's completed. We've done it in the past for several units, but you have to come to a meeting with the plans and get our approval before you can start."

Michelle thought about that for several moments. "I'm not sure I want to buy a condo," she said.

"I wasn't sure either, but that's what was available in my price range. And it's a lot easier now that I'm on the board." Hannah stopped speaking and sighed deeply. "Actually . . . I'm not sure it's easier. It's easier for changes that I'd like to make, but I don't really want any changes. And the board meets twice a month with meetings that last a couple of hours. Now that I think about it, I really don't know if it's worth it."

"Would you rather have a house?"

"Maybe, but then all the headaches would be mine, and all the expenses, too. This way it's a shared responsibility. I'm just not sure which I'd prefer, but this is what I have and I'm happy with it." She stopped and motioned to Michelle. "Come on. My grand prize has to be here somewhere. We need to find it."

They looked in the guest bathroom, but there was nothing there. It was exactly as Hannah had said. The room was too small for anything that needed three football players to carry it.

"The only place left is your bedroom," Michelle said, opening the door to Hannah's room. "Since we've eliminated all the other possibilities, it's got to be in here."

Both women started to enter Hannah's bedroom, but the moment they cleared the doorway, they both stopped dead in their tracks.

"Whoa!" Hannah said, taking a step backward.

"Whoa is right," Michelle breathed. And then they both

simply stared at the huge apparition taking up the space near the foot of Hannah's bed.

"Is that what I think it is?" Hannah asked, turning to face her sister.

"I think so. It looks like one of those all-in-one trainers, the ones that take the place of stationary bicycles, rowing machines, cross-country ski simulators, and treadmills."

"I was afraid of that," Hannah said, frowning deeply. Then she pointed to the front of the machine. "Is that what I think it is between the handlebars?"

"If you're thinking television set, you're right. And I think there's a . . ." Michelle stopped speaking and walked forward to approach the front of the machine. A moment later, she said, "I'm right. It's a television set with a built-in DVD player so you can play exercise videos, or watch regular television while you use the treadmill. It's an expensive piece of equipment, Hannah. You won an all-in-one fancy exercise machine that would make every member of a fitness center drool."

Hannah let out a groan and sat down on the edge of her bed. "Just what I needed. Oh, boy."

"You're being sarcastic . . . aren't you?"

"And how! I don't need an exercise machine. The last time I used one was at Heavenly Bodies Spa in the mall. And you know what happened when I did that!"

"You discovered a dead body." Michelle gave a little chuckle. "I wouldn't worry about that. There's no Jacuzzi here. And it's certainly not a reason to avoid this machine. You won't find a dead body here in your bedroom unless someone breaks in and exercises himself to death."

"That could happen. If I start using this machine, the victim could be me."

"You're going to use it?" Michelle asked, sounding surprised.

"Maybe. My jeans are getting a little tight around the

hips. And it does have a DVD player. I don't necessarily have to watch an exercise tape. I could amble on the treadmill and watch one of my favorite movies."

Michelle looked down at the machine. "Sorry, Hannah. There's no setting for amble. The closest you could come would be fast walk."

"I could do a fast walk, especially if I watched *Chariots of Fire* or a documentary about the life of Roger Bannister."

"That's true. And it might take the onus out of exercising for you. Actually . . . I wouldn't mind using it while I'm here. If you don't mind, that is."

"I don't mind. Have at it. I'm going to go make a dessert for tonight's dinner. Norman's picking up pizza at Bertanelli's."

"He's going to leave the cats in the car while he goes inside?" Michelle asked, sounding worried.

"Of course not. They've got a drive-in window now. Ellie told me that Bert put it in himself. They hired an extra person to man the window and business has increased fifteen percent already."

"I can understand that. Their pizza is the best in Winnetka County. What kind of pizza is Norman getting?"

"He's getting three. Sausage and pepperoni, five cheese, and a garbage pizza with everything on it."

"Who else is coming?"

"Nobody, as far as I know. But Norman wanted us to have plenty of leftovers so we wouldn't have to cook for a couple of nights."

"That's nice of him. What are you making for dessert?"

"I don't know yet, but I'll think of something."

"Okay," Michelle said, paging through the manual that had come with the machine. "It says that this machine can take the place of almost every machine in a well-equipped gym."

"That's interesting," Hannah said for lack of something better to say.

"I'll be there to help you in a couple of minutes. I just want to try this thing out and see if it does what they say it can do."

"No hurry," Hannah told her, turning to leave. "Knock yourself out, but not literally, of course."

Hannah was frowning slightly as she walked down the hallway to the kitchen. She wasn't head-over-heels delighted about her grand prize, but she had to admit it was impressive. Unfortunately, they'd given it to the wrong person. She could think of several people right here in Lake Eden who'd really enjoy it and would use it every day. Giving it to her was almost like throwing money up in the air and watching it blow away. She might use it, sooner or later. And it would probably be later, if she were entirely honest about it. But she wasn't thrilled by the prospect. At least Michelle seemed to appreciate it and that was good. Now that she thought about it, there were several people she knew who might appreciate it. She'd show it to Norman when he got here and get his opinion, and she'd certainly show it to Mike the next time he came over. Mike was the expert when it came to exercise equipment. He'd ordered all of the fitness machines for the gym at the sheriff's station, and Bill had told her that they had the best equipped law enforcement exercise facility in the whole state of Minnesota.

Hannah entered the kitchen, flicked on the lights again, and took an apron out of the drawer. Then she opened the refrigerator to see what was there. Perhaps Michelle had gone shopping while she was in jail, and there would be some special ingredient she could use for her dessert.

"No such luck," Hannah said aloud, staring at the empty shelves. Lonnie and Michelle must have gone out to eat or brought in takeout every night that she was gone. It was time to try the pantry and hope she could find something there.

Of course the basic ingredients for cookies were in her pantry. She kept them on hand in case of fire, flood, earthquake, blizzard, or any other natural disaster. Cookies made everything bearable. Hannah and every one of her customers at The Cookie Jar would testify to that!

What could she put in the cookies to make them interesting and different? She had several different flavors of chips including white chocolate, semi-sweet chocolate, milk chocolate, butterscotch, and peanut butter, but she wanted something more special than a variation on her Chocolate Chip Crunch Cookies. The only item that was even remotely promising was a packet of sweetened dried cranberries that had been on her shelf since Christmas before last. Hannah read the "use by" date on the package. It was good until September this year. Of course the sweetened, dried cranberries were still good. Nothing affected sweetened dried cranberries if the package hadn't been opened. And this package was not only unopened, it had also been sitting untouched on her pantry shelf ever since she'd bought it at Florence's Red Owl grocery store twenty months ago.

What could she do with the cranberries? Hannah thought for a minute. Of course she could always make a batch of Boggles. She had all the ingredients including the oatmeal right here in her pantry. But she'd baked three batches of Boggles today and she didn't feel like baking them again. What other dessert used sweetened dried cranberries? She could use the cranberries in Imperial Cereal, but she didn't have enough dry cereal for that. And Imperial Cereal was more of a snack than a dessert. Her third choice was Cranberry Scones, but those weren't a dessert either.

"Whoa!" Hannah breathed as she visualized a beautiful lacy cookie with sweetened dried cranberries and white chocolate chips. She could do it! She'd use her recipe for Christmas Lace Cookies as a guide and go from there. It was fun to come up with a new cookie and Hannah was smiling as she walked to the living room to print out the recipe on her home computer.

Once she'd printed the recipe for her Christmas Lace Cookies, she carried the paper back to the kitchen. If the cookies turned out as well as she thought they would, they'd add them to the menu at The Cookie Jar. And that meant she had to come up with a descriptive and catchy cookie name. She didn't want to use the word *lace* in the name. That was unique to their Christmas Lace Cookies.

"Airy Berry Cookies?" Hannah asked herself out loud as she assembled the ingredients on the kitchen counter. Yes, that cookie name was perfect. Now all she had to do was mix up and bake the cookies to see if they were good and the name actually fit. She was about to start mixing the cookie dough when the phone on the kitchen wall rang.

Hannah made a beeline for the phone and lifted the receiver. "Hello?" she answered the call.

"I'm glad I caught you, dear. You're not going to leave to go out to eat or anything, are you?"

"No, Mother," Hannah said, squelching the uncharitable urge to groan. It wasn't that she didn't like talking to her mother. She enjoyed their conversations. It was just that Delores could keep her on the phone for what seemed like hours on end and she had cookies to bake before Norman arrived.

"Good! Doc asked me to call. He needs to talk to you, Hannah. He says it's very important and it'll only take a minute or two."

"Okay. Put Doc on the phone."

"No, dear. Doc needs to talk to you in person. We'll be leaving the hospital immediately and we'll drive right out. I just didn't want you to leave before we got there."

"What does Doc want to talk to me about?" Hannah asked, feeling a bit apprehensive. The last time Doc had asked to talk to her in person was on the night Bill had come to arrest her.

"I don't know, dear. I asked, but he won't tell me. The only thing I know is that it's not bad news. I asked him that because I didn't want you to worry."

"Thanks for asking, Mother."

"Certainly, dear. It's all right if we come over, then?"

Hannah did the only thing she could do. She agreed. "Okay then," she said, but it sounded rather curt even to her own ears, so she added, "Would you and Doc like to join us for dinner? Norman's bringing pizza from Bertanelli's."

"That would be lovely, dear. Thank you. Shall we pick up anything on the way?"

"I don't really need anything, unless . . ." Hannah stopped and began to grin. "Are you wearing silk stockings?"

Delores laughed. "Yes, and I have some fish-shaped, salmon-flavored treats for Moishe in the glove compartment of Doc's car. I'll carry them in with me so I can bribe Moishe."

Hannah was still smiling as she said goodbye and hung up the phone. Delores knew the drill. If she wore silk stockings and arrived without Moishe's favorite kitty treats, there could be another pair of shredded hose to add to the two dozen or so that had gone before them.

The phone rang again and Hannah picked it up. Delores must have forgotten to tell her something. "Hello again, Mother."

But it wasn't her mother. It was Norman. She recognized his laugh immediately. "You just got off the phone with your mother?" he asked.

"Yes. I'm glad you called, Norman. If you haven't gone to Bertanelli's yet, will you pick up some garden salads? Mother and Doc will be joining us for dinner."

"Eight salads, and I'll order a small Canadian bacon and pineapple pizza for your mother."

"That would be great. I know she loves . . . wait a second." A puzzled expression crossed Hannah's face. "We're only five for dinner. Mother and Doc, Michelle, you, and me."

"Five so far," Norman said.

"What do you mean?"

"Dinner at your place always grows by the time I get there. I'll play it safe and get eight salads. And I'd better get a couple orders of meatballs, too."

"Do you know something I don't know?"

"A lot of things. I know how to do a root canal, and you don't. And I can extract a tooth painlessly, which I'm willing to bet you can't do."

Hannah laughed. "Not dental things. I admit I don't know much about those. I meant, do you know anyone else who's going to come here for dinner?"

"Not for sure, but I figure there's a fifty-fifty chance that Lonnie and Mike will drop by."

Hannah thought about that for a moment. "You're probably right. Lonnie will want to see Michelle."

"And Mike was at the courthouse this morning. He'll probably drop by to see how you're doing."

"You could be right. But that's only seven people. Who's the eighth?"

"Andrea if she's still mad at Bill. Do you know if she is?"

"She's still mad. I talked to her on the phone earlier."

"Then she might drop by your place so she doesn't have to talk to Bill."

Hannah thought about that for a moment. "That's possible," she said. "I hope you don't mind picking up more food. When you get here, I'll pay you back."

"Don't be silly. They're my friends, too. And I need to talk to Doc, anyway."

"About the tooth?"

"The tooth and other things. And before you ask, I didn't

find out anything definitive about the tooth except that the diamond is real."

"*Real* as in *real* valuable?" Hannah quipped.

"Very funny. And yes, it is *real* valuable. In fact, it's worth a small fortune. I'll tell you all about it when I get there. Right now, I have to call in another couple of pizzas and order the green salads, put the cats in the carry crate, and get on the road. I'll see you in a while, Hannah. I love you."

"I love you, too," Hannah said, hanging up the phone and heading back to the kitchen counter again. She *did* love Norman. Perhaps she didn't love him enough to marry him, or . . . perhaps she did. She'd have to think about that when she had more time. Right now, she had cookies to bake before Norman and everyone else came through the door.

AIRY BERRY COOKIES

Preheat oven to 350 degrees F., rack in the middle position.

1 and ½ cups rolled oats *(uncooked dry oat-meal—use the old-fashioned kind that takes 5 minutes to cook, not the quick 1-minute variety)*

½ cup salted butter *(1 stick, 4 ounces, ¼ pound)*

¾ cup white *(granulated)* sugar

1 teaspoon baking powder

1 teaspoon flour *(that's not a misprint—it's only one teaspoon!)*

½ teaspoon salt

1 teaspoon vanilla extract

1 large egg, beaten *(just whip it up in a glass with a fork)*

½ cup sweetened dried cranberries *(I used Craisins)*

½ cup white chocolate chips *(I used Ghirardelli's)*

Measure the oatmeal and place it in a medium-sized bowl.

Melt the butter and pour it over the oatmeal. Stir until it's thoroughly mixed.

In a small bowl, combine the white sugar, baking powder, flour, and salt. Mix well.

Add the sugar mixture to the oatmeal mixture and blend them together thoroughly.

Mix in the vanilla extract.

Add the beaten egg and stir until everything is combined.

Mix in the half-cup of sweetened dried cranberries. Then add the white chocolate chips and stir them in thoroughly.

Hannah's 1st Note: I once used cherry-flavored Craisins in these cookies. That means I had to re-name them Airy Cherry-Berry Cookies.

Line cookie sheets with foil, shiny side up. Spray the foil lightly with Pam or another nonstick cooking spray.

Drop the cookie dough by rounded teaspoonful onto the foil, leaving space for spreading. Don't crowd these cookies together. Place no more than 6 or 8 cookies on each cookie sheet.

Hannah's 2nd Note: Lisa and I use a 2-teaspoon cookie scoop to form these cookies down at The Cookie Jar. It's the perfect size.

Bake your Airy Berry Cookies at 350 degrees F. for 12 minutes. Remove them from the oven and cool them on the cookie sheet for 5 minutes.

Pull the foil off the cookie sheet and onto a wire rack.

Let the cookies cool completely on the sheet of foil before you try to remove them.

When the cookies are completely cool, peel them carefully from the foil and store them in a cool, dry place. *(Your refrigerator is NOT a dry place.)*

If you want to dress up these cookies for special company, wait until they're cool and then drizzle them with melted chocolate chips mixed with juice, milk, or a berry or coffee liqueur. The recipe is below:

CHOCOLATE DRIZZLE

$\frac{1}{2}$ cup semi-sweet chocolate chips *(or milk chocolate chips, or white chocolate chips— it's your choice)*
6 Tablespoons juice, milk, or liqueur

Before you start, lay out sheets of wax paper and place the completely cooled cookies close together on the wax paper.

Place the chips and the liquid you chose in a microwave-safe bowl and heat them on HIGH for 30 seconds.

Let the bowl sit for at least 15 seconds and then stir it smooth with a spoon or a heat-resistant spatula. If you can't stir it smooth and the chips are still lumpy, microwave the mixture in 20-second intervals until you can stir it smooth.

Check the consistency of your mixture. If it's too thick to drizzle, add additional liquid until it's the proper drizzling consistency. If it's too thin, add a few more chips and microwave again until those are melted and can be stirred into the drizzling mixture.

Place the bowl right next to the wax paper with the cookies and use a big spoon to drizzle the cookies with lines of chocolate sweetness. You can go all one way to make parallel lines or you can drizzle lines that crisscross each other. The design is up to you.

Let the chocolate drizzle harden on top of the cookies and then store them between sheets of wax paper in a cool, dry place.

Yield: One batch of Airy Berry Cookies makes about 2 and $\frac{1}{2}$ dozen cookies.

Chapter Fourteen

"Oooh! Pretty!" Michelle said, coming into the kitchen just as Hannah was taking the last pan of cookies out of the oven. "What are those?"

"Airy Berry Cookies. We're having them for dessert with ice cream."

"Do you think there's enough for one more?"

"Let me guess. Lonnie's coming?"

"Yes. He just sent me a text message."

"And you told him yes?"

"No. I said I'd find out and let him know."

"Then text him back and tell him to come. Norman's bringing enough pizza and salad for eight."

"Eight? Who else is coming?"

"Mother and Doc. Mother called to ask if they could come. And Norman thinks Mike will show up, and possibly Andrea if she wants to avoid Bill when he gets home."

Michelle laughed. "Norman's probably right. Mike always seems to come over when we're eating, and Andrea's still mad at Bill."

Hannah put the last pan of cookies on a wire rack to cool and turned to look at her sister. "You'd better text Lonnie and then grab a quick shower before he gets here. You're all sweaty."

"That's because I had a great workout. I tried out everything the manual said your machine could do."

"Did it live up to its claims?"

"Yes. It's really an amazing all-in-one gym, Hannah. Wait until Lonnie sees it. He's going to be really envious."

"Does Lonnie know a lot about exercise machines?"

"Not as much as Mike knows, but Lonnie knows enough to appreciate this one. I wonder what Norman will think of it."

"We'll find out when he gets here."

"I think you should have Doc take a look at it, too. It's got all sorts of medical monitors like heart rate and things like that."

"Do you think I should ask Mother, too?"

"Why bother?" Michelle gave a little laugh. "Mother doesn't know anything about exercise machines. She never uses them and she doesn't need them. She just naturally has a perfect figure."

"I know. If she weren't my mother, I'd hate her."

"Me, too. Don't ask her about the machine, though. I think it would be a mistake."

"Why?"

"Because she's bound to have an opinion," Michelle said with a grin. "She'll tell you that the color on the handlebars clashes with your bedspread."

Hannah laughed. "You're probably right, but I'll show her anyway. I don't want her to feel left out." She glanced up at the kitchen clock and gave Michelle a little push toward the living room. "You'd better get a move on if you want to text Lonnie and take your shower before Norman gets here with the food."

When Michelle left, Hannah cleaned up the kitchen. There wasn't much mess. She usually rinsed off things after she'd used them so it was simply a matter of placing utensils in the dishwasher and wiping down the counters. She was just thinking about pouring herself something to drink when she heard Michelle coming down the hallway.

"What can I do to help?" Michelle asked as she entered the kitchen.

Hannah took one look at her youngest sister and blinked in surprise. Michelle was wearing snug white jeans and the tightest pink lace tank top that Hannah had ever seen. "You can go get a sweater to throw over that tank top."

"But this outfit won't look good with a sweater."

"Do it anyway. Mother's coming."

"But what's wrong with this outfit? This top is Lonnie's favorite. I think it's the color."

Hannah just stared at her sister for a long moment and then she sighed deeply. "You think it's the *color* of the tank top?"

"I know it's the color. Lonnie just loves me in pink."

"I see," Hannah said, sighing again. "Go put on something else, Michelle. If you think the color is the only thing Lonnie loves about that tight pink tank top, it's because it's cutting off the circulation to your brain."

As usual, the pizza was great. Bertanelli's pizza always was. They'd just taken their first few bites when Hannah's phone rang.

"It's got to be Mike," Norman said, and then he turned to Hannah. "Do you want me to get it?"

Hannah nodded. It was all she could do. She was still chewing her bite of pizza and her mouth was filled with sausage and pepperoni.

"Hi, Mike," Norman said once he'd picked up the receiver. There was a pause and then he laughed. "Just a lucky guess. We're all here eating pizza and there's plenty for you. Where are you?"

There was another pause. Mike was obviously answering Norman's question. And then Norman spoke again. "Sure. Just come on up and we'll set another plate."

Once Mike had joined the group, they all ate in silence for several minutes. Then Delores turned to Hannah. "Doc has something to tell you, dear."

"Not now, Lori," Doc said. "We're eating."

Delores looked puzzled. "Is it something we can't discuss while we're eating?"

"Yes."

"Then it has something to do with that man Hannah hit?"

Doc looked around the table apologetically. "Sorry," he told them. And then he reached out to take Delores's hand. "This isn't twenty questions, Lori. And it's not appropriate conversation for the dinner table. We'll discuss all this after dessert."

Hannah turned to smile at him. "How do you know there'll be dessert?"

"There has to be dessert. You *always* make dessert. And I'll bet it's something you want us to test. Am I right?"

"You're right," Hannah said. "It's vanilla ice cream with a new cookie I just made." She stopped speaking as she heard a familiar sound. It was a loud thump followed by a quieter thump as the cats jumped from her bed to the floor of her bedroom. "Uh-oh!" she said, reaching for the basket of garlic bread and closing the lid on the closest pizza box. "Feet up, everybody! They're coming fast!"

Everyone knew the essentials when there was a call for "feet up." Norman finished closing the pizza boxes, Michelle steadied the salad bowl, Lonnie put the cover on the containers with the extra meatballs and the freshly grated mozzarella, Doc picked up the extra pitcher of iced tea that sat on the table, and everyone grabbed for their drinking glasses or coffee cups. Almost in unison and just in time, they tucked up their feet as the cats came racing into the room with Moishe in the lead and Cuddles chasing him.

There was another thump as Moishe lost purchase with his claws on the carpet and skidded into the table leg. Whether it was a planned ploy or a simple accident didn't matter. Hannah had given them enough warning to secure everything so that none of their dinner fell to the floor.

"No steak this time, Moishe," Lonnie said, remembering the time his steak has fallen to the floor at Norman's house and the cats had made off with it.

Both cats paused for a moment to stare up at the tabletop and then they raced off again. Hannah heard them go into the laundry room and she turned in her chair to watch as they came out and barreled back down the hallway to her bedroom.

"Is that it?" Delores asked when there were two thumps from the bedroom as the cats jumped back on Hannah's bed.

"Once more," Norman said, still holding the pizza boxes. "I was watching Cuddles and I saw that crazed look in her eyes. She's not ready to give up the chase quite yet."

"And I noticed Moishe's tail," Hannah added. "It was flicking at the very tip and that always means at least one more circuit around the food table."

"You're both right," Delores said, tucking her feet up again. "I just heard two thumps from Hannah's bedroom."

When the cats barreled into the living room the second time, Cuddles was in the lead and Moishe was chasing her. They raced around the table, barely missing the legs of Hannah's standing salad bowl, and then they exited the room.

"Are we done now?" Delores asked.

"As far as Moishe is concerned we are," Hannah replied. "His tail stopped flicking."

"And Cuddles looked tired instead of crazed," Norman added. "I think we can eat the rest of our meal in peace."

Delores looked over at Doc and gave the little giggle that Hannah found both surprising and endearing. It was the joyful laugh of a woman in love and she was glad that her mother had found someone who could make her so happy.

"This may sound crazy," she told Doc, "but every time we go out to the Lake Eden Inn for dinner, I miss the cat races."

Hannah laughed. "Sorry, Mother. The feline speedway is only open at Norman's house and my place."

"She actually tucked her feet up the last time we had dinner out there," Doc told them.

"Simple reflex," Delores explained. "One of the cooks dropped something in the kitchen and I heard it."

"Back to the pizza," Norman said, opening the boxes and placing them in the center of the table again.

"I think I've had enough," Delores announced, turning to Doc. "You're almost ready for dessert, aren't you?"

"Not yet. I haven't had a piece of the Hawaiian pizza yet. I wouldn't want to eat a whole pizza like that, but it's nice for a change."

"Oh, I just thought we were all through and we could have dessert. Or maybe we could talk before dessert while our dinner settles."

"The rest of us are still eating, Mother," Hannah said, knowing precisely what was on her mother's mind. Her great-grandmother had always said that curiosity killed the cat, but in this case, it was almost killing the mother!

Delores looked as if she really wanted to ask them to hurry and finish so that she could hear Doc's news for Hannah. She even opened her mouth to start talking, but before she could reopen the subject, Doc popped a cherry tomato from his salad into her mouth. "We'll talk about it later, Lori."

Everyone laughed and so did Delores, but only after she'd eaten the tomato. "Thank you, dear," she said to Doc. "That was much more delicious than a sock stuffed in my mouth and it had exactly the same effect."

Fifteen minutes later, when almost all of the pizza had been eaten and everyone had eaten dessert and said they thought that Hannah's new cookie was one of the best they'd ever had, Michelle cleared the table. Hannah made a fresh pot of coffee, and they carried it to the table.

"We're through with dessert," Delores said as soon as Michelle had refilled their coffee cups. "Tell us, Doc."

Doc turned to Hannah. "The first part is interesting, Hannah. Marlene managed to isolate that stain on the man's shirt. It's blackberries."

"Really!" Hannah exclaimed. "I didn't expect that. I wonder where he got a stain like that." As everyone began to speculate, she listened with one ear as her mind raced through the possibilities. She'd check with Rose at the café to see if she'd made blackberry pie on Friday. And she'd check with Florence at the Red Owl to see if any of the pre-packaged bakery pies she carried were blackberry or if she carried fresh blackberries in her produce department. "Is Marlene sure it's blackberry and not some other kind of berry?"

"She says she's ninety percent certain. It has to do with acidity, color, and sweetness. She tested for pH value, color density, and brix."

"Brix?" Mike looked puzzled.

"It's a measure of sweetness. Marlene used a refractometer to test for that. She always hedges her bets, so when she told me she was ninety percent sure, that means we can be ninety-nine percent sure."

"That's good enough for me," Hannah said. "It's got to be blackberries."

"Now on to something more serious." Doc took another swallow of his coffee. "Your mother was right, Hannah. What I have to tell you does have to do with the man you killed. Would you like to discuss it in private?"

Hannah thought about that for a moment and then she shook her head. Everyone here was either a relative or a friend. "That's okay," she said. "You can tell all of us whatever it is."

"Something about the autopsy report was nagging me over the weekend," he began, "so I got out the photos of the damage to your truck and compared them with my descriptions of the injuries."

Hannah leaned forward slightly. She could feel her heart rate increase and she felt a flurry of excitement run through her. Was Doc about to tell her that she hadn't killed the man after all? She wanted to ask, but Doc started speaking again.

"I found three sites of trauma that didn't line up with the damage to the front end of your truck."

"Exactly what do you mean?" Mike asked, looking almost as hopeful as Hannah was.

"Our John Doe suffered a massive blow to the cranium, causing several fissures of the frontal bone." Doc noticed Delores's puzzled expression and clarified. "That's the front part of the skull, Lori. And fissures are fractures. At first, I thought that contact with the front bumper of Hannah's truck was the cause of the injury, but this particular trauma was not consistent with the other injuries that were caused by the collision." He stopped as he noticed several other puzzled expressions. "Sorry. I'll try to put it more clearly. These injuries were too severe for the speed that Hannah was traveling. There was also the location of the fractures. They weren't consistent with the other injuries I attributed to the impact."

"Something else hit him before Hannah did?" Mike asked, taking the words right out of Hannah's mouth.

Doc nodded. "Some*thing* or some*one*. I spent most of the afternoon examining him again, and that's the conclusion I reached."

"Then I *didn't* kill him?" Hannah finally managed to ask.

"Let me finish, Hannah. There's more."

Hannah clamped her mouth shut. Doc would tell her exactly what he meant eventually. It was difficult to wait, but she would let him tell them in his own precise way.

"There were two other injuries that were not consistent

with the configuration of Hannah's truck. Both were on the left side of his face, one on his chin and one on his cheek. They were approximately the same size and shape as the configuration of a man's hand clenched into a fist."

"He was in a fight?" Delores guessed.

"That's the conclusion I drew."

"But the fight didn't cause the man's death, either?" Hannah asked, hoping that she was wrong and that someone else had delivered the fatal blow.

"That's correct, Hannah."

"How about the shape and configuration of the fist?" Mike asked. "Is there any way to identify the man who fought with him from the pattern the blows left on his face?"

"No. The problem is that there was nothing distinctive about the marks that were left. I can tell you with some certainty that the person who fought with our John Doe was right-handed, but that's about it. And it may be possible for me to eliminate suspects by the size and shape of their fists if their fists are unusually small or unusually large, but that would be as close as I could come. There is one thing, though."

"What's that?" Lonnie asked, and Hannah noticed that he had already pulled out his notebook and pen and he was taking notes on what Doc told them.

"The person who delivered the blows to our victim wore a ring at least part of the time."

Hannah felt her interest pique. "Part of the time?" she asked.

"Yes. One blow was delivered while he was wearing the ring. The indentation is clear. The other blow was delivered without the ring and with a bare fist."

"A one-two punch?" Lonnie suggested, and then he explained to Michelle, "That's one punch with the right hand and the other with the left hand."

"No," Doc said, and he sounded very certain. "Both blows were delivered with the same fist, the right one. My guess is that the ring slipped off with the first blow. But the man didn't stop fighting to pick it up. He delivered a second blow that was even harder than the first blow. It did some very serious damage."

"How serious?" This time Delores was curious. "You told Hannah that the fight didn't kill him."

"It didn't, but it did cause the inter-cranial hemorrhaging to intensify."

Hannah sat up a little straighter. This was new! "What inter-cranial hemorrhaging?" she asked him. "You didn't mention that before."

"Sorry. I got a little ahead of myself. It's been a very long day." Doc took a sip of his coffee and smiled at Hannah. "There was already some hemorrhaging from the massive blow to the frontal bone. The combination of the two new blows caused him to hemorrhage more rapidly."

Hannah thought she knew exactly what Doc was saying, but she still felt the need to clarify. "And all this was done before I hit him with my truck?"

"That's right. It was prior to the impact."

"How long before the accident was it?" Mike asked.

"It's difficult to tell, but my guess would be shortly before Hannah hit him."

"Can you put a time limit on it?" Lonnie asked, his pen poised to write it down.

"No more than a half hour for the massive blow to the front bone, and the blows to the face came after that. If Hannah hadn't hit him with her truck and killed him right then, he would have died from his other injuries within an hour, perhaps less."

"Let me get this straight," Delores said. "Even if Hannah hadn't hit him, he would have died anyway."

"That's right, Lori. It was inevitable. Even if I'd been right there on the scene, there would have been no way to save him."

"Did you hear that, dear?" Delores turned to Hannah. "He would have died anyway."

"I heard."

"Well, doesn't that make you feel better?"

Hannah thought about that for a moment. "No," she said. "I killed him. It doesn't matter when he would have died. Think about it, Mother. Anybody I hit and killed would have died anyway. Everybody dies, sooner or later."

"Don't say that, Hannah." Delores gave a little shiver. "That's morbid."

"But it's true," Hannah argued. "There's no getting away from it, Mother. I hit him and I killed him. It was an accident and I really don't think it was my fault, but it happened. The person he fought with isn't responsible for his death. I am."

Chapter Fifteen

"Well, that was depressing," Michelle said, propping her pajama-clad legs up on the coffee table, giving Moishe a scratch behind the ears, and taking a sip of the mango iced tea that Hannah had poured for her.

"Not really. I thought about all that while I was in jail. I can't duck my responsibilities, but I don't have to dwell on them. The best thing I can do for that man, at this point, is figure out who he is and exactly why he was there."

"By doing that, you might clear yourself of the charges."

"I doubt it, but that would be nice. I'm still going to have to live with the fact that I hit someone with my truck and killed him."

"Can you live with that?"

"Yes. I have to. The first thing we have to do is find out who the man was and why he was here."

"I know. And then we have to find out who he fought with. That was interesting about the ring. Now we have two rings to investigate."

"Maybe not." Hannah took a sip of the glass of white wine she'd poured for herself.

"What do you mean?"

"It could be the same ring. Doc said the second blow was delivered by a bare fist and he thought the man could have dropped the ring."

"That's possible, especially if it was too loose."

"And if the man's assailant made a quick getaway when he heard my truck coming, the victim could have picked it up and slipped it back on his finger before I hit him."

"I guess it could have happened that way." Michelle thought about that for a moment. "Then the ring you saw on the victim's finger was really the ring his assailant was wearing when he delivered the first blow."

"That's right. That's not to say it happened that way, but it *could* have happened that way."

"I'll go online first thing in the morning and see if I can identify that school seal. Do you think it's a high school ring? Or could it be a college ring?"

"What does it look like?" Hannah asked, trying to recall her high school seal. She'd never bothered to buy a college ring, and she'd opted to use the money her parents would have spent for her high school ring on college expenses.

"It has a pine tree, a tall narrow building, and waves. It doesn't have the name of the high school or college, though. Lonnie and I looked at it under a magnifying glass."

"How about initials engraved inside the band?"

Michelle shook her head. "There aren't any. We looked for that, too."

"Maybe it's not a high school or college ring."

"Then what is it? It's got some kind of a seal on it."

"It could be an organization. Or maybe a branch of some government agency. I'll ask Mike if he can find out. He has access to all sorts of things ordinary people don't have."

"Not anymore. He's suspended, remember?"

Hannah sighed. "For a moment there, I forgot."

"I can ask Lonnie. Mike can tell him how to do it and he can use the computer at work and run a search."

"No, Michelle. I don't want you to ask Lonnie to do that."

"Why not?"

"Lonnie could get into trouble accessing a law enforcement computer for personal use. It's bad enough that Mike is suspended."

"That's true, I guess."

"It would be different if he had Bill's permission, but I doubt Bill would let Lonnie spend his time on something like that." The phone rang and Hannah reached out to answer it.

"Hi, Carly," she said when the caller identified herself. She listened for a moment and then she said, "Sure thing. She's right here."

Michelle took the phone that Hannah handed her and held it up to her ear. "What's up, Carly?" she asked.

Hannah got up to give Michelle some privacy to talk to her friend. She was just flicking the lights on in the kitchen when Michelle called out to her.

"Hannah? Is it okay if Carly comes over for a while? She says she's been driving around for hours, wrestling with a problem, and she needs to talk to someone about it."

"Of course Carly can come. I'm going to turn in soon, anyway. You two can sit up and talk for as long as you want to talk."

"I hate to ask you this. I know it's been a really long day for you, but Carly wants to talk to you, too. She said something's really bothering her about her sister and she needs your opinion."

"Okay," Hannah said quickly, walking back to the couch and sitting down. She'd been looking forward to climbing into her own bed in her own bedroom, and simply relaxing in the luxury of her own home. Staying up to talk to one of Michelle's friends was the last thing she wanted to do, but Hannah had always liked Carly and if Carly needed to talk to her, she was willing to forget about going to bed for as long as it took and try to help Carly any way she could.

"I'm going to bake some chocolate cookies," Michelle said, getting up from her seat on the couch. " If Carly's been driving around for hours, she's really upset and chocolate will make her feel better."

"Good idea. She can eat leftover pizza first and have your cookies for dessert."

"She could, but the pizza's all gone."

"There's *no* leftover pizza?"

"Not even crumbs. Mike polished off the last two pieces. And that means there won't be any pizza for our breakfast."

"We'll go out for breakfast," Hannah said, deciding on the spur of the moment.

"To the Corner Tavern?"

"Not there. We're going to go to Hal and Rose's Café. I need to ask Rose if she served blackberry pie to anyone on Thursday or early Friday morning."

"Good idea," Michelle said, catching on instantly. "But Rose is a member of the Lake Eden Gossip Hotline and Mother said no one was expecting any visitors that didn't arrive."

"Rose didn't know that the man I hit had blackberry stains on his shirt. Nobody knew until Doc told us tonight. She may not have mentioned that someone she didn't know came into the café. She gets strangers there all the time. Sometimes it's someone just passing through, or truck drivers she doesn't know delivering something to a business in town."

"That's true. And it's still fishing season. She gets people she doesn't know from the cabin rentals out at Eden Lake."

"Uh-oh!" Hannah said, and followed it with a big sigh.

"What?"

"I forgot all about the cabin rentals until you mentioned them right now. The man I hit could have rented a cabin at the lake."

"He didn't look like a fisherman," Michelle pointed out.

"That's true, but fishermen aren't the only ones who rent summer cabins. Lots of families do."

"He didn't look like a family man, either."

"I know. Forget about family men. Maybe Grandma Knudson was right. He could have rented a cabin for a week to check out a new venue for his prostitution ring."

Michelle laughed. "I didn't know you heard. I thought I'd just about die when Grandma Knudson said that. I was carrying a tray of coffee cups and I almost dropped them."

"And I was laughing so hard, I had to put my hand over my mouth so I wouldn't be heard in the coffee shop. We'll have to check out the cabins anyway, if only to eliminate that possibility."

"Okay. Maybe Mike can take care of that. Since he's suspended, he doesn't have anything else to do. He might even appreciate having something he can investigate. He said he wanted to do anything he could to help you. Why don't you call him and ask? It's only ten-thirty and he's probably not in bed yet."

"That's a good idea," Hannah agreed, reaching for the phone. She started to punch in Mike's home number, but she stopped in mid-digit. If Mike was home, he always answered his land line. Did she really want to know if Mike was home in his own apartment? Or was it better if she didn't know whether he was home, or not?

Hannah clicked the button to end the call and began to punch in a different number. She'd call Mike's cell phone. If he was sleeping, he wouldn't answer his cell phone. And if he was otherwise engaged, he wouldn't answer it, either. The first option was fine. If Mike was sleeping, she wouldn't want to disturb him. The second option was more problematic. If Mike was otherwise engaged, she didn't want to know what he was doing and whether anyone else was involved in whatever it was. Calling his cell phone would tell her nothing about what Mike had decided to do when he'd left her condo. And since she wouldn't know why he hadn't answered his cell phone, it would preserve her own peace of mind.

* * *

"This is probably silly of me, but I have this feeling I just can't shake," Carly said as Michelle handed her a glass of iced tea.

"Before you start to tell us, would you like a Chocolate Hazelnut Crisp Cookie?" Michelle asked her.

"I'd love one, but you didn't have to bake just for me."

"They're not just for you," Michelle told her with a grin. "I'm going to have one, too. And so is Hannah. Right, Hannah?"

"Right. It's a new cookie of yours, isn't it, Michelle?"

"Yes. I made it with Nutella. I read the ingredients and it's made from hazelnuts and cocoa."

"I *love* Nutella!" Carly said. "When Florence first started carrying it at the Red Owl, Mom and I used to spread it on toast instead of butter and eat it for breakfast if we were in a hurry. I think cookies made out of Nutella would be really good."

"You're about to find out," Michelle said, getting up and heading for the kitchen to get a plate of warm cookies. She was back in record time to set them on the coffee table. "You might have to wait a minute or two. They just came out of the oven when you were walking up the stairs."

"Perfect timing," Hannah complimented her youngest sister. "Is this one of your original recipes?"

"Yes. I made them for a girl in my psychology class who has a peanut allergy."

"But she's okay with hazelnuts?" Hannah asked.

"Yes. In her case, it's just peanuts and anything made with peanut products like peanut oil."

In the space of a minute or two, three cookies had disappeared. All three of them reached for a second cookie and Carly began to smile. "These are great!" she told Michelle. "Will you give me the recipe?"

"Sure. They're simple, too. They're just as easy as peanut butter cookies."

"And they taste a lot better because they have chocolate," Hannah added.

When the first plate of cookies was gone, Michelle brought more from the kitchen. Hannah refilled their iced tea glasses and poured one for herself, and they settled down to talk.

"Thank you both," Carly said. "I was so upset, I forgot to eat all day today."

"I can believe that," Michelle said, " I think you've lost some weight since the last time I saw you."

Hannah could believe it, too. Carly had always been a petite blonde, even in high school, but now she looked almost gaunt. "Didn't you see Carly just a couple of days ago?" Hannah asked her sister.

"Four days ago," Michelle answered, and then she turned to her friend. "Something's really bothering you, Carly. What's going on?"

"It's Jennifer. Or maybe it's not. *That's* the problem."

"What do you mean?" Hannah asked her.

"I mean, I could be cracking up here, but . . . please don't think I'm crazy if I tell you . . . okay?"

"You're not crazy," Hannah reassured her. "Tell us. Both Michelle and I are here to help any way we can."

"Thanks." Carly drew a deep breath and then she blurted it out. "I don't think Jennifer is my sister."

"You mean you don't think Jennifer ever was your sister?" Michelle asked. "Or you don't think the woman who calls herself Jennifer is really Jennifer?"

Carly looked confused for a moment and then the puzzled expression left her face. "Oh, I see. It's no to the first question. I don't have any reason to believe that the Jennifer I knew when I was almost four years old wasn't my sister."

"But there's some question in your mind that the Jennifer who came back after running away isn't the sister you knew in the past?" Hannah asked, seeking to clarify it for all three of them.

"That's exactly right." Carly sighed deeply and took a sip of her iced tea. "I don't think she's really Jennifer. I think she's just pretending to be my sister Jennifer."

"What makes you think that?" Hannah asked the most important question.

"Little things. Just little things, like she didn't remember what I gave her for her birthday right before she ran away."

"How many years ago was that?" Hannah asked, even though she knew the answer to her own question because Michelle and Carly had been in the same high school class and their birthdays were ten months apart.

"Sixteen years ago."

"Do you remember what Jennifer gave you for your birthday that year?" Michelle asked her.

"Yes. It was a doll with blond hair and blue eyes. She told me it looked just like me." Carly stopped and swallowed hard. "I just loved that doll. I still have it. And Jennifer was the one who planned my party. She even baked me a cake with a big number four on it."

"What did you give Jennifer for her birthday?" Hannah asked.

"Bath beads. They were really pretty and they were in a round see-through plastic case. They came in all sorts of colors and they looked like jewels."

"What did Jennifer say when you asked her if she remembered?" Michelle leaned forward, waiting for the answer.

"She said, 'I'm so sorry, Carly. I don't remember. I really don't remember very much about that last year at home. I hope you're not hurt, but I don't want to lie to you and say I remember, when I don't.'"

Michelle nodded. "That was a good answer, Carly. Maybe she really doesn't remember."

"Or maybe she's not really Jennifer and she never knew," Carly said, looking a bit sick at the prospect. "I realize that doesn't prove anything, but it's just one of several things."

"Tell us some of the other things that make you suspect her," Hannah said.

"Well . . . there's the bath. Jennifer loved baths. I remember that. It's why I gave her the bath beads. They melted when you put them in the bottom of the tub and ran bath water in, and they smelled so good." Carly turned to Hannah. "I'm not sure they even sell them anymore, but you know what I'm talking about, don't you?"

"I know," Hannah told her.

"Jennifer didn't sleep well the night before last, so before I went to bed last night, I asked her if she wanted me to run her a nice, relaxing bath. She used to love taking long baths right before bed. She'd give me a bath and then she'd clean out the tub and take one herself while Mom was reading me a bedtime story."

"That's nice," Michelle said.

"I know. It's one of my fondest memories. But when I asked her if she'd like to take a bath, she said thank you for offering, but she preferred showers to baths."

"People do change their preferences," Hannah pointed out.

"I did," Michelle said. "I used to love taking baths, but now I'd rather take showers."

Carly sighed. "I know all that. I prefer showers now, too. It's just that . . . well . . . something's not right about Jennifer. I asked her what she used to hide in her napkin and pass to me, and she didn't remember what I was talking about."

"What were you talking about?" Hannah asked her.

"Sweet potatoes. Jennifer really hated yams and sweet potatoes. She used to take a small helping just to please Mom, but she'd hide the pieces in her napkin when no one was looking. Then she'd pass it to me and I'd get up to get more milk or something and throw her napkin in the trash. It was our secret."

"That was years ago, Carly," Michelle said. "Maybe she just didn't remember."

"Maybe, but one of these nights when I don't have to work, I'm going to make sweet potatoes and see if she eats them."

"Does she remember anything about her life with you before she ran away?" Hannah posed the question that was uppermost in her mind.

"Yes. That's part of the problem. She remembers a lot. And some days I'm sure she's really Jennifer. But other days, I think she's not."

"Does she know things that only Jennifer would know?" Hannah followed up on her initial question.

"Yes. She remembered all the names of her teachers, even the ones that aren't there anymore. And she described the cabin we used to have on Eden Lake. And when Mom got out the birthday tablecloth she always used for us when we were kids, she remembered that." Carly looked from Hannah to Michelle and then back again. "Do you both think I'm crazy for doubting her?"

"No," Hannah said, before Michelle could reply. "But if she's not the real Jennifer, why is she here pretending to be Jennifer?"

"That's what I can't figure out. It's not like we're rich or anything like that. And we don't have anything valuable to steal. As far as I can see, there's nothing for her to gain by pretending to be Jennifer."

"Have you told your mom about your suspicions?" Michelle asked the question before Hannah could.

"No. I wouldn't do that to Mom. What if I'm wrong?"

"Do you think your mother believes she's Jennifer?" Hannah asked the next question.

"I know she does. Mom's so happy that Jennifer's back. She's all relaxed now and she smiles all the time. I don't think I've ever seen her so happy."

Hannah felt a surge of sympathy for Carly. No wonder she needed to talk to them! "So even if you have doubts, you feel you can't discuss them with your mother?"

"That's right, especially because I can't put my finger on anything concrete. It's just a gut level feeling I have. And I only have it once in a while."

"But do you still like Jennifer?" Michelle asked.

"Yes. That's the strange thing. Even when I doubt she's really my sister, I still like her a lot."

"Do you think part of your doubt is due to jealousy that your mother is so happy about someone other than you?" Michelle asked. "Think about that before you answer, Carly. If you do feel jealous, it would be entirely natural."

Hannah held her breath. Michelle had asked a very difficult question of Carly.

"I've thought about that," Carly answered. "And I don't think it's due to jealousy on my part. I'm more concerned with seeing Mom hurt if I'm right and she's really not Jennifer." Carly turned to face Hannah. "That's why I wanted to talk to you, too. I know you've solved a slew of murders in the past couple of years. And that means you're a really good investigator. Would you . . . could you . . . investigate Jennifer and find out if she's really my sister?"

CHOCOLATE HAZELNUT CRACKLES
(Nutella Cookies)

Preheat oven to 375 degrees F., rack in the middle position.

> 1 cup melted butter *(2 sticks, 8 ounces, ¹/₂ pound)*
> 2 cups brown sugar *(pack it down in the cup when you measure it)*
> 2 teaspoons vanilla
> 1 and ¹/₂ teaspoons baking soda
> 1 teaspoon baking powder
> ¹/₂ teaspoon salt
> 1 cup Nutella *(like peanut butter, but made with chocolate and hazelnuts)*
> 2 beaten eggs *(just whip them up with a fork)*
> 3 cups all-purpose flour *(no need to sift)*

Microwave the butter in a microwave-safe mixing bowl to melt it. Add the brown sugar and the vanilla. Stir until it's blended, then add the baking soda, baking powder and salt. Mix well.

Measure out the Nutella. *(I spray the inside of my measuring cup with Pam so it won't stick.)* Add it to the bowl and mix it in.

Pour in the beaten eggs and stir them in.

Add the flour and mix until all the ingredients are thoroughly blended.

Form the dough into walnut-sized balls and arrange them on a greased cookie sheet, 12 to a standard sheet. *(If the dough is too sticky to form into balls, chill it for a half-hour or so and try again.)*

Push the dough balls down just a tiny bit so they won't roll off the sheet when you slide them into the oven. *(Yes, that's happened to me—it's a horrible mess, even with a self-cleaning oven!)*

Bake at 375 degrees F. for 8 to 10 minutes. The balls will flatten out, all by themselves.

Cool the cookies on the cookie sheet for 2 minutes and then remove them to a wire rack to finish cooling.

Yield: 5 to 6 dozen chocolaty, nutty treats, depending on cookie size.

Chapter Sixteen

It was the best night's sleep she'd had in four days. Hannah woke up at four-thirty and sat up in bed. Moishe was purring beside her, curled up on his own pillow for a change, and he opened one eye, his good one, to stare at her in surprise.

"Who did you expect? Norman?" she asked, smiling at her furry friend. "You're home, and so am I. And doesn't it feel absolutely wonderful?"

Moishe didn't comment. She didn't expect him to. He just rolled over so that she could rub his back and scratch the base of his tail. Hannah chuckled softly under her breath. She talked to Moishe frequently, just as if he could understand her and answer her questions when she asked them. She was thinking about what she'd do if he opened his mouth and answered her in a tiny cat voice. She'd be so shocked that she'd probably have a heart attack on the spot. And that would put an end to her silly questions.

"Daylight in the swamp," she uttered her usual morning greeting to him. "Let's go out to the kitchen and see if the cat fairies left you something good to eat."

Almost as if he were responding to her words, Moishe got to his feet, gave a little shake, and dropped down again in a belly stretch with his front legs extended as far as they could reach toward the foot of the bed and his back legs stretched out behind him so that they touched the edge of his pillow. Stretched out like that, Hannah noticed that he covered well over half the length of the bed.

"You're a really long kitty," she told him. "No wonder you're always trying to take over my half of the bed. And this is a king size bed. They don't come any bigger than king size."

"Rrrrroww!" Moishe responded, just as if he were answering her.

"Okay. Let's go." Hannah sat up on the edge of the bed and reached for her slippers. She pulled them on, shrugged into her robe and padded down the hall with Moishe playing tag with the belt of her robe.

The kitchen light was on and fresh coffee was in the pot. Hannah poured herself a cup, fed Moishe, and was just sitting down at the kitchen table to drink her coffee when Michelle came out of her bedroom.

"Morning, Hannah," Michelle greeted her.

"Good morning, Michelle."

"Are you going to take your shower right away, or can I use your exercise machine for a quick five-minute workout?"

"You can use it. My eyes aren't fully open yet. The last time I wasn't fully awake for my shower, I slumped to the floor, fell asleep on my back with my mouth open, and almost drowned."

"Really?" Michelle looked shocked.

"No. I'm just kidding. But it'll be at least twenty minutes before I'm ready to take a shower. Go work out and have fun . . . if that's possible."

"It's possible," Michelle said with a smile. "I love to work out first thing in the morning. It's so invigorating." Then she turned on her heel and headed back the way she'd come.

"She loves to work out first thing in the morning," Hannah repeated to Moishe. "At times like this, I feel like Carly.

You heard what she said about Jennifer last night. If Michelle likes to work out first thing in the morning, she can't possibly be my sister."

They were standing outside Hal and Rose's Café when Rose McDermott flicked on the lights, turned the sign that hung on the door from closed to open, and unlocked it to let them in. Hannah and Michelle trooped in and sat at the first booth so that Rose wouldn't have to walk far.

"What'll it be?" Rose asked, coming up with two cups and the coffeepot without being asked.

"Coffee, please," Hannah answered. "I didn't get my full four cups this morning. And then you can tell us what's good for breakfast."

"Everything's good," Rose gave her standard answer. "If it wasn't good, I wouldn't have it on the menu."

"Do you have toast cups this morning?" Michelle asked her.

"I always have toast cups, honey. Do you want one?"

"Yes. I just love your toast cups. I tried to make them, but mine don't turn out as good as yours do."

Rose looked puzzled. "But you watched me make them the last time you were home from college. There's no mystery about them."

"I know, but I must have done something wrong."

"Did you pre-cook the bacon?"

"Yes. And I drained it on a paper towel."

"Did you use a three and a half inch cutter for the bread?" Michelle nodded. "Yes, just the way you do."

"And you buttered the muffin cups?"

"I did."

"You put the shredded cheddar in the bottom right after you put the bread rounds in?"

"Yes, exactly the way you said I should."

Rose looked puzzled. "Then I don't understand it. That's exactly what I do."

"Maybe it's because I have an electric stove. Your oven is gas, isn't it?"

"Yes, but that shouldn't make any difference. Did you preheat the oven to four hundred degrees?"

"*Four* hundred?!" Michelle looked surprised. "But I saw you turn your oven to three seventy-five!"

"That's because my oven runs hot. You've got to know your oven, honey. If yours doesn't run hot, you should set it for four hundred degrees. You won't get the toast crisp enough if you don't."

"Got it," Michelle said, looking pleased. "Thanks for clearing that up, Rose. When I get back to college, I'm going to try to make them again."

"Good." Rose smiled at her. "Do you still want one today?"

"Yes, I do. I just love them for breakfast."

Rose turned to Hannah. "How about you?"

"I'll have one, too. And then we're going to have dessert."

It was Rose's turn to look surprised. "Dessert for breakfast?"

"Why not? There's no rule that says you can't have dessert for breakfast. And that reminds me . . . I have a question for you, Rose."

"What's that?"

"Did you have blackberry pie for sale last Thursday or Friday?"

"No."

The answer had come so quickly, it made Hannah wonder if Rose had taken time to think about it. "But you have lots of different kinds of pies. It's important. Are you sure you didn't have blackberry pie?"

"I'm positive. And that's because I never serve it. Some of the people who come here for pie are slobs. And if they drop a forkful of blackberry pie and I don't notice it right away, it'll stain my white countertop. It's just like beets. I don't serve beets, either."

"Okay. Thanks, Rose." Hannah mentally crossed Rose off her to-do list.

"So what do you want for dessert?" Rose asked. "Pie?"

"I want a chocolate doughnut," Michelle said, making up her mind immediately. "Why don't you have one too, Hannah? Unless you don't want chocolate, of course."

"Bite your tongue!" Hannah said with a laugh. "I always want chocolate."

Rose nodded. "Almost everybody who comes in here needs a little chocolate. It seems to just set people up for the day. I know that because I always have to order four times more chocolate doughnuts than I do of any other kind."

It was eleven in the morning and Hannah stood in the kitchen at The Cookie Jar, mixing up yet another batch of cookies. It seemed everyone in Lake Eden wanted to listen to Lisa's story of how they had driven through the terrible summer storm, and Hannah had hit and killed the stranger no one in town or the surrounding towns seemed to know.

Today something new had been added to Lisa's story and everyone had turned out to hear what it was. Hannah had listened to Lisa talk about the injuries Doc Knight had described from the fight the man had been in with an unknown assailant, and how the assailant's ring had slipped off and could be the very same high school or college ring the stranger had been wearing.

Lisa was just coming to the part about the blackberry stain on the stranger's white shirt when Hannah popped more pans of cookies in the oven. She set the timer, poured herself another cup of coffee, and tried not to listen. Unfortunately, trying not to listen was a bit like trying not to jiggle a sore tooth. The more the tooth loosened, the more you jiggled. Hannah found herself listening with rapt attention as Lisa described the blackberry stain on the man's expensive white shirt.

"Blackberries?" Hannah heard a shocked voice say. "Are you sure it was a blackberry stain?"

"Yes, we're sure," Lisa said. "Doc Knight tested the stain in the hospital lab."

"Well, Winnie Henderson's the only one who raises blackberries around here," someone said. "Maybe he raided her blackberry patch, or ate a piece of her blackberry pie. I know she made some for her grandson's birthday party. I took my boy there and I had a piece myself."

Hannah thunked the side of her head with her hand. Of course! Winnie had told her on Friday morning that she had to bake another blackberry pie because one of hers had been stolen.

The stove timer dinged and Hannah went to take the cookies out of the oven. She'd just placed the last sheet of cookies on the baker's rack when there was a knock at the back door.

Hannah hurried to open the door. Perhaps it was Norman, on break from the dental clinic. But when she pulled open the door, she saw her mother standing there.

"Hello, Mother," Hannah said, trying not to sound disappointed.

"Hello, dear. I just popped in for coffee."

"You're in luck then. I made a fresh pot no more than five minutes ago and I've got fresh cookies that just came out of the oven."

"Perfect timing then," Delores said, taking a seat at the stainless steel work counter. "I'm considering butterscotch tarts for dessert at the wedding reception, dear."

"Butterscotch tarts?" There was a question in Hannah's voice when she repeated her mother's choice. "Do you think they'll be festive enough for a fancy dinner?"

"I don't know. That's one of the reasons I came over here. I was thinking that perhaps we could decorate them in some way."

"I'll have to think about that. But I thought you wanted something chocolate."

"I did. I still do, but it's not just for me, dear. Doc is Scottish and I thought we should have something to reflect his heritage."

"There's your main course, Mother. You could have haggis."

"What's that, dear? I don't think I've ever tasted it."

"It's the chopped organs of a sheep mixed with oatmeal and stuffed in a sheep's stomach."

"Ohhh!" Delores gave a delicate shiver. "That sounds simply dreadful!"

"I understand it is, but I've never eaten it either."

"Forget Doc's Scottish heritage for the moment. I'd much rather have a half Cornish game hen with apricot glaze."

"But I thought you'd decided on individual Beef Wellington."

"That did sound marvelous, but I've reconsidered. And I've decided on the colors for the bridesmaid dresses. I want something in lavender lace."

It was Hannah's turn to shudder. Lavender was a shade of purple and she'd never been able to wear any shade of purple. Of course, there was no sense in getting upset about it. Her mother was bound to change her mind at least a dozen more times before the wedding.

"Would you like to have a cookie, Mother?" Hannah asked, hoping to change the subject. Wedding planning with Delores was always frustrating and the last thing she needed today was more frustration.

"Cookies would be lovely, dear. I'm not sure I'll have time for lunch. I have to run out to the hospital this afternoon. Doc has some filing for me to do."

It was love, pure and simple Hannah decided on her way to the baker's rack to get cookies for her mother. Delores hated filing. She hated office work of any type. She'd never done any office work at Hannah's father's hardware store. But here she was manning Doc's office in addition to heading the Rainbow Ladies, the hospital volunteer group. Yes, it had to be love. There was no other explanation for it.

Hannah thought about this while her mother munched a Molasses Crackle. Like her mother, Hannah wasn't fond of office work. She knew how to file and write a business letter, but would she do it for either of the men she dated and loved? Norman didn't need her to do his office work. He had a part-time helper from the Jordan High business class for that. And Mike didn't need her either because he used the secretarial pool at the Winnetka County Sheriff's station.

"Why so thoughtful, dear?" Delores asked, finishing the last of her coffee.

"Oh, I don't know. Maybe it has something to do with spending three days and nights in jail."

"Why would that make you thoughtful?"

"Because there was nothing else to do while I was there. When the lights went off at ten o'clock, I couldn't read any longer. And no visitors were allowed after ten at night, so the only things I had for entertainment were my own thoughts."

Delores looked pensive. "That must have been boring, dear," she said.

"Not at all. I carried on imaginary conversations with people, I speculated on quite a few what-ifs, and I tried to imagine what my life would be like ten years from now."

"Ten years from now?" When Hannah nodded, Delores began to smile. "I would hope you'd be married with at least two children. And still in love with your husband."

"I knew you'd say that, Mother," Hannah said, her mind busily searching for a way to change the subject. There was no way she'd tell her mother about her daydream of being a contestant in a food channel contest, winning the competition, and becoming a famous dessert chef. She'd mentioned her flight of fancy to Michelle, but she certainly didn't want to discuss it with her mother! "How about you, Mother?" she asked, turning the tables so quickly her mother actually looked a bit off balance.

"Me?" Delores stalled for time.

"Yes, you. Where do you think you'll be in ten years?"

"I should hope I'd be right here in Lake Eden, happily married to Doc and doing almost the same things I'm doing right now." There was a slight narrowing of Delores's brown eyes. "And I would hope that *all* my grandchildren would be right here around me, and Doc and I would all be enjoying time with them."

"That's assuming you'll be marrying Doc."

"Of course it is! I'm certainly not going to be marrying anyone else, *except* Doc!"

"But you might not be marrying him."

"What do you mean by that?"

Hannah took a deep breath and repeated her great-grandmother's saying in her mind. *In for a penny, in for a pound.* She'd opened the subject and now it was time to tell her mother that her continual wavering about the wedding plans had gone on long enough. It wouldn't be nice, and it wouldn't be pretty, but Hannah was about to put an end to it. "You've changed your mind about everything else that concerns the wedding. For all we know, you might change your mind about marrying Doc, too."

"I'd never do that!"

"Okay. That's written in stone then. But think about this, Mother. You might not be marrying at all since you can't make up your mind about your dress, the bridesmaid dresses, the flowers, and the menu and decorations for the reception. I don't even think you've chosen a wedding invitation yet . . . have you?"

"Well . . . no. No, I haven't. But I've narrowed it down to four and there's still time as long as I don't have the invitations hand-addressed by a calligrapher."

"Yes, you probably missed the ticket on that one." Hannah prodded a little harder. "I hope you get them in the mail in time for the postal service to deliver them. You know, Mother . . . I'm really beginning to wonder if you want to get married at all. You're certainly dragging your feet when it comes to making wedding decisions."

"But . . . but . . ." Delores sputtered, and then she took a deep shaking breath. "Just because I've changed my mind a few times doesn't mean I don't want to marry Doc. I just want everything perfect, that's all. It's very important to me."

"It's important to us, too. You raised three daughters and you put us in charge of the wedding," Hannah reminded her. "And you know, full well, that perfection isn't our long suit. We're trying, but you're knocking down every one of our ideas. And when, and it's a *big* when, you finally agree on something, you change your mind again within a week. You said you didn't care, that we should do it and you'd go along with anything we planned."

"Well! I didn't mean I'd go along with absolutely *anything* you planned."

"Okay, let's keep this simple. Are you going to let us do it? Or are you going to fight us every step of the way?"

Delores sighed and put her head in her hands. She stayed that way for a long moment and then she took her hands away. "All right, Hannah," she said. "You're right. I've been vacillating too long and I haven't been fair to you girls. Give me three choices on everything and I'll decide."

"You promise?"

"Yes, dear. I promise. We'll have another planning meeting tomorrow morning. I'll listen to all your suggestions and then I'll make a choice."

"For the flowers, the dresses, the music, the decorations, *and* the menu?"

"Yes. I'll choose everything tomorrow."

"Thank you, Mother," Hannah said. And then, because she thought she might have been too harsh, she got up and came around the work island to give her mother a big hug. "We love you, Mother."

"I know you do. And I admit I'm being difficult. It's not for me, Hannah. Doc's never had a wedding before. I just want this wedding to be one that Doc can remember with pride."

"It will be, Mother," Hannah said, walking her mother to the door. "I promise you that Doc will love it and remember it with pride for the rest of his life."

When Delores went out and she had closed the door behind her, Hannah walked back to the workstation and sat down again. She'd said what she needed to say, and Delores had agreed. On the surface, everything was fine, but Hannah had the awful premonition that nothing she'd said would do any good when morning rolled around and their next planning meeting convened.

BACON, EGG, AND CHEDDAR CHEESE TOAST CUPS

Preheat oven to 400 degrees F., rack in the middle position.

6 slices bacon *(regular sliced, not thick sliced)*
4 Tablespoons *(2 ounces, ½ stick)* salted butter, softened
6 slices soft white bread
½ cup grated cheddar cheese
6 large eggs
Salt and pepper to taste

Cook the 6 slices of bacon in a frying pan over medium heat for 6 minutes or until the bacon is firmed up and the edges are slightly brown, but the strips are still pliable. They won't be completely cooked, but that's okay. They will finish cooking in the oven. Place the partially-cooked bacon on a plate lined with paper towels to drain it.

Generously coat the inside of 6 muffin cups with half of the softened butter.

Butter one side of the bread with the rest of the butter but stop slightly short of the crusts. Lay the bread out on a sheet of wax paper or a bread board butter side up.

Hannah's 1ˢᵗ Note: You will be wasting a bit of butter here, but it's easier than cutting rounds of bread first and trying to butter them after they're cut.

Using a round cookie cutter that's three and a half inches *(3 and ½ inches)* in diameter, cut circles out of each slice of bread.

Hannah's 2ⁿᵈ Note: If you don't have a 3.5 inch cookie cutter, you can use the top rim of a standard size drinking glass to do this.

Place the bread rounds butter side down inside the muffin pans, pressing them down gently being careful not to tear them as they settle into the bottom of the cup. If one does tear, cut a patch from the buttered bread that is left and place it, buttered side down, over the tear.

Curl a piece of bacon around the top of each piece of bread, positioning it between the bread and the muffin tin. This will help to keep the bacon in a ring shape.

Sprinkle shredded cheese in the bottom of each muffin cup, dividing the cheese as equally as you can between the 6 muffin cups.

Crack an egg into a small measuring cup *(I use a half-cup measure)* with a spout, making sure to keep the yolk intact.

Hannah's 3rd Note: If you break a yolk, don't throw the whole egg away. Just slip it in a small covered container which you will refrigerate and use for scrambled eggs the next morning, or for that batch of cookies you'll make in the next day or two.

Pour the egg carefully into the bottom of one of the muffin cups.

Repeat this procedure for all the eggs, cracking them one at a time and pouring them into the remaining muffin cups.

When every muffin cup has bread, bacon, cheese and egg, season with a little salt and pepper.

Bake the filled toast cups for 6 to 10 minutes, depending on how firm you want the yolks. *(Naturally, a longer baking time yields a harder yolk.)*

Run the blade of a knife around the edge of each muffin cup, remove the Bacon, Egg, and Cheddar Cheese Toast Cups, and serve immediately.

Hannah's 4th Note: These are a bit tricky the first time you make them. That's just "beginner

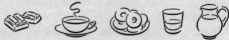

nerves". Once you've made them successfully, they're really quite easy to do and extremely impressive to serve for a brunch.

Yield: 6 servings *(or 3 servings if you're fixing them for Mike and Norman)*.

Chapter Seventeen

Hannah was just wondering which cookie recipe she should bake next when she remembered what she'd been discussing with Michelle and Rose at breakfast this morning. They'd all agreed that everybody needed a little chocolate and there were no chocolate cookies on the bakers rack. Perhaps she'd try a new cookie, a chocolate cookie. Michelle had given her a new chocolate cookie recipe. It was from her friend, Julia Meister, a dance major she'd worked with in several theater productions. Michelle said she'd baked the cookies that Julia called Triple Chocolate Cookies and they were the deepest, darkest, fudgiest cookies she'd ever tasted. If they were as good as Michelle said they were, they were bound to be a hit in the coffee shop.

Hannah was just taking pans of cookies from the oven when there was a knock at the back door. *I hope it's not Mother coming to tell me she changed her mind about the wedding plans again!* she thought as she crossed the kitchen floor and opened the back door.

"Mike!" she said, giving him a big smile. "I'm really glad to see you."

"Thanks, Hannah," Mike said, looking pleased. "That's the warmest greeting I've gotten all day. I ran into Bill at the

Corner Tavern and he wouldn't even look at me. He was sitting all by himself and he sure didn't look happy."

Hannah snapped her mouth closed and went to get him a cup of coffee. She'd been about to tell him that she'd expected her mother and had been relieved to see him instead, but that might make him feel bad.

"Thanks," Mike said, accepting the cup of coffee she handed him and reaching for a cookie from the plate she'd set on the work counter. "Do you know if Bill's made up with Andrea yet?"

"Not that I know of. I do know that she was still mad at him yesterday. It might be a while before she forgives him for arresting me. I know from experience that Andrea can hold a grudge for a long time."

"What experience was that?"

"Just something that happened when we were kids. I got a red bicycle for Christmas and she got a gold one. She wanted the red."

"Why didn't you switch?"

"Because I'm just as stubborn as she is. Red was my favorite color, even back then. I wasn't about to give up a red bicycle. Besides . . . there was another consideration."

"What was that?"

"Andrea's younger and she was a lot smaller than I was. Maybe she could have reached the pedals on mine, but if I'd tried to ride her little bike, I would have banged my knees on the handlebars."

"That sounds like a valid reason to go with what you were given," Mike said, and then he handed her the bag he'd carried in with him. "Here," he said. "I found this at the crime . . . I mean the scene of the accident."

Hannah opened the bag and peered in. There was a metal pan inside. "What is it?"

"Looks like one of those pans you bake pies in to me. I thought you'd know what it was."

"Can I take it out of the bag?"

"Sure, but you'd better use a napkin or something."

"To preserve any fingerprints?"

Mike shook his head. "It was out in the rain. If there were any fingerprints, there won't be any left now. I just didn't want you to get your hands dirty, that's all."

Hannah grabbed a napkin and lifted the pan out of the bag. "You're right," she told him. "It's a pie tin. There's still some crust sticking to the bottom and . . ." She stopped and took the plate to the window to examine it in the sunlight. "Yes! There's a little bit of some kind of berry sticking to the crust. This could have been from the blackberry pie that was stolen from Winnie's window ledge."

"If you're right, Winnie's pie was stolen by the dead man. There are coincidences in police work, but not all that many. And Doc said the man had a blackberry stain on his shirt. Do you think Winnie might recognize this pan so that we can confirm that the pie came from her?"

"I don't know. Maybe. At least she'll know if it's the same size as hers."

"They're not all the same size?"

Hannah laughed. "No. Pie plates come in several sizes. And some are deep dish while others aren't. They're made of different materials, too. Some are metal, some are glass, and then there's the disposable kind that are made of aluminum foil. This one doesn't look expensive, and Winnie bakes a lot of pies. It's possible that she has a whole set of these in her cupboard at the ranch."

"Do you have more cookies to bake right now?" Mike asked her.

"No. Why?"

"I was thinking we could run out to Winnie's and see if that pie pan is hers."

"Okay. I can go with you." Hannah was pleased. Mike could have gone by himself, but he'd asked her to come along.

"Do you have to tell anyone where you're going?"

Hannah listened. Lisa was still talking to the audience and she didn't want to disturb her. "Not really. I'll just leave a note so Michelle and Lisa will know where I've gone."

Hannah wrote a note and propped it up on the counter where Lisa and Michelle would be sure to see it there. Then she grabbed the bag with the pie plate and was about to go out the door when she thought of something. "Hold on," she told Mike. "I need to get something."

The photo they'd used for the flyers was in a folder on the counter. Hannah grabbed it, folder and all. It wouldn't hurt to ask Winnie, Connor, and the ranch hands if any of them had seen the dead man hanging around on the morning Winnie's pie had been stolen.

Once Hannah was settled in the passenger seat of Mike's Hummer, she leaned back and enjoyed the ride. Winnie's ranch was out in the country surrounding the town of Lake Eden and it took a full twenty minutes to get there. The farm next to it belonged to Carly's mother, Loretta, and Hannah peered out the window to see if she could catch a glimpse of Carly's sister, Jennifer. Someone was out in the yard and Hannah assumed that it was Jennifer since she looked just like an older version of Carly.

"What's so interesting?" Mike asked, noticing that she was peering out of the window.

For one brief moment, Hannah thought about telling him what Carly had confided last night. Perhaps Mike could help her with her promise to find out if Jennifer was really Carly's long-lost sister. But she quickly squelched that impulse. Carly had told them her suspicions in confidence. It wouldn't be right to tell Mike without asking Carly if that was all right with her.

"Hannah?" Mike asked again, and Hannah knew she had to say something. The best way to reply would be to tell him the truth, or at least part of it. "I think I just saw Carly's sister out in the yard. I'm almost sure that it was her. She looks just like an older version of Carly."

"Is Carly okay with her sister coming home after all this time?" Mike asked.

"I'm not sure," Hannah said, not wanting to lie, but shading the truth just a bit. "Michelle said that Carly likes Jennifer a lot."

"That's all to the good then." Mike made a sharp left and pulled onto the private road that led to Winnie's ranch house. They bounced along the gravel road for another few minutes and then Mike pulled up and parked in front of the house. "Here we are," he said. "I just hope she's home."

Hannah glanced at her watch. "I'm sure she is. It's almost noon and she's probably fixing lunch for Connor and the ranch hands."

Winnie answered the door herself. She was wearing an apron and she wiped her hands on a towel before she shook Mike's hand and gave Hannah a hug. "Hi there. What brings you out here all this way?"

"This," Hannah said, getting right to the heart of the matter by pulling the pie plate out of the bag. "Is this one of yours, Winnie?"

"Looks like it," Winnie said, taking the pie tin from Hannah's hand. "If it is, somebody sure doesn't know how to wash dishes!"

"I found it in the woods close to here," Mike explained. "And Hannah said you'd had a blackberry pie stolen on Friday morning so we thought it might be yours."

"Is there any way you can tell for sure?" Hannah asked, hoping for a positive identification.

"Sure is. Follow me to the kitchen. I'll just give it a soak and then I can tell." Winnie led the way to the kitchen and dropped the pie pan into the sink, which was already full of soapy water. "Have a seat at the table."

"Something really smells good in here," Mike said as they sat down at the big, round, oak table.

"Don't know what that could be unless it's fried chicken, biscuits, green beans and carrots, and Graham Cracker Cake. You two hungry? There's plenty enough for two more. Connor and the boys will be trooping in here to eat about five minutes from now."

Mike shook his head. "Thanks, Winnie, but I had a big breakfast less than three hours ago."

"I didn't ask you when you ate breakfast. I asked you if you were hungry."

Mike grinned. "So you did. I'm not hungry, but that fried chicken smells really good. I think I could choke down a leg or two."

"That's what I thought. Your mouth started watering the minute you stepped through the door to my kitchen. Coffee while you wait?"

"No, thanks," Mike said quickly, and Hannah knew he remembered Winnie's extra-strong, boiled coffee. He'd managed to drink one cup the last time they were here together, but Hannah suspected that it had probably given him indigestion.

"How about you, Hannah? You hungry?"

"I was born hungry, Winnie. I can't eat too much, though. I'll have one piece of chicken, one of your biscuits, and a piece of that Graham Cracker Cake. I've never had Graham Cracker Cake before."

"You'll like it. And you'll like it even better when I write out the recipe for you. It's so easy that making it's like falling off a log." Winnie walked over to the sink and pulled the pie pan out of the dishwater. "That's better. Just let me rinse it off and I can tell you if it's mine or not."

Mike and Hannah watched while Winnie rinsed the pan and dried it on a dishtowel. Then she carried it to the window and peered at the inside of the pan. "Yup," she said. "It's mine, all right."

"How can you tell?" Hannah asked her.

"There's an *S* scratched inside. That's for Sadie, my mother's name. She baked a lot of pies just like me, and she gave a lot away. That way, if people gave her back the wrong pie tin, she knew right away that it wasn't hers."

Hannah was about to ask another question when the outside kitchen door opened and four men came in. One was Connor. Hannah recognized him, but she didn't know any of the other three.

"You recognize Hannah, don't you, Connor?" Winnie said to her head horse wrangler and ranch manager.

"Sure do. Hi, Hannah." Connor hung his hat on the hook by the back door and gave Hannah a friendly smile. "I recognize Mike, too. Hello there, Mike."

"Hello, Connor," Mike said, smiling back. "What happened to your hand?"

Connor looked a little sheepish. "I let a horse get the best of me instead of the other way around. I finally got him to behave, but it wasn't easy."

"He's a new one and I named him Diablo," Winnie told them. "If the rein hadn't snapped, that stallion would have broken Connor's hand."

"It's true, but Diablo didn't break it, and the swelling's better today. I think I'll be able to take off the bandage by the end of the week."

"Glad to hear it," Winnie said, gesturing toward the three younger men. "You boys go ahead and introduce yourselves to Miss Swensen and Deputy Kingston. And when you're through with the niceties, go wash up for noon dinner."

Hannah turned toward the three ranch hands. One was a bit older than the other two, but she suspected that if the three of them added up their ages, the sum wouldn't be more than sixty years. "You're working summer jobs?" she asked them.

"Yes, ma'am," one of the boys said. "I'm Brad and this is my little brother, Dave. And this here's a friend of ours, Jim."

"Connor knows their father," Winnie explained. "He's a breeder from Mankato and these boys grew up around horses. They're real hard workers and we're lucky to have 'em for the summer. They're not like some of the slackers that come here looking for work."

It was the perfect opening and Hannah seized it by taking out the flyer with the photo of the dead man. "Do you boys know that someone stole one of Winnie's blackberry pies on Friday morning?"

"We heard," Brad said, the obvious spokesman for the group.

"Did any of you see this man hanging around outside?" Hannah handed the flyer to Brad. "He could be the one who stole Winnie's pie."

Brad looked at the photo and shook his head. "Not me. I was working in the paddock and these two were mucking out the stalls in the barn. Miz Henderson asked us before if we saw anyone." He turned to Winnie and grinned. "We think she thought we took it. We really like her blackberry pies. They're somethin' else!"

"I didn't think that for a second," Winnie said, laughing a little. "You boys don't have to steal. If you wanted one, you could have just asked for it and I would have handed it over."

After the boys had left to wash up, Hannah pushed the flyer over to Connor. "How about you, Connor? Have you ever seen him before?"

"I don't think so," Connor said after studying the photo for a moment. "He doesn't look familiar to me. Of course, I meet a lot of people at the horse auctions and I don't remember them all. I think I might remember this guy, though, especially with that jewel in his tooth."

Hannah handed the flyer to Winnie. "How about you, Winnie? Does he look familiar?"

Winnie studied the photo for a moment. "Yes. I'm pretty sure I've seen him before, but I can't place him. He's older here so it must have been a while ago. And he didn't have that kind of tooth back then. It'll come to me, Hannah. I'll remember where I met him." Winnie stopped and chuckled. "I'll probably think of it at three in the morning. That's how it usually happens."

"If you do, call me. I won't mind waking up to that call. It's important, Winnie."

"Then this must be the man you hit with your truck," Winnie said. "I can tell he's dead in that picture. He looks dead. Why do you want to know who he is?"

"It's a mystery," Hannah answered.

"I can understand that. I'll think of it, Hannah. Trust me. It might not be tonight and it might not be tomorrow night, but it'll come to me eventually."

The kitchen door opened and the boys came back in to take chairs at the table. As Hannah helped Winnie serve their lunches, she wondered exactly how long it would take her friend to remember where she'd seen the dead man. She hoped it wouldn't take long. This was a mystery she wanted to solve so that she could devote her full attention to discovering whether Jennifer was really Carly's sister, or not.

GRAHAM CRACKER CAKE

Preheat oven to 350 degrees F., rack in the middle position.

¹⁄₂ cup salted butter, softened *(1 stick, 4 ounces, ¹⁄₄ pound)*

³⁄₄ cup white *(granulated)* sugar

1 teaspoon vanilla extract

2 large eggs

2 teaspoons baking powder

¹⁄₄ teaspoon salt

2 and ¹⁄₄ cups graham cracker crumbs

1 cup whole milk

1 cup chopped nuts *(measure after chopping— I used walnuts)*

――――――――――

8 and ³⁄₄ ounce can crushed pineapple WITH juice

¹⁄₄ cup white *(granulated)* sugar

Hannah's Note: You can either crush your own graham cracker crumbs by placing graham crackers in a bag and rolling the bag with a rolling pin, crushing them in the food processor by using the steel blade, or you can buy ready-made graham cracker crumbs at the store.

Spray a 9-inch square baking pan with Pam or another nonstick cooking spray and sprinkle the inside with flour. Shake out excess flour. You may also use Pam spray for baking, which contains a coating of flour. Both will work well.

In an electric mixer, cream the butter and the sugar, adding the sugar gradually with the mixer on MEDIUM speed.

Add the vanilla extract and mix it in thoroughly.

Beat in the eggs, one at a time, incorporating the first egg before you add the second.

Add the baking powder and the salt, beating until they're thoroughly mixed.

Mix in half of the graham cracker crumbs with half of the milk. Beat well.

Mix in the other half of the graham cracker crumbs with the remaining half of the milk.

Remove the bowl from the mixer and fold in the chopped nuts by hand.

Pour the Graham Cracker Cake batter into the prepared pan and smooth the top with a rubber spatula.

Bake your cake at 350 degrees F. for 30 minutes.

Take your cake out of the oven, turn off the oven, and place the cake on a wire rack to await its topping.

In a saucepan on the stovetop, combine the contents of the can of crushed pineapple and juice with the white sugar.

Cook the pineapple mixture over MEDIUM HIGH heat, stirring constantly until it boils.

Turn the burner down to LOW and cook the pineapple mixture for an additional 10 minutes, stirring frequently.

Pour the hot pineapple sauce over the hot cake. Cool in the pan.

Serve the Graham Cracker Cake with sweetened whipped cream or vanilla ice cream.

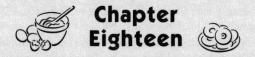

Chapter
Eighteen

When Hannah walked back into the kitchen at The Cookie
Jar, she was feeling much better. Winnie's fried chicken
had been wonderful, her biscuits were as light as a feather,
the helping of mashed potatoes and chicken pan gravy she'd
indulged in despite her resolve had been goodness itself.
Then there was the Graham Cracker Cake. It had been nothing short of incredible. But the good lunch she'd enjoyed
wasn't the only reason she was in a good mood. Mike had
discussed the quest for the dead man's identity with her and
he'd come up with some great tactics.

Mike had already spoken to Lonnie, who had used the
sheriff's department facilities to run the man's fingerprints.
He wasn't in the national database so if Grandma Knudson
was correct and the man was either a pimp or a drug dealer,
he hadn't been arrested for his illegal activities. It was disappointing that the dead man had no criminal record. That
would have made it easy to learn his name and last known
address. But Mike had come up with another investigative
technique that should work very well. He was going to drive
to Minneapolis to talk to Stella Parks, the head detective at
the Minneapolis Police Department. He'd show her the flyer,
see if she personally recognized the dead man, and leave
some flyers with her so that she could ask officers in other

departments. Since Stella was a friend of Mike's and she'd
met Hannah before, Mike would tell her the whole story of
how Hannah had hit the stranger and killed him. Stella liked
her and Hannah was almost certain that Stella would find
out who the man was if he came from the Minneapolis area.

Lisa was telling the story again. Hannah could hear crowd
noises through the swinging door that led to the coffee shop.
She glanced at the bakers rack and blinked several times in
surprise. Lisa was really attracting an audience today. The rack
had been loaded with cookies when Hannah had left with
Mike, and now it was at least half empty. It was lucky she'd
stashed the Triple Chocolate Cookies in the walk-in cooler
to try out on anyone who dropped by her condo tonight, or
they'd probably be gone, too!

Hannah had just taken her last pan of bar cookies out of
the oven and poured herself another cup of coffee when
there was a knock at the back door. She went to answer it and
smiled as she saw Norman standing there. "Hi, Norman!"
she greeted him. "Come in."

"I brought you some lunch," Norman said, heading for
his usual stool at the workstation.

"Thanks, Norman," Hannah said, hating to disappoint
him by telling him that she'd already eaten lunch at Winnie's
ranch with Mike. At least she'd had a fairly light lunch, if
you didn't count the Graham Cracker Cake and the biscuit
with honey and butter. She went to fetch coffee for both of
them and then she sat down across from him at the workstation.

"I got a little news today, Hannah," Norman said, opening
the conversation.

Hannah was almost afraid she'd jinx it by asking, but she
did. "About the dead man's tooth?"

"That's right. I e-mailed a copy of the photos and a detailed description of what I'd noticed when I examined the tooth to the dental professor who gave the symposium on tooth jewelry and embellishments."

"He got back to you?" Hannah asked, hoping she was right and Norman had learned something that would help them.

"Within the hour. He didn't know whose work it was, but he had a roster of names from the symposium. There's one dentist he remembered in particular who was very interested in providing that service for his patients. His name is Leland Jones and he has a practice on Munsington Street in Minneapolis."

"That's a great lead, Norman!" Hannah beamed at him. "As a matter of fact, Mike is driving to Minneapolis right now to show the photo of the dead man to Stella Parks."

"I remember her. She was a nice lady."

"And a really good detective," Hannah added. "We already know the dead man doesn't have a rap sheet. Mike had Lonnie run his fingerprints on the department computer. But if the dead man's from Minneapolis, someone in their department might have had a run-in with him. Why don't you call Mike and tell him what you learned about that dentist? Maybe he'll have time to check out his office."

"It's worth a try," Norman said, pulling out his cell phone. "Shall I have him meet us for dinner if he gets back in time?"

"Sure. I don't want to wait until tomorrow to find out if he learned anything. I'll cook. Both of you can come to my place."

"I'll take you out. You've got too much on your mind to bother making dinner."

"Is it your mission in life to feed me?"

Norman laughed. "Just because I brought you takeout

last night, and lunch today, and I'm taking you out to eat tonight?"

"Yes. What did you bring today?"

"Chinese. I've got pork chow mein, kung pao chicken, won ton soup, and brown rice."

"Sounds like a feast," Hannah told him, wondering if she could swallow more than a couple of bites. Luckily, everyone said that Chinese food was mostly vegetables and an hour after you ate, you were hungry again. Too bad Winnie hadn't served Chinese food. Then she would have been hungry by now.

"What's the matter? Aren't you hungry?"

There was nothing to do but tell Norman the truth. Hannah sighed deeply and plunged into deep waters. "I ate lunch out at Winnie's ranch at noon."

You left out the part about Mike, her conscience prodded her. *I know I did,* her rational mind answered. *There's no sense in telling Norman all that. He'd only be hurt because he brought me lunch and I had lunch with someone else first.* Her conscience took umbrage at this excuse. *Mike is his arch rival,* it reminded her. *He's more than just someone else.*

"Hannah?" Norman asked, and Hannah realized that he was looking at her questioningly.

"Sorry. I was just thinking about something. I'd love some pork chow mein, Norman. It's my favorite. I'll get us some plates and silverware while you call Mike and tell him what you know."

Fifteen minutes later, Hannah was stuffed beyond belief. "I'm sorry, Norman. I can't eat anymore," she said, looking down at her half-finished plate. "It's really delicious and I want to eat more, but I think I'm going to burst if I do."

"We don't want *that*," Norman said, chuckling. "Just sit

here and keep me company, Hannah. You don't have to eat. If I know Winnie, she fed you half to death."

"I think the Graham Cracker Cake finished me off."

"I've had that!"

"You have?"

"Winnie gave us lunch when Doc Hagaman and I went out to take care of Tina's tooth."

"Tina?" Hannah was confused. As far as she knew, Winnie didn't have any grandchildren named Tina. And even if she did, why would he go out to the ranch with Norman?

"Tina is Winnie's prize milk cow. Dr. Bob tranquilized her and I pulled her tooth. It was an interesting experience. I'd never worked on a cow before."

Hannah laughed. "That's Lake Eden for you. So far you've treated Mr. Whiskers, the guinea pig at Kiddie Korner, and Tina, Winnie's milk cow. What's next? False teeth for sharks?"

"I wonder if that's possible," Norman said, and Hannah began to laugh. Norman joined in until they heard someone come through the swinging door from the coffee shop.

"What's so funny?" Lisa asked, smiling at them.

"False teeth for sharks," Hannah answered, and the perplexed expression on Lisa's face sent them both into another paroxysm of laughter.

"It's not false teeth. It's dentures, or appliances," Norman corrected Hannah. "You have to learn to use the correct dental term."

"Appliances?" Lisa looked thoroughly puzzled. "You mean like refrigerators? And washers?"

"No, like false teeth or bridges." Norman could barely speak, he was laughing so hard. "That's what dentists call them. I know that it sounds a little weird when you put it that way, but that's what we call them."

"Okay," Hannah said, "It's a different terminology. What

do you call that little rubber sheet you put over the tooth in a patient's mouth when you work on it?"

"It's a dam."

"It's a *dam* nuisance," Lisa said. "I hate those little rubber sheets." And then all three of them cracked up again.

TRIPLE CHOCOLATE COOKIES

Preheat oven to 325 degrees F., rack in the middle position.

Hannah's 1st Note: This cookie recipe is from Michelle's friend, Julia Meister. It won grand prize at a fair and if you bake it, you'll know why!

1 cup all-purpose flour *(pack it down in the cup when you measure it)*

¼ cup Dutch-process cocoa powder *(if your store doesn't carry it, use the same dark cocoa powder you use for the following ingredient)*

¼ cup dark cocoa powder *(such as Hershey's Special Dark)*

½ teaspoon baking soda

¼ teaspoon salt

½ cup salted butter *(1 stick, 4 ounces, ¼ pound)*

4 ounces bittersweet chocolate *(I used Baker's Bittersweet—4 squares)*

1 teaspoon vanilla extract

2 large eggs, beaten *(just whip them up in a glass with a fork)*

1 and ¼ cups white *(granulated)* sugar

1 and ½ cups bittersweet chocolate chips *(I used Ghirardelli 60% cacao chips)*

Hannah's 2nd Note: Florence doesn't carry Dutch process cocoa powder or dark chocolate cocoa powder down at the Red Owl. Not only that, she doesn't carry any bittersweet chocolate, either in one-ounce squares or in chips. I wanted to make these right away so I used Hershey's regular cocoa powder in place of the two cocoa powders, regular semi-sweet baking chocolate to melt with the butter, and regular chocolate chips. Despite all these substitutions, the cookies were still incredibly superior chocolate cookies. I made them again once I'd managed to find the Dutch process cocoa powder, the Hershey's Dark Cocoa Powder, the bittersweet baking chocolate, and the bittersweet chocolate chips. The resulting flavor was deeper, darker, and absolutely marvelous. My point here is that even if you can't find some of the ingredients at your store, this is still a superb chocolate cookie recipe.

Hannah's 3rd Note: Bittersweet chocolate is any chocolate with 60 percent cacao.

Line your cookie sheets with parchment paper or baking paper. *(I also took the precaution of spraying my parchment paper with Pam. With all the substitutions I made in the original recipe, I was afraid the cookies might stick.)*

Mix the flour, cocoa powders, baking soda, and salt together in a small bowl with a whisk. Whisk until they are evenly combined.

Place the stick of salted butter in a microwave-safe bowl. Roughly chop the bittersweet chocolate and add it to the bowl with the butter. Melt in the microwave for 1 minute at full power.

Let the butter and chocolate mixture sit in the microwave for another minute and then attempt to stir it smooth. If it's not yet melted enough to do this, heat it in the microwave in additional 20-second increments until you can stir it smooth. *(You can also do this on the stovetop over low heat, but make sure to stir it constantly.)*

Stir the vanilla into the melted butter and chocolate mixture. Let it cool on the counter.

Use an electric mixer to beat the eggs and sugar together at MEDIUM speed until the mixture is light yellow in color and fluffy. *(This takes 3 to 4 minutes.)* You can also do this by hand, but it takes some muscle.

Turn the mixer down to LOW speed and slowly pour the chocolate and butter mixture into the mixer bowl. Mix this until it's well combined.

Leave the mixer on LOW speed, and sprinkle in the flour mixture. Mix until it is combined, but DO NOT

over-mix. *(This is like brownie batter. Mix it too much and it will lose its fluffiness.)*

Take the bowl out of the mixer and fold in the chocolate chips by hand.

Scoop out rounded tablespoons of dough and drop them on the cookie sheets. *(Lisa and I use a 2-Tablespoon cookie scoop to do this down at The Cookie Jar.)* The cookies should be at least 2 inches apart, no more than 12 cookies to a regular size cookie sheet.

Bake the cookies at 325 degrees F., for 12 to 13 minutes, or until the outside of the cookies are "set", but the insides are still soft and slightly under-baked. *(Just like brownies.)*

Remove the cookies from the oven and transfer the cookie sheets to a wire rack. Cool the cookies on the cookie sheets for 4 minutes. Then pull out the cookie sheet, leaving the cookies and parchment paper on the wire rack to completely cool.

Store these cookies in an airtight container at room temperature. Julia says they are best enjoyed within a week, but I'm almost certain they won't last even half that long!

Yield: 2 and ½ to 3 dozen incredible chocolate cookies, depending on cookie size.

Chapter Nineteen

It was just past five-thirty in the afternoon when Hannah and Michelle pulled into Hannah's parking spot at the condo. Hannah led the way up the outside staircase to Hannah's second-floor unit while Michelle carried a large bakery box with three dozen Triple Chocolate Cookies for them to test after dinner tonight.

They were cooking dinner together. Michelle had planned it all out. She would start the Smothered Chicken and Hannah would assemble one of her favorite side dishes, Oodles of Noodles. Once the chicken was in the pan and the heat had been turned down to low, Michelle would do her evening workout on Hannah's new exercise machine while Hannah put a green salad together and got the coffee ready to go. Then Michelle would take her shower and Hannah would relax on the couch with a glass of something cold and wet.

"I'll catch him this time," Hannah said, setting her grocery bags on the landing and inserting her key in the lock. "You've got your hands full with those . . ."

"What is it?" Michelle asked when Hannah stopped speaking abruptly and stepped back without turning the key or opening the door.

"I don't know," Hannah said in a low voice. "I thought I heard something inside."

"Moishe?"

"No. It sounded like a . . . a humming."

"Humming as in music?"

"No. Humming as in noise. It sounded like something was running . . . a mixer, or a blender, or something like that."

"Did you leave the television on for Moishe?"

"Yes. I always do."

"Then maybe it's a cooking show and it actually is a blender or a mixer. Let's go in and check it out."

Hannah hesitated for a moment. There were no signs of forced entry. The door was still locked, the living room window was open a bit, but she'd left it that way this morning. It was still broad daylight and would be until at least eight o'clock tonight, and she lived in a secure condo complex with a guard at the gate. It was extremely unlikely that a burglar had broken into her home and was blending drinks or mixing up a cake in her kitchen. "Okay," she said, turning her key in the lock and opening the door.

The cat who hurtled out to meet her almost knocked her off her feet. Somehow Hannah managed to catch him and carry him back inside. Whatever she'd heard was no longer audible. Perhaps the humming noise hadn't been coming from her unit at all. Since it was summer, most of her neighbors kept their windows open during the day and it was possible that Sue Plotnik, her downstairs neighbor, had been using her mixer or her blender.

"I don't hear anything," Michelle said, stepping in behind Hannah.

"Neither do I . . . now. Maybe it was coming from somewhere else. Sometimes the acoustics are strange in this building. Sound bounces off these walls because the units are so close together."

"Let's check out the other rooms just to make sure," Michelle said, grabbing the baseball bat that Hannah kept leaning in a corner next to the door.

They checked the rooms one by one, even peering under the beds and inside the closets. Everything was just as they'd left it this morning.

"There's nothing here," Hannah said, heading down the hall toward the kitchen. "We'd better get started on dinner. I told everyone to come at seven."

Hands washed and aprons on, the two sisters started their preparations. Hannah reached into the grocery bags and took what she needed for the noodle casserole. "Here's the chicken," she said, handing the white, butcher-paper package to Michelle.

"Why so many chicken breasts?" Michelle asked after she'd opened the package.

"Because extra people are bound to show up. It always happens when we make dinner."

"But what if we're only five tonight?"

"Then we'll have leftovers of Smothered Chicken for dinner tomorrow night."

"On leftover noodles from tonight?"

"If there *are* any leftover noodles. And if there aren't, we can have the chicken and sauce over biscuits or rice."

"True," Michelle agreed, opening the drawer under the lower oven and getting out Hannah's biggest frying pan. She put in a combination of butter and olive oil, and prepared to brown the chicken.

While the chicken was browning, Hannah assembled the noodle casserole and slipped it into the top oven. "I'm all ready," she said to Michelle.

"So am I." Michelle sprinkled the rest of the herb and flour mixture on top of her chicken and put the lid on the frying pan. She turned the heat down to simmer and went to wash her hands again. "Do you want me to set the table? Or should I do my workout now?"

"I'll set the table while you work out," Hannah said. "Go ahead, Michelle."

"Okay." Michelle turned to look at Moishe, whose head was buried in the food bowl Hannah had just filled. "Are you going to come and watch me work out, Moishe?"

Moishe lifted his head to look up at Michelle and then he followed her out of the kitchen. Hannah was amazed. Food had always been Moishe's number one priority, but it seemed that watching Michelle on the exercise machine was even more interesting than eating.

After she'd set the table and checked the progress of the chicken, Hannah settled down on the couch with a tall glass of iced tea. She was just about to turn on the television to watch the evening news when she heard Michelle calling her from the bedroom.

"I'm here," she called back. "What is it?"

"Come here, Hannah. You've got to see this to believe it."

Hannah got up and walked down the hallway. Michelle must have discovered something new that the fancy exercise machine could do. She took one step inside her bedroom and stopped to stare in utter disbelief.

Michelle was walking on the treadmill, but she wasn't the only one. Moishe was walking right in front of her, keeping pace with the speed of the machine.

"See what I mean?" Michelle asked, grinning at Hannah. "He just watched me this morning, but the minute I turned on the treadmill part of the machine and started to walk, he hopped right up here in front of me and he's been here ever since."

"This is just . . . amazing!" Hannah knew the word she'd used to describe this feline feat was too tame, but she was at a loss for words. She had a cat who liked to pace on the treadmill. She'd never seen anything like it before. "Do any other cats do this?" she asked Michelle.

"I don't know, but he really seems to like it. I wonder what'll happen if I speed up the machine a little." Michelle reached forward to the console and turned a switch.

The treadmill began to go faster. Hannah could tell because Michelle had to jog to keep up. So did Moishe, but he stuck with it, running along and wearing what Hannah thought of as his kitty-grin. "I think he likes it faster," Hannah said.

"Maybe he does, but I'm not ready to jog that fast. I'm going to slow it down all the way and then I'll shut it off."

Michelle turned the machine to a slower speed for a few seconds. When she lowered the speed even more, Moishe turned around to glare at her. He gave a yowl that would have curdled milk, and jumped off in a huff to stalk past Hannah and down the hall.

"I don't think he liked that," Michelle said quite unnecessarily.

"I don't think so, either. I've got to check with Doc Hagaman and Sue. I've never heard of a cat exercising on a treadmill before."

"Maybe you won't have to put him on a diet," Michelle said, stepping off the machine and wiping her face on a towel. "If he exercises every time I do, he'll lose weight on his own."

Hannah was thoughtful as she walked back to the living room and her iced tea. Perhaps Michelle was right and Moishe would lose weight without dieting. And if Michelle was right about Moishe, perhaps *she* should try the fancy exercise machine to see if *she* could lose weight without dieting. It was worth a try. Nothing was worse than being on a diet, and everyone said that exercise was good for you. She'd ask Michelle to show her just how the exercise machine worked and give it a try.

Five minutes later, Hannah was using the treadmill with Moishe walking in front of her. His tail was swishing back and forth and Hannah could tell he was having a wonderful time. On the other hand, she was getting tired even though she'd only been walking for a minute or two. That meant that she was really out of shape and she simply had to find time to use her grand prize every day.

"That's enough, Moishe," Hannah said, lowering the speed until the machine stopped.

"Rrowwww!"

Hannah glanced at her feline roommate. There was no doubt in her mind that Moishe was protesting her action. "We'll do it again tomorrow," she told him. "I promise. And Michelle will, too. And don't forget that Michelle works out twice a day. As long as she's visiting us, you'll have at least three opportunities to ride on the treadmill every day. And Norman's bringing Cuddles over for dinner tonight. If you didn't get enough exercise walking the treadmill, I'm sure you can talk her into playing chase."

That information seemed to appease Moishe, at least temporarily, and Hannah went off to take her shower. Ten minutes later, she was dressed in clean jeans and a summer top, and sitting in her favorite spot on the couch, drinking the small glass of wine that Michelle had poured for her.

"So how do you like your new exercise machine?" Michelle asked her.

"I like it, at least the treadmill part. It's the only thing I've tried so far. And Moishe obviously loves it."

Moishe, who was sitting on top of his Kitty Kondo, turned around to regard her solemnly. He was perched on the top tier so that he could peer out the picture window that overlooked the outside staircase, and he was obviously waiting for Norman to arrive with Cuddles.

"Who would have guessed that any cat of mine would turn out to be an exercise buff," Hannah commented to Michelle. "It's certainly not behavior that he learned from me!"

Michelle laughed. "Maybe it's behavior that you'll learn

from him. Exercise makes you feel good, Hannah. It's fun if you don't overdo it. You have to set realistic goals, goals that aren't out of your reach."

"Four times a week on the treadmill," Hannah said. "That's how often I'll do it. There are some days that I just want to come home and collapse after work. That's why I won't say I'll exercise every day."

"Exactly right," Michelle said, smiling at her. And that was when they both heard an excited yowl from Moishe. "Norman must be here." Michelle got up to look out the window. "I don't see him yet."

"Moishe must have heard Norman's car pull into the garage. He always gives me an early cat warning." Hannah got up from her spot on the couch. "I'll pour some iced tea for him."

"Better wait. It might be somebody else's car."

"It's not. Moishe hasn't ever been wrong. He loves Norman and now that Norman has Cuddles, he positively adores Norman."

There was another yowl from the top tier of the Kitty Kondo and then Moishe began to purr. His purr turned into a loud rumble and he jumped down to stand by the door.

"Shall I catch him so he doesn't get out?" Michelle asked.

"No need. He'll follow the cat carrier when Norman comes in the door. There's no way Moishe is going to run out and miss an evening of playing with Cuddles."

Once Norman arrived and let Cuddles out of her carrier, the two cats ran off to get into whatever mischief their combined kitty brains could cook up. Hannah poured a glass of iced tea for Norman, checked the progress of their dinner, and went to sit on the couch with him.

"Do you think Mike will have any news?" Norman asked her.

"I don't know. I haven't talked to him since I called to tell him to come here for dinner. And that was when he was parking in the lot at Minneapolis Police headquarters."

"Do you think he would have called if he learned anything important?" Michelle asked.

Hannah shrugged. "I don't know. Either he didn't learn anything useful, or he's waiting to tell us in person."

Just then there was a knock at the door and Michelle got up to answer it. "That must be Mike now."

"Or Lonnie," Hannah reminded her. "Actually, it sounded more like Mother."

"You invited Mother?"

"I didn't invite her, but she feels she can drop by without notice. If Doc's busy doing something else, it could be her."

"Or Andrea, if she's still mad at Bill," Michelle said, considering the possibilities.

"Open the door," Norman said, chuckling at the two of them. "The suspense is killing me."

Michelle laughed and opened the door. "Mother!" she said.

"I know I wasn't invited, dears, but Doc had late rounds and the telephone tree came up with something that may or may not be useful to you. May I come in?"

"Of course," Hannah called out. "Join us for dinner, Mother. There's plenty."

"Plenty for two more?"

Hannah glanced at the doorway, but there was no one standing behind her mother. "Is there someone with you?"

"No, but Andrea was parking in the guest lot when I came up the stairs. Naturally, I assumed she was coming here."

"I imagine she is," Hannah said, and called out to Michelle who had gone into the kitchen to get their mother a glass of iced tea. "Will you set two more places, Michelle? Andrea will be here in a minute or two."

Michelle delivered the iced tea, along with the can of cat treats. "Here, Mother."

"But I'm wearing slacks."

"I know, but those are linen, aren't they?" Michelle waited until Delores nodded. "It's the same problem, Mother. If Moishe catches a thread in those slacks, he'll damage them."

Delores glanced down at her slacks. "Oh, dear. If I'd thought of that, I would have come prepared." She turned to Hannah. "Do you have a bath sheet I can use for my lap, dear?"

"Of course." Hannah got up to find the beautiful new bath sheet her mother had given her after a trip to the mall. Since she hadn't used it yet, she pulled off the tag on her way back to the living room, and stuffed the evidence of non-use into her pocket. "Here you go, Mother," she said when she reentered the living room.

"Thank you, dear." Delores took the towel and spread it out so that it draped over her legs. "What a pretty towel! Where did you get it?"

"From you," Hannah couldn't resist saying.

"From me?"

"Yes. You picked it out for me at the mall the last time you were there. I think it's beautiful, too."

"It's lovely," Norman said. "I should have you choose my towels, Delores. They're getting old and I'm not sure which color to buy."

"Of course I will, dear," Delores said, causing Hannah and Michelle to exchange glances. They'd thought that *dear* was reserved for them, but now it evidently included Norman.

The doorbell rang and Hannah tabled any questions she might have about her mother's terms of endearment. She got up to answer it and ushered Andrea in.

"I hope you don't mind," Andrea said, pulling Hannah

aside. "I just don't feel like talking to Bill yet, and he's mad at me too, and . . . well . . . it's not very comfortable at home."

"I'm glad to see you, Andrea," Hannah reassured her. "Come in and I'll get you something to drink. Then you can join us for dinner. There's plenty."

"Who else is coming?" Andrea asked, stepping into the living room and giving a little wave to the group that was assembled there.

"We're waiting for Lonnie and Mike and then we'll eat. Have a seat and I'll get you a glass of white wine."

"That would be wonderful," Andrea said, sounding very relieved.

As Hannah went off to the kitchen to pour Andrea's wine, she wondered what her sister would have said if she hadn't invited her to dinner. She didn't think Andrea would have gone back home and ended her stalemate with Bill. That just wasn't in the cards quite yet. Would she have gone somewhere else, perhaps out to her high school friend Lucy Dunwright's place in the country? Or would she have parked in the garage and stayed in her car until she was sure that Bill was in bed? It must be terrible to fight with the man you loved. And it must be doubly difficult if you were Andrea. Andrea was as stubborn as they came and she wouldn't back down easily. And unfortunately, although Hannah knew that Bill loved Andrea to distraction, he was just as stubborn as Andrea was and he wouldn't be the first to back down. This could go on for weeks with neither of them giving an inch. Hannah knew that she would have to do something to get them back together soon, before the wall of contention between them became a permanent barrier.

"Here you go," Hannah said, handing the glass of Cost-Mart's cheapest jug wine to her sister. Andrea fancied herself as a wine snob and Hannah had taken care, over the years, never to let her see the green gallon jug she kept in the bottom of her refrigerator.

"Oh, thank you, Hannah!" Andrea said after she'd taken her first sip. "I just love this wine. It has such depth and complexity."

"Glad you like it," Hannah said, and left it at that. She knew that if she ever told Andrea that the wine she privately called Chateau Screwtop had cost less than ten dollars a jug, Andrea would never drink it again.

Hannah had just taken a seat next to Norman on the couch when the doorbell rang again.

"I'll get it," Michelle said, rushing to the door. When she came back to usher in two more dinner guests, Michelle was beaming and Hannah knew that was because one of the guests was Lonnie.

"Hi, Lonnie," Hannah greeted him and then she turned to Mike. "Sit down, Mike. It's been a long day for you."

"Not as bad as usual," Mike said, sitting down on the couch on the other side of Hannah. "I put in longer days than this when I was working for the department."

"How about you, Lonnie?" Hannah asked him.

"This is my day off so I went down to the Cities with Mike," Lonnie said, accepting the glass of iced tea that Michelle had brought for him.

"Tell us all about it after we eat," Hannah said, getting up from her spot on the couch. "Please find places at the table and I'll get us started with the salad."

With Andrea and Michelle helping, the dinner was served in practically no time at all. Once they were all seated and the serving dishes were on the table, everyone helped themselves family style. There were praises for the salad, the Oodles of Noodles casserole, and the Smothered Chicken.

"Smart move with the extra chicken breasts, Hannah," Michelle said under her breath as both Mike and Lonnie helped themselves to third helpings of chicken.

"Thanks," Hannah said in the same quiet tone of voice.

During the meal, conversation had been at a minimum.

The comments that were made were either praise for the food, or requests for a tablemate to pass a serving dish for another helping. When everyone put their silverware down and wore expressions of hunger satisfaction, the three sisters cleared the table, made the coffee, and carried it to the table.

"What are these?" Norman asked when Hannah brought out a plate of cookies.

"Triple Chocolate Cookies. It's a new recipe so you have to tell me how you like it."

"Then I'd better take an extra so that I give it a fair test," Delores said, and since she hadn't yet taken a bite, Hannah knew she was reacting to the fact that the cookies were chocolate.

The taste test was a huge success. Hannah knew because no one offered an opinion until they'd eaten at least three cookies. Then the comments were all superlative and she made a mental note to add the cookies to their menu at The Cookie Jar.

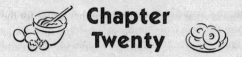

Chapter
Twenty

"I really can't believe this," Delores said, after Hannah had brought more cookies and Michelle had refilled their coffee cups.

"Believe what?" Michelle asked her.

"We haven't had to put our feet up once tonight for a Moishe and Cuddles chase."

"Moishe's tired, Mother," Hannah explained. "He walked for miles this afternoon."

"He got out?!" Delores was clearly shocked.

"No, Mother. He exercised." Hannah turned to Michelle. "You explain."

"I was using Hannah's new exercise machine right before you got here. I had it turned to the treadmill setting, and Moishe hopped on right in front of me and trotted along."

Mike's eyes narrowed in disbelief. "You're joking . . . right?"

"No. He really did it. I called Hannah and she came in to watch. Moishe likes walking on that treadmill. He likes it so much that he got a little perturbed at me when I shut it off."

Mike turned to look at Hannah. "True?"

"True. I'll use it tomorrow morning and we'll see if he'll get on it with me again."

"You're going to exercise?" Delores asked in the very

same tone she would have used if she'd inquired whether her eldest daughter was truly going to the moon.

"I thought I'd give it a try for a couple of mornings to see if I like the machine," Hannah said, being deliberately casual about it. "If Moishe walks along with me, I'll let you know when we have our meeting tomorrow morning." Delores nodded and Hannah turned to Mike. "Okay Mike," she said. "Tell us what you learned in Minneapolis today."

"Not enough to suit me," Mike said, looking disgruntled. "When Lonnie and I got to their headquarters about noon, Stella was just going on a break. We walked down the street to a little coffee shop that Stella and I like, and I showed her the flyer."

"Did Stella recognize the picture on the flyer?" Hannah found that she was crossing her fingers for luck, just as she'd done when she was a child.

"No, at least not by name. But she promised to pass the flyer around. She did think she'd seen him before and he was a—" Mike stopped and glanced at Delores. "Stella thought he looked like a man she'd seen with a woman who was walking the streets in a notoriously crime-ridden area of Munsington Street."

Delores laughed. "You don't have to mince words around me. I know what a streetwalker is. It's the oldest profession in the world and I just wrote about a streetwalker in my latest Regency romance novel. They called them *opera girls* or *round heels* back then."

"That's funny, Mother," Michelle said, "Especially the round heels name."

"It wasn't funny if you *were* one. Prostitutes in Regency England didn't have the benefit of modern medicine or antibiotics. Disease was prevalent and most opera girls lived a very short life."

"Did Stella say the man was soliciting the woman?" Hannah asked Mike.

"Stella was pretty sure he wasn't. She'd seen him before with a couple of other girls she'd identified as known prostitutes. She didn't think he was a customer. She was almost positive that he was a . . ." Mike stopped and glanced at Delores again.

"A pimp?" Hannah provided the word.

"Yeah. That's what Stella thought."

"So Grandma Knudson might have been right!" Michelle said, laughing as she remembered what Grandma Knudson had said when Lisa told her story at the coffee shop.

"Grandma Knudson?" Delores questioned Hannah.

"That's right. Grandma Knudson saw the picture of the dead man when Lisa was telling the story at The Cookie Jar and she said he looked like a pimp."

Delores burst out laughing. "Leave it to Grandma Knudson to tell it like it is. That dear lady is a breath of fresh air, even if Reverend Bob doesn't appreciate it sometimes."

Hannah turned to Mike again. "But Stella didn't know for sure that he was a pimp . . . right?"

"That's right. She suspected he was, but she wasn't sure. She told us she'd pass the flyer to the vice squad when they came back to the station."

"We know more than we did this morning," Hannah said, noticing that Mike still looked disappointed.

"Yes, but we don't know anything for sure. I really thought we could wrap this up today."

Hannah felt a bit like chiding him for being unrealistic, but perhaps that was a trait all detectives had. The desire to wrap up a case quickly might be the reason Mike was so successful and worked so tirelessly.

"How about Doctor Jones, the dentist?" Norman asked him. "Did you get a chance to talk to him?"

"No. His office was closed. I called and got a recorded message that said he only takes patients by appointment."

"Did you make an appointment?" Delores asked.

"I left my name and cell phone number. If he calls back, I'll make an appointment."

"So you don't really know much about him?" Hannah asked.

"Not really. I'm waiting for his call to find out more."

"I know something about him from that phone message," Norman said. "If Doctor Jones only takes patients by appointment, he's either independently wealthy, or he's receiving money from a secondary source. A dentist can't support a practice if he's only open by appointment. If your office is a storefront, you have to take walk-ins."

"Did you meet Doctor Jones at the dental conference last year?" Delores asked Norman.

"Not that I can remember. All I know about him is that he took a seminar in tooth embellishment."

Mike turned to Norman. "And you didn't take that seminar?"

"No. I did embed some tooth jewelry when I worked at the clinic in Seattle, but there's not much call for it here in Lake Eden."

"Unless some college student asks you to play a joke on her older sister," Michelle said, and Hannah knew she was reminding him of the removable caps with rhinestones he'd made for her.

"True," Norman said, smiling at Hannah and then turning back to Mike. "I might have run into him at the conference. There were over eighteen hundred dentists there. But if I did, he must not have made a lasting impression on me."

"We drove past his office," Lonnie said. "It was really small, just a storefront."

"That's right," Mike took up the story. "The plate glass window in front has heavy curtains and we couldn't see inside. It's in a high crime area, very close to the area where Stella thinks she saw the man on the flyer. It all fits together, especially if Jones is the dentist who put that diamond in the tooth." Mike turned to Norman again. "You said you took the diamond to a jeweler to have it appraised?"

"Yes, and it's worth over twenty thousand dollars according to the jewelers at the mall. I took it to three places to make sure, and the lowest appraisal they gave me was twenty thousand."

"Could a pimp afford something like that?" Delores asked Mike.

"Depending on how many girls he has in his stable, sure he could afford it. But he probably didn't buy it from a jeweler and he probably paid a lot less than twenty thousand for it. Chances are it's stolen property and he bought it from a fence."

"Is there any way you can tell if it's stolen?" Michelle asked.

Norman shook his head. "Not according to the jewelers at the mall. I asked about that. Sometimes you can identify stones by the type of setting they're in and this one is simply embedded in the tooth. And that means there's no way to identify it from the setting. The only other way anyone can trace the background of a gem is if it has some distinguishing characteristic like an unusual color or cut. All three jewelers agreed that this diamond doesn't have any distinguishing characteristics."

"I think he probably stole it," Delores said. "Either that or one of the girls in his . . . What did you call it, Mike?"

"Stable."

"Yes, stable. That's really a denigrating term, isn't it?"

Hannah nodded. "Yes, it is, Mother. I don't think pimps really care if their girls have low self-esteem."

"It probably works in their favor," Michelle said. "Otherwise, the girls might decide they could do something better with their lives and leave."

Hannah happened to be watching Mike when Michelle made her comment. The corners of his mouth twitched in laughter, but he didn't comment.

"They can't leave, dear," Delores said, addressing Michelle. "These girls depend on their pimps for their very survival."

Michelle frowned. "Then what happens when their pimp dies? If we're right and the dead man was a pimp, what happens to the girls in his stable?"

"They're up for grabs," Mike answered. "There's always another pimp in the wings who'll take them on."

"But can't they run away before that happens?"

"They could if they had somewhere to run and the money or the means to get there. But most of them don't have that desire. They stay where they are and do what they've been doing all along. Most of them are so beaten down by their circumstances that they don't even think of trying to get out."

"That's just sad!" Michelle said.

Mike nodded. "You're right. It *is* sad. Life on the street is never easy."

They were all silent for a moment and then Delores posed another question. "Is it possible that one of the girls in the dead man's stable stole that diamond from a client?"

"Happens all the time," Mike said. "The pimps encourage it as long as the girls turn over the money, or the jewelry, or whatever to them. Unfortunately, when a girl rolls a John, the John's usually too embarrassed to report it. That means we don't hear about the crime and there's nothing the authorities can do about it."

"So the diamond could have been stolen, one way or the other," Delores clarified.

"That's right," Mike agreed.

"All right then," Delores squared her shoulders. "We have to talk to one of the girls in the dead pimp's stable."

"First things first," Mike told her. "First, we have to find out if Stella was right and he *was* a . . ." Mike reached into his pocket and pulled out his cell phone to look at the display. "It's Stella," he said. "I've got to take this."

They all watched as Mike got up and stepped into the kitchen for privacy before he answered his cell phone. The room went quiet as they listened to his end of the conversation, but Hannah quickly realized that she could learn nothing from his one-word replies.

"Will you feel better if he was a pimp, dear?" Delores asked her.

Hannah shrugged. "I don't know. I shouldn't, but maybe I will." She looked at their puzzled faces and hurried to explain. "I know I shouldn't feel better . . . morally, that is. A man is dead because of me and his character or lack of it shouldn't change that fact."

"But you *might* feel better?" Delores followed up on her earlier question.

"Maybe I would. And if I did, then that would be a fault in *my* character."

Just then Mike came back into the living room, effectively taking Hannah off the hook. She didn't want to answer any more questions from her mother about the dead man.

"He's a pimp." Mike confirmed it. "Stella showed the photo to Vice and a couple of them knew the dead man. They hadn't seen him in the last couple of days and they were wondering what happened to him."

"Do they know his name?" Hannah asked.

"Keith Branson. At least that's what it said on his driver's license when they pulled him over for running a red light."

"But you have to show your birth certificate to get a driver's license, don't you?" Delores asked.

Mike smiled at her and Hannah knew he was thinking something like, *What a babe in the woods you are!* "They make fake birth certificates and they're good forgeries," he told her.

"I know they do," Michelle said. "I have one. That's how I got my fake driver's license."

"I didn't hear that," Mike said, and then he turned to Lonnie. "Did you hear that?"

"Hear what?" Lonnie asked. "I didn't hear anything."

Delores turned on her youngest daughter so fast that Hannah almost burst out laughing. "Why do you have a fake birth certificate and a fake driver's license?"

Michelle didn't quite meet her mother's eyes. "Oh, just to see if I could get them. I had to do some research for a psychology class I took last year."

"They told you to get a fake birth certificate and a fake driver's license?" Delores looked shocked.

"Not exactly. But I had to get into a club to do the research and they carded at the door. It was twenty-one or older."

Delores looked up at the ceiling and Hannah suspected she was thinking, *Where did I go wrong?*

"I wrote a really good paper and I got an A in the class."

Hannah watched her mother alternate between worry and pride. "Well . . . I guess it's all right as long as you didn't use it for anything illegal. You didn't *drink*, did you?"

"Only iced tea, Mother. And I don't mean Long Island Iced Tea."

Everyone laughed, even Delores, at Michelle's little joke, and Hannah knew it was time to change the subject before her mother started asking Michelle about more illegal activities.

"So did Keith Branson have a rap sheet?" Hannah asked Mike.

"No. All they had on him were a couple of traffic tickets he paid right away, and one charge of misdemeanor indecent public exposure."

"What was *that*?" Delores asked him, and Hannah knew her mother was imagining the worst.

"Nothing serious. A highway patrol officer happened to come along when he was urinating by the side of a gravel road in a wooded area of Anoka."

Delores didn't say anything to that and Hannah wondered if her mother wished she hadn't asked the question.

"Stella did find one charge that was disturbing," Mike said. "The vice squad worked with Stella's detectives to get Branson on aggravated assault or attempted murder, but they couldn't gather enough evidence to turn it over to the district attorney."

Hannah noticed that Lonnie didn't look surprised. "Was it that prostitute Stella told us about? The one who died in the condemned building?"

"Yes. All they had was the phone call from her friend, claiming that Branson was the one who beat her. And the friend didn't show up at the station to give a statement."

Hannah wasn't sure if she should feel good or bad about that. It seemed the man she'd killed had been a pimp, an abuser, and perhaps even a murderer. She noticed that Delores was leaning toward her and she quickly framed another question before her mother could ask her again how she felt about that. "Did Keith Branson have any relatives that we should notify?"

"Not that the MPD knows of. Don't forget, we don't even know, for certain, that Branson is his real name."

"Are you going to try to find out more about him?" Andrea asked Mike.

"I was going to drive down there tomorrow to see if any of the girls on Munsington Street knew him."

"You were going to?" Hannah noticed the qualifier in Mike's statement. He hadn't said, *I'm going to drive down*. He'd said, *I was going to drive down*, which meant he no longer planned to go. "Why aren't you going?" she asked him.

"Stella advised me not to try it. She said too many people on the street remembered me from when I worked Vice. And then she made a suggestion that I immediately rejected."

"What was it?" Delores asked him.

"Stella wants Hannah to go down to talk to one of Keith's girls. None of them have ever seen her and Hannah wouldn't pose a threat, especially if she tells them she's visiting from Wisconsin or something like that. Stella thought Hannah would get a lot more information than I could."

"Stella's probably right," Delores said, "but I can get even more information than either one of you."

Hannah just stared at her mother. "*You* want to go with me?"

"Yes. I'm very good at talking to people."

"Mother!" Andrea looked properly shocked. "You want to go along to talk to a bunch of prostitutes?"

"Not a bunch, dear. Just one. It would be interesting."

Andrea still looked astounded. "But, Mother! What about Doc?"

"Oh, Doc can't go, dear. He's far too busy at the hospital. And even if he wasn't busy and *could* go, the girl might think he was a . . . a customer, and I wouldn't like that at all!"

Andrea gave an exasperated sigh. "That's not what I meant and you know it! If you're going along with Hannah, I can't stop you, but I'm going along, too. Someone has to keep you two from getting into trouble."

"The child becomes the mother," Hannah quipped, winking at Delores. "How about you, Michelle? Do you want to join the family party?"

"No, thanks. I've driven past that area and it's not exactly a scenic delight. I'd much rather stay here and help Lisa in the coffee shop."

"That's fine, dear," Delores said, smiling at Michelle.

Michelle looked as if she were uncertain about saying something because she took a deep breath before she said, "Just for your information, when you drive through that area you'd better keep the windows rolled up and the doors locked."

"It's *that* bad?" Delores asked her.

"Not during the daytime. Then it's just this rundown, dilapidated, and filthy area with graffiti sprayed on every building left standing. But I wouldn't want to walk there alone at night. The creatures of the night come out when it gets dark, and I'm not talking about werewolves and vampires."

"Are we going to be there at night?" Delores asked Mike, and Hannah could tell that she was worried.

"No. You'll be out of there long before nightfall. Stella wants you to come to her office at three. I'll give you directions. She's going to send an undercover vice unit with you, but they'll lay low and stay in their car. They'll just be there if you need them. She said the girls go out about four o'clock, so that they can meet up with the guys who get off work at the insecticide factory a couple of blocks down the street."

"Lovely," Delores said. "Is there a restaurant around there? Or shouldn't I ask?"

"You'll have to ask Stella when you see her. That area changes frequently. There's a soup kitchen, or there used to be one, and every other month or so some local church group opens a storefront coffee shop that makes it for a few weeks and then goes under for lack of funds. There's a bar, of course. There's always a bar close to a factory. Little Dingo's has been there forever. And in this neighborhood, two years counts as forever."

Hannah glanced at Andrea, who was staring at Mike open-mouthed. It was the only time in Hannah's life when she hadn't seen her middle sister confident that she could handle everything and still look like she stepped off the cover of a fashion magazine.

"Andrea?" Hannah reached out to touch her arm.

"Yes?" Andrea's voice was a bit shaky, even uttering that one-syllable word.

"You're out, Andrea," Hannah said, hoping she sounded both firm and loving.

"But . . . why? I'm perfectly willing to go with you."

Hannah thought fast. "It's your sheriff's wife persona. You've been paired with Bill in the press one too many times. If only one of these girls reads the papers, or if anyone working the same area has seen your photo with Bill's in the paper, word will get out and they'll know you're the wife of the Winnetka County Sheriff."

"Oh," Andrea said. "I didn't even think about that."

Hannah sat back and hoped that someone else would pick up on her cue. She'd laid the groundwork and that was all she could do.

"Hannah's right, dear," Delores chimed in so quickly that Hannah was amazed. "If you're with us, you could blow our cover. And then not only would we fail to get the information we needed, we might be in danger."

"Oh, dear!" Andrea looked horrified. "I never thought of that. But I don't think Bill and I were ever photographed together in any of the . . ."

"Yes, you were," Hannah interrupted her. "How about that election night photo?"

Andrea sighed. "You're right, Hannah. I even have the clipping. Our photo was in the *St. Paul Pioneer* and one of my high school friends sent it to me." Andrea turned to Delores. "I'm sorry, Mother. I never thought of that when I offered to go along. I was only trying to help."

"I know you were, dear."

"Is there anything else I can do?"

"I'm sure there is," Hannah replied quickly as her mind

raced to find something else, anything else, that Andrea could do to feel helpful. "I know," she said, giving her mother a warning glance. "If you have time, you could pack us some sandwiches."

"You want me to pack sandwiches?" Andrea asked, looking delighted at the prospect.

"Yes, dear," Delores said, interpreting Hannah's warning glance correctly. "Both Hannah and I will be working tomorrow and I doubt we'll have time for lunch."

"That's right," Hannah agreed. "If you could pack some sandwiches for us to take with us, we won't have to stop on the way for food."

"I can do that! How about some peanut butter and jelly sandwiches? Bill says I make the best peanut butter and jelly sandwiches in the world."

"That would be great," Hannah said, maintaining her pleasant expression by deliberately putting all thoughts of her sister's peanut butter and jelly sandwiches out of her mind. She'd eaten Andrea's sandwiches before and while there was nothing really wrong with them nutritionally, Andrea's special combination of peanut butter and mint jelly on cinnamon raisin bread was one culinary experience she didn't really care to repeat.

"How about after you make the sandwiches? Are you free then?" Michelle asked Andrea.

"Yes, I'm free. Tracey's in Vacation Bible School, and Bethie's going shopping with Grandma McCann right after she wakes up from her nap."

"Good. Do you think you could help me out at the coffee shop?"

"I could do that. Do you want me to wait tables?"

"Yes, until we close. And after that, if you want, you can help us bake."

"You want *me* to help you bake?"

"Yes. We need to make some more whippersnapper cookies. Lisa and I were talking about that yesterday, after we locked up at the shop. People have been asking for them."

"They *have*?" Andrea looked inordinately pleased when Michelle nodded. "Oh, then of course I'll help. Maybe I can even think up a new whippersnapper cookie when I get back home tonight."

Chapter
Twenty-one

"You're right, dear," Delores said, closing the bag with their lunch tightly and reaching back to drop it on the back seat. "It's mint jelly."

"You're sure?"

"Yes, I'm sure. I don't think I've ever seen any other jelly that's bright green."

"Neither have I. It's got to be mint. Was it on cinnamon raisin bread?"

"Yes. Shall I throw the sack out the window?"

"No!"

"You mean . . . you're actually going to eat the sandwiches?"

"No, but I don't want to get pulled over for littering. We can always pass out the sandwiches to any homeless people we meet."

"But, dear . . . they're already homeless. Would it be fair to make them eat Andrea's sandwiches, too?"

Hannah laughed, but she kept her hands on the wheel and her eyes on the road. This was the first time she'd driven since the accident that had killed Keith Branson and she was being extra careful. "You're right, Mother. We'll just drop them in the first trash can we come to."

"Do you think we should write a warning on the sack?"

"No, Mother. They're not poison or anything like that. And they're not unhealthy. They're just . . . unpalatable."

"That's a very nice way to put it, dear. And they *were* beautifully wrapped. Andrea used the prettiest foil with little pine trees all over it. She must have picked it up at Christmas. I don't think they make printed foil any other time of the year. What do you have in the little bakery boxes?"

"Butterscotch Brickle Bar Cookies. One box is for the two officers we're going to meet, and the other box is for the woman you're going to interview."

Delores looked slightly dubious. "I can understand bringing the officers something, but why are you going to give bar cookies to a streetwalker?"

"Because everybody likes cookies and it might make her trust us a bit more."

"Oh. I guess that makes sense, especially since I doubt that any of the men she meets bring her anything. It's certainly a nice gesture, dear."

They rode in silence for a few minutes and Hannah thought about what a good morning she'd had. It had started out beautifully when she'd walked down the hall to the kitchen at a quarter to five and found the coffee ready and Michelle just removing the piping hot Bacon, Egg, and Cheddar Toast Cups from the oven.

After a delicious breakfast, Hannah had turned on the exercise machine and set the treadmill at a speed that wouldn't be too exerting for her. She hadn't gone more than five steps before Moishe jumped up to prance in front of her. He appeared to really enjoy the exercise and she'd stayed on the machine for longer than she had intended. Then she'd taken a quick shower while Michelle did her workout, dressed for work, and the moment Michelle had showered and dressed, they'd driven to The Cookie Jar for the daily baking.

At eight-thirty sharp, a half hour before they were due to open for business, both Andrea and Delores had joined them in the kitchen. Hannah had been dreading this wedding planning meeting, but Delores had kept her word. She'd chosen the flowers, yellow roses, and decided that the bridesmaid dresses should be ice blue, a shade lighter than the brushed satin suit she planned to wear. The wedding colors would be yellow and blue, two of Doc's favorite colors. She'd even decided on the tableware, invitations, place cards and decorations, and the menu for the reception dinner. All this had taken less than ten minutes. It seemed that Delores had planned it all out right after Hannah had concluded their mother-daughter talk. Everything was set in stone. Delores had sworn to that. And the pressure was off for the Swensen-Knight nuptials as far as Lisa and all three of the Swensen sisters were concerned.

Hannah was smiling as she drove down the city streets. Everything had gone beautifully so far. She could only hope that this afternoon with one of Keith Branson's prostitutes would go equally well.

"I think this is the place, dear," Delores said, interrupting Hannah's happy thoughts. "Yes! I'm sure it is!"

"Where?" Hannah asked, slowing the car.

"Over there on the left, right next to the car wash. Do you think that's the green Chevy van that Stella told us about?"

"It could be. Let's drive by and see. If they pull out and follow us, we'll know it's them and they picked us up."

Hannah drove by slowly, as if she were looking for a parking spot. They hadn't gone more than a few yards before the green van backed out of its spot and began to follow them. "It's them," she said to Delores, slowing so that the van could pass them.

"How do you know?"

"They're too polite. Any other driver would have honked at me for going so slow."

Hannah followed the van for about a mile before they pulled over and stopped. Stella had told them to drive forward half a block and park. Then they were supposed to wait while the two officers drove past the block where Keith Branson's girls worked and came back to reconnoiter with them.

"I don't look too prim and proper, do I, dear?" Delores asked, flipping down the mirror on the visor and glancing at her reflection.

"Prim and proper?" Hannah turned to look. Delores was wearing a pair of designer jeans and a silk blouse. "No, Mother. You don't look prim and proper at all. But you may look a little too . . ." She paused to think of exactly the right word.

"Too what, dear?"

"Too . . . fashionable."

"But I deliberately dressed down!"

Hannah laughed. "Yes, but your idea of dressing down is most people's idea of dressing up."

"Oh." Delores was silent for a moment. "Would it help if I changed shoes?"

Hannah glanced at her mother's shoes. They were perfectly plain, but quite obviously expensive black flats. "No, but I would lose the watch and the bracelet."

"But what shall I do with them?"

"Put them in your purse. We're not going to take our purses anyway. We'll give them to the officers in the van to watch."

"But what if I need my credit card?"

"You can't use it, anyway. We're going by fake names, remember?"

"Of course. You're right, dear. But what shall we do for money?"

"I've got cash in my pocket."

Delores considered that for a moment. "That's probably wisest, considering the neighborhood. It's certainly not very . . . genteel."

Hannah was about to laugh at what she thought was an attempt at humor on her mother's part, but then she noticed that Delores was shivering slightly. The temperature inside the car was on the warm side since the air-conditioning wasn't all that efficient. Why was Delores shivering if she wasn't cold?

Reality dawned for Hannah and she came very close to gasping in surprise. Coming here was completely out of her mother's sphere. Delores had lived in Lake Eden all her life and she'd always been surrounded by family and friends. She knew about the homeless, and drug dealers, and gangs. You couldn't live in the world of today without hearing about the underbelly of society, but experiencing it firsthand was another matter entirely.

"Why don't you stay with the officers, Mother?" Hannah said, doing her best to sound convincing. "I can take care of this interview myself."

Delores squared her shoulders. "No, dear. I'm going with you. It's just as I told you last night. I can help and I want to do it."

"But you won't be much help if you're scared to death," Hannah said. The words hung in the air just long enough to make Hannah wish she'd phrased her comment more tactfully. "What I mean is . . ." she started to say, but her mother interrupted her.

"I know what you mean," Delores said, reaching out to pat Hannah's arm. "You think that I'll be more of a liability than an asset. But that won't happen, Hannah. You'll see. I have a plan and I'm determined to go with you. I refuse to argue about it, so let's just drop the subject and concentrate on what we came here to do."

There was steel in those carefully chosen words, and Hannah recognized it. Her mother was indeed determined and Hannah could do nothing to change her mind. "All right, Mother," she said, giving in as gracefully as she could.

262   *Joanne Fluke*

And then, before the situation could grow even more uncomfortable, the green van pulled up beside them and the
passenger window lowered.

"Hi," Hannah said, reaching in the back to retrieve the
bakery boxes and handing one through the open window.
"These are for you. Thanks for being here for us."

"What's in there?" the driver leaned over to ask her.

"Something called Butterscotch Brickle Bar Cookies.
They've got chocolate and butterscotch."

"Hey, thanks!" the officer in the passenger seat said. "You
got a live one out there. Bleached blonde, red dress, black
boots. Name's Starlet."

"Scarlet?" Hannah asked.

"No, Starlet. Like a movie *star*."

"Oh. Okay. Starlet."

"She's real young. Maybe sixteen. We picked her up a
couple of months ago, and her pimp bailed her out. That one
was a piece of work!"

"Starlet is a piece of work?" Delores asked him.

"No, the pimp. At least *he's* gone. And good riddance."

Hannah wasn't sure what to say, so she said nothing. The
officer obviously didn't know that she was the one who'd
killed Starlet's pimp.

"Did someone else take his place?" Delores asked.

" 'Course they did. This new one's a woman. We hear
she's one nasty . . ." he stopped, obviously considering the
fact that he was talking to a genuine lady. "One nasty you-
know-what," he finished. "Name's Lady Die."

"Like Princess Di?" Delores asked.

"No. It's Lady Die, like in make you dead. Which one of
you is going to talk to Starlet?"

"Both of us are," Delores answered before Hannah could
even open her mouth. "Where's Starlet now?"

"Around the corner and a block up. We'll stay here with

the windows rolled down. Did Mike give you that whistle to blow?"

"I've got it," Hannah said, patting her pocket. "Will you take our purses with you?"

"Sure thing." He grabbed the two purses Hannah handed him. "How about that sack in the back? Anything valuable in there?"

"Just a couple of sandwiches."

"Want us to take them? Somebody could get 'em if you leave 'em back there. Most people around here can break into a locked car in thirty seconds flat and eat your lunch."

"More power to them," Delores said, sotto voce. Hannah turned to grin at her and then she turned back to answer. "That's okay. They probably need them more than we do and we're going to stop for something to eat on the way home anyway."

"Hi there." Delores walked right up to the smiling girl in the red dress who had struck a sexy pose on the street corner. "I hope you're doing what I think you're doing."

Hannah came close to groaning. Whatever was her mother doing?!

"What'cha think I'm doing, Church Lady?" Starlet asked, never losing her smile.

"I'm hoping you're soliciting on this corner. And I'm not a church lady. I'm a romance writer."

Starlet's smile slipped slightly. "You're a . . . what?"

"I'm a romance writer and I write Regency romances. That's why I need to interview an opera girl."

Starlet gave a derisive laugh. "Then you're out of luck! All we got around here are pimps, Johns, and pieces like me!"

"Not opera, dear," Delores said sweetly. "Opera *girl*. And you just said that was what you were."

Starlet's smile slipped all the way and she suddenly looked young and almost naïve. "Opera girl, huh? Maybe I shouldn't ask 'cause I'm probably talking to a wack job here, but what's this opera girl thing?"

"That's the name they gave to ladies of the night in Regency England."

Hannah watched Starlet's face. She was beginning to look a bit curious. Perhaps her mother's approach wasn't a mistake, after all.

"Where's Regents England?"

Hannah held her breath. Here's where Delores could blow it. If she corrected Starlet, her curiosity might disappear to the point where she'd tell them to get lost, that they were hurting her business.

"It's England, the same England that the Beatles came from."

"Oh, yeah. But the Beatles were a long time ago."

"I know. And Regency England was even longer ago than the Beatles."

"You mean like ancient history?" Starlet asked, clearly fascinated now.

"That's exactly what I mean." Delores smiled at her. "I write about romance way back before they even had electric lights. My story is about a prince who falls in love with an opera girl and wants to marry her."

"Really?" Starlet began to smile. "I like that." But as Hannah watched, her eyes narrowed. "Wait a minute. Does this book of yours have a happy ending?"

"Oh, my yes! The prince ends up marrying the opera girl and she becomes a princess."

"Oh, good! I think I might want to read that book. I don't get time to read much, but that one sounds good."

"I hope it will be, and that's why I need your help. I need

to know what life is like out here on the street, so I can write my opera girl's thoughts before she meets and marries the prince."

"Yeah, but I don't know what it was like on the street way back then. All I know is what it's like now."

"That's good enough for me. I really don't think it's changed that much. Do you?"

"Naw! Men are all the same." Starlet fluffed her hair and put on her concept of an enticing smile at the sole male occupant of a car as he drove slowly past. "So ask me a question, church lady, but make it fast. I'm working this corner and things are gonna start to pick up soon."

"I know. I'd like to interview you, and I know I'm cutting into your working day. That's the reason I want to pay you for your time."

"You want to *pay* me?" Suddenly Starlet was intensely interested. "How much?"

"Fifty dollars an hour. And if it doesn't take an hour, you can keep the whole fifty. I really need your advice for my story."

"Oh! Well! That's just fine with me! Go ahead. Ask me questions."

"Not here," Delores said. "It's much too noisy. I was thinking of somewhere quieter."

Hannah held her breath. This was a mistake on her mother's part. Now Starlet might become suspicious. After all, there were two of them and only one of her.

Starlet's eyes narrowed. "You mean . . . quiet like in a hotel room?"

"No, dear. I was talking about a coffee shop where we can get something to eat. Or . . . even a bar if it's quiet this time of day. Do you know any place like that?"

Starlet smiled as she nodded and this time the smile was genuine. "Sure, I do. And that's okay then." Starlet turned to give Hannah an assessing look. "Who's the other one? Is she coming, too? And what's in that box?"

"Butterscotch Brickle Bar Cookies," Hannah answered, flipping the top on the box to show her. "Have one. They're really good."

Starlet looked suspicious again. "Only if you have one, too." She turned to Delores. "And you, too."

"I don't blame you for being cautious," Hannah said, taking a bar cookie from the box and biting into it. "These are my absolute favorites. I baked them this morning." She held out the box to Delores. "Mother?"

"Mother?" Starlet asked, grabbing a bar cookie the moment Delores had taken a bite of hers.

"Oh, I'm sorry, dear," Delores said. "I forgot to introduce you. My name is Kathryn and this is my daughter, Anne. And what shall Anne and I call you? This interview is completely confidential so we don't need to know your real name if you don't want to tell us."

"Okay. Just call me Starlet. That's what they all call me, but it's not my real name."

"That's fine with us."

Starlet turned to Hannah. "You made these, Anne? They're as good as a candy bar."

"Thanks," Hannah said, smiling at her.

"Where shall we go, Starlet?" Delores asked, getting back to business.

"Little Dingo's is just down the block. He'll give us a booth in the back and make sure nobody bothers us. Let me stash those candy bars here, though. The other girls know better than to touch my stuff and Little Dingo won't let you bring in food. I'll give 'em back to you later."

Hannah shook her head. "They're yours. I brought them for you."

"Whoa! Thanks, Anne."

Starlet left her corner and raced off to what looked like a vacant building. She opened the door, ducked in, and came right back out again. There was a huge smile on her face and it was clear that she could scarcely believe her good fortune. That made Hannah wonder if this was the first time anyone had ever given her anything without expecting something in return.

"Is Little Dingo's okay with you, Anne?" Starlet asked her.

"It's fine with me. I'm just along to take notes and check off that list of questions Mother gave me to make sure she doesn't forget to ask something. I'm acting as Mother's secretary, but you're getting paid. I'm not."

Starlet laughed. "That's the breaks, " she said, and led them down the street.

Less than five minutes later, they were settled in the back circular booth of the grungiest bar Hannah had ever seen in her life. The floor was wavy with the residue of spilled drinks and other fluids of unknown origin that had probably never been mopped up, and the tabletop was sticky with dried substances that Hannah didn't want to try to identify. The walls were dingy and reeked with an odor that combined cigarette smoke and urine in unequal proportions, and the lighting was almost nonexistent.

"It's very dark in here," Delores said, and Hannah noticed that her mother was deliberately not touching the tabletop. Hannah wasn't touching it, either. She was too busy wondering whether the whistle Mike had given her would work in here to summon the officers who were waiting for them.

"Yeah, it's dark," Starlet said. "Dingo wants it that way. Some of the guys that come here don't want to be seen, if you know what I mean?"

"I know exactly what you mean," Delores said. "Do they serve food here, Starlet?"

"Yeah, but I wouldn't eat it. I know a guy that used to cook here and he told me there were rat traps all over the kitchen. And I know for a fact that the new cook bangs on a pan when he opens the door to scare all the roaches back into hiding. If you want something to eat, you should stick with things in bags like chips or pretzels. And don't get anything to drink in a glass. Dingo's got beer and wine in bottles, and that's okay if you drink it right out of the bottle."

"Thanks for the advice," Hannah said. "What do you want to drink, Starlet?"

"Oh, I don't drink when I'm working. I gotta be on my toes, you know? You got to order something though," Starlet informed them. "Dingo put us in this special booth and he'll expect some kind of payment for it. It's not like he's renting space here, you know."

But I bet he could, Hannah thought. *And maybe he does. And that could be why this is called the "special" booth.*

"Of course we'll order something," Delores said, even though they were the only customers in the bar and it wasn't like there was a waiting line for the special booth. "Does he have water in bottles?"

Starlet shook her head. "He doesn't carry anything fancy like that. It's just beer and wine in the bottles. He waters the hard stuff so don't ask for that. Besides, then you got to drink it out of one of his glasses and you don't want to do that."

"How about Coke?" Hannah asked her.

"Coke?" Starlet repeated, and her eyes narrowed again.

"Coke, like regular Coke, or Diet Coke. Does he have that in plastic bottles or cans?"

Starlet look relieved at the answer and she smiled. "Sure, he does. And it comes in cans. He doesn't have Diet Coke though. People around here don't get enough to eat anyway, so they don't have to go on diets. No offense, okay Anne?"

Hannah bristled slightly, but she took care not to let Starlet see that her comment had hit home. "No offense taken," she said and handed Starlet two twenty-dollar bills. "How about if you go up to the bar and get all three of us something safe to drink. Spend it all and that should make Dingo happy."

"Oh, it will. I'll be back with the stuff. Don't start without me, okay?"

Hannah waited until Starlet was well out of earshot and then she leaned close to Delores. "I bet she says that to all her customers," she quipped, and then she wished she hadn't said anything. Delores might not appreciate her slightly off-color comment at this juncture.

But Delores laughed. "I think you're probably right. I'll have to remember to tell Doc what you said. He'll get a real kick out of it."

Hannah was gratified. Even though her mother was still visibly nervous, Delores hadn't lost her sense of humor. She was doing a really good job with Starlet, so far. The girl had bought the cover story Delores had given her and Hannah had no doubt that they would get the information they needed from her.

"Okay, we got all this," Starlet said, coming back to the booth much faster than they had expected. "Just look."

Hannah looked. Three cans of Coke and three packages of barbecued potato chips in bags sporting a brand Hannah had never heard of. Forty dollars was a lot to pay for three Cokes and three small bags of off-brand potato chips, but it would be worth it if Starlet kept cooperating with them.

"Nice," Hannah said, picking up a can and popping the top.

"Thank you, dear," Delores said to Starlet and then she opened her can. "I'm not really hungry so you can have my chips."

"Mine, too," Hannah added. She wasn't entirely sure that the microscopic bugs that were bound to live on the tabletop couldn't somehow crawl into sealed bags.

"You sure?" Starlet asked her.

"I'm sure," Hannah said. "You go right ahead. And while you're eating, I'll read you the first of Mother's questions."

BUTTERSCOTCH BRICKLE BAR COOKIES

Preheat oven to 350 degrees F., rack in the middle position.

2 cups *(no need to sift)* all-purpose flour
1 cup cold salted butter *(2 sticks, $\frac{1}{2}$ pound)*
$\frac{1}{2}$ cup brown sugar *(pack it down when you measure it)*

-----

2 sticks salted butter *(1 cup, 8 ounces, $\frac{1}{2}$ pound)*
1 cup brown sugar *(pack it down when you measure it)*
$\frac{1}{3}$ cup butterscotch ice cream topping *(I used Smuckers)*
1 cup butterscotch chips *(6-ounce package by weight—I used Nestle)*
1 cup semi-sweet OR milk chocolate chips *(6-ounce package by weight—I used Nestle)*
$\frac{1}{2}$ cup finely chopped salted nuts *(OPTIONAL—I used pecans, but any type of nut will do.)*

Line a 9-inch by 13-inch cake pan with heavy duty foil. Start with a big piece of foil so that you will have enough to go up the sides and leave little "ears" of foil

sticking out. That way, when your bar cookies are cool, you can simply pull the foil up and lift them out of the pan.

Spray the foil with Pam or another nonstick cooking spray. *(You want to be able to peel it off later, after the bar cookies cool.)*

Put 1 cup of flour in the food processor.

Cut 1 stick of cold salted butter into 8 pieces and arrange it over the flour in the food processor.

Sprinkle the second cup of all-purpose flour over the chunks of butter in the food processor.

Cut the second stick of cold salted butter into 8 pieces and arrange it over the flour in the food processor.

Sprinkle the $\frac{1}{2}$ cup of brown sugar over the chunks of butter.

Process with the steel blade in an on and off motion until the resulting mixture looks like coarse cornmeal.

Pour the mixture into the prepared cake pan and press it down with your impeccably clean palms or with the back of a metal spatula.

Bake at 350 degrees F. for 15 minutes. Then remove from the oven and set the cake pan on a wire rack to cool, but DON'T SHUT OFF THE OVEN!

Spray the inside of a ⅓-cup measuring cup with Pam or another nonstick cooking spray. *(This will make for quick and easy removal when you pour in the butterscotch ice cream topping.)*

Pour or spoon the butterscotch ice cream topping into the measuring cup and have it ready at the side of the stovetop.

Combine the butter with the brown sugar in a saucepan. Bring it to a boil over medium high heat on the stovetop, stirring constantly. *(A full boil will have breaking bubbles all over the surface of the pan.)* Boil it for exactly five *(5)* minutes, stirring it constantly. If it sputters too much, you can reduce the heat. If it starts to lose the boil, you can increase the heat. Just don't stop stirring.

When the time is up, pull the saucepan off the heat and onto a cold burner. Add the butterscotch sauce quickly and stir it in quickly.

Pour this mixture over the baked crust as evenly as you can.

Hannah's Note: When I do this, I pour about 4 lines of hot brickle that run the length of the pan and then turn the pan to pour about 4 lines of hot brickle that run the width of the pan. If your lines of brickle don't completely cover the crust, spread them out a bit with a heat-resistant rubber spatula. Work quickly before they harden too much. Don't worry if there are some gaps. They will spread out a little when you bake them in the oven.

Slide the pan into the oven and bake the bar cookies at 350 degrees F. for another 10 *(ten)* minutes.

While the pan of butterscotch brickle is baking, put the butterscotch chips and the chocolate chips in a bowl. Mix them together with your impeccably clean fingers.

When the time is up, remove the pan from the oven and sprinkle the butterscotch and chocolate chip mixture over the top. Give the chips a minute or two to melt and then spread them out as evenly as you can with a heat-resistant rubber spatula, a wooden paddle, or a frosting knife.

If you decided to use chopped nuts, sprinkle them on now while the chips are still soft.

Slip the pan into the refrigerator and chill it thoroughly.

When the pan has chilled, peel the foil from the cookies and break them into random-sized pieces.

Yield: A whole cake pan full of yummy treats that are a cross between a cookie and a candy.

Michelle says that when I make these, it always reminds her of Christmas.

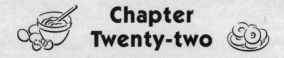

Chapter Twenty-two

"Good job, Mother," Hannah said, glancing at her watch as she parked in front of her mother's house. It was six-thirty at night and that was less than an hour later than she usually got home from The Cookie Jar.

"Thank you, dear. I must say, I had a good time today. I can hardly wait to tell Doc all about it!"

As Hannah watched, the front door of her mother's house opened and Doc stood there, waiting for Delores. "Doc's at your house?" Hannah asked, realizing that her mother must have given him a key.

"Yes, dear. It's Wednesday and we always stay here on Wednesday nights. It's my place Monday, Wednesday, and Friday. And his place Tuesday, Thursday, and the weekends."

"TMI, Mother."

"What is TM . . . whatever those initials were that you just rattled off?"

"TMI. It stands for Too Much Information. I don't need to know where you are every night of the week, and I certainly don't need to know that you're spending nights with Doc!"

Delores gave an exasperated sigh. "Doc's right. I raised a prude."

"What?!"

"Both Doc and I agree that you'd be much happier if you had a fulfilling love life."

Hannah's mouth dropped open and she closed it again with a snap. She took a deep breath and swallowed hard. "Mother!"

"Don't Mother me. It's true."

"Maybe it is, but you shouldn't be telling me that. What are you encouraging? Promiscuity?"

"Of course not. I just want you to settle down with a man who loves you. And I want you to be as happy as I am."

Hannah thought about that for a moment. Actually, she wanted the same thing for herself. The problem was that she seemed incapable of choosing which man it would be. But there was no way she wanted to get into that now, at six-thirty at night, after a long day with her mother. It was best to either ignore it, or make a joke of it.

"Am I correct in assuming that you're saying this because you love me and want me to be happy?"

"You certainly are."

"And am I correct to think that Doc also loves me and wants me to be happy?"

"Of course he does.

"Then you're right, Mother," Hannah said.

"I am?" Delores was clearly surprised at the admission. She seemed pleased for a moment, but then, as she thought about it, she looked a bit dubious, as if she were waiting for the other shoe to drop.

"Yes, you're right," Hannah said, getting ready to fling the other shoe at the floor. "I want to settle down with a man who loves me and wants me to be happy. And you said Doc loves me and wants me to be happy. Unfortunately . . . Doc's already taken."

* * *

Hannah pulled into her garage at seven o'clock on the dot. She'd shared a good laugh with her mother and Doc, and her long day was almost over. Michelle was here and Lonnie's car was parked in her second space. Obviously, Lonnie had brought Michelle home from The Cookie Jar and they were both waiting for her upstairs. Perhaps they'd even have food. That would be wonderful. Delores had decided that she wanted to drive straight home to Lake Eden and not stop to eat on the way. That meant Hannah hadn't eaten anything since breakfast and she was as starved as a bear after a long winter's hibernation.

When she'd locked the loaner car and climbed the steps to ground level, Hannah glanced at the visitor's parking lot. It was full and that was unusual for seven o'clock on a weekday night. She didn't really look at the individual cars until she noticed a Hummer parked illegally on the ring road that ran around the pond. Only one person parked there if Hannah's parking spots were taken. And that was because the guard at the gate knew his car and wouldn't call it in. Mike was here.

Hannah turned and her eyes scanned the cars in the visitor's lot. Yes, Norman was here. And so was Andrea. It seemed it was company night again, and she'd been planning to have a bite to eat with a glass of wine, and then relax on the couch in front of the television with Moishe purring in her lap.

How much did her legs weigh anyway? Hannah thought about that as she climbed the stairs. Weren't people's legs supposed to be a quarter of their weight, or something like that? But that didn't make sense. Then her legs would weigh . . . no, she didn't want to think about dividing how much she weighed by any percentage at all. If she did that, she'd have to recall what she'd weighed the last time she'd stepped on the scale, and that was a three-digit figure she'd rather forget. Her legs weighed a lot, though. With each step she climbed, they seemed heavier and heavier. She knew that was probably because she was dreading the thought of acting bright and cheerful for company. Although they were her best friends and dearest family members, and she loved each and every one of them, she truly didn't feel like putting on a happy face when she was so utterly exhausted.

There's nothing for it but to do it, Hannah repeated one of her great-grandmother Elsa's favorite sayings in her mind. She forced a smile on her lips and told herself to *Always look on the bright side*, another one of her great-grandmother's favorite sayings. They would have eaten already and saved her some leftovers. And Andrea certainly couldn't finish a whole jug of wine by herself . . . or could she?

As she neared the door of her condo, Hannah could hear voices and laughter coming from inside. She stopped at the door and raised her hand to knock. Then she dropped her arm to her side again, feeling rather foolish about what she had been about to do. It was her condo. She owned it. She didn't have to knock on her own door!

Just then the door opened and Michelle stood there looking as cute as a button in white shorts and a royal blue top. "Hi, Hannah. I thought I heard you coming up the stairs. Kick off your shoes and go make yourself comfortable on the couch while I pour a glass of wine for you. We've got food, too. I came back here at noon and put dinner in the Crock-Pot and Andrea brought her new whippersnapper cookies. They're really, really good."

Hannah walked in and greeted everyone with a smile. Then she went straight to her spot on the couch and sat down. Her earlier ruminations seemed silly in retrospect.

As usual, Hannah was the filling in a Mike and Norman sandwich, sitting between them on the middle cushion, but tonight she didn't mind at all. It might have had something to do with the fact that Norman started rubbing the kinks out of her neck while Mike spread some of his Busy Day Pate on a cracker for her. Michelle came in to hand her a chilled glass of wine and a full plate of food, and Hannah felt her spirits rise from the soles of her feet all the way up to the ceiling. She had thought she was bone-tired, but now she was beginning to feel happy and full of energy. What a great welcome! It was wonderful to be home with the people who loved you. As the conversation flowed around her and she ate Michelle's excellent dinner, she felt renewed and refreshed.

"Try my new cookies, Hannah," Andrea urged her. "They're called Golden Raisin Whippersnappers and I really like them."

Hannah's eyebrows shot up in surprise. "But you don't *like* raisins."

"I know, but I like these cookies. I think it's the golden raisins. It's the brown ones I don't really like."

Hannah reached for a cookie and took a bite, chewing and swallowing quickly. "These are great, Andrea! They're as light as air and they have just the right amount of sweetness. Is that cinnamon I taste?"

"Yes. It's in the powdered sugar I used when I coated them. I figured cinnamon went with raisins."

"Oh, it does," Michelle jumped into the conversation. "And everybody who had one at the coffee shop thought so, too. Andrea brought them in for us to try, and they were a huge hit."

"Then we'll add them to the menu," Hannah promised, making an executive decision that she knew would please her sister.

"Do we have to leave some for Bill, or can I have another couple of cookies?" Mike asked Andrea.

"Help yourself," Andrea answered. "You don't have to leave any for him."

Hannah came close to groaning. It seemed the ongoing

feud was still going on. And the longer it lasted, the more difficult it would be to resolve.

"Still mad at him?" Mike asked.

"Yes, but I left two dozen on the kitchen counter for him when I left this morning. And I left another two dozen for Grandma McCann and the girls."

Hannah breathed a breath of relief. Andrea might not know it yet, but the feud was nearing its demise. If Andrea was leaving cookies for Bill, it wouldn't last much longer.

"Are you rested enough to tell us what happened in the Cities today?" Andrea asked. "I don't want to rush you, but my curiosity is killing me."

"Let me get you another glass of wine first," Mike said to Hannah. "How about you, Andrea? Do you want a refill?"

"Yes. I just love this wine, but make it only half a glass, please. I promised Tracey I'd be home by eight so we could read a chapter in her new book before bedtime."

"I'll get it," Michelle said, jumping to her feet before Mike could even get up from the couch. This made Hannah smile. Michelle knew Mike would probably grab the jug and bring it into the living room, never suspecting that they were keeping the brand, price, and source of Andrea's favorite wine a secret from her.

When the coffee cups and glasses were filled, or half-filled in Andrea's case, Hannah told her story. She made it entertaining, but she also gave them the facts they'd learned from Starlet.

"So the upshot was," she concluded, "Starlet confirmed the rumor that one of Keith Branson's girls died from a beating. The girl's name was Sugar, but that was her street name and Starlet didn't know her real name. She also said that she'd heard that Keith was dead and at first she was glad about that. But then Keith's girlfriend, Lady Die, had taken over, and she was even worse than Keith had been."

Andrea looked shocked at this information. "I didn't know that they had women pimps."

"Oh, yeah," Mike said. "Sometimes the women are even tougher on the girls than the men."

"Starlet said the word on the street was that Lady Die was in the hotel room with Keith when he beat up on Sugar. Starlet said she heard that Lady Die was the one who beat her so badly, she died."

Norman just sighed and shook his head. "It's a terrible life for these girls. And most of them get into it young, before they know what's really going on. They don't learn the truth until it's too late for them to get out."

Hannah reached out to squeeze his hand. Norman looked very sad and she knew he was remembering the volunteer work he'd done at the Seattle dental clinic for the unfortunate people who lived on the street.

"There was only one more thing that Starlet told us and it's important," Hannah went on. "She said Keith left last week for some little town because he was chasing a girl who ran away so he could take her back."

"Who?" Mike asked.

"Someone she knew as Honey, but I'm afraid that doesn't help us much. We don't even know if Honey passed through Lake Eden. Keith may have just stopped here on his way to somewhere else."

"How about the diamond in the tooth?" Norman asked her. "Did Starlet know anything about that?"

"No. Starlet was relatively new to the street. She said she'd been working for less than a year, and Keith had the diamond in his tooth when she met him."

"Where did she meet him?" Mike asked.

"In her hometown in Wisconsin. She didn't mention the name of the town, and we didn't want to press her."

"Okay," Mike said. "How about the ring?"

"She knew nothing about that. She said she didn't think that Keith ever wore a ring. I think Doc's theory is right and that Keith picked it up after the man who fought with him lost it."

"Did she say any more about Lady Die?" Lonnie asked.

"Not really, just that she was really nasty and mean."

"I'll call Stella and give her Lady Die's name," Mike said. "Or better yet, I'll talk to some of the guys I know in Vice."

"If you talk to Stella, thank her for me," Hannah told him. "And . . . ask her if there's any way she can arrest Starlet for something so that they can bring her into the station. Lady Die sounds dangerous and if she finds out that Starlet talked to us, Starlet could be in big trouble."

Mike shook his head. "It's not going to work, Hannah. Stella's got enough juice to do it, but she can't keep Starlet there indefinitely."

"I know, but maybe Starlet will tell Stella where she's from and she can get out of Minneapolis and go back there."

"I'll mention it, but it's probably not going to happen," Mike said and he sounded sad and very weary. "You can't rescue somebody who doesn't want to be rescued. And it doesn't sound to me like Starlet wants to go back home quite yet."

Hannah thought that over for a moment. Perhaps Mike was right. Starlet had expressed no desire to go back home and she had seemed content to stay on her corner.

"You did a good job, Hannah," Norman said, "and so did your mother."

"That's right," Mike agreed, and Hannah knew he was making a deliberate effort to be upbeat for her benefit. "You can't save them all, Hannah."

"I know. It's just a shame, that's all."

Mike gave a humorous chuckle. "Why do you think I got out of Vice and became a homicide detective? Murderers are a lot more fun than pimps and prostitutes."

They all stared at Mike for a moment and then Hannah burst into laughter. That broke the ice and everyone laughed.

"I've got to go," Mike said when they'd quieted down. "Hannah's tired and I've got an early day tomorrow."

"You're back at the department?" Andrea asked him, and Hannah noticed that she sounded hopeful.

"Nope. Your husband's as stubborn as a mule, but he'll come around eventually. I've just got some loose ends to tie up, that's all."

"And I have to read a whole chapter to Tracey." Andrea stood up and turned to Mike. "Walk me down to my car?"

"Sure thing."

"Both of us will," Norman said, rising to his feet. "I've got an early day, too."

Lonnie glanced at his watch. "So do I, and it starts at midnight. They've got me on swing shift tonight."

Once goodbyes were said, the living room emptied out quickly. In the space of a couple of minutes, Michelle and Hannah were the only two left.

"It's bedtime for me," Michelle said, yawning widely. "How about you, Hannah?"

It had to be true that yawns were contagious because Hannah yawned, too. "I'll turn in now." She looked down at the cat who was curled up in her lap. "And I think Moishe has already turned in."

There was a sleepy yowl from Moishe as she stood up to follow Michelle down the hall. "Come on, then," Hannah told him. "I'm so tired tonight, you can probably steal my pillow and I won't even notice it's gone."

GOLDEN RAISIN WHIPPERSNAPPER COOKIES

Preheat oven to 350 degrees F., rack in the middle position.

For the Cookies:

$\frac{1}{2}$ cup boiling water

1 teaspoon brandy extract

$\frac{1}{2}$ cup golden raisins *(Andrea uses golden raisins, but you could use regular raisins if you prefer)*

1 large egg

2 cups thawed, not frozen Cool Whip *(measure this—Andrea said her tub of Cool Whip contained a little over 3 cups.)*

1 package *(approximately 18 ounces)* spice cake mix *(Andrea used Duncan Hines)*

For Rolling Cookie Balls:

$\frac{1}{2}$ cup powdered *(confectioner's)* sugar

$\frac{1}{2}$ teaspoon ground cinnamon

Either boil the half-cup of water on the stove and then pour it into a microwave-safe bowl OR heat the half-cup of water in a microwave-safe bowl *(Andrea used a one-cup Pyrex measuring cup)* for 60 seconds

on HIGH. This might not be boiling, but it will be hot enough for your purposes.

Add the brandy extract to your hot water.

Sprinkle in the raisins and set the bowl on the counter while you prepare the cookie sheets.

Chill 2 teaspoons from your silverware drawer by sticking them in the freezer. You want them really icy cold. This will make it a lot easier to form the cookies after the dough is mixed.

Prepare your cookie sheets by spraying them with Pam or another nonstick cooking spray, or lining them with parchment paper, which you will then spray with Pam or another nonstick cooking spray.

Whisk the egg in a large mixing bowl.

Measure out 2 cups of Cool Whip and stir them into the egg.

Check your raisins to see if they've plumped up. If they have, drain them and then pat them dry with a paper towel. If they haven't plumped, give them a little more time before you drain them and dry them off.

When your raisins are plumped and drained, add them to the mixing bowl and stir them in by hand. Mix very gently and don't over-stir. You don't want to stir all the air out of the Cool Whip.

Sprinkle the cake mix over the top of your mixing bowl. Fold it in very gently, mixing only until everything is combined. The object here is to keep as much air in the cookie batter as possible.

Place the ½ cup of powdered sugar in a separate small bowl. *(You don't have to sift it unless it's got big lumps.)*

Add the cinnamon to the bowl and stir it all up with a fork. Mix until the cinnamon is thoroughly combined with the sugar.

Take your teaspoons out of the freezer and drop the cookie dough by chilled and rounded teaspoonfuls into the bowl of powdered sugar and cinnamon. Roll the cookie dough ball around in the bowl with your fingers to coat it on all sides.

Hannah's 1st Note: Roll only one cookie dough ball at a time. If you roll too many at once, they'll stick together and you'll have a real mess. This dough is very sticky, so you must keep your fingers coated with the sugar-cinnamon mixture.

Hannah's 2nd Note: If you're really having trouble with the sticky dough, refrigerate your mixing bowl and dough for one hour. Then take it out and try it again. If you do this, don't forget to turn off your oven. You can preheat it again a few minutes

before you take the cookie dough out of the refrigerator.

Place each coated cookie dough ball on the cookie sheets you've prepared, 12 cookies to each standard-size sheet.

Bake the cookies at 350 degrees F. for 12 to 15 minutes, or until they are firm to the touch when tapped very lightly on the top with a fingertip.

When the cookies have baked, take them out of the oven and let them cool on the cookie sheets for 2 minutes. Then remove them to a wire rack to cool completely.

Hannah's 3rd Note: If you used parchment paper, all you have to do is wait 2 minutes and then pull the whole sheet of parchment paper onto a wire cooling rack. Just leave the Golden Raisin Whippersnappers on the parchment paper until they're cool, and then simply peel them off.

Yield: 3 to 4 dozen delicious cookies, depending on cookie size.

Andrea likes these cookies even though she doesn't like raisins. I think it may be because of the brandy extract.

Chapter Twenty-three

Someone was shining a light in her eyes and she could hear trucks in the distance. Were the police interrogating her right next to a freeway? Hannah sat bolt upright in bed and blinked in the strong sunlight coming through her bedroom window. It was daylight and it wasn't Sunday. At least she didn't think it was Sunday. And if it wasn't Sunday, she'd overslept and she was late for work.

The trucks were still rumbling outside. They must be doing some construction work in the condo complex. That was very odd. She was on the homeowners' association board and she hadn't heard about any repairs or new construction.

The heavy equipment, whatever it was, must have frightened Moishe, because he was nowhere in sight. No Moishe on her pillow, no Moishe at the foot of the bed. No Moishe tunneled under the blankets and no Moishe on top of the dresser, staring at her with yellow eyes. But Moishe was blind in one eye. Doctor Hagaman had told her that. So how could he stare at her with yellow eyes if he could only see with one eye? But it would sound silly to say that Moishe was staring at her with his yellow eye when both of his eyes were yellow. And she'd never have known that he was blind in one eye if Doctor Hagaman hadn't told her. What should she say? Or should she say nothing since Moishe wasn't on top of the dresser and he wasn't staring at her, anyway?

It was too complicated a conundrum for this time of the morning, whatever time it was. Hannah managed to turn the body that suddenly seemed unwieldy to her, so that she could look at her digital alarm clock. "Ten-fifteen?!" she exclaimed so loudly that the sound bounced off her bedroom walls. The slits that had been her eyes opened all the way at her own loud exclamation, and that's when she saw the note propped up on her bedside table.

Coffee in thermos on kitchen table, it read. *Blue Apple Muffins in basket. Take your time. Lisa and I have it covered. She picked me up this morning.*

Hannah rubbed her eyes and reached for her slippers. Thank goodness for that truck! She might have slept until noon if the noise hadn't awakened her. But something strange was happening to the hum of the truck motor. It didn't appear to be coming from the outside, the way she'd initially thought. Now it seemed to be coming from the corner of her own bedroom!

Her head swiveled toward the sound and her eyes opened wide in surprise. Her exercise machine was on! The belt on the treadmill was running in an endless loop, and there was Moishe, walking on the exercise machine!

"Moishe!" Hannah could scarcely believe her eyes. "How did you ever manage to . . . ?" but she didn't finish her question as a logical explanation of this strange phenomenon suddenly occurred to her. Michelle must have come in to ride the treadmill this morning while Hannah was sound asleep. And when she was through, Michelle had forgotten to shut off the exercise machine.

The lure of hot coffee and Blue Apple Muffins, whatever they turned out to be, was too strong to deny. Hannah thrust her feet into her slippers, got up out of bed, and shut off the machine. "Come on, fitness fanatic," she said to Moishe. "It's time for both of us to have breakfast and then I have to get to work."

* * *

Hannah mixed up yet another batch of cookies and tried not to listen to Lisa's new story. Michelle must have told her Hannah's account of their encounter with Starlet because Lisa was telling the story to a packed house. It was great for business, Hannah would be the first to admit that, but it was also a bit embarrassing. Thank goodness Delores was busy at the hospital and hadn't popped in to have coffee with her!

"I just knew he was a pimp!" It was Grandma Knudson. Hannah recognized her voice. "Just wait until I tell my friend Nola that I was right! I'll make her eat fricasseed crow!"

There was a roar of laughter from the crowd and even Hannah had to smile as she measured out the cocoa for another batch of Triple Chocolate Cookies.

She'd just added the melted chocolate and butter to her dough when the phone rang and she hurried to answer it. "This is The Cookie Jar, Hannah speaking," she greeted the caller.

"I'm glad I caught you, Hannah."

It was Winnie Henderson's voice and Hannah knew it wouldn't be a long conversation. Winnie was always blunt and she didn't waste time on chatter. "Hi, Winnie," she said. "Do you have another grandson's birthday?"

"Nope. It came to me last night, Hannah."

"What's that, Winnie?"

"Where I'd seen that man in the picture before. Turns out I saw him right here on the ranch. He worked for me."

"He did?"

"You bet your boots, he did. I never forget a face. Nowadays it takes me longer to remember, but I never forget."

"I wish I could say that," Hannah told her. "When did the man work for you?"

"It's got to be ten or more years ago. He didn't last long. Less than two weeks the way I remember it. I had to fire him."

"Do you remember why?"

"I sure do. He was lazy and shiftless. Jimmy, the other ranch hand I hired that summer, couldn't stand him. Said the new guy was trouble with a capital T. His name was Keith-something-or-other. I don't remember his last name off-hand."

"Keith Branson?"

"That's right! Just like Branson, Missouri, where they put on all those shows. I went there once with one of my husbands. I don't recall which one. Anyway, I thought you'd want to know that I remembered about Keith."

"Thanks, Winnie. I'm glad you remembered."

"So am I. It was bothering me more than a sore tooth. I hate it when I can't remember something."

"So do I. How's Connor's hand?"

"It's in a cast and he's madder than a wet hen that he can't ride for a couple of weeks. That man lives for horses. Turns out his hand is broken. I told him that when I first saw it, but he didn't believe me. You know how men are. They just hate to admit that you're right and they're wrong. It must be in the genes."

"You're probably right."

"I tell you, Hannah, it takes a bulldozer to push that man into going to the doctor. I finally got fed up and told him I'd fire him if he wouldn't go."

Hannah was curious. "Would you really have fired him?"

"I don't know. And I'll never know because he went. Diablo really did a number on him, Hannah. Connor blames the storm that came up that morning. He thinks the lightning spooked him, but I think Diablo is just plain crazy. "

"That's too bad about Connor's hand."

"No, it's not. I got him doing left-handed things around the house. He's painting the living room right now and complaining like crazy about having to use the roller in his left hand. You should hear him. He keeps muttering about not being able to wear his ring and that silly copper bracelet he swears is good for his arthritis." There was a pause and then Winnie spoke again. "Say, Hannah? I just thought of something. How did you know that boy's last name was Branson?"

"Mike checked with a friend of his at the Minneapolis Police Department, and some members of the vice squad recognized him. Keith Branson was a pimp in the Cities."

Winnie laughed. "So Grandma Knudson was right! I bet that tickled her pink. But I guess it figures, now that I think about it. He was a real good-looking boy and he was trouble from the git-go. He used to sneak off to the swimming hole every afternoon to hang around with the local kids. Now that I know how he turned out, it makes me wonder if he was selling them dope or something like that."

Hannah had just finished slipping the pans of Triple Chocolate Cookies onto her revolving racks in her industrial oven when there was a knock at the back door. She listened for sounds from the coffee shop before she went to answer it, but there was only the buzz of conversation. Lisa had finished telling her story for this hour. If Delores was at the door, Hannah would keep her in the kitchen and warn Lisa not to start anther performance until she'd left.

"Loretta?" Hannah was clearly surprised when she opened the door and saw Loretta Richardson standing there. Loretta would have been the inspiration for the old song, "Silver Threads Among the Gold." She was a pretty woman in her middle fifties and her blond hair had begun to gray. Loretta had chosen not to color it because, as she'd told Carly and Michelle, Loretta's mother had possessed the most gorgeous head of silver-white hair she'd ever seen and Loretta was waiting to see if she had inherited the same lucky genes from her mother.

"Hi, Loretta," Hannah said, greeting her warmly. "Are you on break?"

"I am and I wanted to talk to you. Do you have a few minutes you can spare for me?"

"I've got all afternoon as long as you stay in the kitchen with me. All I'm doing today is baking."

"Smells good in here," Loretta said, stepping into the kitchen and taking the stool at the workstation that Hannah indicated.

"It's my second batch of Triple Chocolate Cookies. Would you like a couple from the first batch? They're cool by now."

"Thanks, Hannah. I'd love to taste them."

"Coffee with cream and one sugar, right?"

Loretta was clearly impressed that Hannah had remembered her preferences. "Do you remember how everyone who comes into the coffee shop takes their coffee?"

"No. Sometimes I goof. And that's why I always check." Hannah poured coffee from the kitchen pot, added cream and one sugar, and carried it over to Loretta. Then she took two cookies from the bakers rack, placed them on a napkin, and delivered those as well. "What's up, Loretta?" she asked.

"It's Carly. We had a talk last night and she told me that she confided her fears about Jennifer to you and Michelle."

"That's true. She did."

"She really doesn't think that Jennifer is her sister and I don't know what to do about that."

Hannah was silent, waiting for Loretta to go on. There were times to talk and times to listen, and this was a time to listen.

"She gave me her reasons and they do make some kind of sense, even to me, but it's simply not true, Hannah."

"What were her reasons?" Hannah asked, even though she already knew some of them.

"She was upset that Jennifer didn't remember the birthday present she'd given her before she'd left." Loretta shook her head. "I can see where that would be very disappointing to Carly, but even I didn't remember what Carly had given Jennifer that year. And Carly thought that Jennifer wasn't Jennifer because she liked to take baths when she was young and now she'd rather take a shower. They're all things like that, Hannah."

"I know. Carly told me. Michelle and I asked her if she could be jealous because Jennifer was back and you were so happy about it."

"What did she say?"

"She said she didn't think so, that she really liked Jennifer. It's just that she doesn't think Jennifer is her sister."

"But I *know* Jennifer is Carly's sister. I'm Jennifer's mother and she was my first baby. I didn't work back then and I was with her all day and all night. Jennifer is back even if Carly doesn't believe it, or doesn't want to believe it. I'd know my daughter anywhere!"

"And you don't think it could possibly be wishful thinking on your part?"

"No. The minute I set eyes on her again, I knew. Oh, she looks different now. A lot of years have passed, but I knew right away. You have no idea what a shock it was when she called and said she was coming home. I was so happy, I rushed right out to the store and I managed to find the fabric that I'd used for her old bedspread. I stayed up for hours making her a new one that was just like the old one for her room."

"And did Jennifer say anything about the bedspread when she saw it?"

"Oh, yes. It was one of the happiest moments of my life. She said, *Mom! My room is just the same as it was when I left!* And then she went to the closet, pulled open the door, and started talking about the clothes she remembered from school."

"And you never had any doubts?"

Loretta dabbed at her eyes with a tissue. "Never. I know my own daughter. It's Jennifer and she's back with us again."

"Did you tell Carly all that?"

"I did, but I don't think it did any good. She told me she likes Jennifer. It's not that. And she doesn't think Jennifer is trying to cheat us or hurt us in any way. She just doesn't believe that Jennifer is her sister and I can't think of any way to convince her."

"How about a DNA test?" Hannah suggested.

"Maybe. It would settle the question once and for all. But I worry about hurting Jennifer's feelings by asking her to agree to the test."

"You wouldn't necessarily have to ask her to agree."

"I know. I realize that all you need is hair from a hairbrush, or saliva on something, but I really don't want to do something like that behind Jennifer's back. It's just not . . . honest."

Hannah thought about the problem for a moment and then she sighed deeply. "You're really in a jam, Loretta. I don't see any way out of it. You can't please both Carly and Jennifer."

"I know that. And I also know that I can't let this go on for too long without a resolution. It's a bad situation, Hannah, and it's getting worse with each passing day. The tension is growing and I don't know how long I can stand it. When Carly told me about it last night, I didn't sleep a wink. I love both of my daughters, and I just don't know what to do."

Loretta looked so depressed that Hannah's heart went out to her. "Let me think about it for a day or two," she said, even though she didn't think it would do any good. "Maybe I can come up with something."

After that, they sat and talked for a few minutes, and then Loretta got up to go back to work. And at that exact instant, Hannah had an idea. She believed everything Carly had told her. And she believed what Loretta had confided today. When you believed two people with conflicting views about a third person, perhaps you should meet that third person to sound her out for yourself. When you did that, you could make up your own mind about what you thought was the real truth of the situation.

"How late do you work today?" Hannah asked her.

"Until six. Then Trudi comes in to sell supplies for the seven o'clock embroidery class."

"How about Carly? Is she working today?"

"Carly works Monday through Friday. Why do you want to know?"

"Because I'd like to talk to Jennifer and I'd prefer to talk to her when neither one of you are there. Would you call her and tell her I'd like to drop by this afternoon to meet her?"

Loretta looked nonplussed for a moment and then she nodded. "Of course. I'm sure she'd like to meet you, too."

"I'll take her some cookies as a welcome home present. Does she like chocolate?"

"She likes it, but it doesn't like her. She's the same with peanut butter. I baked peanut butter and chocolate chip cookies when she was a toddler. Jennifer ate one and the poor darling broke out in hives all over."

"Oh, dear! Did you stop baking cookies for her?"

"No. I just tried my mother's oatmeal-raisin cookie recipe and Jennifer adored those. I made a batch the night before she came home and they were gone in less than a day."

"Thanks for telling me, Loretta. I won't take her anything with chocolate or peanut butter. When you talk to her, tell her I'll be there at four. That'll give us time to talk."

"Talk about what?"

There was a wary tone in Loretta's voice and Hannah thought fast. She seized the most plausible explanation she could devise on such short notice and answered, "I want to ask Jennifer about a job, but I need to talk to her for a while first. I'm thinking about hiring someone to help out here at The Cookie Jar and it just occurred to me that Jennifer might like to ride in with you a couple of mornings a week and work here."

"Oh. Well . . . I don't really know if she's looking for work right now."

"If she says no, that's okay. At least I'll get a chance to say hello and welcome her back to Lake Eden. Actually, she may be overqualified for a little part-time job like mine. What kind of work did she do before she came back home?"

"Oh. Uh . . . Jennifer was a . . . a shop girl, a clerk in a department store. You know. That type of thing."

"That's nice. Where did she work?"

"A couple of places. I don't remember the names. They were big stores, though, and she made a good wage."

If it walks like a duck and quacks like a duck, it's got to be a duck, Hannah thought, repeating one of her great-grandmother's favorite sayings in her mind. Loretta was acting like someone who was lying by hesitating before she answered Hannah's questions, and then refusing to meet Hannah's eyes when she did. As far as Hannah was concerned, that meant Loretta was a liar and she wasn't very good at it.

After Hannah had walked Loretta to the door, she came back to sit on her stool again. She had to think of a good cookie to bake for Jennifer, one that would serve as a test of her real identity. She wouldn't use chocolate and she wouldn't use peanut butter. If Jennifer was really Jennifer, giving her an allergic reaction could be dangerous. Perhaps she'd make a sweet potato cookie. According to Carly, Jennifer had always hated sweet potatoes. Jennifer might take one to be polite, but she certainly wouldn't eat more than one.

Once that was decided, Hannah got up to flip through her file of recipes. She didn't have a sweet potato cookie recipe, but she could adapt one of her existing recipes to incorporate them. As she gathered ingredients and began to mix up cookie dough, Hannah was even more determined to find out why Loretta was lying to her and what she was trying so desperately to hide.

BLUE APPLE MUFFINS

Preheat oven to 375 degrees F., rack in the middle position.

The Muffin Batter:

¾ cup melted butter *(1 and ½ sticks, 6 ounces)*
1 cup white *(granulated)* sugar
2 beaten eggs *(just whip them up in a glass with a fork)*
2 teaspoons baking powder
½ teaspoon salt
1 cup fresh or frozen blueberries *(no need to thaw if they're frozen)*
2 cups plus one Tablespoon flour *(no need to sift—pack it down in the cup when you measure it)*
½ cup whole milk
½ cup apple pie filling *(I used Comstock)*

The Crumb Topping:

½ cup sugar
⅓ cup flour
¼ cup softened butter *(½ stick)*

Grease the <u>bottoms only</u> of a 12-cup muffin pan *(or line the cups with double cupcake papers—that's*

what I do at The Cookie Jar.) Melt the butter. Mix in the sugar. Add the beaten eggs, baking powder, and salt. Mix it all up thoroughly.

Put one Tablespoon of flour in a plastic food storage bag with your cup of fresh or frozen blueberries. Shake it gently to coat the blueberries and leave them in the bag on the counter for now.

Add half of the remaining two cups of flour to your bowl and mix it in with half of the milk. Then add the rest of the flour and the rest of the milk. Mix thoroughly.

Put the contents of the can of apple pie filling in a bowl and chop up the apples with a sharp knife. *(You will want some apple pieces in each muffin so the pieces have to be fairly small.)* Measure out ½ cup of pie filling and add it to your muffin batter. Stir it in thoroughly.

Hannah's Note: You will have approximately ½ cup of apple pie filling left over. Put it in a small freezer bag, label the bag, and stick it in the freezer with the rest of the frozen blueberries that you didn't use. Then you'll have the fruits together the next time you want to make Blue Apple Muffins.

Fold the frozen or fresh blueberries into your muffin batter. Mix gently so that the blueberries will stay intact.

Fill the muffin tins three-quarters full and set them aside. If you have any batter left over, grease the bottom of a small tea-bread loaf pan and fill it with your remaining batter.

To make the Crumb Topping, mix the sugar and the flour in a small bowl. Add the softened butter and use a fork or a knife to "cut" it into the dry ingredients until the resulting mixture is crumbly. *(You can also do this in a food processor. Just layer the dry ingredients with chilled butter that you've cut into chunks, and then process it in an on-and-off motion with the steel blade until it looks like coarse cornmeal.)*

Fill the remaining space in the muffin cups with the crumb topping. Then bake the muffins in a 375 F. degree oven for 25 to 30 minutes. *(If you had muffin batter left over and put it in a tea-bread pan, it should bake about 10 minutes longer than the muffins.)*

When your muffins are baked, set the muffin pan on a wire rack to cool for at least 30 minutes. *(The muffins need to cool in the pan for easy removal.)* Then just tip them out of the cups and enjoy.

These are wonderful when they're slightly warm, but the apple and blueberry flavors will intensify if you store them in a covered container overnight.

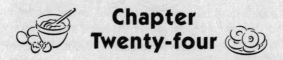

Chapter
Twenty-four

The Minnesota Twins were playing a doubleheader and Hannah had the game on in the kitchen of The Cookie Jar. The Twins and Detroit were battling it out at Target Field. The Twins were winning, four to three, but the bases were loaded with Tigers. It was the ninth inning and the new relief pitcher for the Twins, who had been recently brought up from the minors, was struggling.

"Strike him out!" Hannah instructed the pitcher, just as if he could hear her instruction through the tiny screen of her kitchen television set. "You can do it! Come on!"

It was a full count. It had been a full count for the past four pitches. The Tiger at bat, their second baseman, kept hanging in there by hitting foul balls. As she watched, the batter fouled off another three pitches. Would this inning ever be over? How long could a pitcher pitch? And how long could a batter hit foul balls that were uncatchable?

The inning seemed endless as another three pitches were delivered and fouled off. Hannah was surprised that the announcer wasn't giving statistics about the record for the number of pitches fouled off by a single batter.

Two more pitches, two more uncatchable foul balls, and Hannah turned away to take a peek at the timer to see how many minutes her cookies still had to bake. And that was when the crowd roared. Something had happened!

Hannah's head immediately swiveled toward the television set. Instant replay. Normally she hated instant replays, but this time she was grateful for the technology that generated the replay footage.

"Wow!" Hannah gasped as the pitcher threw a wild pitch, and the Tiger on third base sprinted all-out for home plate. The catcher got out of his crouch much faster than Hannah had thought was humanly possible, retrieved the ball that had ricocheted off the wall between home plate and first base, and threw a missile to the pitcher who had correctly dashed off the mound to cover home plate. The Tiger approaching home slid in feet first, the pitcher reached down to tag him before his foot reached the plate and that was it. Game over, and the Twins had won! Mike had once commented that he thought baseball was as boring as watching paint dry, but he'd obviously never seen a game like this one!

Hannah was smiling as her timer dinged and she opened the oven door to take out her cookies. They looked good and she was eager to taste one.

"Oh, good!" Michelle said as she came into the kitchen and saw that the bakers rack was full. "We're almost out in the coffee shop. Lisa's story is really pulling in the customers today."

"Let's just hope it doesn't pull in Mother. I don't think she'd appreciate the people in Lake Eden knowing she pretended to interview Starlet for one of her books."

"You're right. She wouldn't. I'll keep my fingers crossed that she doesn't come in."

"Thanks for letting me sleep," Hannah said, smiling at her youngest sister. "But I think you should be the one to sleep in tomorrow."

"I'm all right. Really, I am. I get more sleep here than I do when I'm at school."

"Then you'd better get some more sleep at school. I know you didn't get enough sleep last night."

"How do you know that?"

"You were so tired this morning that you left my new exercise machine on after you used it."

Michelle looked at her blankly. "But I didn't exercise this morning. I was afraid I'd wake you if I did."

"You didn't use the treadmill?"

"Not this morning. Why?"

"Because it was running when I got up this morning. Moishe was walking on the treadmill and I woke up to the humming of the machine."

Both of them were silent for a moment, not willing to accept the only plausible explanation, and then Michelle shook her head from side to side.

"Uh-uh. There's no way. I just don't believe it."

"I don't either. Maybe it was a poltergeist."

"I don't believe in ghosts, either."

"Neither do I, but that exercise machine didn't turn itself on."

"That's true. It has to be Moishe. There's no other explanation."

"Okay, it was Moishe. But how did he learn how to turn on the machine?"

"By watching me do it. He stared at me every time I turned it on. I thought he was just curious, but he must have been figuring out how to do it by himself. You've got a really smart cat, Hannah."

"I know. Sometimes he's too smart for his own good. I just hope he never learns to bake. He'll put me out of business."

Michelle laughed. "I think you're safe on that score. And that reminds me, how did you like the muffins this morning?"

"They were phenomenal! I meant to tell you when I came in the door, but you were busy and I forgot. And then I got busy back here and I forgot I hadn't told you. Did you write down the recipe?"

"I did. I'm going to call them Blue Apple Muffins because they've got apples and blueberries in them. They're really simple to make in a hurry. All you have to do is keep a can of apple pie filling in the cupboard and a bag of frozen blueberries in the freezer. If you've got those, you can make them anytime you want to."

"Can you make them again tomorrow?"

"Sure if you want me to. I've got half a bag of frozen blueberries left and there's some leftover apple pie filling. But are you sure you want the same breakfast you had today?"

"I'm positive. Your Blue Apple Muffins were some of the best breakfast treats I've ever had."

Michelle had just finished filling two display jars to take back to the coffee shop when the phone rang. "I'll get it," she said, setting the cookie jars down on the counter and reaching for the phone on the wall. "The Cookie Jar. Michelle . . . oh, hi Mother. Hannah told us what a wonderful job you did in Minneapolis yesterday."

Hannah rolled her eyes and Michelle winked to acknowledge it. Both of them knew it paid to keep their mother happy.

"What's that, Mother?" Michelle asked, and then she turned to give Hannah a shocked glance. "You're going to change your mind about the bridesmaid dresses?"

Hannah sat down on a stool and put her head in her hands. Delores was at it again despite the promise she'd made to choose something and stick with it.

"The menu, too?" Michelle asked, sounding even more shocked. She listened for a moment and then she started to frown. "But I thought you didn't want salmon."

As Hannah watched, Michelle pulled up a stool and sat

down. Then she reached for the shorthand notebook that Hannah always kept by the phone. "Just a minute, Mother. I have to find a pen."

As Hannah watched, Michelle grabbed a pen from the coffee mug with the broken handle that Hannah kept handy by the phone. Then she began to write. She wrote line after line until Hannah couldn't stand the suspense any longer. Delores was obviously giving Michelle instructions and Hannah had to see what her sister was writing. She got up, walked over to the counter, and glanced at the long, narrow, spiral-bound page.

The first line was blank except for one word with an exclamation mark after it. *Buttercups* it read in Michelle's perfect script. And below it, on the next line, were the words, *Where the Sam Hill are we supposed to get buttercups this time of year*, followed by three question marks. On the third line, Michelle had written two words, *burgundy dresses*, and she'd underlined the first word, *burgundy*. And under it was the following inscription, *Oh, yeah. Hannah will be sooo happy about this*, followed by an exclamation point.

Hannah's eyes widened as she read the fifth line. *Lobster Bisque, Salmon in Phyllo Dough, White Asparagus with Caviar, Heart-Shaped Rolls with Our Initials*. This was followed by a sixth line that read, *Don't want much, do you, Mother*, followed by another three question marks.

Michelle was still writing and Hannah leaned closer to read the next line. *Butterscotch Champagne* it read. She grabbed the pen out of Michelle's hand and wrote *She expects us to invent it*, followed by three question marks on the following line.

"Got to go, Mother," Michelle said in a voice choked with laughter. "They need me in the coffee shop. Call me later, okay?" and then she hung up the phone and turned to Hannah.

The two sisters faced each other for a moment, both of them too stunned to speak. Then Hannah slowly shook her head. "No way," she said. "This has gone on long enough. I'm calling Doc. If anyone can talk some sense into Mother, it's him."

The words had no sooner left her mouth when the phone rang again. "I'll get it," she said, plucking the instrument of Michelle's previous torture from the holder on the wall. "The Cookie Jar, Hannah speaking."

She listened for a second and then she gave Michelle the high sign. "Oh! Hi, Doc! I was just about to call you." She listened for another couple of seconds and then she responded. "Well . . . sure. I'd love to and I'm sure Michelle, Andrea, and Lisa would too. And we agree with you wholeheartedly. See you at six, then."

That said, Hannah hung up the phone and turned to Michelle, who was having trouble containing her curiosity. "I didn't have to tell Doc about it. He walked in when Mother was talking to you and walked back out to call me from the front desk. We're meeting him tonight at the Lake Eden Inn for dinner at six. Mother won't be joining us until seven, so we'll have an hour to discuss the problem. Doc says he has a solution in mind if we all agree."

"Sounds great to me," Michelle said. "I'll agree with anything at this point. I'm so frustrated by the whole thing that I don't know *what* to do."

"Matricide is not an option," Hannah told her, and she felt a lot better when Michelle laughed. At least they hadn't lost their senses of humor quite yet.

"I'm surprised that Mother didn't insist on joining us right away," Michelle said. "What excuse did Doc use for getting away early?"

"He didn't need an excuse. The Rainbow Ladies are hosting a wedding shower for Mother at the hospital. It starts at five-thirty and she'll be tied up until seven or maybe a little later. Doc's going to ask her to meet him for dinner at the

Lake Eden Inn as soon as her shower's over. He already told her that we're coming, too."

"This all sounds good to me," Michelle said. "Anything Doc can suggest to help will be great. Mother just doesn't seem to understand that we can't plan her wedding and reception dinner if she changes her mind every time the wind blows."

"Right. Let's hope Doc's got something good in mind because I'm fresh out of ideas. Go tell Lisa about it, will you please? Doc wants her to come to the dinner, too. And ask if you can ride out to the Lake Eden Inn with her. I'll call Andrea and tell her to meet you and Lisa in the dining room. Doc wants the whole wedding planning committee to be there."

"You're coming too, aren't you?"

"Of course. I wouldn't miss it for the world!"

"But you asked me to ride with Lisa. Where will you be?"

"I have to run home to feed Moishe. And then I need to drive out to Loretta's farm to meet Jennifer at four."

"Jennifer asked to talk to you?" Michelle sounded surprised.

"No, it's the other way around. I asked to talk to Jennifer. I need to check her out for myself. Loretta came to see me this afternoon and she's in a really bad situation. She knows Carly doesn't think Jennifer's her sister, but Loretta told me that she knows Jennifer is."

Michelle stared at Hannah for a moment and then an expression of doubt crossed her face. "Wouldn't you think Loretta would know? Jennifer didn't run away until she was a teenager."

"Yes, I think a mother would know. Maybe not if Jennifer had been kidnapped when she was a baby, but she wasn't. Loretta knows."

"But then . . ." Michelle stopped and took a deep breath. "You think Loretta's lying, don't you!"

It was more accusation than question, and Hannah nodded. "I think she could be."

"But you don't know for sure and that's why you have to go out there?"

"Precisely. I want to talk to Jennifer alone, without Loretta or Carly anywhere around. I need some answers from her."

"Better take some cookies with you. Sweeten her up first and then ask the hard questions."

Hannah chuckled. "Has Lonnie been giving you interrogation lessons?"

"No, you have. I've seen you do that sort of thing before."

"Did it work?"

"Beautifully. Most people will tell you anything you ask after a couple of your cookies. You could probably sell them as a substitute for truth serum."

Hannah was still chuckling softly as she began to bake yet another batch of cookies. She just hoped that Michelle was right and her sweet potato cookies would be a good substitute for truth serum. In any event, Yummy Yam Cookies, the name she'd given them, would be a double-edged sword. Either Jennifer would love them and Hannah would know she was a fraud, or or she would hate them and Hannah would know that she was the real Jennifer after all.

YUMMY YAM COOKIES
(Sweet Potato or Yam Cookies)

Preheat oven to 350 degrees F, rack in the middle position.

½ cup *(1 stick, 8 Tablespoons, 4 ounces)* salted
    butter, softened

1 and ½ cups brown sugar *(pack it down in the*
    cup when you measure it)

2 large eggs

4 teaspoons baking powder *(that's 1*
    Tablespoon and 1 teaspoon)

½ teaspoon nutmeg *(freshly grated is best)*

1 teaspoon ground cinnamon

1 teaspoon vanilla extract

1 teaspoon lemon zest *(zest is the yellow part*
    of the lemon peel, finely grated)

1 and ¼ cups mashed yams or sweet potatoes
    (You can buy these in the produce depart-
    ment, cook, peel, and mash your own OR
    use canned yams that you drain, pat dry,
    and mash.)

2 and ½ cups all-purpose flour *(pack it down in*
    the cup when you measure it)

¼ cup chopped dried papaya *(If you can't find*
    this in your store, you can substitute
    chopped and dried almost anything—I've

used chopped and dried dates, chopped and dried apricots, and chopped and dried candied ginger—all were delicious)

$\frac{1}{2}$ cup chopped pecans

Approximately 30 marshmallows, cut in half horizontally. *(I used kitchen scissors dipped in water to cut these.)*

Hannah's 1ˢᵗ Note: This is much easier if you use an electric mixer, but you can also mix up the cookie dough by hand.

In a medium-sized bowl, beat the softened butter and the brown sugar together until they are light and fluffy.

Add the eggs, one at a time, mixing them in thoroughly.

Mix in the baking powder, nutmeg, cinnamon, and vanilla extract. Beat until everything is well blended.

Mix in the lemon zest.

Once your yams or sweet potatoes are mashed, measure out one and a quarter cups. Add them to your mixing bowl and blend them in.

Add the flour a half-cup at a time, mixing after each addition.

Mix in the dried papaya and the half-cup of chopped pecans.

If the cookie dough is too sticky to work with, cover it with a piece of plastic wrap, pressing it down around the dough itself, and refrigerate it for one hour. *(Overnight is fine, too.)*

Hannah's 2nd Note: If you decided to refrigerate your dough, don't forget to shut off your oven and preheat it again right before you take your chilled cookie dough out of the refrigerator.

Prepare your cookie sheets by spraying them with Pam or another nonstick cooking spray or lining them with parchment paper and spraying that.

Drop the cookie dough by rounded Tablespoon onto the cookie sheet, 12 cookies to a sheet. *(Lisa and I use a 2-Tablespoon scooper down at The Cookie Jar when we make these.)*

Use the back of a small spoon or your impeccably clean thumb to make an indentation in the center of each dough mound.

Press a half-marshmallow, cut side down, into the indentation.

Bake the Yummy Yam Cookies for 10 to 12 minutes, or until the side of the cookie feels firm when lightly touched with a fingertip.

Cool the cookies on the baking sheet for 2 minutes and then transfer them to a wire rack to cool completely.

Yield: Approximately 5 dozen soft and tasty cookies, depending on cookie size.

Hannah's 3rd Note: Andrea says Tracey's friends love these because of the marshmallows and they don't realize they're eating vegetables that are good for them.

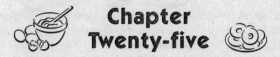
Hannah felt slightly guilty when she left The Cookie Jar at two-thirty in the afternoon, the cookies she'd baked especially for Jennifer sat on the seat beside her in one of her signature bakery boxes. She'd been at work for only three hours, and she usually put in at least ten hours a day.

She told herself that it didn't matter, that she'd baked cookies for the entire time she'd been there, but her conscience was bothering her a bit as she unscrewed the top on a bottle of cold water and drove out of town. It felt almost like playing hooky, something she'd done only once. It had happened when she was in grade school and she hadn't played hooky deliberately. It had just worked out that way.

She'd left school at a quarter to eleven in the morning for her annual fall dental checkup. Her appointment with Doc Bennett had been canceled at the last minute because of an emergency, but she hadn't known that when she'd left her classroom. Doc Bennett's receptionist had delivered the news and Hannah had walked away from his dental office intending to go straight back to school. But the fact that she wasn't expected to return for at least an hour had made her feel as free as the proverbial bird.

Why go back? the little imp that resided in her mind had

asked her. *No one at school will know you're not at the dentist. This is a lucky break for you. Go do something you want to do.*

It had seemed like a wonderful idea at the time and Hannah had put aside her scruples and stopped at the park a block from the school. A sidewalk ran all the way around the perimeter of the park in a huge circle and Hannah had walked slowly around the circle. Usually the sidewalk was filled with mothers pushing strollers, kids on tricycles and older kids on bicycles. Today there was no one on the sidewalk circle except her.

It was almost eleven in the morning and the park was deserted this time of day. The kids who rode bicycles were in school and mothers with small children had taken them home for morning naps and were busy fixing noon lunch. The park would be crowded again by two in the afternoon, but for now Hannah was the only kid around.

The swings hung straight and listless on their heavy chains. Hannah sat down on the highest one. Some were lower for smaller children and one was a baby swing with a little seat, two leg holes, and a strap to hold a small child secure. Since Hannah was tall for her age, her feet dragged a bit when she tried to swing on the smaller swings and the big swing, the one she had now, was almost always taken by someone else. At last she had it all to herself, but the thrill she'd thought would be hers when she swung high on the big swing wasn't nearly as thrilling as she'd imagined.

It was no fun swinging alone, not even on the big swing, and Hannah let the chains slow their back and forth motion and eventually come to a stop. She hadn't expected kids in the park, but she'd thought that there might be people sitting on the benches reading newspapers or flipping pages in a magazine. No one was here, not a single soul, not even anyone cutting through the middle of the park on their way to somewhere else. There weren't even any cars on the street. She was all alone and she suddenly missed her classmates. Playing hooky was no fun if you had to do it alone.

She had glanced at the watch her grandparents had given her for her birthday. Only five minutes had passed since she'd left Doc Bennett's office and it seemed much longer than that. Maybe she should go back to school. At least she wouldn't be lonely there and it was a little strange here, all by herself. It was so quiet, it was almost scary.

Hannah came out of her trip down memory lane with a snap when she turned into her condo complex. She used her key card, waved at Norma, the guard in the kiosk who kept solicitors out and made sure that nonresidents had permission to visit, and drove down the ramp that led to the underground garage.

The garage was mostly deserted. The only other car in her section belonged to Phil Plotnik, her downstairs neighbor, who worked the night shift at Delray Manufacturing. Phil would be getting up in a couple of hours to go to work, but since it was summer, he'd actually get to wake up and see the sun. This didn't happen in the winter because Minnesota was a northern state and the days were shorter in the winter. Then Phil would have to drive home from work in the dark, get up in the dark to go back to work, and only see the sun on the weekends.

As she climbed the outside staircase to her second-floor unit, Hannah heard a noise emanating from the bedroom. This time she knew what it was and she smiled in amusement. Moishe was on the treadmill again. If this kept up, she wouldn't have to put him on a diet. He'd lose the weight on the grand prize she'd won in the Jordan High raffle.

She unlocked her front door, but Moishe didn't come out to jump into her arms as he usually did. He must not have heard her over the humming noise of the treadmill. She walked down the hall and her smile grew wider as she watched her cat exercise. He obviously loved it and that was fine with her.

"Hey, Moishe!" she said, her voice carrying over the sound of the machine.

Moishe turned to look at her and hopped off the belt, hurrying over to rub against her ankles.

"I know. I'm early and you didn't expect me. But you can exercise anytime you want. I have to get dressed in something presentable because I'm going out to dinner with Doc and Mother."

The ridge of hair began to rise on Moishe's back, a sure sign that he'd recognized the *M* word. "Don't worry," she told him. "Mother's not coming back here. Let's shut off the machine and I'll feed you dinner early tonight."

Moishe followed her down the hallway and into the kitchen and observed her as she filled his food bowl. "Salmon tonight?" she asked him.

"Rrrrowww!"

That was definitely a yes. Hannah got a small can of salmon out of the cupboard, opened it, and spread it on top of his kitty crunchies. "Here you go," she said, setting his bowl on the floor. "I'm going to take a quick shower and I'll be right back."

As she passed the desk in the living room, she noticed that the middle drawer was slightly ajar. Moishe was a genius at opening drawers and cabinets, so she pulled it open to check the contents. Everything appeared to be there, but she opened the jeweler's box where she had stored the ring that Keith Branson had been wearing, just to make sure it was still there.

Ring. Man's ring. Her mind replayed the conversation she'd had with Winnie on the phone today. Connor couldn't wear his copper bracelet or his ring because his hand was in a cast. But what if the cast wasn't the only reason that Connor couldn't wear his ring? What if the reason was that he'd lost it and hadn't found it yet? And what about Connor's hand? He'd blamed his horse, but was that the real reason? Had Connor broken his hand in a fight with Keith Branson?

Connor was usually a truthful man. Hannah knew that. He said he hadn't known Keith Branson when she'd shown him the photo, but perhaps that was true. You didn't have to know someone to get into a fight with him. And the evidence certainly pointed to the fact that Keith had stolen Winnie's pie. Was that enough to make Connor hit Keith so hard that he caused an intracranial hemorrhage?

Something had made Connor absolutely furious and Hannah didn't think that the theft of Winnie's pie would do it. He would be angry, but not *that* angry. She stood there in her sunny living room, trying to think of what would make Connor fighting mad. When she couldn't think of anything, she decided to go after her scenario from another angle. What was a pimp like Keith Branson from Minneapolis doing in Lake Eden? Was he coming after Honey, the girl who'd run away from his stable?

It all began to fall in place when Hannah realized that there was only one new girl in town and that girl was Loretta's long-lost daughter, Jennifer. What if Keith had come here for Jennifer and Jennifer's street name was Honey? Winnie's ranch bordered Loretta's farm, and Keith had worked a brief time for Winnie. Jennifer had lived right next door and Keith could have met her that summer. Winnie had mentioned that Keith had slipped away to spend time with the local kids at the swimming hole. It was one of the reasons she'd fired him. What if Keith had met Jennifer there and convinced her to run away with him?

Hannah's mind spun with the possibilities. If she was right and Jennifer had run away with Keith, he knew where she lived. What if Keith had come back to Lake Eden, found Jennifer, and was dragging her back to his car when Connor rode up on Diablo? Carly had said something about Jennifer falling down in the woods and hurting herself, but what if those scratches and bruises were from her efforts to resist Keith?

Connor would have fought for Jennifer. Hannah was sure of that. Connor was a good man and he would have done his best to rescue Jennifer from Keith.

"This ring goes with me," Hannah said out loud. Perhaps she was indulging in a wild flight of fancy, pulling assumptions and connections out of thin air. But perhaps she wasn't. This could be Connor's grandfather's ring from a high school that no longer existed. That would explain why they hadn't been able to find the seal on the Internet.

There was only one way to find out if she was right and Hannah put the ring in her purse. It was a good thing she'd made a batch of Easy Pralines this morning before she'd left for The Cookie Jar. She'd planned them as a surprise for Michelle, a thank you for baking the Blue Apple Muffins, but she'd stop at Winnie's ranch on her way to Loretta's farm and give a box of them to Winnie. It would be a good excuse for dropping by, and Connor would probably be there, painting the inside of the ranch house. She'd say she'd found the ring, and watch him carefully to see if he gave any sign he recognized it.

Hannah realized that her hands were shaking on the wheel as she turned onto the gravel road that ran past the wooded area where she'd hit and killed Keith Branson. She shivered slightly as dark clouds gathered in the sky. There just couldn't be another summer storm. Not now. Not when she was about to pass the very spot where it had happened.

The sky darkened momentarily as the cloud passed across the sun, but within the space of several heartbeats, it was sunny again. Hannah breathed a sigh of relief and rolled down her window for a breath of summer air. It was hot, but there was a slight breeze as she drove by the swimming hole the local kids used and she could smell damp earth, fresh water, and the sweet scent of red clover on the currents of air.

Hannah saw three beautiful mares standing by the white fence that separated Winnie's ranch from the neighboring farms. Seeing the mares made Hannah smile. It looked as if they were watching for cars to pass by and speculating on where the drivers and passengers were going. The one in the center neighed as she drove past, almost as if she were saying hello.

An open field was next, bare of trees and planted with low ground cover. Hannah began to shiver slightly as she passed it. This was the field where the lightning had struck so violently and so frequently on that fateful morning. There was room for her to have pulled over here. The shoulder was certainly wide enough to have parked there to wait for the storm to cease. But if she had, she would have been exposing both Lisa and herself to the raging elements and what had seemed to Hannah to be probable electrocution.

Hannah slowed as she came around the bend and into the tree-lined area. The huge branch was gone, but there were round chunks of wood piled by the side of the road. A county road crew must have come out with chain saws to remove the branch from the roadway.

Winnie's ranch was just ahead, and Hannah turned onto the winding road that led to the ranch house. It was a beautiful area and Winnie kept the white fences painted and the ground free of debris. The rolling green hills reminded Hannah of the pictures she'd seen of the English countryside. She'd like to go to England someday, but for now, the Lake Eden countryside was certainly beautiful enough for her. Hannah pulled up at the ranch house, got out of the car, and walked up to Winnie's front door. She still wasn't sure how she would handle this. She just hoped that the right words would come to her when she needed them.

"Hi, Winnie," Hannah said when Winnie opened the door. "I brought you something on my way to Loretta's place."

"That's nice of you, Hannah." Winnie took the box that Hannah handed her. "What's in it?"

"Pralines. One of my college friends gave me the recipe and I made them this morning. She was from New Orleans and she claimed they were authentic."

"Did I hear you say *pralines*?" Connor appeared in the doorway.

"Nothin' wrong with the man's ears," Winnie said, smiling at him and then turning back to Hannah. "Coffee? I just made a fresh pot."

Hannah counted the days. Winnie always washed the giant, blue-enameled pot and made fresh coffee on Sunday mornings. On the other days of the week, she just kept the pot on the stove until the level of coffee was low and then she added more coffee and water, and brought it up to a boil again. By Saturday, Winnie's coffee could double as nail polish remover. Hannah and Mike had suffered through a Saturday night cup once and neither one of them had done it again. Winnie claimed that her mother had made coffee that way and she didn't see any reason to change it.

This was Thursday and that was over halfway through the week. She was living dangerously if she accepted Winnie's offer, but it wouldn't be politic to refuse. "Sure," she said. "I'd love a cup of coffee, Winnie."

Winnie poured cups for all three of them and they sat at the kitchen table. They talked for a minute or two and then Hannah pulled out the ring.

"I found this on the way in," she said, handing the ring to Winnie. "It looks like a man's ring to me. Did somebody around here lose it?"

"Looks like yours." Winnie handed it to Connor.

As Hannah watched, Connor's face turned pale. "It's mine," he admitted.

"Why didn't you tell me you'd lost it?" Winnie asked. "I would've put the boys on lookout for it."

" 'Cause I wasn't sure . . ." Connor stopped and took a deep breath. "I didn't know where I'd lost it." He turned to Hannah. "Where did you find it?"

"In the woods right next to the place where I hit Keith Branson with my truck."

Connor's face turned even paler. "Yup," he said. "I was afraid of that."

"What were you doing there?" Winnie asked.

Connor sighed again. It was the sigh of a man who knew he'd been caught red-handed, doing something he shouldn't have been doing. "I was fighting with him," he told her.

"Why didn't you tell me?" Winnie's eyes flashed angrily.

"Because you said you could never love a fighting man. And I want you to love me, Winnie."

Hannah could see the angry expression on Winnie's face fade. "Why did you fight with him, Connor?"

"He was dragging a woman through the woods. I came across them at the fence line so I jumped the fence and punched him. And then I punched him again so hard that it knocked him out."

"He was hurting a woman?" Winnie waited until Connor nodded and then she got up, went around the table, and hugged him. "Who was it?"

"I don't know. I never saw her before, but she was scared. I know that. And the minute I pulled him away from her, she ran away."

"You dummy!" Winnie said, and there was love in her voice. "When I said I could never love a fighting man, I meant a man who was a bully and picked fights. I never meant you shouldn't fight to defend a woman. That's what a man ought'a do."

"I've got to go," Hannah said, standing up. "I'll let myself out. I've got somebody else I have to see. Enjoy those pralines, both of you."

"I didn't know you liked pralines," Winnie said as Hannah left the table.

"I love 'em. I had some in New Orleans when I was there for the PBR Rodeo."

"What's PBR?"

"Professional Bull Riders. They put on events at the New Orleans Arena."

"You were a bull rider?" Winnie sounded impressed.

"That was my dad, not me. I've always been partial to horses."

Hannah pulled open the front door and went out. One part of her investigation was over. She now knew that Connor had been the man who'd delivered the lethal blow to Keith Branson's head. She hadn't seen any reason to tell Connor or Winnie that, not when she was the one who hit him with her truck and actually killed him. Connor had defended an unknown woman in the woods. And Hannah thought she knew exactly who that woman was.

EASY PRALINES

1 cup buttermilk
2 and ½ cups white *(granulated)* sugar
1 teaspoon baking soda
2 Tablespoons dark corn syrup *(I used Karo Dark)*
½ cup salted butter *(1 stick, 4 ounces, ¼ pound)* at room temperature
1 teaspoon vanilla extract
1 cup pecan pieces OR 1 cup pecan halves *(Halves are fancier, but also more expensive.)*

Before you start, get out a 4-quart saucepan and spray the inside with Pam or another nonstick cooking spray. Make sure to spray the sides of the saucepan. Get out your candy thermometer. Place the thermometer inside the saucepan with the sliding clamp on the outside. Slide the thermometer through the clamp until it's approximately one-half inch from the bottom of the pan. *(If the bulb touches the bottom of the pan, your reading will be wildly off.)*

Take the candy thermometer out of the pan, making sure you don't move the sliding clamp. You'll be attaching it again later.

In the saucepan, on a cold burner, combine the buttermilk, white sugar, baking soda, and dark corn syrup. Stir the mixture until it is smooth.

Hannah's 1ˢᵗ Note: If you do this step ahead of time and let everything come up to room temperature in the saucepan, it will take only 3 minutes or so to come to the boil and you'll cut your standing at the stove and stirring time in half.

Turn your burner on MEDIUM HIGH heat. STIR the candy mixture CONSTANTLY until it boils. *(This will take about 6 minutes if you decided NOT to let the ingredients come up to room temperature, so pull up a stool and get comfortable while you stir.)*

When the mixture boils, move the saucepan to a cold burner, but don't turn off the hot burner. You'll be getting right back to it.

Add the butter to your candy mixture and stir it in. Stir until the butter is melted.

Carefully attach the candy thermometer to the pan again, making sure it hasn't moved up or down from its earlier position. Wiggle it slightly to make sure it's not scraping the bottom of the pan.

Slide the saucepan back on the hot burner and watch it cook. STIRRING IS NOT NECESSARY

FROM THIS POINT ON. Just give it a little mix when you feel like it. Pull up a stool and relax. Enjoy a cup of coffee while you wait for the candy thermometer to come up to the 240 degree F. mark. *(240 degrees F. is the soft ball stage in candy making.)*

When your thermometer reaches 240 degrees F., give the pan a final stir, turn off the burner, and remove your saucepan from the heat. Stir in the vanilla extract. *(This could sputter a bit so be careful.)*

Let the pan cool on a wire rack or a cold burner for 10 minutes. *(If it's a hot day and it's hot in your kitchen, you'd better give it 15 minutes.)*

While your candy cools, lay out sheets of wax paper on a cutting board or a bread board. Then sit down and relax until the cooling time is up.

When your praline mixture has cooled the required number of minutes, beat it with a wooden spoon until it loses its glossy look and thickens. *(My candy took approximately 5 minutes to reach this stage.)*

Quickly stir in the pecans.

Use a tablespoon from your silverware drawer to drop the Easy Pralines on the wax paper. Don't worry if your pralines are not of a uniform size. Once your

guests taste them, they'll be hunting for the bigger pieces.

Yield: 2 dozen of the best pralines you've ever tasted.

Hannah's 2nd Note: Andrea adores this candy. She asks me to make it for her every Christmas. Michelle likes it too, but she wants me to substitute a teaspoon of maple extract for the vanilla extract. She's made it that way and she says it tastes a lot like the candy we used to get from Canada that was shaped like little maple leaves. Mother loves this candy, but she wants me to try dipping it in melted chocolate. That doesn't surprise me. Mother is a confirmed chocoholic.

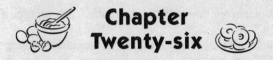

Chapter
Twenty-six

It took less than three minutes to get to Loretta's land. Hannah passed more deeply wooded areas and barbed wire fences until she came to Loretta's mailbox. She turned down a winding gravel road and drove until she saw the pale blue farmhouse in the distance.

She stopped by a massive oak tree and took several deep, calming breaths. She was almost at the farmhouse and she wanted a clear head to ask the questions that she needed to ask Jennifer.

Hannah had no sooner pulled up in front of the farmhouse when the front door opened and a pretty young woman came out. It was the same young woman Hannah had seen when she'd driven past from the opposite direction on her way to Winnie's ranch with Mike.

"Hi, Hannah!" the young woman greeted her. "Mom said you liked coffee so I put on a fresh pot. Come into the kitchen."

She's friendly, Hannah thought, turning off the ignition and following Jennifer up the sidewalk to the house. "It's nice to meet you, Jennifer," she said, as Jennifer walked through the living room and led Hannah to the kitchen.

"Mom said you took it black," Jennifer said, waiting for Hannah's nod before she brought Hannah's cup of coffee to the kitchen table. "Sit down. Mom was absurdly pleased that you remembered how she took her coffee. She told me all about it."

"That's nice," Hannah said, but her mind was taking a very different approach. *Better take control*, it told her. *Jennifer's trying to run the show and you can't let her do that.*

"So Jennifer," Hannah said, motioning to the chair across the table. "Is it good to be home after all these years?"

"Oh, yes! It's just wonderful to see Mom again. And Carly! She's all grown up now and she was so little when I left."

Get her, Hannah's mind said quite unnecessarily because Hannah had already thought of her next comment. She smiled and delivered the first pitch. "It must be a little shocking for you to see her now, considering that Carly was only a toddler when you left."

"Oh, she wasn't a toddler. Carly was five when I left," Jennifer said, her bat connecting solidly with Hannah's pitch.

"Carly wasn't five. She was four," Hannah corrected her, watching the pitch Jennifer had hit roll foul. "You should have remembered that since you baked the cake for her party and put a big number four on it."

Jennifer seemed at a loss for words and Hannah announced the play in her head. *Foul ball. The count is no balls, one strike.*

"Of course you're right. I just forgot for a moment." Jennifer looked a bit uncomfortable. "Mom said you own a wonderful cookie and coffee shop in town."

"It's nice of her to say that," Hannah responded. "As a matter of fact, I brought you some cookies." She produced the bakery box, set it on the table, and raised the lid. "I call these Yummy Yam Cookies. They're made with sweet potatoes or yams and marshmallows."

"That sounds wonderful!" Jennifer said, smiling broadly. "I just love sweet potatoes and yams."

Strike two! Hannah's mind kept the tally as Jennifer's bat failed to connect with Hannah's second pitch. Carly had told Hannah and Michelle that Jennifer hated sweet potatoes and yams. But was Jennifer just being polite? Hannah had to make sure.

Hannah watched Jennifer reach for a cookie and eat it eagerly. "These are great cookies!" she said.

"Thanks," Hannah answered, but her mind was announcing the progress of the game. *If the batter takes another Yummy Yam Cookie, the count is no balls, two strikes.* And Jennifer reached for another cookie.

One more strike and she had her! Hannah got ready to throw the next pitch. She hadn't asked about Jennifer's new bedspread yet. "I hear you're back in your old room," she said, watching Jennifer reach for a third cookie. For a girl who hadn't liked sweet potatoes and had hidden her portion in her napkin, this was a telltale sign.

"Yes. Everything's just the same, except for the bedspread, of course. And the clothes in the closet don't exactly fit me anymore."

"The bedspread is different?" Hannah asked, picking up on what she knew to be an untruth.

"Yes. Oh, it's the same design as the one I had when I left home, but Mom found the same material and made me a new one."

Hannah felt like groaning, but she managed to keep the pleasant expression on her face. She thought her last pitch would strike Jennifer out of the game, but she'd managed to fend it off. *Foul ball*, the announcer in Hannah's mind called out. *The count remains at no balls, two strikes.* Jennifer was staying in the batter's box for another pitch, at least.

After five more pitches and five more foul balls, Hannah was getting desperate. No matter what she did, she couldn't seem to get Jennifer to completely strike out. If she searched her heart, she'd have to side with Carly. She didn't think that

Jennifer was her sister. But there was nothing in Jennifer's manner or demeanor that branded her as a liar. There was another emotion beneath her exterior, something Hannah was searching to identify. It was a powerful emotion, one that could drive a person to lie. But what was it?

The answer came to her when Jennifer picked up her coffee cup. Her hands were trembling and Hannah realized what was driving this young woman to lie. It was fear! Jennifer was terrified of something or someone. It was time to pull the best pitch out of her arsenal and force Jennifer to tell her why she was terrified. Whatever the source, it had convinced Loretta to lie for her, and to pretend that Jennifer was her daughter. Hannah knew that she could keep pitching and Jennifer could keep fighting off her pitches longer than Hannah wanted to play the game. Then nothing would be accomplished. Alternatively, Hannah could borrow a tactic from the Twins game she'd seen. She could throw a wild pitch and see what happened.

"I'm so glad you like these cookies," Hannah said. "I almost brought you some Treasure Chest Cookies instead."

"I love these, but the Treasure Chest Cookies sound interesting, too. What are they?"

"They're a basic sugar cookie dough with a hidden surprise baked inside. I used miniature Reese's Peanut Butter Cups in the last batch I made."

"That would be incredibly good!" Jennifer's hands stopped trembling for several seconds as she thought about it. "I just love the combination of peanut butter and chocolate. I used to make myself peanut butter and chocolate fudge sandwiches. I bought the fudge ice cream topping, you know? It's not expensive and it goes a long way. And it's so good! I remember one week when I ate peanut butter and chocolate fudge sandwiches three meals a day."

Strike three, batter out! the announcer in Hannah's mind declared. *Team Hannah has won the game!*

"Okay, that's it," Hannah said, grabbing Jennifer's hand and holding it tightly. "I know you're not Jennifer Richardson. And I can tell you're terrified. I also know you convinced Loretta to lie and say you're her daughter. I'm wise to you Jennifer, or whatever your name is, and you have to tell me what's going on if you want me to help you out of the jam you're obviously in."

"And what if I don't want your help?" Jennifer's voice was shaking, but she'd obviously chosen to take the high ground. "What are you going to do then?"

"I'll call my friend Mike at the Winnetka County Sheriff's Department. And I'll tell him exactly what happened here this afternoon. I'm sure he'll be happy to take you right back to your corner on Munsington Street so that you can go back to work and deal with Lady Die all by yourself."

Chapter
Twenty-seven

O f course Jennifer had caved in. She was too frightened
to do anything else. And Hannah's head was swimming
as she drove back to her condo. What Jennifer had told her
wasn't exactly a surprise. Mike had often said that there
were no coincidences in homicide investigations and this
investigation had turned out to be a homicide. It was a homicide that hadn't occurred in Lake Eden, but it was a homicide nonetheless.

The real truth was even more shocking than Hannah had
imagined. The woman who'd pretended to be Loretta's
daughter had been the real Jennifer's best friend when they
were on the streets together in Minneapolis. They'd both
been in Keith Branson's stable and neither one of them had
seen any way out of the life they'd been duped into leading.
Loretta's daughter had been known as Sugar, and Sugar was
dead. Keith Branson and Lady Die had beaten Sugar so
badly when Sugar had attempted to come back home that
she'd died of her injuries. The woman who'd pretended to be
Jennifer was Honey and she'd been the one to find Sugar
after the beating. Honey had managed to move Sugar to an
abandoned building and she'd done her best to nurse her
back to health. Nothing Honey had done had helped, but at
least Sugar had been comforted by a friend when she'd died.

It had taken Sugar five days to succumb and she'd talked

about her happy memories of Loretta and Carly at home in Lake Eden. It had seemed idyllic to Honey who had never known more than a series of foster homes before she had run away with Keith. Near the end of Sugar's brief and unhappy life, she had made Honey promise that she would go to Lake Eden and tell Loretta how much she regretted what she had done and how she'd never stopped loving her mother and her little sister.

Honey had used the last of her money to buy a bus ticket to Lake Eden. In reality, she'd had no choice. Keith and Lady Die were already searching for her and she knew exactly what would happen if they found her.

Hannah looked over at her passenger. Honey was crying softly. "When did you tell Loretta?" she asked her.

"The first day when I got there. Carly was at work and I told Loretta everything. She invited me to stay right there at the farm. She said she'd figure everything out and the farm was the safest place for me. Since I looked so much like Sugar, she said to pretend I was her daughter."

"But Keith figured out where you were."

"Yes. And Lady Die sent him to bring me back. That's how I got hurt that day in the woods. I told Loretta and Carly that I tripped and fell, but it happened when I was trying to fight Keith off."

Hannah turned off the gravel road and onto the highway. "Did you punch Keith in the face?"

"No. The man did that. He was a really good fighter. I could tell that with the first punch he landed."

"Do you know who the man was?" Hannah glanced at Honey, but she quickly focused on the road again. Traffic was heavy and she needed to pay attention to her driving.

"I don't know who he was. He just came out of the woods on a horse and pulled Keith away from me. And when they started to fight, I ran away as fast as I could."

"Where did you go?"

"Back to the farmhouse. I was going to pack a bag and run, but Loretta came home. She said she heard that there was a man killed on the road that ran past the farm and she drove right home to make sure I was all right. "

Honey gave a little sob and Hannah looked over at her passenger again. Honey's face was still tear-streaked, but she looked more at peace than she had since Hannah had first met her. Perhaps that was because the truth was out and Hannah had promised to help her deal with the fallout.

"Are you okay?" Hannah asked her.

"I'm okay. It's just that nobody ever cared that much about me before. And I'm worried about Loretta and Carly. What if Lady Die figures out where I went and she comes out to the farm to kill me?"

"You won't be there. That's why you're going to my place. I called Mike and left a message for him. He'll probably be waiting for us at my condo. Between Stella and Mike, they'll figure out a way to keep you safe until it's time to testify against Lady Die and put her away for good!"

"But will Loretta and Carly be safe?"

"I'll call the shop and tell Loretta to stay with Trudi tonight, just in case. And Carly can stay at my place with Michelle, or go to stay with any of her other friends. If Lady Die does drive out to the farm, the only person she'll find there is a deputy who'll arrest her."

"Okay then. That's all good." Honey breathed a deep sigh of relief as they pulled into Hannah's parking spot. "Are we here?"

"We're here, but I guess Mike's not, at least not yet. He would have parked in my other spot."

Hannah motioned to Honey and both of them got out of the car. Hannah led the way up the stairs, unlocked the door, and caught Moishe in her arms. This elicited a laugh from Honey, the first laugh Hannah had heard from her, and they went inside.

"I called Norman to come and stay with you so you won't be alone," Hannah told her. "He should be here any minute. Just help yourself to anything you want in the refrigerator, and don't let anyone in."

"How about this Norman? I'm supposed to let him in, aren't I?"

"You don't have to let Norman in. He has a key. And he'll probably bring his cat to play with Moishe. Her name is Cuddles."

"That's a cute name. I like cats," Honey said quite unnecessarily since she was standing by the back of the couch scratching Moishe under his chin.

Hannah was just getting ready to leave when there was a knock on the door. "That'll be Mike," she said, not bothering to look through the peephole before she opened the door.

"Wrong," a female voice said, and Hannah found herself staring into the barrel of a pistol that was pointed at her head. "Back up, lady! Where's Honey?"

A million thoughts flashed through Hannah's mind in the space of a nanosecond, but none of them did much good. She'd miss her mother's wedding if she died right now, Honey would end up dying too, and Norman and Mike would discover their bodies. Delores would grieve for her, that was certain, and she'd probably wear ugly black outfits for years. Hannah's mind clicked. Her last thought had been so incongruous, it had given her an idea.

She made a motion behind her back that she hoped Honey would catch. It was a wave that was intended to tell Honey to run and hide in the safest, most obscure place she could find. And then Hannah deliberately took a step closer to the woman in the doorway.

"Where *ever* did you get that incredibly *horrible* outfit?" Hannah asked in her best authoritarian voice.

"Wha . . . ?" Lady Die was clearly taken aback, and she

did as Hannah hoped she would do. She looked down at the outfit she was wearing.

"Mistake!" Hannah said, grabbing the barrel of the gun and knocking it away. At the same time she planted her foot in Lady Die's midsection and kicked her back as hard as she could.

It worked almost like it had in the movie Hannah had seen with Mike. There was only one exception. She didn't have a black belt in any martial art. The pistol *did* fall over the rail to the ground below just like it had in the movie. And Lady Die *did* stagger back a half-step or two. But she recovered her balance much more quickly than the villain had in the movie. And she came after Hannah with a vengeance.

As Hannah turned to run, she knew not where, she heard a sound she recognized from the end of the hallway. The exercise machine was on and the treadmill was running! Hannah dashed down the hallway and into her bedroom, making a sharp turn just inside the doorway. She saw an orange and white streak as Moishe jumped off the treadmill and slid under the bed at high speed. At almost the same instant, Hannah scrambled over the mattress and dropped to the rug between the wall and her bed, feeling frantically for the bowl of flour she kept under the bed. She pulled it out and popped up just in time to see Lady Die step squarely on the belt of the treadmill.

Time slowed to a crawl for Hannah as she watched Lady Die recover her balance once. The woman must be in incredibly good shape, probably enhanced by using Keith's "girls" as punching bags. Then Lady Die managed to stay on her feet a second time by windmilling her arms and grabbing at the handlebars. Surely she couldn't maintain her balance for long. Or could she?

Hannah didn't want to take the chance. There was too much at stake. She sidestepped around the edge of the bed and planted herself in front of the handlebars. Then she ripped off the lid she kept on the top of the bowl.

"This is for Sugar," Hannah exclaimed, throwing the bowl of flour squarely into Lady Die's face.

Lady Die let out a sound that was part scream and part growl as she lost her grip on the handlebars and fell, head-first, on the belt. The belt kept moving, carrying her backward and she crashed into the bedroom wall at the back of the machine. It should have been over, but Lady Die would not give up. She attempted to make her way to the handlebars again by crawling.

"Hands up!" a male voice yelled, and Hannah's head swiveled toward her bedroom doorway in time to see Norman sprint forward to pull the plug on the machine. "I said, hands up! I'm a dentist!"

What happened next made it fairly obvious to Hannah that Lady Die must have suffered some brain damage when she fell and hit her head on the machine. She just sat there wiping the flour from her eyes and laughing.

"So whatcha gonna do, Mr. Dentist?" she asked. "Pull my teeth?"

"I don't pull teeth for free," Norman replied, raising Lady Die's pistol and pointing it at her head. "But I do occasional charity work and ridding the world of someone like you falls into that category. You can put your hands up, or you can be my next tax deduction. It's your choice."

"Thanks, Norman. I got her now," another male voice said.

Hannah glanced at her bedroom doorway to see Mike standing there, and she watched as he grabbed Lady Die, hauled her to her feet, and cuffed her. "Good job," he said to Norman.

"Thanks."

"Do you even know how to shoot that pistol?" Mike asked.

"Not really, but I saw you pull in right before I came through Hannah's door and I knew all I had to do was create a diversion until you got up here."

That was when Hannah heard a sound behind Mike and she moved to a better vantage point to see Honey standing there with her hands held up to her face.

"Honey! Where were you?" Hannah asked her.

"In your laundry room. I hid in your dryer since it's one of those big ones. Do you know you have wet clothes in there?"

"Uh-oh! I did a load this morning, and I was going to dry it, but I guess I forgot. Are you okay?"

"I'm okay."

"You're safe now, Honey. Lady Die's in cuffs and you don't have to cry."

"I'm not crying," Honey said removing her hands from her eyes. "I'm laughing. Your cat was on the treadmill, you threw a bowl of flour in Lady Die's face, a dentist with a gun he doesn't even know how to use came in the front door, and there's a cute little cat out there in the living room looking totally confused. This place is a zoo!"

Hannah burst into laughter. "I guess it is. Are you really sure you want to stay here in Lake Eden?"

"Oh, yes!" Honey said, and she sounded very certain. "Sugar told me she left because her hometown was boring, but it's not boring at all. If everybody else in Lake Eden is as much fun as you guys are, this is the perfect place for me."

Chapter
Twenty-eight

"Sorry I'm late," Hannah said, sliding into her place next to Andrea at the big round table in the Lake Eden Inn dining room. "I got tied up."

"Literally?" Michelle asked, chuckling slightly at her own joke.

"Almost literally. I'll tell you all about it later." Hannah turned to their host. "It's nice of you to invite us to dinner, Doc."

"I enjoy your company, but that's not the only reason I invited you to join me here tonight. I waited until you got here to start, but I planned this evening as a dinnervention."

"Dinnervention?" Hannah asked, beginning to laugh.

"That's right. It's a combination dinner and intervention. Lori's causing a problem for all four of you and I have a solution. All I need is your word that you won't tell anyone about my solution until Lori and I are married."

"You have my word," Hannah said quickly.

"Mine, too," Michelle chimed in.

"And you have mine," Andrea promised. "We almost went crazy trying to plan this wedding."

"Lisa?" Doc turned to the only one of them who hadn't spoken.

"I agree, but I'm not too happy about it," Lisa told him. "When I married Herb we promised we wouldn't have any secrets from each other, except for Christmas and birthday presents, and little things like that. But this isn't little and it's a secret."

"You can tell Herb," Doc assured her. "I'd like you to warn him not to tell anyone else."

"I can do that. Herb will never tell. He keeps secrets better than anyone I've ever known."

"It's fine then." Doc looked around at each of them. "If Lori gets even a hint of this, it's not going to work."

Hannah was about to ask what Doc's solution was when Sally brought an appetizer tray. "Check this out," she said, setting it in the center of the table. She turned to Doc and asked, "Did you tell them yet?"

"Not yet. We were just waiting for Hannah to get here. You can bring the drinks, Sally. And once you do that, please sit down and join us. You're a part of this, too."

Sally hurried to the bar and picked up a tray of martini glasses that she carried back to the table. "These are Blackberry Pie Martinis," she explained as she set a glass in front of each of them and took one for herself. "Dick came up with the recipe."

"Thanks, Sally, but I really shouldn't . . ." Michelle started to say, but Sally put a hand on her shoulder.

"No worries," Sally said. "Yours is nonalcoholic. So is mine. I have to cook tonight."

"These are incredible," Lisa said, after she'd taken a sip.

"Yes, they are," Hannah agreed with a smile.

That was everyone's cue to compliment Dick's martinis and Sally looked very pleased. "I'll tell Dick you liked them."

"So what's your solution, Doc?" Hannah asked, unable to contain her curiosity any longer. She hoped it was a good solution. Someone had to take charge of this runaway wedding train, and Doc Knight was the only one who could do it.

"I'll tell you in a minute," Doc said, motioning toward the

pretty Lazy Susan that Sally had put in the center of the round table. "What do you think of Sally's appetizers?"

"I think I'm happier than I've been all day," Hannah said, helping herself to a toast point with smoked salmon and herb-studded cream cheese. She pointed to the neighboring section on the swiveling tower. "Are those Bill Jessup's Misdemeanor Mushrooms?"

"You betcha!" Sally said, grinning from ear to ear as Hannah added two to her appetizer plate. And then Sally proceeded to name the appetizers in each section of the tiered tray.

"My favorite deviled eggs!" Michelle said, taking one with smoked salmon and another with ham salad. "What could be better than this?"

"Baked Brie with apple and cinnamon," Andrea said, helping herself to a big slice.

"These olives stuffed with bleu cheese are the best," Lisa offered her opinion.

"No, the haggis is."

"Haggis?!" Hannah gasped, staring at Doc's side of the Lazy Susan. "Where's *that*?"

"It's not haggis. It's Mike's Busy Day Pate," Sally told them. "It just looks different because I piped it on a triangle of pumpernickel bread."

"We only have ten minutes or so until Mother gets here," Hannah said, glancing at her watch as they finished their martinis and Sally's busboy arrived to take away the appetizer tray. "You'd better tell us your solution now, Doc."

"It's simple," Doc said, smiling at all of them. "I'm going to kidnap Lori and drive her to the airport. We'll board a plane to Las Vegas, first class of course, and get married at the Little White Wedding Chapel."

"By Elvis?" Lisa asked, who had obviously heard of the Little White Wedding Chapel.

"No, by a minister. They have regular services, too. I

called to find out. After the ceremony, you girls will spend the night there and fly back to Lake Eden in the morning to get ready for the reception dinner. Lori and I will stay a second night and then fly back in time for the reception."

There was silence for a full minute as they all thought about it. It was an incredible plan. And then Sally spoke. "Does Delores know about this?"

"Of course not. Lori would never agree. I'm just going to kidnap her from her house and bundle her into a waiting limo that'll drive us to the airport."

"That's romantic," Lisa said, blinking back the moisture that had formed in her eyes.

"That's not romantic. That's necessary," Hannah contradicted Lisa. "Mother's never going to make up her mind and none of us can take any more of these changes in the wedding plans."

"And that's why I decided to save us all the aggravation," Doc explained. "Your mother will be so happy by the time the reception rolls around, she'll love anything you decide to do. Just put up with her in the meantime and know that the final decisions are entirely yours. Can you do that?"

"We can do that," Hannah said. "Is there anything we can do to help you arrange things?"

"All you have to do is pack a suitcase for Lori on the day we leave and bring it out to me at the hospital. Then we'll be all set." Doc looked around at their shocked, but delighted faces. "So what do you think of my solution?"

"It's brilliant," Hannah spoke for all of them and there were nods all around the table. "We'll be grateful forever, Doc. You saved us a lot of grie . . ." She stopped speaking as she glanced at the door to the dining room. "Uh-oh! Here she comes!"

All eyes swiveled toward Dot Larson, who was leading Delores into the dining room. Sally got up to go back to the kitchen, stopping to greet Delores on the way, and Delores gave a little wave around the table as she sat down in the vacant chair next to Doc. Then she zeroed in on Hannah. "Are you all right, Hannah?"

"I'm fine, Mother. Why?"

"There was a rumor floating around at the hospital when I left. Mike and Bill brought in a woman in handcuffs, and she had a head injury. Jenny was on, and Mike told her that the woman tried to kill you!"

"That's true," Hannah admitted.

"Jenny also said that Mike told her Norman held a gun on the woman until he arrived to cuff her."

"That's true, too."

"Oh, my!" Delores put her hand to her chest and took a deep breath. "I'm so glad you're all right! Mike told Jenny and Marlene that you were, but I was still worried. Tell me, dear . . . is it true that Norman didn't even know how to shoot that gun?"

"That's what he said after Mike arrived."

"Well, for heaven's sakes! What was Norman planning to do with it?"

"He was planning to figure it out before he had to shoot, Mother."

Andrea started to laugh. "Did that last sentence of yours have a comma in it, Hannah?"

For one brief second, Hannah didn't get it, but when she did, she was delighted. Andrea had made her first joke about grammar. Perhaps all the nights she'd spent helping Andrea with her grade school grammar lessons had borne fruit after all!

"It has a comma," Hannah told her. "Norman wasn't planning to shoot Mother."

There was laughter around the table for several minutes and then Sally arrived with a split of champagne. "Delores?"

she said, pouring it for Delores and giving her a glass. "I know you've already eaten so I brought you a sweet treat to go with your champagne."

Delores looked down at the gold box on the table. "Is that what I think it is?"

"Yes," Sally said. "The last time you were here with Doc, you mentioned that you loved chocolate, so I made some fruit truffles for you."

"Wonderful!" Delores said, "Truffles are one of my favorite things." She gave Sally a grateful smile and reached into the box for one. She took a bite and her smile grew even wider. "This one is strawberry and they're wonderful, Sally!"

"Thank you. And now I'd better get the rest of the entrees Doc and the girls ordered. Doc said you'd be having refreshments at the bridal shower, but are you sure you don't want something else to eat?"

"Well . . . a little chicken salad sandwich with the crusts cut off only goes so far. Do you have your oso bucco tonight?"

"We do."

"Then I'll have that. And what I don't finish, Doc will probably have for breakfast . . . right, Doc?"

"TMI, Lori."

Delores laughed. "Too much information. I learned that just the other day from Hannah." She turned back to Sally. "Please forget you heard that."

"Consider it forgotten," Sally said. She patted Delores on the shoulder and then she hurried back to the kitchen.

"I have a toast," Delores said when Sally had left. "I want to thank all of you for being so patient with me. I know I promised I wouldn't change my mind again, but I just had the best idea for the wedding."

The three Swensen sisters and Lisa exchanged glances. It

was clear that all four of them were thinking the same thought. *Uh-oh! She's going to do it again!*

"What's your idea, Mother?" Hannah asked.

"Pink! Wouldn't pink be a perfect wedding color?"

Hannah came close to groaning. With her red hair she did not look pretty in pink. "Does this mean you're going to wear pink on your wedding?"

"No, dear. I was thinking about the bridesmaid dresses and the bridal bouquet. I think little pink roses mixed with something white would be absolutely perfect. Pink and white. It's a simply lovely combination. Yes, I've decided. I want white for the other wedding color."

"You're planning to wear white?" Lisa asked.

"Heavens no! I'd never wear white. This is a second wedding for me and I'm not exactly the blushing bride, you know."

Doc laughed. "You can say *that* again!"

While Hannah, Michelle, Andrea, and Lisa struggled to contain their laughter, Delores turned to Doc in shock.

"Doc!" she exclaimed, her eyes flashing fire.

"Relax, Lori. Three of the four girls sitting at this table are your daughters, and I delivered all three of them. I know you're not the blushing bride."

"Oh," Delores said, and her angry expression turned into a smile. "Of course you know. You were my doctor."

"I'm still your doctor."

"Yes, you are." Delores turned back to them again. "I'm sorry I've been so indecisive about the wedding plans. It's just . . . well . . . I want everything to be perfect."

"That's okay, Mother," Hannah said, and she meant it.

Andrea nodded. "Don't worry about it, Mother."

"We're fine with anything you decide," Michelle said.

"It's your wedding, after all," Lisa added her comment. "You're the one who has to decide."

"But I've been changing my mind too much after I promised Hannah I wouldn't." Delores looked contrite. "I want to apologize and tell you that I plan to do my very best to stick with what I decided."

"Fine with us," Hannah said, and everyone else nodded their agreement.

"Oh, good!" Delores looked very relieved. "For a moment there, I thought you were about to give up on me."

"We'd never do that," Hannah responded for all of them.

"Well, you're all very understanding and sweet," Delores said, and then she turned to Doc. "I have good girls, don't I, dear?"

"The best in the world," Doc said, winking at them before he pulled Delores into his arms and hugged her.

Andrea smiled at Delores. "We're all very happy for you, Mother."

"And we're very happy to plan your wedding," Hannah added.

It was a happy moment. The wedding planners were saved future aggravation and Doc had accomplished that. As far as everyone at this table was concerned, Delores was marrying the perfect man for her . . . and for them, too!

And then the roof came crashing in, metaphorically of course, because Howie came up to their table. "You all look very happy," Howie said.

"We are," Delores said, smiling at him. "What's the good word, Howie?"

Howie looked slightly embarrassed. "I'm afraid it's not very good, Delores. Can I see you in private, Hannah?"

Hannah felt her heart rate escalate. Howie looked very solemn. "Of course," she said.

"Is this about the trial?" Doc asked him.

"Yes. When is the wedding?"

"September twentieth," Delores told him. "And of course you and Kitty are invited. I'll get the invitations out soon."

"Thank you," Howie said politely, and then he turned to Doc again. "I really should talk to Hannah in private."

Hannah made a move to get up, but Doc motioned her back down to her seat. "If this is about the trial, it concerns all of us. What is it, Howie? Spit it out."

"Hannah?" Howie turned to her.

Hannah swallowed hard. She was terribly afraid that their happy evening would be spoiled, but now that Howie had brought it up, there was nothing to do but discuss it in front of her family. "Go ahead, Howie. Tell us all."

"Your trial is scheduled for the first week in September, Hannah. That means it should be over by the time your mother gets married."

"Thank goodness for that!" Delores said, looking very relieved. "Hannah's a bridesmaid, you know."

"I know," Howie said, turning back to Hannah. "I need you in my office next week to discuss strategy."

Hannah nodded. Her mouth was too dry to speak. She wanted to ask him if everything was going to be all right, but perhaps the question was better left unasked for now.

"I'll be there," She forced out the words, and then she turned to her mother. "Don't worry, Mother. You heard Howie. Everything will be settled by the time you get married."

Delores smiled and motioned for Sally to bring an extra chair for Howie. "Champagne?"

"Just one glass. I have to meet a client at my office."

"At this time of night?" Doc asked him.

"Yes. It's an assault and battery charge and this case is complicated."

"You work too hard, Howie," Delores said as Dot arrived with a chair for Howie and poured champagne for him.

As the conversation flowed around her, Hannah managed to keep the smile on her face. Howie wanted to have a strategy meeting. What did he mean by that? Was her case even more complicated than the case he was discussing with another client tonight?

Somehow Hannah managed to keep the fixed smile on her face, but she didn't meet anyone's eyes, especially not Howie's. She was afraid she'd burst into tears. Was Howie going to try to convince her to accept a plea bargain? And should she do that if he said it was advisable? If she did, would she be locked in prison so that she couldn't be a part of her mother's wedding to Doc?!

BLACKBERRY PIE MARTINI

To make this drink you will need a martini glass, a martini shaker **OR** a pitcher filled with ice, and a drink strainer.

The Rimming Mixture:

$\frac{1}{2}$ teaspoon ground cinnamon
$\frac{1}{4}$ teaspoon ground nutmeg *(use the store-bought kind—it's ground finer than if you grate it)*
$\frac{1}{4}$ cup white *(granulated)* sugar

The Drink:

2 ounces of Tito's Handmade Vodka
1 ounce Triple Sec
$\frac{3}{4}$ ounce fresh lemon juice
2 ounces Torani Blackberry Syrup *(or fresh or frozen blackberry puree)*

The Garnish:

blackberry as a garnish

Mix the cinnamon, nutmeg and sugar together in a saucer or small salad plate that is slightly larger than the rim of your martini glass. *(I used the cap of my*

flour jar turned upside down to do this—it fit perfectly.)

Dip your impeccably clean fingertip in a bit of lemon juice and run it around the rim of the martini glass. (*The object here is to make it wet on top of the rim so the rimming mixture will stick.*)

Turn the glass upside down in the shallow bowl and move it around a bit so that the rimming mixture coats the tip of the rim.

Set the rimmed glass on the counter while you make the drink.

Combine the drink ingredients in a martini shaker. Add ice and shake for 5 to 10 seconds, but not long enough to melt the ice cubes.

Strain the mixture into your rimmed martini glass, add the blackberry garnish, and serve.

Alternatively, you can make this in a pitcher filled with ice, stir until the mixture is icy cold (but not long enough to melt the ice—you don't want it to dilute the martini), and strain the mixture into your rimmed martini glass.

Drop a fresh or frozen blackberry into your martini as a garnish.

Yield: 1 delicious martini that tastes like blackberry pie!

Hannah's Note: If you're only making one Blackberry Pie Martini, you'll have some rimming mixture left over. Put it in the cupboard and use it to sprinkle on hot buttered toast in the morning to make cinnamon toast.

BLACKBERRY PIE COOLER
(NON-ALCOHOLIC BLACKBERRY PIE "MARTINI")

The Rimming Mixture:

$\frac{1}{2}$ teaspoon ground cinnamon
$\frac{1}{4}$ teaspoon ground nutmeg *(use the store-bought kind—it's ground rather than grated)*
$\frac{1}{4}$ cup white *(granulated)* sugar

The Drink:

2 ounces white cranberry juice
2 ounces fresh lemon juice
2 ounces Torani Blackberry Syrup OR fresh blackberry puree

The Garnish:

1 fresh or frozen blackberry as a garnish

Mix the cinnamon, nutmeg and sugar together in a saucer or small salad plate that is slightly larger than the rim of your martini glass. *(I used the cap of my flour jar turned upside down to do this—it fit perfectly.)*

Dip your impeccably clean fingertip in a bit of lemon juice and run it around the rim of the martini glass. *(The object here is to make it wet on top of the rim so the rimming mixture will stick.)*

Turn the glass upside down in the shallow bowl and move it around a bit so that the rimming mixture coats the tip of the rim.

Set the rimmed glass on the counter while you make the drink.

Combine the drink ingredients in a martini shaker. Add ice and shake for 5 to 10 seconds, but not long enough to melt the ice cubes.

Strain the mixture into your rimmed martini glass, add the blackberry garnish, and serve.

Alternatively, you can make this in a pitcher filled with ice, stir until the mixture is icy cold (but not long enough to melt the ice—you don't want it to dilute the martini), and strain the mixture into your rimmed martini glass.

Drop a fresh or frozen blackberry into your drink as a garnish.

Yield: 1 delicious non-alcoholic "martini" that tastes like blackberry pie!

Hannah's Note: If you're only making one Blackberry Pie "Martini", you'll have some rimming mixture left over. Put it in the cupboard and use it to sprinkle on hot buttered toast in the morning to make cinnamon toast.

BLACKBERRY PIE MURDER
RECIPE INDEX

Baking Conversion Chart

These conversions are approximate, but they'll work just fine for Hannah Swensen's recipes.

VOLUME

U.S.	*Metric*
½ teaspoon	2 milliliters
1 teaspoon	5 milliliters
1 tablespoon	15 milliliters
¼ cup	50 milliliters
⅓ cup	75 milliliters
½ cup	125 milliliters
¾ cup	175 milliliters
1 cup	¼ liter

WEIGHT

U.S.	*Metric*
1 ounce	28 grams
1 pound	454 grams

OVEN TEMPERATURE

Degrees Fahrenheit	*Degrees Centigrade*	*British (Regulo) Gas Mark*
325 degrees F.	165 degrees C.	3
350 degrees F.	175 degrees C.	4
375 degrees F.	190 degrees C.	5

Note: Hannah's rectangular sheet cake pan, 9 inches by 13 inches, is approximately 23 centimeters by 32.5 centimeters.

"What's next, Hannah?" Michelle wiped her hands on a kitchen towel and turned toward the counter where Hannah was brushing the pastry top of the entrée she'd just assembled with egg wash.

"They'll start coming in the door any minute now, so you can preheat the top oven to three-fifty. I won't start to bake this until they come. It won't take that long and we'll have the appetizers and wine first."

Andrea walked into the kitchen. "The table's all set," she said, and then she came over to give Hannah a hug.

"What's that for?" Hannah asked her, smiling to show that she was pleased at this show of affection.

"That's because you're the best big sister in the world for inviting Bill. He was so happy. He thought you'd never forgive him for arresting you." Andrea stopped and took a deep breath. "You have forgiven him, haven't you?"

"Of course I have. Bill had to do what he did and I know he didn't want to do it. You've forgiven him, too, haven't you?"

"Yes. I still don't like what he did, but I do understand." Andrea gestured toward the decorated packages of puff pastry on the cookie sheets. "What's that, Hannah? It's pretty."

"It'll be prettier when it's baked. Then the top will be golden brown."

"But what is it? You never told us what we're having for dinner tonight."

Hannah smiled as she turned to face her sisters. She was confident that one or perhaps both of them would appreciate her little joke. "We're having Pate on Pumpernickel Appetizers, Salmon Wellington, and Rainbow Parfait with Scottish Shortbread for dessert."

"Wait a second," Andrea said, frowning slightly. "Mother doesn't like pumpernickel bread. And she doesn't like salmon, either. Remember what she said when Doc ordered salmon at the hospital luncheon for the board members?"

"She said she'd just push the salmon around on her plate because she didn't like it," Michelle recalled.

"You're right," Hannah agreed. "But that was *last* week."

"And this is *this* week," Andrea finished the thought for her. "I know it sounds impossible, but I keep forgetting how changeable Mother is."

"Parfait and shortbread for dessert," Michelle repeated what Hannah had said. "Didn't you suggest a fancy parfait and shortbread right after Mother told us she wanted a dessert that would reflect Doc's Scottish heritage?"

Hannah didn't say anything. She just smiled the smile that her Regency romance writer mother would have attributed to the *cat that got into the cream pot*.

Michelle interpreted her expression and started to laugh. "I get it. Your menu tonight is everything that we suggested and Mother rejected."

"Not quite *everything*," Hannah told her. "I didn't think we could eat a twenty-six course dinner."

All three sisters laughed and then Andrea asked, "Why are you doing this?"

"I'm just trying to prove a point. Let's see what Mother says when we serve it. I'll bet she loves my whole menu *this* week."

* * *

Everyone around Hannah's dining room table must have been hungry because the tray of Pate on Pumpernickel appetizers disappeared almost as fast as the first bottle of chilled champagne. Hannah handed another bottle of champagne to Norman to open, along with a refill of ginger ale for him, and went back to the kitchen to get the second tray of appetizers.

"Oh, good!" Delores exclaimed as Hannah set the tray on the table. "You made more appetizers. These are just delicious, dear. And I love the way you decorated them. So festive!"

"Thank you, Mother," Hannah replied, not daring to look at either of her sisters for fear they'd all burst out laughing.

Once the second bottle of champagne was ancient history and there were only crumbs of pumpernickel left on the tray, Hannah motioned to her sisters and they went into the kitchen to get the entrées.

Hannah cut the first piece of Salmon Wellington in half and arranged it on the plate in a vee-shape. She quickly cut another piece for the second plate and added two spears of tender cooked asparagus and one wedge of cooked carrot to each presentation. Then she gave one plate to Andrea and the other to Michelle. "Serve Mother and Doc first," she instructed them. "Turn the plates so that the cut ends face them. I want Mother to see how pretty the layers are."

As Hannah prepared the next two plates, she heard a gasp from the dining table. "How lovely!" Delores exclaimed, loud enough to be heard in the kitchen. "Please tell Hannah that this is the prettiest entree she's ever served."

"Lovely," Hannah said under her breath. "But will she also think it's delicious?"

Hannah had her answer sooner than the expected. It came the moment she carried her own plate to the table.

"This is just delicious, dear!" Delores complimented her.

"And so pretty! I hope you serve this again. It would be lovely for a Christmas dinner."

Hannah thanked her mother and accepted the compliments of everyone else. And then she heard little cat feet pounding down the hallway in a race for the salmon. "Feet up!" she warned.

"Secure your plates!" Norman added. "Cuddles and Moishe love salmon!"

"I've got the wine," Bill said, grabbing the bottle.

"And I've got the water pitcher," Lonnie announced.

"Rrrrrow!" Moishe yowled as he barreled into the room and ran straight into the back of the couch, which Hannah and Michelle had repositioned so that they could add another leaf to the old-fashioned dining room table.

Cuddles gave Moishe a passing glance, but she headed straight for the table. She raced around it and made an attempt to climb Mike's pant leg.

"Oh, no you don't!" Mike said, laughing as he plucked her off and set her back on the rug. "I'm not a tree, you know."

"I'll take care of this." Hannah got up from her chair. "Come with me, Cuddles. You too, Moishe. I've got salmon for you in the kitchen."

Less than five minutes later, the cats emerged from the kitchen. They were no longer running but walking sedately as they climbed up on the couch to stretch out contentedly.

Once the plates had been cleared, the three sisters busied themselves in the kitchen. Michelle put on the coffee, Andrea rinsed the dishes and put them in the dishwasher, and Hannah removed her desserts from the freezer. She lined the parfait glasses up on the counter and took out the shortbread she'd made.

"Coffee's on," Michelle announced coming over to look at the colorful desserts. "Those are gorgeous. What do you call them?"

"Rainbow Parfait."

"And this?" Michelle pointed to the two pie plates that Hannah had taken out of the cupboard.

"Scottish Shortbread," Hannah told her.

"Doc should like that," Andrea commented, coming over to look.

"I hope so. The recipe's authentic, or at least I think it is. I got it from Grandma Knudson and she said she got it from someone named Fiona who lived in Scotland."

Hannah got out a cutting board large enough to accommodate the pie plates and flipped them over on the board. The shortbread came out and she turned it right side up.

"What are those marks on the top?" Andrea asked her.

"The little holes are from pricking the dough all over with a fork. The lines are a guide to cutting it. I scored it before I baked it."

Hannah reached for a knife and cut both rounds of shortbread in pie-shaped wedges. By that time, the sherbet in the parfait glasses had thawed enough to be eaten. She handed the first two parfait glasses to Michelle and gave the plate of shortbread to Andrea. "Serve Mother first, and then Doc. And then come back for more. I'll pour the coffee and put it on a tray."

The serving went quickly and once everyone at the table had coffee and dessert, Hannah joined them. She sat down but before she could even sample her dessert, Delores spoke.

"This is so attractive! And this cookie is marvelous, too."

"It's shortbread," Doc told her, and then he turned to Hannah. "Where did you get this recipe? Most American shortbreads have too much sugar in them for me. This one is exactly like the shortbread my mother used to make."

"Grandma Knudson gave me the recipe years ago. She said she used to correspond with someone who lived in Scotland and they exchanged recipes."

"Was the woman's name Fiona?" Doc asked.

"Yes. How did you know?"

"My mother's name was Fiona. She mentioned that she was corresponding with someone in town, but I had no idea that it was Grandma Knudson and they were exchanging recipes."

"Would you give me a copy of the recipe, dear?" Delores asked Hannah. "I don't bake, but if it's not too difficult, perhaps you could teach me how to make it for Doc."

Love. It had to be pure love, Hannah thought as she promised her mother she would. Delores had never baked for anyone before. And she'd certainly never asked Hannah to teach her to bake!

Conversation flowed around the table as they finished their parfaits and drank more coffee. And then Delores cleared her throat.

"I really hate to do this, especially after I promised I wouldn't, but is it too late to make a few changes to the reception dinner?"

There was no way Hannah could look at either of her sisters. "What changes, Mother?"

"Your Salmon Wellington was simply delicious and I think it would be perfect as the entrée. And the Pate on Pumpernickel is wonderful and it could be passed around on trays when we have champagne. And then there's the parfait. Is it difficult to make, dear?"

"Not at all. Sally could make it ahead of time and keep it in the parfait glasses in the freezer. Then all she'd have to do is take it out a few minutes before serving. The shortbread's very easy, too."

"Well then, I'd like to include this whole dinner in the menu. If it's still possible, that is."

"Is there anything else you'd like to change, Mother?" Michelle asked, deliberately avoiding Hannah's eyes.

"Why yes! Now that you mention it, I'd like to coordinate the wedding colors with the parfait colors. Wouldn't that be lovely? And then, of course, we'll change the colors of the bridesmaid dresses, the napkins, the tablecloths, the decorations, and the flowers. Did I leave anything out?"

"If you did, I'm sure you'll think of it," Hannah said, doing her best not to sound sarcastic. And then she somehow managed to turn to her sisters without laughing. "What do you two think? Is it too late to change everything?"

Michelle was the first to respond. "Well, it *is* late, but I think we can do it."

"Of course we can," Andrea said, smiling at Delores and nudging Hannah under the table.

"Hannah?" Delores turned to her. "If I promise that this is it and I won't change my mind again, is it all right with you?"

Somehow Hannah managed to keep the grin off her face as Doc winked at her. She'd serve this exact dinner any time her mother requested it, but it couldn't be at the wedding reception dinner. Delores didn't know about Doc's plans to elope with her and she had no idea that the menu was already set for the party two days after her whirlwind Vegas wedding. "Of course it's all right with me, Mother," Hannah said. "You can change your mind right up to the last day. It's *your* wedding, after all."

PATE ON PUMPERNICKEL

4 ounces braunschweiger *(or liverwurst—I used Farmer John brand)*

4 ounces cream cheese *(not whipped—I used Philadelphia brand)*

⅛ cup minced onion **OR** ⅛ cup sweet pickle relish

1 hard-boiled egg, finely chopped

1 loaf appetizer-size pumpernickel bread *(either rounds or squares—if you can't find that, most stores have black bread you can cut in small pieces)*

Hannah's Note: If you like sweet, use the pickle relish— if not, use the onion.

Garnish:
slices of green olive with pimento
slices of cherry tomato
slices of pimento
small purple onion rings
slices of pitted ripe olive
slices of miniature bell peppers in assorted colors

Place the braunschweiger and the cream cheese in a microwave-safe bowl. Heat it on HIGH in the microwave for 40 seconds.

Mix the braunschweiger and cream cheese with the minced onion **OR** the sweet pickle relish.

Mix in the finely chopped hard-boiled egg.

Refrigerate for 20 minutes to thicken the pate to the consistency of thick frosting.

Use a small rubber spatula or a frosting knife to spread a layer of pate on the pumpernickel bread.

Top your Pate on Pumpernickel with any of the above garnishes, place them on a tray, and serve. If you do not serve immediately, cover with plastic wrap and refrigerate the tray until 5 minutes before serving.

Yield: approximately 2 dozen pieces, depending on bread size.

SALMON WELLINGTON

2 ounces salted butter
4 six-ounce salmon filets, skin removed
1 package frozen puff pastry *(I used
     Pepperidge Farm Puff Pastry Sheets,
     17.3 ounce package with 2 sheets.)*

1 small package fresh baby spinach leaves
salt and pepper
honey mustard *(I used Beaver Sweet Honey
    Mustard)*

Salmon Toppers:
canned mushroom slices *(optional)*
capers *(optional)*
black olive slices *(optional)*
¼ to ½ cup minced onions *(optional)*

Egg Wash:
1 large egg
1 teaspoon water

Melt the butter at MEDIUM HIGH heat in a frying pan large enough to hold the 4 salmon filets.

Add the salmon and fry it for 2 and ½ minutes.

Flip the salmon over and fry the other sides for 2 and ½ minutes.

Remove from the pan. Cover and refrigerate the salmon filets for 1 hour or until cold.

If you decided to top your salmon with minced onions, use the butter remaining in the frying pan to fry your onions until they are translucent.

Take the onions out of the frying pan with a slotted spatula or slotted spoon, cover them, and refrigerate them.

Hannah's 1st Note: You can fry the salmon filets and the onions up to 24 hours in advance. This will save you time on the day you want to serve the Salmon Wellington.

Take out 2 sheets of puff pastry and let them thaw according to the package directions. *(My package said to either thaw them in the package in the refrigerator overnight or thaw them at room temperature for 40 minutes.)*

Once the pastry sheets are thawed, spread them out on a lightly floured surface. *(I used a bread board.)*

Preheat your oven to 400 degrees F. *(NOT a typo—that's four hundred degrees F.)*

Measure the puff pastry. If the sheets are not 11-inches by 17-inches, use a rolling pin to roll them to that size. Trim the excess with a sharp knife and save it.

Cut each sheet of pastry into 2 pieces with a sharp knife. Make your cut from the middle of one 17-inch side to the middle of the other 17-inch side.

Lay one salmon filet lengthwise on the bottom half of one piece of puff pastry. Center it one inch from the edges. Notice how much space it takes.

Remove the salmon and lay out a bed of spinach leaves, three leaves deep, the size of the salmon filet.

Sprinkle the bed of spinach with a little salt and pepper.

Place the salmon on top of the spinach.

Using a small rubber spatula or a frosting knife, slather honey mustard all over the top of the salmon filet.

Choose a salmon topper if you want it *(you have 4 choices above)* and sprinkle your choice over the top of the mustard.

Fold the bare half of the puff pastry over the salmon and "snuggle" it up to the salmon. If the pastry crust extends more than an inch beyond the salmon, cut off the excess with a sharp knife and save the extra pieces.

Make the egg wash by beating the egg with the water.

Flip up the top pastry crust and use a pastry brush to brush the egg wash on the lip of the bottom pastry. Put the top crust back in place and press both pieces together with your fingers to seal them.

Either crimp the edges together as you would for a pie crust, or use the tines of a fork held flat to press them together.

Place your salmon on a baking sheet lined with foil *(shiny side down)* or with parchment paper.

Repeat this technique with the other 3 salmon filets.

Brush the egg wash over the tops of the salmon "packages". When you bake them, this will give them a golden glossy finish.

If you like, cut out little decorations to stick on the tops of your salmon packages from the excess puff pastry that you saved. Don't forget to brush the decorations with egg wash before you bake the salmon packages.

Cut a slit on top of each salmon package to let out the steam.

Bake the salmon at 400 degrees F. for 25 minutes, or until the pastry is golden brown on top.

Cool for five minutes, cut in half so that your guests can see the layers, arrange on a plate, and serve.

Yield: 4 gorgeous and delicious servings.

RAINBOW PARFAIT

Small container of frozen original Cool Whip
Parfait glasses
3 differently colored containers of sherbet *(I
used raspberry, lemon, and orange)*

The night before you want to make the Rainbow Parfait, take the container of frozen original Cool Whip out of the freezer and put it in the refrigerator.

In the morning, line up your parfait glasses up on the counter.

Take the 3 containers of sherbet out of the freezer and let them sit on the counter until they are just soft enough to scoop.

Working quickly, fill an inch at the bottom of each parfait glass with Cool Whip. Smooth the layer with the back of a spoon or a rubber spatula.

Again working quickly, scoop out enough of the first sherbet to make a layer approximately 1-inch thick on top of the Cool Whip. Smooth out the layer. Do this in all the parfait glasses.

Repeat for the second color of sherbet.

Repeat for the third color of sherbet.

Alternating colors, fill the parfait glasses with sherbet layers to within an inch and a half from the rims.

Fill the remaining space with Cool Whip, cover the tops with plastic wrap, and stick the glasses, standing them upright, in your freezer.

Take the glasses of Rainbow Parfait out of the freezer 5 minutes before serving. Serve with Scottish Shortbread or another type of cookie. Alternatively, you can decorate the tops of the glasses with fresh fruit.

SCOTTISH SHORTBREAD

Preheat oven to 350 degrees F., rack in the middle position.

¾ cup *(1 and ½ sticks, 6 ounces)* salted butter
¼ cup white *(granulated)* sugar
1 teaspoon pure vanilla
1 and ½ cups all-purpose flour *(pack it down in the cup when you measure it)*
½ cup rice flour *(or cornstarch)*
⅛ to ¼ cup white *(granulated)* sugar to sprinkle on top after baking.

Melt the butter in the microwave or in a pan on the stovetop. Let it cool to slightly above room temperature.

In the bowl of an electric mixer *(or by hand but it'll take some muscle)* beat the white sugar with the butter until it's smooth and creamy.

Add the vanilla and mix it in.

In another bowl, mix the all-purpose flour and the rice flour *(or cornstarch)* together.

With the mixer running, add the flour mixture to the bowl in half-cup increments, mixing well after each addition.

Turn the dough out on a lightly floured board and cut it in half.

Spray the inside of two 9-inch pie plates with Pam or another nonstick baking spray.

Press the dough into the pie plates and smooth it out with your impeccably clean hands.

Prick the two pans of dough all over the tops with the tines of a fork.

Make shallow cuts with the tip of a sharp knife to divide each "pie" into 8 wedges. *(These shallow cuts are called "scoring".)*

Bake your Scottish Shortbread at 350 degrees F. for 25 to 30 minutes or until the edges are beginning to turn golden.

Sprinkle sugar over the tops of the shortbread immediately after taking it from the oven.

Cool in the pie plates on a wire rack or on cold stovetop burners.

When the shortbread is completely cool, tip it out of the pie plates, cut it into pieces using your scored lines as a guide, and store it in an airtight container until you are ready to serve it.

Yield: 16 pieces of delicious shortbread.

Life in tiny Lake Eden, Minnesota, is usually pleasantly uneventful. Lately, though, it seems everyone has more than their share of drama—especially the Swensen family. With so much on her plate, Hannah Swensen can hardly find the time to think about her bakery—let alone the town's most recent murder . . .

Hannah is nervous about the upcoming trial for her involvement in a tragic accident. She's eager to clear her name once and for all, but her troubles only double when she finds the judge bludgeoned to death with his own gavel—and Hannah is the number one suspect. Now on trial in the court of public opinion, she sets out in search of the culprit and discovers that the judge made more than a few enemies during his career. With time running out, Hannah will have to whip up her most clever recipe yet to find a killer more elusive than the perfect brownie . . .

Please turn the page for an exciting sneak peek of Joanne Fluke's newest Hannah Swensen mystery DOUBLE FUDGE BROWNIE MURDER coming in March 2015!

 # Chapter One

"**R**rrowww!" Hannah Swensen's orange and white cat gave an irate yowl as he jumped out of her arms.

"Sorry," Hannah apologized. She must have been hugging him too tightly, a reaction to her anxiety about the day that was just beginning to unfold. She finished the last sip of her coffee, set the empty mug on the end table, and attempted to explain. "I didn't mean to scare you, Moishe. I guess I'm just a little nervous, that's all."

"Rrrow."

This time the yowl was softer and it was accompanied by a purr as Moishe jumped up to resume his favorite position on the back of the couch. It was obvious he'd accepted her apology by coming back into hugging range. He perched there, staring down at her and watching to see what she'd do next. Moishe knew that this was not a typical morning. For one thing, the sun was up and it was past five A.M., the time that Hannah usually left for work. For another thing, she usually fed him, drank her coffee at the kitchen table, and took a quick shower just as soon as her eyes were fully open. Then she dressed for work and tossed him several kitty treats before she picked up her keys and went out the door.

"I know. It's different this morning," Hannah told him

past the lump in her throat. "I don't have to leave for work early because my trial starts today and Howie is picking me up to take me to the Winnetka County Courthouse."

Moishe made a sound that was halfway between a growl and a purr, and Hannah interpreted that to mean that he was sympathizing with her.

"It's going to be okay," she reassured him. "Howie told me the only thing that's going to happen today is jury selection. I'll be home tonight . . . probably earlier than usual."

Moishe had no reaction to that statement, either verbally or physically. He simply stared at her with a perfectly blank kitty expression.

"Howie said not to worry, so you shouldn't worry either."

"Rrrrow."

This was definitely a response to her words and Hannah took it as such. "I know. It's impossible not to worry, but I want you to think about what's going to happen when I come home tonight. I'm going to call Michelle and Andrea when court is adjourned for the day and they're going to come over with Chinese takeout. They're both helping out at The Cookie Jar today since I can't be there."

"Rrroww?"

This time Moishe's response was definitely a question. Hannah was sure of that. "That's right. Chinese takeout. Andrea and Michelle know that you like shrimp and they promised to bring extra. It'll be a nice family dinner."

As Hannah watched, Moishe's expression changed. His eyes widened in what appeared to be alarm and the fur began to stand up on his back. She was initially puzzled by his reaction and then she realized what she'd said.

"You can relax, Moishe. I know I said *family dinner*, but Mother's not coming. She's still on the cruise to Alaska. I think today's the day they're going to Taku Point in a seaplane to see the glaciers and have a grilled salmon shore lunch."

"Rrrrrrow!"

Hannah laughed. She'd done it again. She'd used one of the words Moishe knew well. "I know. I said *salmon*. I'll go get you some salmon treats, and then it's time for me to leave. Howie should be pulling up any minute now. And Howie's always punctual."

Hannah retrieved the treat canister from the kitchen and returned to the back of the couch where her feline roommate was waiting, his tail swishing back and forth like a metronome beating out a march tempo. "Here you go." She shook out several of the fish-shaped, salmon-flavored treats and placed them next to Moishe. "That ought to tide you over until I get home."

People claimed it was impossible for cats to smile, but Hannah was positive that Moishe's expression was close to glee as he stared down at his favorite treats. Then his gaze shifted back to her and he purred loudly.

"You're welcome. I'll see you tonight then. And we'll have dinner with Andrea and Michelle."

Hannah gave him a final scratch under the chin and made herself walk to the outside door. She didn't want to leave, but she knew she had to. She opened it, stepped through the doorway, and shut the door behind her, testing it once to make certain that it was locked. Then she stood there on the landing for a brief moment, blinking back the moisture that welled up in her eyes.

"Silly!" she chided herself, descending the outside staircase and squelching the urge to glance up to see if Moishe was watching her from the living room window.

It was a chilly Minnesota morning, colder than usual for the third week in September, and Hannah shivered as she took the sidewalk that wound around the condo buildings. There was a light sprinkling of frost on the yellow and dark orange chrysanthemums in the planters that separated the buildings. Soon the gardeners would dig up the bulbs and store

them for the winter. All that would be left in the planters
would be the evergreen shrubs which would provide spots of
green against the white winter snow.

The arrival of the first snowfall in Minnesota was unpre-
dictable. It could occur at any time from the month of October on. It was not at all unusual for it to snow on Halloween,
and mothers made sure that a warm coat and warm pants
could fit under their children's Halloween costumes.

Minnesotans had to be prepared for a winter with sixty to
seventy inches of snow. Of course some of it melted in the
early months, but the banks of snow the plows left at the side
of the road could reach heights that were taller than the roofs
of cars. Snow season could last for six months, starting in
October and tapering off to end in April. Delores and Doc
both said they remembered one year, they thought it had
been in the seventies, when there had been a blizzard in May.

As she walked, Hannah thought about the long, cold winter that stretched out before her. She couldn't help but wonder if she'd be around to shovel the sidewalk at The Cookie
Jar, her coffee shop and bakery. If she was convicted and had
to go to prison, would her partner, Lisa, keep their business
running? Would there be enough income for Hannah to continue to make the monthly mortgage payments on her condo?
And what would happen to Moishe? Could she rely on Norman to take care of Moishe until she got out of prison?

"Don't borrow trouble!" Hannah told herself sternly. Then
she looked around quickly and was relieved to find that no
one else was on the sidewalk. None of her neighbors had
heard her talking to herself.

Howie's car was parked right where he'd said it would be,
in the first space of the visitor's lot. Hannah hurried toward
the black Lexis, an appropriate car for Lake Eden's finest
lawyer. Howie gave his clients notepads with that sentiment
printed on the top of every page. It was his little joke since
he was also Lake Eden's *only* lawyer.

"Good morning, Hannah," Howie greeted her as she slid into the leather-covered passenger seat.

Is it a good morning, Howie? Hannah thought, but she didn't voice the question. Instead she responded, "Good morning, Howie. Did you bring coffee for Judge Colfax?"

"We'll stop on our way to the courthouse."

"Okay. When you give him the coffee, give him this, too." Hannah handed him a small white bag.

"What is it?"

"One of my Double Fudge Brownies. I figured it might sweeten him up. But don't tell him it's from me. I don't want to get accused of bribery on top of everything else."

"Got it." Howie place the bag on the back seat. "Say, Hannah . . . that brownie isn't poisoned, is it?"

"No!"

"Just kidding. I had one of your Double Fudge Brownies yesterday. They're great."

Hannah shivered again as Howie put the car in gear and pulled out of the parking lot. This time it wasn't from the cold. It was a shiver of fear at what might happen to her if Judge Colfax found her guilty of vehicular homicide.

"Relax, Hannah. Everything will be fine. Judge Colfax isn't a bad judge. He's just incompetent."

"Is that supposed to make me feel better?" Hannah couldn't help but ask him.

"No, it's supposed to make you laugh." Howie turned to smile at her. "You're taking all this too seriously, Hannah."

"Maybe that's because I'm the one on trial and you're not."

"Yup. That could account for it. Lean back and relax. This'll all be over much sooner than you think."

Only if you're planning to ram your car into a bridge abutment, Hannah thought as Howie turned onto the access road that led to the highway.

* * *

"Mr. Levine?" the bailiff approached Howie and handed him a folded note. "Judge Colfax thanks you for the coffee and brownie. And he told me to tell you he needs to see you and Miss Swsensen in his chambers before the trial begins."

Howie unfolded the note, read it quickly, and nodded. "Okay."

"He's tied up for a couple more minutes and he wants you to wait in the anteroom until he calls you in," the bailiff explained. "Just follow me, please."

Hannah and Howie followed the bailiff down the hall and took seats in the anteroom. The bailiff had just left when Howie's phone rang.

"Uh-oh!" Howie glanced down at the display. "I've got to take this, Hannah. I'll be right outside the door. Just poke your head out in the hall and alert me when Judge Colfax calls us in."

Hannah nodded, wishing that she could stand out in the hall with Howie. It would be more comfortable than sitting in in the anteroom, waiting. For one thing, the wooden chairs in the anteroom were terribly uncomfortable.

There was a clock on the wall and Hannah watched the seconds tick by. There was no sound from the room next door and Hannah wondered if Judge Colfax had left his chambers and forgotten that he'd summoned them. She wished she were somewhere else, anywhere other than sitting in a hard wooden chair that must have been designed by a sadist in this small room smelling of old furniture, stale sweat, and dread.

Hannah shut her eyes to block out the sight of the clock which was moving much too slowly. She hadn't gotten much sleep last night and she was bone tired. If she hadn't been so uncomfortable, she might have dozed off. At least then the time might have passed faster.

There was the sound of a crash, followed by a heavy thud

from the room next door. Hannah's eyes flew open and she jumped to her feet. Had the sounds she'd heard come from the judge's chambers? Or had she fallen asleep and dreamed it?

She could feel her heart beat hard as she tiptoed to the interior door. She didn't hear anything alarming so she put her ear to the surface of the door. If she heard pages rustling as Judge Colfax read a brief, or the sound of his voice talking on the phone, she'd know he was all right. The temporary judge she'd drawn for her trial was elderly and had come out of retirement to fill in for Judge Flemming, the regular judge. It was entirely possible that Judge Colfax had slipped and fallen. And if that had happened, perhaps he was unable to get up and needed help.

Hannah hesitated one more moment and then she decided that she had to do something. The defendant in a trail couldn't just burst into the judge's chambers. That was not only impolite, it could even be grounds for further changes against her. Her hand trembled slightly as she knocked on the door and waited for a response. The interruption might make Judge Colfax angry, but she would explain that she had heard a crash and a thud, and she had just wanted to check to make sure he was all right. Surely he couldn't object to that!

There was no answer, no sound at all from within the chambers. Hannah took a deep breath and knocked a second time. What if Judge Colfax couldn't answer her knock, or even call out for her to come in? What if he was stretched out on the floor, unconscious from his fall?

There was only one thing to do and Hannah did it. Carefully, silently, she pushed the door open a crack and peered in.

At first glance, the room appeared empty. Then Hannah saw something that made her push the door open all the way and rush in. That something was a wooden gavel on the floor near the far corner of Judge Colfax's desk. And the gavel was only inches from a pool of blood.

Hannah stepped over the gavel, avoided the pool of blood,

and raced around the side of the desk. And there she found Judge Colfax, crumbled in a heap on the floor, his desk chair upended beside him.

The scene was horrific and Hannah averted her eyes. If only she'd rushed in the second she'd heard the sounds! But another glance at Judge Colfax's head told her that it wouldn't have made a difference. She was no doctor, but she was almost certain that there was no way Judge Colfax could have recovered from the massive damage done by the gavel to the side of his skull.

Get help! Hannah's shocked mind told her and her shaking legs carried her across the room to the door that led to the hall. She opened it, stepped out, and motioned frantically to Howie who was pacing near the water cooler, his cell phone to his ear.

Hannah watched as Howie ended his call and approached her. "Judge Colfax called us in?" he asked.

Hannah opened her mouth to answer, but she couldn't seem to find her voice. She shook her head from side to side, cleared her throat, and somehow managed to choke out the words she needed to say.

"Get help! The judge is dead. He was murdered!"

Catering and Capers with
Isis Crawford!

A Catered Murder	978-1-57566-725-6	$5.99US/$7.99CAN
A Catered Wedding	978-0-7582-0686-2	$6.50US/$8.99CAN
A Catered Christmas	978-0-7582-0688-6	$6.99US/$9.99CAN
A Catered Valentine's Day	978-0-7582-0690-9	$6.99US/$9.99CAN
A Catered Halloween	978-0-7582-2193-3	$6.99US/$8.49CAN
A Catered Birthday Party	978-0-7582-2195-7	$6.99US/$8.99CAN
A Catered Thanksgiving	978-0-7582-4739-1	$7.99US/$8.99CAN
A Catered St. Patrick's Day	978-0-7582-4741-4	$7.99US/$8.99CAN
A Catered Christmas Cookie Exchange	978-0-7582-7490-8	$7.99US/$8.99CAN

Available Wherever Books Are Sold!

All available as e-books, too!

Visit our website at www.kensingtonbooks.com

Grab These Cozy Mysteries
from
Kensington Books